"If I am to make any progress in finding you a bride, you must change, Mr. St. Ledger," Emmaline said.

"I don't care if you're rich as Croesus, I will never be able to find a bride for an ogre."

"Ogre?" St. Ledger's eyes narrowed to angry slits. "Did you say *ogre*, madam?"

Emmaline lifted her chin defiantly. "I did."

He crossed his arms, and the movement drew her gaze to the remarkable contours of is bare chest. But Mr. St. Ledger showed nt the slightest concern that he was offending her feminine sensibilities. He merely stood there, eyeing her darkly.

"I cannot work miracles," Emmaline declared, willing her mind away from his physical assets. "If there is to be any hope for you, you must put yourself in my hands. For at the moment, you have absolutely no chance of making a successful match."

"No chance?" He finally looked taken aback. "Very well—you may do with me as you will."

"Then I'll be on my way." Emmaline edged away from the intoxicating nearness of Mr. St. Ledger's bare chest. It ought to be a crime for a _____ _____ _____ __ attractive.

EILEEN PUTMAN

Never Kiss A Duke

AVON BOOKS
An Imprint of HarperCollins*Publishers*

AVON BOOKS
An Imprint of HarperCollins*Publishers*
10 East 53rd Street
New York, New York 10022-5299 .

Copyright © 2000 by Eileen Putman
ISBN: 0-380-80290-2
www.avonromance.com

First Avon Books paperback printing: July 2000

Avon Trademark Reg. U.S. Pat. Off. and in Other Countries, Marca Registrada, Hecho en U.S.A.
HarperCollins® is a trademark of HarperCollins Publishers Inc.

Printed in the U.S.A.

WCD 10 9 8 7 6 5 4 3 2 1

This book is dedicated to Micki Nuding,
editor *extraordinaire*.

Acknowledgments

I am indebted to John W. Griffith and Charles H. Frey, editors of *Classics of Children's Literature* (Macmillan Publishing Company, New York, 1992), for their provocative work on fairy tales, and especially on Charles Perrault's contribution to that genre. These two gentlemen are in no way to blame for the fact that I have infused *Never Kiss a Duke* with my own entirely irrational ideas on the subject.

"*Is it you, my Prince? I have waited for you a long while.*"

"*Silence, wench. 'Tis a kiss I want, not reproach.*"

"*Nay, my lord. The kiss of a princess comes dear. I shall require that you grovel. And then, perhaps, we will be friends.*"

—With apologies to Charles Perrault (1628–1703) and *The Sleeping Beauty in the Woods*

Chapter 1

London, 1811

"**A** woman of modest beauty, independent means, and a tireless passion for marital, er, relations." Emmaline bestowed a radiant smile on her client. "I am sure I will find just the right lady for you, Mr. Burwell."

"Not too headstrong, mind you, Mrs. Stanhope."

Emmaline looked aghast. "Oh, no, sir. Headstrong is not the thing."

"Her passions must be limited to the marriage bed. I want no intemperate shrew."

"Certainly not," Emmaline agreed, lowering her lashes.

"My work is very demanding. I have no desire at the end of the day to put up with a nagging wife. You're certain you are not available?" He stood on the steps, a speculative gleam in his eye.

Emmaline gave a ladylike cough. "I am afraid not," she said, her voice filled with regret. "My heart will always belong to my poor husband, God rest his soul."

1

"Your husband was lucky to find such a pearl." Mr. Burwell tipped his hat. "I have a feeling that with your help, Mrs. Stanhope, I shall be lucky, too. You have restored my faith in the future. I bid you good day."

Emmaline maintained her confident smile as Mr. Burwell made his way down the walk. It was a lovely spring day, and he gave her a jaunty wave as he walked toward the gate.

"Mind the Mail, sir," she called to him. "The driver never has the courtesy to slow his team. You will wish to cross quickly to avoid dirtying your clothes in his dust."

Mr. Burwell pulled a pocket watch from his waistcoat, which stretched tightly over the ample fullness of his stomach. "Why, 'tis five o'clock. I didn't realize the day was so far advanced."

"Oh, yes," she replied cheerfully. "You can set your watch by the Mail coach. It is neck or nothing with the drivers. I suppose they get a bonus for being on time."

"Well, there is the rent for another month, thank the Lord," muttered a voice at her elbow.

Emmaline turned. "Shhh! He will hear."

"Not with the Mail coming," her aunt Heloise replied tartly. "One of these days I shall have to teach that driver a lesson. He positively ruins my afternoon nap."

"When one lives on the Oxford Pike, one cannot be particular about noise."

"Nor about the company one allows into the house, I suppose." Her aunt's brilliant blue eyes narrowed as she regarded the man stepping into the street. "Just look at him. If his stomach was any larger, he'd not be able to see his shoes. And that scruffy beard—pity the poor woman who marries him! You don't have a prayer of finding someone for him."

"His requirements are rather stringent," Emmaline conceded.

"Like all of 'em. The men want doxies, and the women want dukes. 'Tis a wonder anyone ever weds."

"I never realized that running a matrimonial agency could be so difficult." Emmaline sighed. "I don't know any beautiful, wealthy women with passionate natures."

"Find him a woman who adores the marriage bed and he won't mind about the other."

Emmaline flushed. "Aunt—"

"One of the Covent Garden chits will take him on, once she sees he's a man of some means. In my day, that set was always on the lookout for the main chance. I don't imagine things have changed very much since."

She gave her aunt a pained look. "Mr. Burwell is not seeking a prostitute."

"Nonsense. All husbands want their wives to be whores in the bedchamber."

Emmaline took a deep breath. "You know, Aunt, I don't believe I thought this plan through sufficiently. Ever since I placed that newspaper notice for Harmonious Matrimony, we've been deluged with men of the worst sort. If we don't get more legitimate clients like Mr. Burwell, we'll have to return to fortune-telling."

"I knew I shouldn't have given my crystal ball to Lucy. Bird in the bush, and all that."

"*Hand.* Bird in the hand—"

"Hand, bush—what does it matter? It all boils down to money in the end."

Emmaline could not argue with the truth of that statement. "At least with Mr. Burwell's deposit, we will be able to afford Dr. Evans."

"Throwing good money after bad, if you ask me," Aunt Heloise muttered.

"It is only that we've not yet found the right treatment for you."

Aunt Heloise patted Emmaline's shoulder. "It pains me to see you waste your youth on me, dear. You should be going about the business of finding a husband who can give you the life you deserve. In a just world, you would have had a Season. By now, you'd be married to a duke and readying the nursery."

"A duke!" Emmaline laughed. "That sounds like something Father would have said. But daydreams don't pay the rent, as you well know."

" 'What dreams may come when we have shuffled off this mortal boil—er, coil.' Drat. I can never remember the rest." Aunt Heloise frowned. "What I mean to say is that a woman cannot have too many dreams. By the time she reaches my age, she'll need every one of them."

"Then let me dream of a cure for you," Emmaline said gently. "It is my right—you have just said so."

Aunt Heloise gave a gruff harumph, but her eyes glistened with moisture. Emmaline leaned over and kissed her aunt's cheek. "Come. I will brew us some tea. And you can tell me more of the magnificent Mr. Kemble."

"That man? Hadn't a chivalrous bone in his body. Stepped on everyone's lines. We loathed him."

As Emmaline turned to shut the front door, she saw her client, standing in the street, talking to an elderly woman. He appeared to be giving her directions, for he pointed in the direction of town, then bowed politely as the woman, her back bent with age, wrapped her voluminous cloak more tightly against the breezes and went on her way. It was fortunate Mr. Burwell had good manners; they would go a long way in finding him a wife.

"Mr. Burwell," Emmaline called with alarm, "the Mail is coming—have a care." And indeed, the dust cloud that heralded the coach's arrival was almost upon them. The Mail guard sounded a blast on his tin horn.

Mr. Burwell wrapped his scarf around his neck and smiled broadly. But he did not budge from the street.

"Lives dangerously, that one," Aunt Heloise said darkly.

The thundering of hooves and the rumbling of a heavy carriage roared nearer. Still, Mr. Burwell did not bestir himself. He wore a pleasant expression, as if he were already contemplating the joys of marital bliss.

Horrified, Emmaline ran down the steps. "Mr. Burwell!" she cried. "Sir, you must move this instant!"

Her client gave no indication that he had heard; his features were strangely placid as he smiled at her.

He was still smiling when the Royal Mail ran him down.

Changeling.

If Sir Harry hadn't known beyond doubt that the man behind the desk was Portia's child, he wouldn't have believed it. That his poor deceased sister could have birthed such a cold creature as Adrian St. Ledger was beyond his comprehension. In the weeks since his nephew had ascended to the dukedom, Sir Harry had begun to suspect that the man was thoroughly mad—a conclusion underscored now by his nephew's appearance.

The duke of Trent sat at his vast desk, his features rigid as stone, glowering at a yellow ball of fluff that appeared to be a canary. Next to the bird, which pecked aimlessly at the oak desk top, rested a white bone as big around as a man's thigh.

Macabre images leapt to Sir Harry's mind, but he pushed them aside. Cannibalism was unthinkable, even for his nephew, though the place did exude a rather deathly gloom. The library wore a musty scent, like a mausoleum. A brace of flickering candles on Trent's desk did nothing to chase the shadows from the room.

His nephew hadn't acknowledged his presence by so much as the blink of an eye. The canary hopped to the edge of the desk, however, and greeted him with a melodious chirp.

Might as well get to it, Sir Harry thought grimly. If Trent wanted to turn his library into an aviary, it was none of his business.

"There has been a death," Sir Harry began. "Rather unusual circumstances that fall, as it happens, within your area of expertise. Lord Castlereagh would take it as a great favor if you were to look into the matter."

His nephew's gaze remained fixed on the bird.

"The deceased, William Burwell, was a clerk in the War Office," Sir Harry continued. "He was under investigation for suspected treason."

This statement likewise had no discernible effect.

"Documents have been disappearing," Sir Harry said more loudly, now thoroughly irritated by his nephew's rudeness. "Last month, the French obtained the schedules for our supply ships to the peninsula. One ship was sunk, another heavily damaged."

Sir Harry paused to give Trent the opportunity to commiserate with England's war woes, if he chose. He did not.

"We'd been shadowing Burwell, planning to catch him in the act of turning over papers," Sir Harry said through gritted teeth. "Needless to say, his death has been cause for consternation. We are no closer now than before to identifying those behind this treachery."

Those unnerving gray eyes blinked once.

"The Mail ran him over." With a great effort, Sir Harry restrained himself from grabbing his nephew by the collar and shaking him into attentiveness. "By all accounts, Burwell just stood in its path like a stupid, suicidal squirrel."

An appreciative chirp came from the desk top. Sir Harry glared at the canary. "Can't you do something about that bird? Surely your cook has a recipe for pigeon pie."

"Tough birds, canaries. Most unsatisfactory in a pie."

The voice, low and mellifluous, flowed like honey over Sir Harry's arid tone. It was a legacy from Portia, who'd had a pure, sweet voice as lovely as—well, a canary's.

With a muttered curse, Sir Harry pulled a newspaper clipping from his pocket. He tossed it onto the desk, narrowly missing the canary, who squawked a protest.

"Take a look at that," Sir Harry demanded, pointing to a notice he had circled:

> Gentlemen desirous of meeting satisfactory candidates for marriage are requested to call at Harmonious Matrimony, Number 10 Oxford Pike, where a Respectable Widow will assist them in the process of selecting their future mates. A small fee will ensure the happiest of outcomes.

His nephew glanced at it.

"Burwell answered this notice," Sir Harry explained. "He died in front of her cottage."

Trent's attention had already wandered. He ran his finger along the smooth expanse of the bone, contemplating it gravely, as if the thing held the answer to some pressing question.

With a muttered curse, Sir Harry pulled out a handbill and thrust it under Trent's nose. "This was found in Burwell's pocket."

Fortunes told, wishes fulfilled, the future un-
veiled. Gypsy Flora, Number 10 Oxford Pike.
Appointments not necessary.

Even as Trent glanced at it, Sir Harry turned the handbill over to reveal the drawing of a skeleton in black armor riding a horse. A skull and crossbones adorned the horse's reins. Beneath the drawing, someone had written Burwell's name.

"The tarot death card," Trent said softly.

"Exactly," Sir Harry replied. "Damn it, Trent. If anyone can get to the bottom of this, 'tis you."

The quick narrowing of Trent's pupils told Sir Harry he had the man's attention at last. "The war on the Peninsula is at a turning point," he continued quickly. "We have Massena on the run. Every effort, every thought must be for victory. That is why we must discover who is behind this nefarious scheme. With Burwell dead, the handbill and the woman are our only clues."

"The marriage broker?" Trent arched a brow.

"Matrimony is only her latest venture. As you can see by this handbill, she dabbles in fortunes, too. 'Tis likely she was involved in Burwell's death and possibly the treason, too."

His nephew regarded the drawing thoughtfully.

"The woman lives with an aunt on the other side of the park," Sir Harry said. "Their fortunes have been in decline since the death of her father five years ago. She seems harmless enough— nothing criminal in her background. But appearances can be deceiving, as you well know. I confess, the drawing of that death card has unnerved more than one of my investigators."

Trent's mouth curved upward in what might have been a smile, had he been one to indulge in such frivolity. "I know of no mystic capable of causing a man's feet to stick to the cobblestones as death bears down on him."

"Of course not," Sir Harry quickly replied. "But we lack an explanation as to why the man didn't save himself."

Trent's brow rose another fraction of an inch. "A rational explanation lies at the root of most unusual phenomena."

"Yes, well, we don't have one here."

"I tried to enlighten Parliament about this sort of thing years ago. Our august leaders chose not to listen." Trent picked up his pen. "I've a paper to finish, Uncle. What do you want of me?"

Sir Harry took a deep breath. "Go and see this woman. Pretend to be a client in need of her services. With your background, you'll discern things others might miss."

"No." Trent's pen moved smoothly over the paper.

"You must, dammit."

His nephew looked up. "Not 'must,' Uncle. Never that."

"For God's sake, Adrian," Sir Harry rasped. "Your poor mother would be horrified to see what you have become: a man who cares nothing for his fellowman, who rejects a plea from his country and his own flesh and blood. For Portia's sake, I ask you to do this. There is no one else in

England who possesses your knowledge."

"You dare to invoke her memory?" Trent's eyes narrowed.

Sir Harry's expression softened. "I honor you, Adrian, for what you tried to do in her name. Just because you failed to convince a bunch of idiotic Whigs is no reason to—"

"On the contrary," he said coldly. "It is every reason."

Sir Harry eyed his nephew uneasily. "My dear boy," he began, "I know you have had a difficult past—"

"I am thirty, uncle. My boyhood is a lifetime behind me."

"Yes, of course." Sir Harry rubbed his eyes. Dealing with his difficult nephew had tired him considerably. "But I will always see you as you were that summer Portia took you away from England. So lost, so . . . strange."

"What is her name?"

Sir Harry tried to gather his thoughts, but as he stared into his nephew's enigmatic gray eyes, all else vanished from his mind.

"Her name," Trent repeated in a low voice. He tapped the pen impatiently, then idly moved it back and forth.

"Emmaline Alcott Stanhope." For a moment, as Sir Harry's gaze followed the pen, his vision clouded.

"You look sleepy, Uncle," his nephew observed. "Would you care to rest upstairs? I can have Gibbons prepare a room."

"Damn it, man." Sir Harry took a step backward. "What are you doing to me?"

Trent studied him. "You've done it to yourself, Uncle. The imagination is a powerful thing. It can make the blind see and the deaf hear. Perhaps it can even make a man stand in front of a fast Mail coach. But it's all illusion."

A strange heaviness pooled in Sir Harry's body. Time seemed to halt, overcome by the same lethargy that affected him. He was vaguely aware that his nephew was watching him as intently as he'd studied that bone. Why the devil were Trent's features blurred?

"Very well." Trent sighed in resignation. "I shall discover whether this Mrs. Stanhope is enmeshed in some nefarious treason. You will see how the rational mind, unfettered by the poisonous influence of the imagination, works wonders."

Sir Harry blinked.

"I will serve my country in this small, ridiculous way and then I shall require that you leave me be. I have papers to finish, translations to complete, bones to study. The beauty of science is that it is not dependent on human foolishness."

The canary chirped cheerfully.

"Good day, Uncle," Trent said softly.

Sir Harry beat a swift retreat.

Chapter 2

❦

"A gentleman is downstairs." Aunt Heloise struck a pose in the doorway to Emmaline's tiny bedchamber. "A rather compelling sort."

Emmaline looked up from her diary, where she had been scribbling some of the troubling thoughts that had occupied her of late. "What does he want?"

"Claims to be in search of a bride."

"I hope you told him that my services are no longer available."

"I did no such thing. The rent is due on the fifteenth—had you forgotten?"

Emmaline sighed. "Still, I wish I'd never placed that notice. Poor Mr. Burwell."

"Pity him if you must, but no sane person could stand in the way of a coach and six and hope to live to tell the tale."

"And yet," Emmaline said in a musing tone, "he gave no sign that his wits were addled."

" 'He dies, and makes no sign.' " Aunt Heloise brought her handkerchief to her lips and gave a

13

heartfelt sigh. "If only you could have seen me as Queen Margaret. Of course, that line was Henry's. Shakespeare didn't like women, you know. Gave the best lines to men."

"I hope our visitor is not one of those investigators," Emmaline said worriedly. "There've been so many since last week."

Aunt Heloise nodded. "Beady eyes, dour faces. 'Choked with ambition of the meanest sort,' if you catch my drift."

Emmaline rose. "I will send our caller on his way."

"Oh, no, dear. My instincts never play me false; he is not like the others. He looks to be a gentleman born. His clothes are of good quality but not ostentatious. And he has the most wondrous thick hair. Dark, like Mr. Kemble's. Doesn't speak much, though. He scarcely paid me any mind."

"If he has no manners, I can see why he needs help finding a wife." Emmaline checked her appearance in the mirror. The dark circles under her eyes reflected the sleepless nights she had endured since Mr. Burwell's horrifying accident.

"We must find some other way to raise the rent money. I can't help but think we had a part in Mr. Burwell's death. Out of respect for the poor man we should drop this ill-starred venture."

"Nonsense, Em, dear. No one is to blame for the man's stupidity except himself. As for respect, 'tis a fleeting bit of coin. Won't pay the rent." With a toss of her faded but still-thick copper-colored curls, Aunt Heloise moved down the hall.

Emmaline yearned to crawl into bed, pull the covers over her head, and remain until all difficulties vanished. They wouldn't, of course, but she'd have enjoyed pretending. Between her and the haven of financial security lay a vast chasm that could be crossed only with great difficulty, if at all.

But some things had to be faced. She made her way down the stairs to see what sort of man had so intrigued Aunt Heloise, praying he would be the answer to their financial woes, yet knowing he would not. Miracles did not walk into one's parlor and sit there waiting to be discovered.

Pausing just outside the room, Emmaline took a deep, calming breath. Then she peeked in to see what manner of man awaited.

His gray gaze slammed into hers.

It was as if he'd expected her to appear at precisely that moment, for his eyes were already filled with an awareness of being observed. And those eyes—dear Lord! Gray as gloom but as compelling as a stiletto. A strange sensation stirred in the pit of her stomach—doubtless the result of skipping breakfast this morning.

Mortified that he'd caught her peeking, Emmaline hastily stepped forward. "Good afternoon, sir." She pasted a bright smile on her face. "I am Emmaline Stanhope. I am sorry to have kept you waiting."

One of his brows arched almost imperceptibly. He blinked, once. His eyes were swirling, unfathomable seas, but even as she studied him, a veil descended. So quickly did his gaze transform into an icy aloofness, she might have imagined the momentary vibrancy.

He rose. "I am Adrian St. Ledger."

That odd sensation in her spiraled into a dizzying warmth. What in the world was wrong with her? Quickly, Emmaline extended her hand, though she was not in the habit of doing so to strange gentlemen. To her surprise, he did not take it. Instead, he regarded it suspiciously, as if she'd just presented him with a piece of rotten fish.

Her hand fell to her side and took refuge in the folds of her skirt.

"How may I be of service, Mr. St. Ledger?" she asked briskly, relieved that at least her voice held its own in the face of this unsettling man.

"I am in need of a wife." His voice was rich, resonant, almost spellbinding.

Emmaline wondered how such a man could possibly need assistance. He was not the least deficient in his personal appearance. Besides those extraordinary eyes, he possessed a pair of broad shoulders and a magnificent head of undisciplined dark hair.

But there was a chilly wariness about him. His brow was stern, his nose aristocratic, his mouth set in a grim line. He stood with a stiff vigilance, as if expecting to dodge enemy fire at any moment.

Emmaline hesitated. "I should tell you that an unfortunate accident occurred here last week."

"Accident?" Again, that slightly arched brow.

"One of my clients had the misfortune to be

struck by the Royal Mail. The authorities are pursuing the matter diligently, and investigators tend to drop by at odd moments. I'm afraid I cannot promise that your association with me would remain strictly confidential."

He seemed to consider this news gravely, and Emmaline immediately regretted that she'd been so forthright. Aunt Heloise had the right of it; if Mr. St. Ledger took his business elsewhere, there'd be no hope of paying the rent.

She had little doubt that he could afford her fee. Though his clothes were plain, the facing of his coat was silk serge, if she did not miss her guess. A woman who had to trim her frocks every year to disguise the wear developed an eye for such things.

"I could meet you elsewhere," she offered, "so that we would not risk observation."

He was silent for so long Emmaline feared she had offended him. Or—heaven forbid—inadvertently suggested another kind of rendezvous altogether. When his gaze narrowed, she took a small step backward. But the distance she put between them failed to ease her unsettling awareness of his commanding masculine presence.

"What I meant to say," she added carefully, "is that while I have nothing to hide, I am aware that those who seek assistance in matrimony may have no wish for that fact to be known."

He was not listening. His gaze was fixed on a point slightly behind her, and his lips parted on a scowl. Emmaline turned to see a small black shadow dart around the legs of her chair.

"I cannot abide animals," he said stiffly.

Emmaline quickly scooped up Thomas. "I understand perfectly," she assured him. "Indeed, my father was quite sensitive to cats. They made him sneeze, which is why we never kept one. But Thomas has a gentle nature and is good for business. I don't know why, but people who come to have their fortunes told expect to see a black cat in residence."

"Fortunes?" He said the word with distaste and eyed her as if she had suddenly developed the plague.

Drat her wayward tongue. "My aunt and I tell fortunes now and then," she explained. "Some folks find it amusing."

"Perhaps the fortune-teller is amused," he said softly. "But what of those who take your words to heart, ruining their lives in the process—are they amused, madam?"

His frank hostility took her aback. "We do not ruin lives here, Mr. St. Ledger." She turned away to hide her anger. "I will put Thomas outside."

But Thomas squirmed in her arms, and when one of his claws pierced her sleeve, Emmaline gave a little cry and let him go. He landed at Mr. St. Ledger's feet with a dull thud and proceeded to rub against her guest's leg.

St. Ledger froze. "Get . . . that . . . creature . . . away from me."

The strangled rasp was so different from his rich baritone that Emmaline hastened to do his bidding, though it meant she had to forcibly remove Thomas from his ankle. The cat hissed loudly as Emmaline dashed to the front door and tossed him onto the stoop.

She hurried back into the room, but she needn't have; St. Ledger did not deign to acknowledge her.

Heavens. No wonder his marital prospects were dim. A man with a perpetually stern countenance and insufficient warmth to abide even so independent a creature as a cat would never gain *her* affections, regardless of his income. Fortunately, she wouldn't be the one to marry him.

Indeed, she knew many women would be willing to tolerate his eccentricities, providing he possessed deep pockets and a handsome face. She couldn't vouch for the former, but he was certainly gifted with the latter.

"Perhaps it would be best to go over the terms of my matrimonial services," she said with forced cheer.

When he made no response, Emmaline seated herself in the chair, leaving him to stand or sit as he preferred. He remained standing.

"My fee is twenty pounds," she began. "Half is paid upon the signing of our agreement, the rest falls due when your engagement is accomplished. If, for some unforeseen reason, a marriage fails to occur after the engagement is announced, I will refund a small sum to be applied to a new search through our agency." She smiled pleasantly, giving him time to respond.

He said nothing.

"For my fee," she quickly continued, "I will produce two candidates who fit your qualifications. Would you care to sit down, sir?" Emmaline was weary of looking up at him. She waited, her features arranged in the amicable expression she adopted for business purposes.

Gradually, as if he was returning from a far journey, his eyes lost their blank look. She could see the moment he arrived in the present, for his gaze focused suddenly and sharply on her. He stepped backward until his legs touched the chair. Slowly, he sank into it.

Emmaline suppressed a sigh. The fact that Mr. St. Ledger was not in full possession of his wits would vastly complicate the task of finding him a bride. Still, she'd not flinched at a challenge yet and wouldn't now.

"I can offer testimony from numerous couples who owe their wedded bliss to Harmonious Matrimony," she said pleasantly. "My qualifications are superb. I attended Lady Warwick's School for Young Ladies. Perhaps you have heard of it? 'Tis known far and wide for its excellence."

Actually, she was quite sure no one beyond the village of Hadley, where the school had stood on a tiny piece of land for two decades, had heard of Lady Warwick's. The school's fortunes had deteriorated over the years, until there was nothing left but a shabby building and two elderly teachers who had nowhere else to go.

And though she had not exactly united dozens of couples—not even one, truth be told—Emmaline had no qualms about that small fib. Too much honesty could pose difficulties for a struggling business like hers. All she needed was one blissful match, and they could keep the cottage for a few more months. She'd had high hopes for

Mr. Burwell, but fate had intervened.

Emmaline pulled out a handkerchief. "And, of course, I was married myself." She dabbed at her eyes. "Unfortunately, my husband is no longer living."

This revelation usually caused prospective clients to eye her with compassion, but Mr. St. Ledger showed not even a scintilla of sympathy for her widowhood. Obviously, she'd misjudged him again.

"If the terms are satisfactory," she said, recovering quickly, "we can begin immediately. Once I know your requirements, I will prepare a contract for your signature."

He made no response to this. The man was impossible. "Suppose we begin with the type of bride you had in mind," Emmaline prodded.

He regarded her steadily. "The marrying kind, Mrs. Stanhope."

She flushed. "What I meant was her character, her temperament, that sort of thing. You would, of course, wish her to share your interests."

"I study rocks, madam. I don't care whether she shares my interests. I would doubt her sanity if she did."

"Rocks?" Emmaline repeated with a puzzled frown.

"Fossils, if you prefer." Abruptly, he reached into his pocket, pulled out a banknote and tossed it in her direction. "I must leave to finish a paper I am presenting tonight. Present yourself at the Argyle Rooms at eight o'clock. Use this for the cab. We will continue our discussion then."

With that, he rose to his feet and, without so

much as a glance in her direction, strode from the house.

Any pleasure Emmaline might have derived from the money on her floor was lost in her anger. So the man expected her to grovel for her fee, did he?

Emmaline bent to pick up the money. To Adrian St. Ledger's growing list of undesirable qualities, she added the sin of arrogance. The man was insufferable.

But she would find him a wife, she thought grimly. Oh, yes. And then the devil could take him, with her blessing.

Infinity, Adrian thought darkly, might well be measured in cobblestones. There was no end to them, because someone, somewhere, was always building roads in the name of progress.

Progress: an excuse to avoid reckoning with the past.

He'd sent his carriage home after deciding that walking was a better remedy for his roiling gut than rattling around in a closed vehicle. The distance home was farther than he'd imagined, however, and the rows of uneven cobblestones stretched to forever under his feet. The late afternoon grew into dusk.

Damn the stones and damn Emmaline Stanhope's lovely eyes, which had not quite disguised her disgust of him. He'd had himself under control until that cursed cat appeared and brought the memories rushing back. It amazed him that the old fears still existed, that they'd seeped into the furthest recess of his brain, waiting to be summoned by something as innocuous as a cat. Despite all the years he'd put between himself and the past, terror stalked him still.

He'd acted like an idiot. But he wouldn't apologize to the woman. If he had to apologize every time someone had taken him in disgust, he'd spend infinity in supplication. And God knows, he had no time for that.

The clatter of wheels punctured his dark reverie, and though he'd dismissed the carriage, Adrian was gratified to see it rolling at a sedate pace toward him.

"Your Grace," Gibbons greeted him.

Adrian didn't look at him. "Remind me to pay you better."

Gibbons bowed. "As you say, Your Grace."

"None of that. I'm supposed to be incognito."

"Sorry, Mr. St. Ledger, sir."

Adrian slanted him a suspicious gaze, then stepped quickly into the carriage and collapsed against the squabs. Gibbons sat opposite him as if it were perfectly ordinary to rescue his employer from whatever dire fate awaited a man so foolish as to walk the turnpike at dusk, alone save for his thoughts.

Control. He took three long breaths, mentally repeating the word with each breath. He ran his fingers through his hair and counted backward from ten.

Then, and only then, did he relax.

Chapter 3

"It is possible that the bone derives from an ancient, as yet unrecognized animal. Its diameter and weight would seem to rule out human origin." St. Ledger scarcely glanced at his audience as he held the ghastly bone in his hands.

A colder man she'd yet to meet. With eyes that saw everything and yet nothing, St. Ledger seemed untouchable, remote. Perhaps it was that bone, cold and white and bare of flesh, that made him seem so devoid of sentiment. Perhaps it was that strangely magnetic quality he possessed, which compelled as much as it repelled.

"This delineates the geological section according to age," he said, pointing to a chart, "with the New Red Sandstone strata containing the oldest relics and the Chalk strata the most recent."

His rich voice, so compelling in her parlor, was dry and flat tonight, as if he'd intentionally wrung the life out of it.

From her seat in the back of the room, Emmaline could see that while many in the audience appeared rapt, a few had dozed off. If she hadn't been so fascinated by St. Ledger's transformation from the wildly edgy man in her parlor to this lifeless pedagogue, Emmaline might have nodded off, too.

Fortunately, the Argyle's lavishly decorated Turkish room had much to hold her interest—like the ceiling's large gilded eagle. It clutched a thunderbolt, from which hung an enormous chandelier. There were other distractions, too. Giggles and shrieks filled the corridor as groups of merrymakers made their way to other rooms in the building. St. Ledger seemed oblivious to the noise.

"Diligent study will be required to determine the fossil's origins. It is my recommendation that the Society undertake new excavations at Oxford and Maidstone, the most promising sites of the four I have described." He massaged the bridge of his nose, as if unburdening himself of such weighty information had given him a headache.

Slowly, methodically, he neatened his papers into a precise pile. Finally, he regarded his audience with that flat, gray gaze. Gray was of a piece with the man, Emmaline decided; his lifeless discourse could put even the most earnest scholar to sleep.

Heaven save the world from earnest scholars. Her father had been one, and if he had ever come down from his ivory tower to grapple with something approximating real life, she had missed it.

One by one, the members of the audience be-

stirred themselves as they realized the lecture
was over. Emma could almost hear the creaking
of limbs as each man rose stiffly to his feet. It
was to her gender's credit that no women had
wasted their evenings by coming to hear St.
Ledger. Her father's talks had been well attended
by both sexes, but many of the women came only
to flirt with the handsome widower.

Woe betide any woman who undertook a flirtation with St. Ledger. No matter that his shoulders nicely filled out that plain brown jacket or
that his long, tapered fingers seemed inexplicably sensual—he'd be oblivious to a woman's
needs. As a conversationalist, he was sadly lacking. As a scholar, he seemed determined to
stamp the life out of learning. As a man . . . well,
there were possibilities, but he seemed determined to stamp those out also.

St. Ledger had little to commend him except
his money. Still, he was all that stood between
her and eviction.

A smattering of applause spread through the
room, and St. Ledger bowed in acknowledgment.
A man who had shared the stage with him made
a few closing remarks about having long enjoyed
Mr. St. Ledger's scintillating scholarship.

The room emptied quickly, leaving St. Ledger
to gather his bone and charts. At last, Emmaline
was the only other person remaining. Gathering
her courage, she moved quietly toward the stage.

He had rolled up his charts and was tying
them with a piece of string, his back to her. Not
wanting to startle him, she cleared her throat dis-
creetly.

"Whatever it is you are peddling, madam, be it arcane theories or your person, I am not in the least interested." He did not turn around.

Emma blinked. "But . . . I understood this was urgent."

"There is nothing exigent about fossils." He set the charts aside as he wrapped the bone in parchment. "They have lain in repose for millions of years, and I daresay will do so for millions more."

"I beg your pardon?" Emmaline stared at him.

" '*Exigent*,' " he snarled. "E-x-i-g-e-n-t. Something that requires immediate action. Or was it '*repose*' you did not comprehend? Have you had not even a rudimentary education, madam? All the more reason for you to be on your way. This meeting is for Society members only."

He had not even bothered to look at her.

Emmaline's temper snapped. "I am here at your invitation—nay, 'twas more in the nature of an order. I cannot imagine why you have forgotten our appointment, Mr. St. Ledger, unless the lecture numbed your brain as much as it did mine."

At last, he turned. The annoyance in his gaze gave way to recognition. For a moment, the gunmetal of his gaze flared into a spark. Just as suddenly, the spark vanished.

"Mrs. . . . ?" He frowned at her.

"Stanhope," Emmaline supplied evenly.

"I'd forgotten about you." He pointed to the pile of charts, as if that explained his momentary lapse.

"That, is very flattering of course," she retorted—then immediately wanted to bite her tongue. "I beg your pardon. I should not have given rein to my temper."

A gentleman might have apologized for the insults he'd flung at her, but St. Ledger said nothing. The silence that stretched between them was so awkward Emmaline felt intensely uncomfortable.

"Have you decided whether the terms I outlined this afternoon are acceptable?" she ventured.

He shrugged, as if it were a matter of complete indifference. Then he seemed to recall himself. "I should like to know more about your customer—"

"Client," Emmaline corrected.

He arched a brow. "The man who died. I find myself wondering whether doing business with you puts me in mortal danger."

Emmaline smiled wanly at what she hoped was an attempt at dark humor. "Mr. Burwell seemed in full possession of his senses on the two occasions I met with him. I have no reason to think he found anything in our last meeting to cause him to stand in the path of the Mail."

"Had you found a bride for him?"

"May we sit, Mr. St. Ledger?"

"By all means."

Emmaline sat on one of the wooden chairs on the stage. It was a very odd place to conduct such an interview, but Mr. St. Ledger was a very odd gentleman.

He waited expectantly.

"I generally keep information about my clients

confidential," she began, "but in the case of poor
Mr. Burwell, I suppose it does not matter. He
was not at all suicidal. Indeed, his last words to
me were something on the order of my having
restored his faith in the future."

"How ironic." He took no notice of her indignant glare. "What of the grieving fiancée?"

"Fiancée?"

"Mr. Burwell's chosen bride. Surely she must
be despondent over his fate."

Emmaline shook her head. "Mr. Burwell and I
had not progressed that far. I had only just obtained a thorough understanding of his requirements."

"And they were . . . ?"

"Is it entirely necessary that we discuss this
matter, Mr. St. Ledger? I find it most distressing."

"I merely wondered whether you'd been able
to satisfy his needs." He gave the last word a
slight emphasis, which caused it to linger in the
air between them.

"His needs?" Emmaline eyed him suspiciously. "What are you implying, sir? My business is entirely aboveboard. I hope you do not
suggest otherwise."

She paused in the event he chose to reassure
her, but he did not. "Just because I match couples
in need of companionship, just because our cottage is on the edge of town and ramshackle, is
no reason to assume that I—" She broke off.
"You think me a . . . a *procurer*, don't you?"

An infuriating gleam in the depths of those unnerving gray eyes confirmed her suspicions: He thought her a conniving lightskirt.

Emmaline rose, ignoring the hunger pang that reminded her she'd not eaten dinner, and lifted her chin defiantly. "If you are looking for an abbess, you had best look elsewhere."

"Abbess?" His mouth curled in amusement.

"A-b-b-e-s-s," Emmaline said acidly. She wrapped her cloak around her. "I shall leave you to your bones and rocks."

"Not yet." He moved in front of her, blocking her way.

To her dismay, a wave of dizziness swept her. She'd left what little food they had for Aunt Heloise, but now she wished she'd eaten a morsel herself. Swaying, she reached for St. Ledger's arm.

He stepped adroitly away and Emmaline barely caught herself from falling.

"As to my requirements in a bride," he said, seemingly unaware of her distress, "I have given the matter some thought."

Emmaline leaned weakly against the chair.

"Intelligence, first of all."

She stared at him.

"An aversion to sentiment, a disinclination to hysteria." At her expression, he frowned. "Is there something wrong, Mrs. Stanhope?"

Emmaline tried to gather her wits. "Most gentlemen wish for ladies who are beautiful and, er, passionate."

"I detest passion of any kind."

She blinked. "I see."

"You think that odd?"

"I have always assumed that one of the advantages of marriage is that it allows for the sharing of mutual passions."

"I've never met one."

"I beg your pardon?"

"A mutual passion. 'Tis an illusion created by poets."

"Oh, surely not," Emmaline said uncertainly.

"I yield to your superior knowledge, madam. You have been married. I have not."

Emmaline flushed. "Well . . ."

"You undoubtedly shared such a passion with your husband." His speculative gaze made her cheeks grow warm.

"Our conversation has taken a rather personal turn, Mr. St. Ledger. May we return to the subject at hand?"

"You had no qualms about inquiring into my marital needs."

Dear Lord, the man was trying!

"Yes, but I must know something about you in order to find you a wife," she said in exasperation.

"All you need to know is this: I will not require my wife to share my bed. Therefore, she need not possess passion. Indeed, I prefer that she not."

Emmaline stared at him. "Why, exactly, do you wish to wed, Mr. St. Ledger?"

He frowned. "For the usual reasons."

"In my experience," Emmaline said carefully, "people marry for passion and companionship on the one hand, money and lineage on the other. In the happiest of marriages all of these motives coexist happily."

"Then perhaps you will not be able to find me a wife, Mrs. Stanhope. I have all the money I wish and no desire to perpetuate my line. I have no use for companionship, and I've already given you my views on passion."

Emmaline forced a smile. "If you will give me time, I think I can find the right woman for you, Mr. St. Ledger." She hesitated. "Only—"

"Only what?"

"Have you no interest in love, sir?"

"None at all."

Emmaline tried another tack. "Would you wish to have children?"

Something flickered in his gaze, then was gone. "I think not."

Perhaps that was for the best—it would be dreadful to pass on such madness to another generation.

Her stomach chose that moment to growl rebelliously.

St. Ledger arched a brow, though a true gentleman would have pretended not to hear. "I have a roll in my pouch. Would that interest you?"

"No, thank you," she said quickly, then caught herself. There was no sense in denying what was obvious. "I did not have time to eat," she confessed.

He pulled out the roll and handed it to her. Then, because she could not speak with the bread in her mouth and because he made not the slightest effort at conversation, they sat in excruciating silence while she ate. All the while, she felt his gaze on her. The horrid man. Had he never seen a woman eat?

"As I was saying," Emmaline said at last, thinking she had never felt so uncomfortable in her life, "I am confident that Harmonious Matrimony can find you a wife. As I understand your requirements, she must be smart, practical, even-tempered—"

"Phlegmatic," he corrected.

" *Phlegmatic*?"

"P-h-l-"

"I know how to spell, Mr. St. Ledger. My education was in no way defective." Emmaline glared at him. "You want a woman without an ounce of emotion."

He looked surprised; perhaps he'd thought her a dullard whose knowledge was limited to words of one syllable. Emmaline felt pleased.

"What of her appearance?" she asked.

"What?" He frowned.

"Her looks, Mr. St. Ledger. All of my male clients want someone beautiful, of course, but some prefer dark-haired women, some light; some have a preference for thin women, others for ladies with more . . . fullness."

"Irrelevant."

"I beg your pardon?"

"I don't care what the woman looks like."

Emmaline gaped at him.

"Big as a barn or as thin as a rail. I could care less, just as long as she doesn't get in my way. I am a man of precise habits. Perhaps you should write them down, as it will be essential for my wife to observe them scrupulously."

Emmaline hadn't thought it possible to be surprised by anything the man said, but once again he had astonished her. "That is not necessary. I have an excellent memory."

"Good. I rise at six, go to bed at eleven. I take breakfast precisely at seven, dinner at eight. I am flexible about luncheon; it is at noon, give or take the half hour. After breakfast, I work undisturbed in my study. I expect sherry at dusk, brandy just before I retire."

"Sherry at dusk," she repeated, dazed.

"In the summer I travel to Cornwall to dig in my favorite quarry. Every autumn I prepare a paper on my findings for presentation to the Society. In the winter I teach and translate Latin texts."

"And the spring?" Emmaline managed. "Is that planned, too, or do you leave it to chance?"

"I leave nothing to chance. I spend spring in Sussex. Its sandstone contains a wealth of fossils. Indeed, I am planning a trip there next month. You are looking at me strangely, Mrs. Stanhope."

"It is just that—"

"I lead an ascetic existence," he said, cutting her off. "I have given you all the information you need. How soon can you find someone?"

When hell freezes over. "I will need a few weeks," she said cautiously.

"Prepare the agreement then, and I will sign it." He picked up his charts and bone. "It is late. Nearly time for my brandy. Shall we go?"

"Er, yes." Emmaline reached for the masculine

arm she assumed would be offered her. Again, St. Ledger stepped beyond her reach.

He eyed her expectantly. "Well, Mrs. Stanhope? Are you coming?"

"Yes," she said through gritted teeth, falling into place behind him, "of course."

Mrs. Stanhope was that most offensive of females: a toucher. If he'd given in to the impulse to take her arm, to put a steadying hand at her waist, it would have distracted him from his purpose; for despite her character defects, the woman was alluring—too much so. Thus, he kept his hands fisted at his sides as they descended the grand staircase to the vestibule. She did not utter a word of reproach, but he could tell by the rigid set of her shoulders that she was consigning him to the devil.

As they passed the painted frescoes that adorned the hall, Adrian studied her profile. Her lips were pursed, her expression strained. No doubt he'd treated her badly, but he refused to allow himself to be bothered by that fact. She might be a traitor, she might be a whore—albeit an educated one—but whatever she was, it was nothing to him. He'd promised to do this for the sake of his deceased mother; nothing else mattered. Certainly not Mrs. Stanhope's sensibilities.

Fashionable peers of the realm escorting scantily attired women brushed by them, heading for the ornate ballroom. The Cyprians' Ball was a night of bacchanalia when some of London's most fashionable aristocratic men—many of them married—cavorted openly with their fa-

vorite lightskirts. Adrian recognized a few of his
father's friends—thank God they were too distracted by their partners to recognize him. Lord
Pembroke was too old to cavort with anyone,
though he was trying his best with a woman his
daughter's age. The marquess of Ainsford, an
unpleasant man under any circumstance, was
leering openly at the tipsy woman on his arm.

Adrian had never gone in for debauchery.
Since inheriting the title, he'd shunned all the
trappings of rank, foolish and otherwise. He
lived his life as before, quietly preparing his papers and planning his digs. His fellow academics
and Society members knew him only as Professor St. Ledger, and he meant to keep it that way.
A duke would garner no respect in that circle.

Mrs. Stanhope's eyes widened at the well-
endowed women and their provocative gowns.
Some of the men they passed gave her speculative gazes, but she held her head high.

Somehow, even in her slightly shabby frock
and worn cloak, Mrs. Stanhope exuded dignity.
Her fine auburn hair was pulled sedately off her
face into a coil at the back of her head. Her simple straw bonnet gave her an air of innocence,
though Adrian knew she was anything but. He
hadn't missed the calculating look in her green
eyes, as if she was already spending the fee he
would pay her.

Had she conspired in Burwell's death? Did
evil lurk behind her comely face? He'd discover
the truth, then shed her company as quickly as
possible. Something about her unsettled him.

On Regent Street, carriages were lined up for

blocks to disgorge their passengers. Mrs. Stanhope would have to walk far to find a cab. Adrian hesitated. Whatever she was, he supposed he couldn't abandon her in the crush of drunken dandies and half-naked women.

"I would offer you the use of my carriage, but I walked," he said stiffly. "I shall, however, assist you in finding a cab."

"How kind of you, Mr. St. Ledger."

If her tone held irony, Adrian ignored it. He strode swiftly off toward Regent Street, leaving her to follow. But by the time he reached the corner, he was alone.

Frowning, he turned.

Half a block behind, Mrs. Stanhope stood between two disheveled dandies. One of them pulled her into his arms.

"Mr. St. Ledger!" she called, panic in her voice.

Must the woman be such a trial? If she'd simply told him she meant to finagle her way into the Cyprians' Ball, he'd have happily left her there. But she hadn't mentioned her plan, and it was clear she'd chosen her escorts badly. Anyone could see that those two were trouble. With a heavy sigh, Adrian retraced his steps.

The dandies were foxed. They had removed her cloak, which lay in a formless heap in the street.

"Do stop dallying, Mrs. Stanhope," Adrian said sternly. "Come along, if you please."

She eyed him incredulously. The two men glanced at his unprepossessing attire and dismissed him as a threat.

"Is she yours?" one drawled with a grin.

"Then you ought not to have left her. What do you think, Rob? We found her, so she's ours now, ain't she?"

"Without doubt," the other man replied, putting a proprietary hand on Mrs. Stanhope's shoulder. "Finders keepers, and all that."

Adrian should have been utterly indifferent to Mrs. Stanhope's fate. But as the man's hand dipped lower, he saw that the front of her frock had been torn. When the dandy's hand slipped under the torn fabric to close over her left breast, Adrian felt pure rage.

Whatever the woman was, she didn't deserve this.

"Mrs. Stanhope," Adrian said softly.

Her head whipped around. Adrian saw the tears on her cheeks, the anger and humiliation in her eyes. His rage exploded.

His kick caught the first man in the gut. With an angry cry, the second man shoved Mrs. Stanhope away and launched himself at Adrian. In one fluid motion, Adrian spun away from his attacker and, with a deftly placed kick, dispatched him as well. Both men crumpled to the street.

Adrian plucked Mrs. Stanhope's cloak from the puddle in which it lay. It was dirty and wet, but he tossed it over her shoulders nonetheless. Already a group of curious revelers were moving in their direction, and some of them did not look at all friendly.

"This would be an ideal time," he said quietly, "for us to go in search of that cab."

Chapter 4

S t. Ledger's face was deathly pale.

"I am grateful for your intervention." Emmaline spoke quickly to cover her distress. She clutched her soggy cloak around her. "I imagine you are just now realizing how much danger you risked in taking on those awful men. 'Tis no wonder your nerves are shot."

He did not respond, but sat stiffly on the seat of the coach that had mysteriously appeared at the corner of Little Argyle and Regent streets as they dashed from the scene of the scuffle. His fingers gripped the seat so tightly his knuckles had turned white.

" 'Tis a lovely carriage," Emmaline ventured. "How fortunate that it arrived just in time. Er, do you perhaps know the owner?"

His gaze was blank, and he did not appear to be connected with the world around him. His lips moved slightly, as if he were reciting something to himself. He had said nothing to the driver, who'd cracked the whip as soon as they were inside, sending them barreling through the streets.

"Do you have any notion where this carriage is taking us?" Emmaline ventured.

She tried not to panic, but felt as if she was barely holding on to her sanity. Those horrid men had frightened her badly; she had no illusions about what would have happened had St. Ledger not intervened.

It amazed her that he had. Judging by his reaction, he'd amazed himself as well.

At last he looked at her. His eyes lost their vagueness as he regarded her with an annoyed expression.

"I prefer that you do not speak."

Emmaline bristled. "I beg your pardon. I was merely thanking you for your gallantry on my behalf. Perhaps I ought to thank the coachman instead, as soon as I can ascertain where he is taking us."

"You are angry."

"A brilliant deduction, Mr. St. Ledger. No wonder you held those scholars spellbound for one hour and forty-five endless minutes."

Did she imagine it, or did his mouth curve slightly upward? Impossible. The man had no sense of humor.

"I do not do well in closed carriages."

Emmaline frowned. "Whatever do you mean?"

"I have a loathing of closed spaces. In order to overcome my dread, it is necessary for me to focus my mind entirely on doing so. Conversation is a distraction."

"I have never heard of such a thing."

" 'There are more things in heaven and earth, than are dreamt of in your philosophy.' "

"Oh, dear. Not another one." At his blank look, Emmaline sighed. "My aunt has a passion for playwrights."

"All of them?" he queried, staring at her strangely.

"What I meant is that she is an actress, though she is ill now, and—never mind. You cannot wish to hear about our troubles."

He did not dispute her. Clearly, others' misfortunes did not interest him. Then why, she wondered, had he intervened when those men accosted her?

The answer was obvious. The man needed a wife, and he had no wish to trouble himself to find one. For the moment, at least, he needed her.

Emmaline spared a moment of pity for the woman who would have the misfortune to become Mr. St. Ledger's bride. The difficulties she and Aunt Heloise faced paled to being married to him.

The carriage stopped before a house that looked a hundred years old, maybe more, a grande dame that rose above Brook Street like royalty presiding over its lesser neighbors. Gleaming mullioned windows looked out from gray, forbidding stone that ascended some five or six stories to arched pinnacles. At the apex of the door, presiding incongruously over all, was a ferocious stone elephant. Head thrown back, trunk curled upward, the wild-eyed creature was in the act of trumpeting his might. Another moment and he'd be charging full tilt through the streets.

Emmaline was still staring at the elephant when the door to the carriage opened. St. Ledger exited so rapidly she barely gathered her wits in time to follow him. Moments later, as she stood in the mansion's foyer, Emmaline was convinced she had stumbled into a fantasy. A majestic staircase swept upward, framed by a gilded banister that looked as if it rose all the way to heaven. The foyer itself was polished marble and could have contained their entire cottage.

A distinguished-looking man with a mane of silver hair stood before them, his lined face a careful blank.

"Gibbons," St. Ledger ordered, "find Mrs. Stanhope a dress."

The man did not by so much as an eyelash betray that he thought this an odd request. With a deferential and slightly apologetic air, he studied her with a measuring gaze.

"We have no women in the household, madam, so I shall need to search the attic. I believe His Grace's mother was about your size—"

"Gibbons," St. Ledger barked in a warning tone.

The man bowed slightly. "Forgive me, Your—sir. I will fetch something immediately."

"Mr. St. Ledger," Emmaline whispered when the man had left them. "Where *are* we?"

But he was striding down a corridor, leaving Emmaline no choice but to follow or be stranded in that grand foyer.

Past priceless paintings in gold frames,

through corridors covered with oriental carpets, past a full-length mirror that showed her a woman with tired eyes and a muddied cloak, past more trappings of wealth and grandeur than Emmaline had ever seen in her life, she followed St. Ledger into a musty room where a bottle of fine French brandy stood on a table near a large oak desk.

St. Ledger poured himself a glass, took a sip, then lowered himself into an enormous blue-leather chair that looked more comfortable than anything Emmaline had ever sat on. Curling his fingers around the glass, he closed his eyes. Something like a sigh escaped his lips.

"Be seated," he ordered. "I cannot abide distractions."

From somewhere in the room came a distinct chirp, but Emmaline couldn't see what creature had made the sound. She perched carefully on a tapestry-covered wing chair. "Mr. St. Ledger," she whispered, "where in heaven's name are we?"

He opened one eye. "This is my house. But I'll take no blame for the folderols. I've been here but two months."

"Your house," she echoed numbly. "Dear lord. You are rich as Croesus."

"Unfortunately."

"*Unfortunately?*" Emmaline was appalled. "My dear sir. Most of London suffers in poverty, save for those few like yourself, who wear their good fortune with careless arrogance."

"Good God. You are a liberal. I cannot abide—"

"Liberals," she finished for him. "Yes, I am certain you cannot. Perhaps you do not realize how difficult it is for the rest of us to—"

"Mrs. Stanhope . . ."

Outraged at being interrupted, Emmaline glared at him. *"What?"*

"Your dress. Evidently *you* do not realize it has sustained a mortal injury."

Emmaline looked down at the front of her dress, only to see that her cloak had fallen to one side, leaving the front of her torn frock gaping scandalously. Scarlet, she snatched at the edges of her cloak.

Fortunately, St. Ledger was no longer regarding her. They sat in silence for the next ten minutes, Emmaline clutching her cloak and praying desperately for the arrival of the efficient Mr. Gibbons.

At last he appeared in the doorway, holding several dresses. "I apologize, madam. These are woefully out of date, but perhaps they will serve."

Emmaline rose hastily. "Thank you, Mr. Gibbons," she said. "If you will just show me where I might change—"

"Certainly, madam." He escorted her from the room. "I regret that we have no female to assist you. There is a small chamber off this corridor that might serve your needs. His Grace used it when he grew too feeble to climb the stairs."

"His Grace?"

Gibbons hesitated. "The duke of Trent owned this house, madam. He died earlier this year."

"I see. Mr. St. Ledger has only recently purchased the property?"

Gibbons merely inclined his head.

"Mr. St. Ledger is very wealthy, isn't he?" Emmaline stared at her surroundings in awe.

"Yes, madam. Please ring when you are ready to return to the study."

The chamber Gibbons thought small was larger than her parlor and dining room combined. An enormous bed, its heavy mahogany frame ornately carved, occupied the center of the room. Evidently the chamber had not been used in some time, for it had a slightly musty smell.

Emmaline held up the first of the dresses Mr. Gibbons had brought. It was a teal taffeta, and she immediately adored it. Moreover, it was a perfect fit. Emmaline stared at her reflection in the mirror.

A stranger looked out at her. Her hair was mussed, her eyes too wide and weary, her cheeks flushed. Even so, the gown made her look almost beautiful.

The woman in the mirror frowned. *None of your daydreaming, Em. 'Tis only a dress, and a borrowed one at that. It won't change your circumstances one whit.*

Emmaline sighed. It was best to remember her place.

But why in the world was a man of his wealth paying her to find him a wife?

Adrian glared at the canary, which had hopped onto the table nearest his chair. The bird had fallen down the chimney Monday last. He'd found it in the hearth, looking dazed and out of sorts. Gibbons had unearthed a bamboo cage and cleaned it thoroughly before presenting it to the canary as if the bird were visiting royalty. And though Gibbons had known very well that Adrian could not abide animals, he'd promptly installed the bird in his study.

"Who the devil opened his cage?" Adrian demanded.

"One of the footmen, no doubt," Gibbons replied calmly. "I will speak to him."

Adrian took another sip of brandy just as Mrs. Stanhope appeared in the doorway. He took one look at her and nearly choked.

His mother's gown made the green of her eyes look as fine and rare as emeralds. He had tried to avoid even a glance at the part of her that had been laid bare by that ruffian, but now he could not avert his gaze from that heart-shaped neckline as it dipped just enough to expose the rise of her breasts.

"Is something wrong, sir?" Gibbons asked.

"The gown," he muttered.

Mrs. Stanhope hesitated in the doorway, embarrassment written over features.

" 'Tis a bit much, isn't it?" she said quietly. "I am not accustomed to something so grand."

"And we are not accustomed to females, so you must forgive His—Mr. St. Ledger's lack of tact." Gibbons shot Adrian a dour look.

"Oh, how lovely!" Mrs. Stanhope moved toward the table. "A canary, is it not?"

Of course she would adore the thing. "Gibbons, pour Mrs. Stanhope some sherry."

"Oh, no," she said. "I couldn't possibly—"

"Mr. St. Ledger is right, madam," Gibbons said gently, pouring her a glass. "Spirits have a way of soothing one's nerves."

"That is all, Gibbons," Adrian said pointedly. Gibbons bowed and left the room.

The man had no humility. One of these days, he would have to put a stop to Gibbons's interfering ways. There was no need for the man to keep sending carriages after him, as if Adrian were a helpless child wandering the streets alone—though admittedly, the one tonight had come at an opportune time. Adrian suppressed a sigh as he watched Mrs. Stanhope befriend the canary.

"What is his name?" she asked, stroking its tiny head.

"Name?"

"Never say he doesn't have one! He is so handsome and gallant. You should call him Galahad."

"A bird? Ridiculous."

Her gaze met his. "No more ridiculous than a man who cannot ride in a carriage."

"Name him whatever you wish," he growled. "It makes no difference to me."

Her smile caught him by surprise. "You are quite the curmudgeon, aren't you, Mr. St. Ledger?"

"What I am, or am not, is not your concern, Mrs. Stanhope."

She bit her lip, and Adrian found himself staring at her mouth in some fascination. It was heart-shaped, like the neckline of that dress.

"This evening has been very distressing," she said at last. "I confess I do not know what I am doing here."

He wrenched his gaze away from her mouth. "I could not return you to your aunt in a torn dress. Now that you are suitably attired, I'll have Gibbons drive you home."

"That is kind of you, only—" She gave him an apologetic smile. "I must tell you that there is much about our arrangement that does not make sense."

Surely hell had a special place for prying women. "Such as?"

"You are a wealthy man, Mr. St. Ledger. Scores of women would marry you in an instant, women who move in exalted circles. Why have you come to me?"

A reasonable question, he thought grimly. If only Uncle Harry were here to think of an answer.

"I am not interested in scores of women," he improvised, "or in those who've been taught from birth how to catch a wealthy husband. I seek an uncommon female."

The dubious glint in her eyes told him she found his explanation lacking.

Adrian cleared his throat. "I am not accustomed to females. I do not have them in my home, nor do I escort them about town or any of that nonsense."

"It would be remiss of me not to point out that I, a female, am standing in your house at this very moment."

"An exception." Adrian rose abruptly. "I have

no inclination to increase my meager knowledge of the female gender. That is why I responded to your notice. It is my preference to live alone, but a man can't do that without being deluged with invitations to this or that ball."

"A nuisance," she agreed.

Adrian did not entirely trust the solemn expression on her face. "I don't wish the bother of finding a wife myself, but someone has to run the house, so—"

"I would have thought Mr. Gibbons excelled in that."

"Yes, well, Gibbons is, er, not a wife." Damn. He sounded like a babbling idiot.

She was silent for so long that Adrian mentally congratulated himself for satisfying her questions. He was about to ring for Gibbons to escort her home when she spoke again.

"I have no desire to pry into your personal affairs, sir, but neither will I be party to inflicting cruelty upon some unsuspecting woman."

Adrian blinked. "Cruelty?"

"With all due respect, Mr. St. Ledger, you seem to be something of a misogynist. For all I know, you would beat the poor woman or otherwise abuse her."

"I have never beaten a woman in my life."

"Perhaps that is because you have not had the opportunity," she said with a steely gaze. "I shall not be a party to perversity."

"Perversity? Good God, woman. What do you think I am?"

"I am not sure. What sort of man has no female servants? What sort of man has no desire for passion, or for a wife to share his bed? I find all of this very strange."

Damn Uncle Harry and his persuasive tongue. Adrian closed his eyes and prayed silently for inspiration.

"The truth," he heard himself say, "is that I am inept with women. They do not like me."

She looked around. "A man with all this?"

"I have only lately acquired a fortune. Previously, I taught at one of the colleges, a post that paid very little. I had neither time nor inclination for female companionship. And now . . ." He let his voice trail off, praying he had laden it with the right note of sincerity.

"Now?" she prodded gently.

Adrian sighed. "Now I do not know how to go about it. I don't know how to act around a woman, how to court one, how to please one."

"We are not a foreign species, Mr. St. Ledger."

He shook his head. "I am thirty years of age," he added, readying the coup de grace, "but I have never engaged in . . ." Adrian coughed slightly.

"In . . . ?" She eyed him encouragingly.

"Intimate relations."

Seeing that blush sweep her features almost made this ridiculous scene worthwhile. "I am an innocent, an utter innocent," he said softly.

He didn't think it was possible for anyone to look more stunned than she did at that moment.

"So you see, Mrs. Stanhope, I am afraid of making a fool of myself. That is not something a man cares to admit." He lowered his gaze, congratulating himself on a masterful job of improvisation. Women were vastly pleased when a man humbled himself.

She blinked. "I suppose not. Only—" She broke off.

"Yes?" Now it was his turn to prod.

"You may be eccentric, Mr. St. Ledger, but you do not strike me as fearful."

"Nevertheless, there it is."

"This puts a new light on things," she said. "To be truthful, I thought you somewhat mad. Now I see that you are only . . . unworldly. If I may make a suggestion?"

Adrian drained the rest of his brandy, fearing he'd gone too far—for Mrs. Stanhope looked suddenly inspired.

"If you will put yourself in my hands, Mr. St. Ledger," she said, "I will find you the right mate."

"I will try, madam," he said with a growing sense of dread, "though I am distrustful by nature."

She smiled reassuringly. "I quite understand. But you cannot know how wonderful it is to have a woman in the house. She will supervise your meals, oversee the decorating, handle the social correspondence . . ."

Ruin my life . . . Adrian managed a pallid smile.

"A woman can be a wonderful asset to a man," she assured him. "I will find someone who can show you just exactly what you have missed all these years."

"I cannot abide forward women."

"Not forward," she assured him. "Someone with gentle ways but able to wield a firm hand over the household. There are some things a man just can't manage without a woman. And if you change your mind about having children, needless to say you will need a woman for that."

Adrian nodded as if convinced by her sterling logic.

"You have inspired me, Mr. St. Ledger," she continued. "Already, I have one or two candidates in mind."

"You will warn them about my . . . inexperience?"

She eyed him dubiously. "Something tells me that you are a quick study."

"Nay. I am quite hopeless."

Mrs. Stanhope beamed. "Leave everything to me. I will find you the perfect bride."

Chapter 5

*His eyes reveal nothing, his words little. He is
possessed of rigid habits and loath to relax them.
He is inflexible, cold, and strange, and I cannot
imagine that any woman would truly please
him. He seems without compassion, yet he did
come to my aid tonight . . .*

The words she'd written in her diary summed
up Mr. St. Ledger exactly, Emmaline decided.
No, there was one other.

Untouchable. St. Ledger held himself apart from
the world. In that, of course, he wasn't very different from many scholars—including her father,
who'd insulated himself from life's realities.

Emmaline had learned long ago that problems
couldn't be solved by avoiding the mirror in
which they were reflected. She'd trained herself
to face facts as they were, not how she wished
they would be.

Though that lovely taffeta gown made her feel
like Cinderella, there was nary a prince in sight.

The only thing princely about St. Ledger was his wealth.

Reverently, Emmaline smoothed her hands over the duchess's gown. Long ago she'd believed in fairy tales, in the dreams that made a young girl shiver in anticipation on St. Agnes' Day. She hadn't thought of that custom in years, but tonight the past seemed as tangible as the rustling fabric that slipped through her fingers like rare treasure.

"*Tell me again, Papa.*"

Her father never tired of fueling her imagination with the myths and tales he compiled for his texts. She'd especially liked the story of Agnes, the Roman girl who took a vow of celibacy, spurning all suitors.

"*Why did she not wish to marry, Papa?*"

"*Legend says she was married to her faith. But I suspect she was just particular. That's as it should be, Emmy. Don't wed for any reason except love.*"

Her father had married the woman he loved; when she died birthing Emmaline, he'd never seen any reason to wed again. "*One true love. Remember that, Emmy. He's waiting for you, just as your mother was waiting for me. You'll find him, mark my words.*"

Silly as it seemed now, she'd followed the St. Agnes ritual precisely, fasting every January twentieth and reciting the Lord's Prayer in Latin at bedtime. Then she lay on her back with her hands clasped behind her head, waiting to fall asleep and see the man she was destined to marry. He would come to her in a dream, the legend said, and offer her a drink of water.

Emmaline had long forgotten whether she'd seen any husbandly visions in her dreams. There had been few suitors in real life, though. Her father's death five years ago had put an end to girlish dreams; he'd left a pile of debts big enough to scare off the most ardent suitor.

Aunt Heloise, her father's sister and Emmaline's only living relative, had been her salvation. Though illness had forced her to retire from the stage, her aunt had enough money put away to pay the rent on a small cottage. After the initial shock of discovering that the real world bore no resemblance to her father's, Emmaline had plunged into the task of keeping them afloat.

But even though she could conjugate Latin verbs from dawn till dusk, Emmaline had no marketable skills. Her father had neglected the practical arts. Her needlework was abysmal, her sewing wretched. She couldn't cook if her life depended on it.

It was left to Aunt Heloise to help her see that the market was what one made of it.

"Take Ophelia, dear. Not my favorite role, but I performed it often enough—to raves, of course. Eventually they made me Queen Gertrude, though I always had a girlish way and could have played Ophelia well into my thirties."

"I am certain you were excellent, Aunt, but—"

"The point, dear, is that if you ask people whether they wish to see a young woman get herself spurned by a madman and whine about it endlessly before drowning herself in a pond, most will demur. But throw a bit of poetry in the mix, hint at erotic secrets under the madness, put her in a diaphanous gown, and they love it."

Her father wouldn't have agreed. A purist, he would have put *Hamlet*'s appeal down to universal themes like vengeance and redemption, not something as superficial as Ophelia's gown. But as Emmaline had listened to Aunt Heloise, she'd begun to see that style could be as important as substance.

"In the theater, we invite the audience to laugh or cry with the characters," Aunt Heloise had told her. "They give their imaginations free rein and leave with their dreams satisfied for a time. Needless to say, they feel vastly superior to those on stage. No mystery to it, dear: the key to success lies in creating illusions that feed basic human desires."

Thus had Flora's Fortunes come about.

Telling fortunes was merely a matter of selling illusions. With acting skills as sharp as ever, Aunt Heloise played Flora to a fare-thee-well, while Emmaline copied handbills to slip under doors and nail to posts along the busy turnpike.

They managed to eke out an existence, but though Aunt Heloise was sprightly most of the time, the days she took to her bed came more often. Her petite form grew painfully thin. They consulted doctors when they could afford it, with widely varied results. One physician predicted Aunt Heloise would not live to see Michaelmas. When September came and went, they consulted another, who claimed a tonic of bitters and pine bark would cure her. It had not.

Then Emmaline had played the role of Flora

for a time, but her performance couldn't hold a candle to Aunt Heloise's. The idea for Harmonious Matrimony had come one night as she was pouring out her woes in her journal, wondering why women were fated to marry, bear children, and little else. The moment a woman wed, her property and her person belonged to her husband. Any way one looked at the picture, it was lopsided, with women on the losing end.

What if women had a greater selection of mates, much as a farmer examined his entire herd to find the best cow to take to market? What if a woman could study a large herd of potential husbands?

Though Emmaline had envisioned the agency as a boon to women captive to a paltry crop of local bachelors or parental preferences, Aunt Heloise persuaded her to place a notice in the *Times* to bring in male clients.

"It's men who have the money in this world, and they've no patience for courting. Guarantee them a painless way to find a wife, and they'll flock to our door."

The notice had brought several dozen men to their door—most of whom greatly misunderstood the services Emmaline was offering. She'd found it necessary to invent a deceased husband; widowhood allowed her to depress unwanted advances on the grounds she was still mired in grief for her late spouse. When Mr. Burwell appeared, Emmaline was so relieved he truly wanted a wife, she'd not minded that his requirements for a mate were somewhat crass.

Poor man. He'd never had a chance to find

matrimonial happiness. Emmaline had given his deposit to the constable to pass on to Mr. Burwell's relatives, but there was little else she could do. Perhaps, in some small way, finding a mate for Mr. St. Ledger could help make up for the tragedy Mr. Burwell suffered at her gate.

Emmaline put her diary aside and, with a wistful glance at the duchess's gown, donned her serviceable night rail, which had several holes in the sleeves. She crawled into her bed, pulled up the covers, and wondered who in the world she could pair with Mr. St. Ledger.

She didn't know what to make of his assertion that he had no experience with women. Even her father's students, who hadn't been above twenty, had been clever enough to steal kisses from her when her father was unawares.

Those kisses were but a distant memory now, and Emmaline felt far older than her twenty-two years. Her small bed was hard and uncomfortable; the broken window admitted rain, insects, and cold. She thought of Mr. St. Ledger lying in some enormous feather bed in his grand, comfortable house. She tried to imagine him as one of her father's students, whose gazes had burned with the fire of discovery.

But St. Ledger's eyes were dead and cold, save for the occasional burst of intensity that flared now and then. She thought of his lecture, dull and empty, and his domestic rituals, obsessive and inflexible. She thought of how he'd scarcely looked at the tear in her dress and of how his legs, swift and deadly, had lashed out at her assailants.

Who was the man behind those impenetrable gray eyes?

When she fell asleep, hands clasped behind her head, Emmaline dreamed of a strange, unquenchable thirst.

Adrian awoke to find the canary perched on his chest, studying him from beady black eyes.

"Go away," he growled.

The bird did not move.

Adrian sat up with a jerk, prompting the creature to flee to the bedside table. With relentless cheer, the canary chirped a morning greeting.

The clock on the wall said eight o'clock. Unbelievably, he'd overslept. With a muttered curse, Adrian swung his feet over the side of the bed and plunged them into the waiting bucket of ice water.

Frissons of cold shot up his legs, sped through his chest, and settled somewhere in the vicinity of his heart. He stood for a moment in the frigid water, letting the cold fill him, savoring its bite. Thomas Jefferson had had the right of it: A bucket of ice water each morning got a man off to the right start. Those Americans were an inventive lot.

Reaching for a towel, Adrian reviewed his plans for the day. It would be just the kind of day he liked, filled with solitude and study. He had one more paper to finish, so he'd be far too busy to call upon Mrs. Stanhope and sign that contract.

Mrs. Stanhope—now there was a dilemma. His uncle thought her guilty of murder, treason, or both, but Adrian suspected her only real crime was being a charlatan and cheat. Through fortune-telling and that ridiculous matrimonial agency, she'd probably bilked dozens of unsuspecting victims out of their last penny.

A glass of fresh water sat on the table. Slowly, Adrian drained it. Despite sleeping late, he still felt weary. His sleep had been restless and terror-filled, as it always was when he stayed up too late. Last night Father Hell had marched through his dreams, putting him mercilessly through his lessons. *"Contrition," he'd said, bending over to whisper in Adrian's ear. "C-o-n-t-r-i-t-i-o-n. You can spell that, can't you, boy?"* The sharp crack of the rod on his back sent him spiraling deeper into the past. *"Com-pli-ance. Four vowels, three syllables. Show me, boy. Show me you know what that means."*

It was *her* fault that he hadn't slept well. As punishment for the rash act of bringing that woman into his house, he'd lain awake last night remembering her in that gown, letting it replace the image of her torn frock and all that it had revealed.

Those lies he'd told her held more truth than falsehood. For as she'd stood in the doorway of his study, her beauty limned in teal, Adrian had tasted fear. Though he hadn't touched a woman in a great while, he wanted to touch Emmaline Stanhope. A woman like that could make a mockery of a man's self-control.

Thank God he'd mastered his will long ago. There was no risk that he'd let Mrs. Stanhope's enticing charms beguile him into something rash.

Adrian took a deep breath and walked over to the wardrobe. His clothes hung in neat, orderly rows. Browns together, fawn trousers separated from buff ones. Boots arranged neatly, from high-topped Hessians to the kid slippers for evening wear. Most of these expensive tokens of his rank had been his father's; many—like the canary yellow waistcoat and pink-satin shirt— were, in Adrian's opinion, unwearable. He'd asked Gibbons to remove them, but the man had turned a deaf ear. No doubt he hoped the garments would show Adrian how a proper duke attired himself. With a sigh, Adrian selected a plain pair of brown trousers and a simple muslin shirt.

Breakfast was a satisfying meal of kidneys and coddled eggs. He perused the London *Times,* which had a dispatch from the Peninsula about England's progress against Napoléon. Wellington seemed to have matters well in hand. Whatever harm England faced from Burwell and his treasonous friends had not yet damaged the cause.

But the dispatch was several weeks old, Adrian noticed. Who knew what was really going on? He'd have to pursue matters with Mrs. Stanhope, but for today, at least, he'd give himself a respite from the woman.

When he settled in at his desk and began to write, the words flowed effortlessly from his pen. *It is possible the specimen came from an elephant bought to England centuries ago by the Romans. A comparison with known skeletons of both Asian and African elephants reveals sufficient differences, how-*

ever, as to make it unlikely the Cornwall bone derives from either species as we know them today.

This was what he loved. Fossils and rocks, solid and steady. Mysteries from the distant past, comfortingly remote.

The door opened. Gibbons stood on the threshold, regarding Adrian with solemn eyes. He held some brown, formless thing in his arms.

"Madam left her cloak." Gibbons imparted that news as if it were a weighty matter requiring an immediate and equally weighty response.

Adrian stared at the garment Gibbons held so gingerly. Even at a distance, he detected the distasteful odor of the street.

"Burn it." He scribbled a few more words before he realized Gibbons was still standing in the doorway. Adrian looked up. "Yes?"

"I doubt madam would approve," Gibbons said.

Adrian frowned. Gibbons spoke of the woman in tones one normally reserved for the queen. "The cloak's ruined, Gibbons. Go and burn the thing."

"Perhaps," Gibbons said, "she does not have another."

The man's reproachful tone made Adrian feel like the devil incarnate. He knew Gibbons was manipulating him—doubtless he'd done the same with Adrian's father.

Well, Adrian had never claimed to be the man his father was, thank God. "Gibbons," he said warningly, "please remember that you work for me, not the other way around."

"That fact is always uppermost in my mind, Your Grace."

Gibbons betrayed not a hint of insolence. To the unknowledgeable eye, he appeared the dutiful man of affairs, an image aided by his distinguished silver hair.

Adrian knew better. As a child, he'd been only dimly aware of his father's quietly efficient man of affairs. But two months ago, Gibbons had appeared at the Maidstone dig to inform Adrian that, as he was now duke, urgent matters required his attention. Nor would the man leave his side. To finally gain a moment's peace, Adrian had come to London to attend to his ducal duties, something many letters from his solicitors had failed to accomplish.

Since then, Adrian had learned that Gibbons was anything but compliant. Whatever instinct Gibbons had for appearing just as Adrian needed him also gave the man an uncanny knowledge of exactly where Adrian's weaknesses lay.

Mrs. Stanhope's cloak, for example.

Adrian stared at the ugly brown mass in Gibbons's arms. It was folded neatly, carefully, as if it were some luxurious garment and not a soggy, smelly, disgusting thing that had spent time in the street.

All right. Perhaps she didn't have another. Perhaps the only thing she had to protect her lovely shoulders from the cold was that ugly, putrid brown cloak.

"Very well," Adrian snapped. "Send it back."

"Unfortunately," Gibbons said in a mournful tone, "I have sent the footmen on errands. You had requested alterations in the jacket from Weston's, as well as several books from Hookham's."

"Yes?" Adrian waited for the man to reveal why those things should concern him.

"After you complained about last night's burned dinner, Cook set the scullery boy to cleaning the stove. He's covered in soot and unfit to leave the house. Cook himself has gone to market with a list of the items you requested for dinner. It will take some doing, I'm afraid. He is aware of your fondness for oysters, but the oyster harvest has been very bad this year."

Adrian took a deep breath to quiet his temper. "In short, the fact that no one is available at the moment to return Mrs. Stanhope's cloak is entirely my fault."

"As you say, Your Grace." Gibbons bowed his head, but not before Adrian had seen a glimmer of intrigue in the man's dark brown eyes.

"Then see to the matter yourself."

"Certainly," Gibbons said easily.

Adrian waited. He'd learned enough about his man of affairs to know this subject was not yet closed.

"Although . . ." Gibbons began, his voice trailing off.

Adrian sighed. "Yes?"

"My gout is acting up again," Gibbons said. "A man of my years must constantly battle the reminders of his human frailties."

"You have my deepest sympathies."

Gibbons laid the cloak on a small table near the door. "No doubt I will be well enough in a day or so to undertake such an errand. Perhaps

Mrs. Stanhope will not need her cloak before then, although my elbow aches uncommonly today. 'Tis usually a sign bad weather is approaching."

Adrian watched as Gibbons slipped from the room with the grace and speed of a man half his age.

Gout, indeed.

He stared at the brown pile on the table. He wouldn't be able to get a damned thing done with Mrs. Stanhope's cloak infusing the air with its vile odors. Obviously, Gibbons meant to shame him into returning the thing himself. For reasons known only to himself, Gibbons evidently approved of Mrs. Stanhope.

Well, no matchmaking man of affairs was going to rule his life. Gibbons had reckoned without the steely control Adrian had forged from the ashes of his boyhood.

Adrian grabbed the cloak. The coarse brown wool felt rough and hard against his fingertips. Doubtless it left tiny abrasions on Mrs. Stanhope's smooth, ivory skin, extracting a price for protecting her from the chill.

He inhaled deeply. Yes, it stank of the gutter. But there was another scent, one not wholly eclipsed by the street odor. Lavender, perhaps, or violet—he could never distinguish between the two.

No doubt she'd wash the thing until the mud and street smells vanished, then fling it over her lovely shoulders as she went on her way, seeking her next prey.

Fortune-tellers, seers, mesmerists—they were

all the same, preying on a victim's desire for gratification and happiness, twisting that need into a hope that fattened their illicit coffers.

Even if Mrs. Stanhope hadn't sent that Burwell fellow to his death, she'd led him on, allowed him to believe that she could find the woman of his dreams.

Dreams were idiocy, nothing but vain hopes fed by human folly. Sometimes Adrian wanted to climb to the rooftop to shout that truth to the world.

A nice, healthy fire blazed in the hearth. It would make short work of the ruined garment that had once graced Mrs. Stanhope's shoulders.

Emmaline paused under the very intimidating elephant that guarded the door of Mr. St. Ledger's mansion. She'd never called at a gentleman's home before. It wasn't a proper thing to do, but she'd buried her doubts and her pride under one immutable fact: He had her only cloak.

Her knock sounded loud and brazen to her ears. She pulled her light shawl more tightly around her shoulders, but it was no substitute for a woolen cloak.

Mr. Gibbons opened the door. To her surprise, he did not look at her with disdain, or hint that a respectable woman did not call at a gentleman's home unescorted.

"Good afternoon, madam. Come in out of the chill."

"Thank you, Mr. Gibbons. That is a very fierce elephant, isn't it?"

" 'Tis a relic from the days of Charles I. The king had those who supported him against Cromwell erect statues of fierce animals at their gates, the fiercer the better. Supposedly, they signaled a vast network of safe havens and tunnels the king could use if it became necessary to flee London."

"My goodness." Emmaline studied the elephant anew.

"Most of the houses had no such escapes, however; their owners merely put up the statues to mollify the king. But you didn't come for a history lesson. Mr. St. Ledger is in the study, just down this corridor. Sorry to leave you on your own, but I was on my way out on an urgent errand."

Stunned by Mr. Gibbons's warm but confusing welcome, Emmaline walked through the corridor until she came to a partially closed door. An odd, unpleasant smell wafted from the room. Gingerly, she pushed the door open, then gasped in disbelief at the scene before her.

A half-naked man—not naked, precisely, but alarmingly unshirted—stood before a blazing fire, his back to her as he held a smoking remnant of fabric.

"Shut the door!" St. Ledger barked over his shoulder as smoke suddenly shot from the fireplace.

Realization dawned. "You're burning my cloak!" Emmaline watched, dumbfounded, as the fire leapt up violently, threatening to breach the boundary of the brick hearth.

"Gibbons!" St. Ledger roared, and though Emmaline was quite sure everyone in the house must have heard, no one responded to his summons.

Smoke filled the study. St. Ledger loosed an oath, then rushed past her out of the room. Just like the man to leave her to die in his smoke-filled study.

Coughing and sputtering, Emmaline fumbled for the door. Just as she found it, St. Ledger swept in with a bucket of water. She heard a splash and a sizzle, and a dying cloud of black smoke wafted toward them.

"Open the windows!" he ordered.

Emmaline groped along the wall and fumbled for the latch, but the window wouldn't budge. Suddenly St. Ledger was there, throwing up the sash to admit life-giving air.

Gradually, the smoke thinned.

Emmaline took a deep breath. St. Ledger did the same. As her breathing grew more even, she slanted a gaze at him.

His bare chest had been no mirage.

"W-what happened to your shirt?" she stammered.

"I used it to fight the fire. It was the only thing I had handy after I fed it that cloak of yours. Have you recently stepped in whale oil, madam? Because something on the fabric caused the fire to run wild. I tried to beat it out with my shirt, and was managing quite well until you opened the door and gave the fire all the air it needed to blaze out of control. Damn it, woman, do you not have even a rudimentary understanding of science?"

Emmaline rounded on him. "You, sir, are a rude fellow. You are coarse and churlish and unkind. Your disposition is grating and self-centered. If I am to make any progress in finding you a bride, you must change, Mr. St. Ledger, and quickly. I don't care if you're rich as Croesus, I will never be able to find a bride for an ogre."

"Ogre?" St. Ledger's gaze narrowed to angry slits. "Did you say *ogre*, madam?"

Emmaline lifted her chin defiantly. "I did."

He crossed his arms. The movement drew Emmaline's gaze to the remarkable contours of his bare chest and the faint sheen of perspiration that accented it. But Mr. St. Ledger showed not the slightest concern that he was offending her feminine sensibilities. He merely stood there, eyeing her darkly.

"I cannot work miracles," Emmaline declared, willing her mind from its contemplation of Mr. St. Ledger's physical assets. "You are a thorough miscreant. No woman wants to marry such a man. If there is any hope for you, you must put yourself in my hands."

One brow arched, but his stern expression did not alter.

"I will be frank, sir. My aunt and I are in urgent need of funds. The rent is due soon, and her doctors are costly. But I won't take your money unless I know I can succeed with you. And at the moment, you have absolutely no chance of making a successful match."

"No chance?" He finally looked taken aback.

"None," Emmaline affirmed sternly. "You must not take this lightly, sir."

"Oh, I shan't," he murmured.

"We will require daily lessons," she said.

"Lessons?"

"Oh, yes, Mr. St. Ledger. You are my only client—the publicity over Mr. Burwell's death has nearly ruined us. Without your fee, our landlord will evict us. So you see, I *must* succeed with you, as daunting a prospect as that is."

St. Ledger studied her. "You find me daunting, Mrs. Stanhope?"

Emmaline leveled a gaze at him. "What I find daunting is the task of turning you into a respectable husband. The women of my acquaintance are genteel, with strong hearts and refined sensibilities. I will not foist upon them some ill-mannered oaf so wealthy that no one has had the courage to enumerate his many faults."

For a moment, St. Ledger almost looked offended. "Very well," he said at last. "When do we begin?"

"Today," Emmaline said immediately. "Present yourself at my door at four."

"This afternoon? But I must revise my paper—"

"Either you are serious about this endeavor or you are not. If you have no intention of learning how to make yourself amenable to a woman, then let us end it now—for this is no joke to me. I will need all the time I can get to find another client."

Emmaline fervently hoped he had not noticed the quiver in her voice or the worry in her eyes.

It was too bad their fate was in the hands of such a man. To be sure, he did not look like a monster. The soot on his high cheekbones gave him an appealingly earthy air, and that muscled expanse of bare chest left no doubt as to his manliness. Most women would find him attractive—until they got to know the man underneath that impressive physique.

So intent was Emmaline's scrutiny that she only belatedly realized he was studying her just as thoroughly—and St. Ledger's eyes glinted with something mysterious and a little frightening. Emmaline shifted awkwardly under his inspection.

Had she soot on her nose? Was there something amiss with her frock? She looked down, but she was properly buttoned and her dress covered everything that needed to be covered.

"Very well, Mrs. Stanhope," he said abruptly. "I will present myself at four. You may do with me as you will."

Emmaline tried for levity, to diffuse the thick, oppressive air between them. "You'll see, Mr. St. Ledger: we will turn you into a veritable Prince Charming."

His brows rose. "Will we?"

"Oh, yes." Emmaline smiled. "The ladies will fall at your feet. You'll have your pick of brides."

"That is comforting."

"Well, I'll be on my way." Emmaline edged away from the window, away from the intoxicating nearness of Mr. St. Ledger's bare chest.

It ought to be a crime for a man so beastly to be so attractive.

Chapter 6

The warm-blooded higher vertebrates would seem too fragile to survive through the eons.

Rude, was he? Coarse, churlish, unkind? She didn't know the half of it. But an ogre? Now *that* hurt.

Their young require long gestation and considerable care long after birth; it is unlikely they would weather a volatile climate for long.

She wanted to give him lessons. Very well; he'd let her. And when they were done, he'd have the answer to his uncle's questions and maybe a few of his own. Then he'd put the conniving Mrs. Stanhope out of business. She'd claim no more victims on his watch.

Lessons? Yes, he'd teach *her* a few things. Maybe he'd even let her throw herself on his mercy, barter her lovely person for the privilege of retaining that ramshackle cottage of hers. He'd watch her writhe in sweet agony and marvel at his masculine prowess as he pleasured her—

Or maybe not.

It had been too long since he'd touched a

woman. He'd not last ten seconds with the difficult but captivating Mrs. Stanhope.

Thus, the scientist looks to other species as links to the earliest forms of life.

Adrian thrust Mrs. Stanhope from his mind as his pen moved swiftly over the page. Within the world of scholarship there was no room for guessing or half-truths. Here there were discipline, boundaries, clear lines and expectations. It was the life he had chosen and would continue, dukedom or no dukedom.

He very much wished it was no dukedom. Unlike his two older brothers, Adrian hadn't been trained for the title; two sons had been considered sufficient to preserve the line. Adrian had scarcely known his father, a loud and boisterous man usually steeped in spirits, or his brothers, who'd been away at school most of the time. He'd been nine when his mother took him far away from anything resembling a duke's coddled existence.

As it turned out, two sons were not sufficient to preserve the line. His father's refusal to take the new smallpox vaccine carried him aloft, along with Cameron and Daniel, who'd been just as stubborn.

Adrian had mourned their passing in the only way he knew: by plunging deeper into the rigors of scholarship. He'd skipped the funeral, knowing his father would not have wanted him there. The duke had considered Adrian's existence a blight, not a boon.

Adrian had yet to visit the far-flung estates that were now his responsibility. He hoped they bore no resemblance to this gloomy house or the study that, as a result of this morning's disaster, now reeked of smoke. He had no intention of transforming the mansion into something more pleasant; he meant to be off as soon as he concluded this business with Mrs. Stanhope. The little cottage he'd leased at Oxford for many years beckoned.

There he could mold young minds, help them build the foundation for a lifetime of scholarship. There he measured his days with perfect control. Nothing threatened his orderly world; no squawking birds upset his sleep. No drunken dandies prompted him to violence. Most especially, no woman interfered in his carefully delineated universe.

The canary swooped onto Adrian's desk. It landed near his water goblet and peered at him through the stem of the glass, which distorted its head into something akin to a large iguana. A herbivore, he recalled from his early animal texts. Lizards were a notoriously adaptable species. Over the centuries they'd survived earthquakes and volcanoes, storms and pestilence. Who knew how many years they had been on the planet?

That sparked another train of thought, and soon his pen was moving furiously once more. Charlatans like Mrs. Stanhope might claim to possess the key to life's mysteries, but the true secrets of the universe lay in fragments of its past. Science, not metaphysics. Fact, not illusion. Reason, not lust. Control above all. That was the natural order of things.

The canary let out a squawk. Adrian shot him

a warning glare, daring the creature to interfere with his work. The bird ruffled its feathers and blinked one eye in a fair approximation of a wink. Then he hopped to the center of the desk and regarded Adrian solemnly.

Interesting. The bird was toying with him.

"What are you staring at?" Adrian groused. He rose, secretly glad for the excuse to stretch. His father's chair was deuced uncomfortable. Adrian ambled over to the mantel.

Swooping past his ear, the canary landed next to a candlestick and began to preen disgracefully at its reflection in the brass.

"Now look here," Adrian began sternly. "I'll not have you following me about all day—"

"Well, Trent, what have you learned about the mysterious Mrs. Stanhope?"

Adrian turned. His uncle was in the act of settling himself into a wing chair. Why hadn't he thought to give instructions he was not to be disturbed?

"Nothing." Adrian crossed the room to his desk.

Sir Harry frowned. "The woman's nearly destitute. I'll wager a dinner at White's she's a turncoat. Either that or a whore. Maybe both."

That jarred. Adrian picked up his pen and moved it aimlessly over the paper. He did not reply.

"You detected nothing unusual?" Sir Harry prodded.

Adrian's doodles had formed themselves into letters. *E-m-m-a . . . Emmaline.*

"She's being followed, you know."

Adrian looked up in surprise. "Impossible. I would have discerned that."

"You aren't God, Trent. I'll wager you didn't even notice *our* man."

"Your man?" Adrian said tightly.

"We're following her, too. All of England seems to be following the woman. Our man saw you rescue her from those foxed imbeciles. A brilliant stroke to gain her confidence, Trent. My estimation of your skill grows."

Followed—by *two* men—and he hadn't even known it. Damn. He'd been more distracted than he realized.

"You brought her here," his uncle said.

Adrian stiffened.

"Did you seduce her?"

"Certainly not."

"Pity. Might have loosened her tongue."

Adrian's gaze fell on his paper. *Emmaline . . . seduce*, the doodles read.

"Now that you're on the case, I'll call off our man. He doesn't have a prayer of getting as close to her as you'll be." Sir Harry winked broadly. "For the record, the Foreign Ministry sanctions seduction as a justifiable means to the end. All for Mother England, eh?" He rose and gave Adrian a hearty pat on the back.

Suddenly, the canary swooped from the mantel and launched himself at Sir Harry. With a warlike squawk, he dug his tiny talons into the man's balding pate.

"What the devil?" His uncle flailed at the bird, but the canary mounted a second assault that forced Sir Harry to take cover under a small table.

Having won the point, the bird gave a high-pitched cry and flew back to the mantel.

"Damn and blast!" His uncle glared up at Adrian from the floor. "When are you going to put that bird to the use God intended it? Either eat the thing or teach it manners."

Galahad. His knight and defender.

Adrian stared at the bird, barely aware of his uncle's hasty, blustering departure. "What a strange creature you are. He could have dispatched you with a well-aimed fist."

The canary merely cocked his head.

Adrian's gaze shifted back to his paper. He'd do no more work today; his concentration was shot. Instead of fossils and lizards, his mind's eye gave him the image of a woman in a teal dress, with a neckline that took him down, relentlessly down.

His hand moved to the bellpull, but Gibbons appeared in the doorway before he touched it. "Have the carriage brought round, Gibbons," Adrian said in a resigned tone. "It is time for my appointment with Mrs. Stanhope."

Gibbons hesitated. "Should you like me to come with you, Your Grace?"

"That is not necessary. I am in perfect command of myself."

A dubious chirp came from the vicinity of the mantel. Adrian glared at the canary, which regarded him solemnly from atop the brass candlestick.

* * *

"That nice Mr. St. Ledger is here for his appointment."

Emmaline ran her hand over Thomas's dark fur. "There is nothing remotely nice about that man."

"Then again, nice men are so uninteresting."

Emmaline managed a weak smile. "I have his contract ready. I'll take it down." It had taken her the better part of an hour to prepare the document, which pledged to present him with two candidates in thirty days. This, she suspected, would take a small miracle to achieve. On the other hand, St. Ledger's wealth was bound to be a powerful draw. What was it like to have all the money one wished?

A king without love is a pauper, Emmy. I may not have much money, but your mother's love was a treasure beyond price. Love makes the poorest man a king.

Her father's declaration had made her feel guilty, since it was her birth that deprived him of his true love. Still, he'd reclaimed his happiness. He took pleasure in his students and his passion for teaching.

If there was any passion in St. Ledger, it was tightly controlled. A man whose life held no imagination, no emotion, no joys or disappointments, was a man who gave nothing of himself. Could the right woman find a wellspring of feeling in the man? How would Emmaline find that woman?

"Daydreaming again? I can guess who has put those fantasies in your head." Aunt Heloise smiled.

Emmaline straightened. "There's not a fanciful bone in my body."

"It's not the bones that decide such things. You could do worse than to let that heart of yours do the thinking once in a while."

Emmaline did not pretend to misunderstand. "Mr. St. Ledger is well-favored, but I have no interest in him, save as a client who can keep the wolf from our door."

Her aunt led the way down the stairs. "Wolves aren't all bad—as long as one remembers they are wolves and cannot change their natures."

Just outside the parlor, Aunt Heloise struck a pose. " 'He's mad that trusts in the tameness of a wolf . . . or a whore's oath.' " Her brow furrowed. "Or was that honor? 'Whore's honor'? No, that won't wash."

Her aunt could project her voice to the heavens; St. Ledger had doubtless heard every word. Sure enough, as they entered the parlor his gaze settled on Aunt Heloise.

"Er, 'Whore's oath,' " he said politely.

Aunt Heloise gave a peal of delight. " 'Thou, sapient sir, sit here.' " She sat on the couch and patted the space next to her. " 'Now, you she foxes!' "

Her aunt had been a beautiful woman, with a mane of copper curls and a vivacious sparkle in her blue eyes. Even now, her coy smile was alluring; St. Ledger, Emmaline noticed, was not immune to her aunt's charm.

"You are worlds beyond me, ma'am." He looked embarrassed, but obediently sat next to Aunt Heloise.

"Nonsense," she said. "You merely want study."

At Emmaline's baffled expression, Aunt Heloise laughed. "Do not be so grim, dear. Our guest was but signaling a mutual interest in *Lear*." Aunt Heloise regarded St. Ledger approvingly. "How did you come by your knowledge of drama?"

"As a student, I was compelled to tutor younger students in literature. It was not my field, but—"

"Oh, dear. I was hoping you had been on the stage." Aunt Heloise smiled wistfully. "I am so out of touch these days. Like a fish out of water—or is that a duck? I suppose it doesn't matter."

To Emmaline's amazement, St. Ledger's expression softened. "I imagine you are a gifted actress, ma'am."

"All in the past now, I'm afraid." With a parting sigh for lost pleasures, Aunt Heloise rose and left the room.

Alone with St. Ledger, Emmaline felt suddenly awkward. She thrust the contract at him. He scarcely looked at it, but signed his name and reached in his pocket for her fee.

"Ten pounds," he said, and set the money on the table.

They stared at each other. Emmaline cleared her throat. "I did not properly thank you for rescuing me last night."

" 'Twas nothing," he answered gruffly.

"Nay, you put yourself in harm's way because of me."

"Those men were too foxed to do me any harm."

"You are very skilled with your, er, feet," Emmaline added, then realized how silly that sounded.

"It is an acquired talent. I'd thought to avenge myself on an old enemy. Unfortunately, he died before I got the chance."

Heavens. The man was a bloodthirsty barbarian.

St. Ledger's face was impassive, but his eyes held a swirling intensity that left the space between them churning with currents, foreign and unknown.

An answering agitation warmed her innards.

"I suppose," she said at last, "we ought to begin our lessons."

Her imagination was playing her tricks. There was no reason to think those enigmatic gray eyes held any warmth for her. "The first thing you must learn is conversation."

"Conversation?" He eyed her warily.

"I speak, then you," she explained. "Discourse is essential to a good marriage."

"I can't imagine having anything to say to a wife."

Dear lord, the man was a trial. "When one is courting a woman," Emmaline said evenly, "one must at least pretend to subscribe to the civilized conventions. It's like this, Mr. St. Ledger: A woman expects a man to talk to her."

"My father never talked to my mother or anyone else he didn't care to."

"I suppose that explains why *you* turned out

so well." Instantly, Emmaline put her hand to her mouth. She hadn't meant to speak so; the words had somehow tumbled out.

St. Ledger's gaze narrowed. "You ought to leave off the sarcasm, Mrs. Stanhope. It doesn't become you."

"I beg your pardon." She deserved his reprimand. She'd made them antagonists again, shifted the mood from one of unsettling possibilities to outright hostility. Then again, perhaps that was for the best. "I only meant that you must learn to carry on a conversation with a woman."

"If it's anything like the one we're having now, I'd just as soon not."

Emmaline took a deep breath. "Somehow, you bring out the worst in me, sir. My rudeness is not your fault, of course. 'Tis only—"

"If this is your notion of conversation, madam, it's uncommonly silly."

"Yes, I suppose it is." Emmaline tried to gather her wits. "Let us start again, shall we?"

"I would say that the question of whether we started in the first place is open to debate."

Exasperated, Emmaline rose. St. Ledger leaned back against the cushions, as if he were in the comfort of his own horridly grand house.

"Now, *that* is not the thing," she said sternly. "If I rise, you must also."

"Must I?" One brow arched.

Her heart was beating alarmingly fast. There was a strange fluttering in her stomach, especially when Mr. St. Ledger's gaze roved over her like that.

"Yes, you must," Emmaline said firmly. "It is proper to rise when a woman does. You must give her to understand that you respect her, that you hold her in uncommon esteem. You cannot do that if you are lolling about on the sofa."

"I see." Slowly, Mr. St. Ledger got to his feet. He was a full head taller than Emmaline and stood much closer than she would have liked. "Now what?"

"Conversation," Emmaline said swiftly. "I will say that the weather is lovely, and you agree in a pleasant tone."

"If I agree, what is the point of talking about it?"

Emmaline sighed. "The *point*, sir, is that you must say something in response to my remark. Then I reply. It is how conversation is done. Back and forth, give-and-take. You cannot simply stand there, refusing to grant the other person any ground, making her feel like a complete idiot."

"If you are an idiot, madam, I take no responsibility."

Emmaline stared at him. "I was speaking metaphorically," she said through gritted teeth. "You have not made me feel like an idiot, exactly—"

"Glad to hear it."

Emmaline brought her hand to her temple, which had begun to throb mercilessly. "You are an infuriating man."

"Aren't you obliged to say something pleasant and meaningless that I can agree with?"

"You are doing this on purpose," she said in

a small, furious voice. The man was an intractable oaf. No woman would wish to spend more than five minutes in his company.

He merely arched those infuriating brows again. "Perhaps you would like to change the subject?"

"Not in the least." Emmaline glared at him. " 'Tis lovely weather we're having, don't you think, Mr. St. Ledger?"

"I don't think about the weather."

Resolutely, she ignored him. "Now if I had a fan, I might move it so—" Emmaline fluttered an imaginary fan.

"What the devil are you doing with your hands?"

" 'Tis another kind of communication. I am flirting with you."

"And here I thought you were only clawing at the air."

Emmaline stamped her foot. "Stop it! That handsome face of yours will only take you so far. No woman in her right mind will tolerate—"

Handsome face. Had she actually said the words aloud?

To her utter amazement, St. Ledger reddened. "Perhaps we should continue this lesson another time."

"Yes, of course." Emmaline took a step backward, trying to put space between them. She had thoroughly disgraced herself. Another minute and he'd think she was throwing herself at him.

"Tomorrow?" he suggested.

"Er, yes. That would be convenient."

"I believe it is going to rain."

She blinked. "Rain?"

"It was an observation about the weather. I was trying to begin a conversation. Though since I am leaving, that appears to be unnecessary."

Emmaline sighed. "At least you have come away with something from this afternoon's lesson."

He tilted his head. "Yes. Good day, madam."

"Good day, Mr. St. Ledger."

He turned toward the door.

"Mr. St. Ledger?"

As he glanced back at her, his eyes glimmered with something quite . . . stimulating.

"I will try to start off on a better foot next time. I'm afraid that I—" Moving forward, Emmaline's foot caught the corner of the frayed cotton rug that covered the parlor floor.

To her complete and utter mortification, she toppled forward into his arms.

Adrian's instincts bade him to release her, but it was too late. His senses were awash.

The crisp muslin of her dress brushed his skin. Her hair spilled out of its pins, tumbling over her shoulders like a silken veil, sliding over his hand like a caress. Her faint floral scent evoked a field full of wildflowers.

Vast, paralyzing sensations swept him. He stared down at her, wondering how one woman could make herself such a nuisance. As she struggled to right herself, his arms closed around her.

Her head came up, embarrassment plain on

her features. "H-how clumsy of me," she stammered.

His hands gripped her arms. They slid slowly down her sleeves to the point where the fabric stopped and her bare skin began. His thumbs grazed the pulse points on the inner part of her wrist.

"Mr. St. Ledger," she murmured.

Adrian decided he had never seen anything quite as appealing as her pink, trembling lips.

"Mrs. Stanhope," he acknowledged.

"So clumsy," she said again.

"I have noticed that about you, madam. You are forever requiring my assistance."

She tried to pull away, but his hands refused to release her. "Wh-what are you doing, Mr. St. Ledger?"

Adrian sighed. "I have no idea."

Her eyes widened; her lips parted. What he saw in her gaze might have been invitation or just plain horror at finding herself at his mercy. He hadn't tried to read a woman in ages; he had no idea how to do so now.

"You—you didn't let me fall." Her lips curved into a shy smile. "How gallant of you."

"As I said before, madam, sarcasm doesn't suit you." Adrian wanted to release her, but his will deserted him.

She bit her lip. "You are the strangest man I have ever known."

"I imagine you've known quite a few," he said, unaccountably irritated by that fact.

The sudden silence sizzled with awareness. A slow, burning heat began in his gut, and spread throughout him. With a will of its own, his hand stroked her forearm.

"I have noticed," Mrs. Stanhope said suddenly, "that my gentlemen clients sometimes develop a tendre for me."

Adrian's hand froze.

"I suspect this is because, in the course of talking about a potential mate, we are forced to speak of rather intimate things," she added.

"You do not suggest that I—"

"Oh, no," she quickly assured him.

"I have no interest in you, Mrs. Stanhope, other than as the woman who will find me a wife," he said stiffly.

She hesitated. "Then you do not mind removing your hands from my, er, person? I feel it most improper to—"

He jerked his hands away.

"Until tomorrow," she said.

"Good day, Mrs. Stanhope." Adrian grabbed his hat and fled.

Outside, he climbed onto his curricle and set the horses toward town. His mind searched for something, anything, to dispel the perturbing sensations that lingered still.

But the wheels clattered over the cobblestones, drumming a cadence through his brain:

Emmaline. Emmaline. Em-ma-line.

Chapter 7

"Mesmerism. 'Tis your only hope, I'm afraid."

Emmaline studied the large, bespectacled man who hovered over her aunt. Dr. Evans's office was dark and dingy; gloom permeated its dusty corners. "Could you elaborate, Doctor?"

"Certainly." He turned toward her, his bulging eyes assessing. "I can find nothing wrong with your aunt. Therefore, the origin of her illness is in her brain."

" 'Tis not the brain that aches," Aunt Heloise grumbled. " 'Tis all over."

Evans gave her a condescending smile. He lowered his bulky form into the chair opposite Aunt Heloise. To Emmaline's surprise, he took her aunt's hands between his.

"You have a strong pulse, you are not overweight, your breathing is even and deep. You have no outward injuries, and you are not bilious. You are beyond the possibility of childbirth, so you cannot be afflicted with morning sickness or any other debilitation associated with pregnancy. Your back is straight, without obvious misalignment. Your skin is dry and of normal temperature. Your complexion is clear—one might almost say glowing—"

"Thank you." Aunt Heloise trained her blue eyes on him.

"You are attractive for your age—"

"How kind of you," Aunt Heloise murmured meekly, but Emmaline caught an unsettling glint in her gaze.

"Numerous physicians have found nothing wrong, and neither can I. In short," Evans said in a patronizing tone, the nostrils of his bulbous nose flaring, "I can account for your aches and fatigue in no other way, Miss Alcott, but to say that they are all in your head. 'Tis a rising theory in medicine that holds some promise. It is possible your problem is only your imagination run amok."

"I disagree," Emmaline protested. "Her illness is quite real. There are some days she cannot even get out of bed."

Dr. Evans gave Emmaline a pitying look. "I do not doubt her symptoms, Mrs. Stanhope. It is the cause I am seeking, and it does not seem to be organic. That is why I intend to work on your aunt's mind."

Emmaline shook her head in bewilderment. "I do not understand."

" 'Tis simple, dear." Aunt Heloise eyed Evans consideringly. "He wishes to mesmerize me."

Evans beamed. "You are a quick study, Miss Alcott. We will put you in a trance and tell your symptoms to disappear. It is not quite as simple as that, of course; even Dr. Mesmer did not succeed every time. Often many sessions are needed to complete the cure."

"Several of my former colleagues used mesmerism to rid themselves of stage fright," Aunt Heloise offered.

"Did it work?" Emmaline asked skeptically.

"I'm not sure," her aunt replied in a musing tone. "But my friend Sarah developed a particular regard for her mesmerist. I believe she came to look forward to her sessions. Something about the laying on of hands."

"Ah, yes." Evans eyed Aunt Heloise warmly. Emmaline might have called his expression a leer. "The women do like that part of it."

"*Stimulating* was the word Sarah used," Aunt Heloise said, her eyes thoughtful.

Emmaline frowned. "What occurs during these sessions?"

Aunt Heloise looked at her in surprise. "You've not heard of the mesmerism cure, dear? 'Tis all the rage on the Continent, especially among women. Should I continue, Doctor, or would you prefer to explain it?"

Evans's gaze filled with admiration. "Please go on, Miss Alcott. You are doing an excellent job." He stroked Aunt Heloise's hands with a steady, almost anticipatory enthusiasm.

Emmaline thought this an excessive familiarity, but the man was a physician, after all, and Aunt Heloise hadn't pulled away. She didn't even look uncomfortable. Yet something about the intensity of the man's regard made Emmaline uneasy.

What disturbed her most, however, was the wide-eyed innocence that suddenly filled her aunt's eyes.

"It is necessary to find a mesmerist of the highest integrity and discipline," Aunt Heloise said solemnly.

Evans nodded. "Yes, indeed. I have heard of unethical men who abuse their access to the patients, but I assure you, dear lady, I am not one of those. I am most scrupulous in all my dealings with female patients."

"I am so glad to hear that, Doctor." Her aunt hesitated. "For I have heard alarming stories about some of these sessions. Why, Sarah told me that she was put into a trance that was almost—I blush to say it—*erotic*."

Evans looked taken aback. "My patients would never say such a thing."

"Certainly not," Aunt Heloise agreed. She paused for a heartbeat. "Though I must say Sarah's description was . . . intriguing."

Emmaline slanted her a gaze. "In what way, Aunt?"

"Sarah said the mesmerist sat facing her," Aunt Heloise replied. She adjusted her position accordingly, drawing closer to Evans so that her skirts brushed his trousers. "He required that her knees touch his."

"Completely necessary," Evans assured her. "There must be a flow of energy between patient and doctor."

"That her knees were *between* his, I should have said," Aunt Heloise amended. Quite sedately, she inserted her knees in the space between Dr. Evans's legs.

"Yes, of course. To be absolutely accurate, that is . . ." Evans's voice faltered as Aunt Heloise nudged his thighs ever so gently.

"As I understand it," she continued softly, "the mesmerist strokes the patient's abdomen."

Emmaline blinked. Dr. Evans was rubbing her aunt's hands with a good deal more warmth than before. Was it her imagination, or was that a thin bead of perspiration on the good doctor's brow?

"Upon occasion," he conceded. "The doctor is, of course, most dispassionate during what some would consider an inordinate intimacy."

"Sometimes," Aunt Heloise said in a husky voice, "he strokes her lower down . . . in the region of the ovaries."

Dear heavens. Emmaline swallowed a gasp. Evans's face was florid. A deep sense of foreboding seized her at the look in her aunt's eyes.

"Eyelids become moist, respiration is short and spasmodic, and the *breast* rises tumultuously," her aunt continued, absently toying with the neckline of her frock.

"Yes," Evans murmured softly.

"The touching is then extended over *numerous* areas." She emitted a breathy sigh.

"Aunt, I believe it is time to go," Emmaline said. Neither her aunt nor the doctor paid her any mind. Dr. Evans's breathing had grown quite labored, alarmingly so.

"Often in the vicinity of the most *sensitive* parts of the body," Aunt Heloise added.

Evans uttered a heartfelt sigh.

Emmaline rose. "We *must* go, Aunt."

"I have not finished, dear," her aunt said calmly.

"Yes, by God," Evans rasped. "Let the lady finish!"

"Often," Aunt Heloise murmured, turning her attention once more to Evans, "the physician passes his hand around the woman's body." She clasped one of Evans's hands and drew it around her waist. Despite her weight loss, her form was still wondrously proportioned—a fact that did not seem lost on the doctor, for he gave a shuddering sigh.

"Essential," Evans managed in a strangled voice. With one hand he kneaded Aunt Heloise's waist. With the other he massaged her hand with such vigorous passion Emmaline marveled that he could speak at all.

"They move toward one another." Aunt Heloise leaned forward. Her lips were mere inches from Evans's. "Their faces nearly touch," she murmured. "Their breaths mingle."

Evans's eyes had closed. He looked to be in great pain. "Yes," he declared. "Oh, *yes*."

"They share *all* their physical reactions," Aunt Heloise said softly. "The mutual attraction of the sexes acts with *full* force."

"By God, you have the right of it!" Evans cried, kneading her aunt's hand for all he was worth. Sweat now poured down his face. His legs began to jiggle as he pressed the balls of his feet to the floor and moved his heels up and down.

"Tremors begin," Aunt Heloise whispered. "Lovely, uncontrollable tremors."

Evans gave a hoarse cry and rocked back and forth in the chair.

"There is extreme agitation," Aunt Heloise added quickly, "but it is important not to stop the therapy."

"No, by *God*, don't stop!" Evans rasped. "Don't . . . ever . . . stop."

Aunt Heloise gently disengaged her hand from his, but Evans did not notice. His rocking quickened.

"And then," her aunt declared in a deeply resonant voice that had brought many appreciative audiences to their feet, "come the *spasms*."

Evans gave a cry the likes of which Emmaline had never heard before. He stiffened violently. His tongue sagged from his mouth, as if he'd suddenly lost control of it, and he emitted a low, animal-like groan.

Emmaline could only gape as her aunt rose calmly, picked up her gloves, and walked toward the office door.

"Come along, dear."

Mutely, Emmaline followed her out of the room to the outer office, where the doctor's bored young assistant sat reading some papers. He looked up.

"The doctor's fee—" he began.

"Has been paid," Aunt Heloise said sweetly, not even breaking her stride.

Out in the street, as they waited in a chill drizzle for a hackney, Emmaline could not think of a word to say.

"Oh, pray, do not look at me so reproach-fully," Aunt Heloise said. "I told you the man was a charlatan, didn't I? My years on the stage have served me well. I can almost always tell when someone is not what he seems."

"Dr. Evans—"

"Is a lascivious brute. Can you imagine what he does to unsuspecting and defenseless women all day? They think they're undertaking a cure, when all they're doing is satisfying the man's sensual appetites."

"I-I wonder if he will send us a bill."

"He will not. He knows that we are on to him. And that he disgraced himself in front of not one but two women."

Emmaline's face was warm. "I cannot believe that you—that we—" She gave up, shaking her head in amazement.

The cab pulled up at that moment. "Don't think badly of me, Em, dear. I have never made any secret of the fact that I've led a rather worldly existence."

Emmaline gave her aunt a hug. "I don't think ill of you. It is just that I've never witnessed anything quite like that—"

"And you shouldn't have, but I just couldn't help myself. The odious man was so condescending, as if he was doing us a great favor to see us, making us come to his office when I'm sure he pays house calls on women of more elevated stations. Then he demeans my condition, implying that I caused my own illness. Does he think me a lunatic?"

"I am sure he does not," Emmaline replied.

Aunt Heloise grinned. "No doubt there are any number of other words that have occurred to him, however."

Emmaline smiled gamely.

"I know I behaved badly back there." Her aunt grew somber as they seated themselves in the cab. She fingered the edges of her burgundy cloak. It had been grand once but, like her riotous mass of reddish curls, had faded. "Sometimes I think worldliness is the only asset I possess. I've seen and done things that would put a young woman like you to blush. But I've kept my head above water, if only barely sometimes."

Aunt Heloise looked so forlorn that Emmaline immediately enveloped her in her arms. "You are wonderful, and I love you," she said softly.

Her aunt wiped away a tear. "I should never have exposed a chaste young woman to such a sordid scene. You've had no experience with men like Evans—no experience with *any* man, I'll warrant. What will you think of me?"

"What I think," Emmaline said gently, "is that you are a marvelous actress."

Aunt Heloise smiled through her tears. "Yes," she said, "I am, aren't I?"

"Off for today's appointment, Your Grace?" Gibbons was unusually cheerful as he helped Adrian into his jacket. "Mind the rain; I don't like the looks of that cloud. 'Tis just a drizzle now, but it could be a downpour before long."

Sometimes Gibbons was as solicitous as a mother hen. "There's no need to hover, Gibbons.

I'm quite capable of seeing myself out the door."

"Yes, Your Grace." Gibbons took a step back. "I sent madam a new cloak, so you needn't worry that she'll take cold."

Adrian blinked. "You did *what?*"

"Moss green, with lilac trim. It will go well with her coloring, especially those lovely eyes. A nice wool, with a soft but sturdy weave."

"Why the devil did you do such a thing?" What color were her eyes, anyway? Adrian racked his brain. Green—yes, definitely green.

Gibbons looked surprised. "You ruined hers. We had a responsibility to make her whole."

"We?" Hell. Gibbons was probably right. Still, it chafed to have his man of affairs act as his conscience. He heartily wished Gibbons would leave him be. A sudden suspicion filled him.

"You didn't enclose a card from me, I hope."

"As a matter of fact, I did."

Adrian took a deep breath. "Gibbons, you must stop interfering in my life."

"I would never interfere, Your Grace. Besides, the cloak was so lovely I knew you would want to send it."

"What did the card say?"

"The card?" Gibbons furrowed his brow. "To tell you the truth, I can't recall. But it was quite acceptable. And I made sure to sign your given name, so as to maintain your, ah, masquerade. But madam seems possessed of a keen intelligence, Your Grace. You may wish to consider informing her about your title. I can't think that she would like to discover it on her own."

"Gibbons," Adrian said evenly.

"Yes, Your Grace?"

"Listen to me."

"I always do, sir."

Adrian forced his voice to remain calm. "I am seeing Mrs. Stanhope as a favor to my uncle."

"You aren't the sort to do favors, Your Grace, if you don't mind my saying."

"The point, Gibbons, is that I'm not courting the woman. Not now, not ever. You must put that thought far from your mind. I know you nurture hopes for me in that vein, and I cannot imagine why. Certainly I have done nothing to suggest I would even consider such a thing."

Gibbons looked impassive. "No, Your Grace."

"Even if the woman were not of dubious character, I do not intend to marry her," Adrian said. "I do not intend to do anything with Mrs. Stanhope except fulfill the request my uncle has made of me."

"Yes, Your Grace."

Adrian eyed him suspiciously. No matter how polite Gibbons's assurances, the man would do and think exactly as he wished. How had he ended up with such an interfering man of affairs?

"Have you considered seeking other employment, Gibbons?"

The man looked startled. "Not at all, Your Grace. I have always served the duke of Trent, as my father and grandfather before me."

"Surely they couldn't have all been like you."

"I beg your pardon if I have offended or annoyed you, sir. No one has ever questioned my loyalty before."

"I am not questioning your loyalty, Gibbons. In the weeks we've been together, I've seen that you have my interests uppermost in your mind."

"That's so, Your Grace. It would never be otherwise."

Adrian sighed. "But damn it, man, you go too far. It's one thing to be a loyal employee and quite another to send young women cloaks in my name."

"Mrs. Stanhope is a fine woman who's fallen on hard times, sir. With all due respect, she needed that cloak."

The man was almost as stubborn as he was, Adrian decided as he strode out to the drive and his waiting curricle.

"She will think well of you for sending it," Gibbons called.

Adrian was certain nothing would alter Mrs. Stanhope's dismal opinion of him. He climbed onto the seat, flicked the reins, and guided the vehicle into the street. He felt ridiculous driving something as insubstantial as a curricle, and had no admiration for the dandies who dashed around town in the many-caped coats that signaled their driving expertise. Still, the top folded back. It was the vehicle's only virtue, but for him that was everything. The wind on his face was a gift. His thoughts promptly strayed to the woman he was about to see.

Many more of Mrs. Stanhope's "lessons" and he'd end up a babbling idiot. Already he'd lost track of his task: to ascertain whether she was a murderess and traitor.

Had she read the tarot for Burwell, drawn him

that death card, and sent him to his doom? Even a stolid Englishman like Burwell might believe in the power of mysticism. One had only to look at the success enjoyed by that Frenchwoman, Le Normand. She'd predicted Napoléon's rise; now the wealthy and powerful fawned over her.

Perhaps Burwell had been so shocked by Mrs. Stanhope's dire forecast that he'd not noticed the Mail coach. Perhaps she'd drugged him, so that he'd been unable to detect the approaching vehicle.

Every instinct Adrian had—and he thought he'd purged instinct from his character long ago—told him she was innocent of those crimes. But could he trust his judgment? She left him off-balance; wild impulses he thought long buried came to the fore. Yesterday, when she tumbled into his arms, Adrian had *almost* wanted to kiss her.

Kiss Mrs. Stanhope? It did not bear considering. He'd never humble himself that way, never risk giving her the slightest weapon with which to wound him.

He must remember he was a master of control. He could kiss a woman and remain unfazed; he'd done it plenty of times. The soft seductiveness of a woman's lips was nothing to him.

Nothing.

So, come to think of it, why *shouldn't* he kiss Mrs. Stanhope? He might gain her confidence, induce her to reveal something incriminating in an unguarded moment.

An outright confrontation would put her on the defensive; he'd never learn anything that way. He had to get her to let down her guard.

A kiss, then. Maybe.

Chapter 8

❦❦❦

"This is not a battle, Mr. St. Ledger," Emmaline admonished sternly. "Pray do not keep fighting me."

St. Ledger glared at her. "I would fight anyone intent on making me look the fool, madam."

Emmaline sighed. "You would not look the fool if you learned the steps. They are *not* difficult."

"I fail to see why I must learn them."

Putting her hand to her aching head, Emmaline sank gratefully onto the divan. "You have the most irritating need for control."

St. Ledger stood stiffly in her parlor, hands balled in fists by his side. She had not expected him to be an enthusiastic pupil, but his performance had failed to meet even her low expectations. He'd copied her demonstration of the minuet halfheartedly, but the cotillion was quite beyond him. He'd stepped on her feet so many times they were swollen.

Emmaline wouldn't have minded if he had merely been clumsy, but she'd seen the swift, lethal grace with which he dispatched those dandies. No, he'd simply closed his mind to the necessity of learning to dance. He had defied her all afternoon, refusing even to take her hand.

"You simply *must* learn a dance or two," Emmaline said. "A woman expects a bit of entertainment now and again."

"Surely women can entertain themselves without making spectacles of men. Why do I have to don breeches and slippers to jump around a ballroom like a crazed rabbit?"

Emmaline prayed for patience. "Dancing is a most graceful activity."

"Graceful is for tulips of the *ton*—like the ones who pawed you outside the Cyprians' Ball. Is that what you would have me aspire to?"

Emmaline flushed. "How unkind of you to embarrass me by mentioning that horrid episode."

"I didn't mean to embarrass you."

"No, I'm sure you do not intend these constant little mortifications you put me through, Mr. St. Ledger. Nevertheless, you do it incessantly."

He crossed the room and sat at the other end of the divan. He didn't glance at her, but stared morosely at her threadbare carpet. They sat in silence for several minutes.

"You know," he said wearily, "I feel as if I've just gone several rounds with Gentleman Jackson."

Emmaline sighed. "I am not a boxer whom you must pummel into submission. I am simply trying to make you a more appealing marriage prospect."

"I won't change for any woman."

"Nor even try to accommodate her wishes, I see. Very well, Mr. St. Ledger. Let us forget the dancing. Let us forget about the need to make your poor wife's existence a little brighter by pretending that you enjoy the social intercourse common to civilized societies."

"Social intercourse?" His tone was dubious. "Sounds obscene."

Emmaline reddened. Unbidden, the shocking scene her aunt had staged in Dr. Evans's office came to mind. "I refer to the polite discourse and civility that is evidently foreign to your nature. A wife is not a possession to be tucked away in a closet and dusted off once or twice a year for public display, Mr. St. Ledger. She expects to be escorted to social occasions, danced with, spoken to—all the things men do with their wives to show how pleased they are with their mates."

"Is that how your husband treated you?"

St. Ledger's blunt intensity took her aback. "My life has been very different from yours," she said quietly.

"You think my wealth makes me something you are not?"

"Your fortune will admit you to Almack's, to court—anywhere you wish," she said, unable to keep the scorn from her voice. "You may not have a noble pedigree, but money provides a most acceptable substitute."

He studied her curiously. "What if I don't wish admittance to any of those places? They sound intensely boring."

Emmaline gave a bitter laugh. "Ask the fox

when he has sampled the grapes if they were sour."

"Money is not the measure of a man. Or woman. You strike me as one who knows that better than most."

"Be careful, Mr. St. Ledger," she said with a shaky laugh. "I might take that for a compliment."

He arched a brow. "Would that be a crime?"

Emmaline eyed him in surprise. She might have said his expression was sheepish, if his mouth hadn't pulled into a scowl at the last moment.

"Any woman who provokes you into a compliment will be a rare treasure indeed." She gave a little cough. "Well, what will it be, Mr. St. Ledger? Shall we continue the dance lessons or abandon all hope?"

"Abandon hope."

To her amazement, he shot her a quick, fleeting grin. It was a pity he didn't smile more often, for it gave him a breathtaking allure. The combination of those fierce eyes and tentative smile radiated an intriguing vulnerability that made her wish to know what had caused it.

Emmaline gave herself a mental shake. St. Ledger was no better than he seemed: an impossible curmudgeon with a demeaning view of the opposite sex. It would not do to imagine how he might be in other circumstances. "Very well," she said. "Let us adjourn for the day. Tomorrow we will work on something more pleasant."

He eyed her warily. "Like what?"

"Politics, perhaps. It is important for a gentleman to be informed—"

"My loathing for dancing is exceeded only by my loathing of Parliament."

"What a curious thing to say. Have you had personal experience with our august leaders?"

"In a manner of speaking. I once tried to persuade some narrow-minded Whigs that it was in their best interest to outlaw people such as yourself."

Emmaline stared at him. "On what grounds?"

"That they prey on the weak. Don't worry, you are safe. Turns out that Parliament pays lip service to the public good but has no abiding interest in protecting it. Excuse me. I must be going."

Glowering, he grabbed his hat. Emmaline sighed. To his other insensitivities, she would have to add bigotry. And yet . . .

"Mr. St. Ledger?"

"Yes?" he barked.

"Thank you for the cloak. It is beautiful. I would not have imagined you would be so thoughtful."

He looked as if he would speak again. Instead, he strode to the front door and opened it so forcefully she thought he might rip it off its hinges. At the last moment, he turned to her.

" 'Tis a fine day. Would you care to take a walk?"

Emmaline looked past him to the street. Raindrops dotted the puddles that had been gathering in the street since early afternoon. It wasn't quite a deluge, but neither was it a day for taking the air.

"Why, yes," she heard herself say. "I'll get my cloak."

How did one go about kissing a woman in the rain? Adrian felt like the world's biggest fool. He hadn't bothered to look outside before he'd issued his proposal, and now, as they stood at Mrs. Stanhope's gate waiting for the carriages to pass, he had no idea how to proceed.

He'd had in mind a comfortable stroll in the amber glow of the late-afternoon sun. Unfortunately, rain lent the cobblestones a slippery sheen, and the carriages churned up mud that splattered their clothes.

It was a wet, miserable day, and from the looks of the gathering clouds, would soon get a lot worse.

The copse of trees next to the blacksmith's shop across the street would offer some shelter on this wretched afternoon. Adrian led the way. Mrs. Stanhope followed, picking her way around the mud puddles. As they crossed the stable yard where the smithy plied his trade, the heavy scent of manure, made newly pungent by the rain, wafted toward them.

Mrs. Stanhope huddled in the folds of her new green cloak, looking uncomfortable and damp. Adrian had to concede that the fabric looked nice against her skin, which was all pink and dewy in the chilly drizzle. Moss green, Gibbons had said. Yes, it definitely brought out the green of her eyes. How did Gibbons know these things?

They found an ancient oak tree that shielded them from the rain, if not the damp. Neither of them spoke as they stood watching the earth around them turn to mud. What was there to say? Rain was rain, after all.

"I should like a reading," he said suddenly.

"A reading?" She looked bewildered.

"The tarot. I wish you to tell my fortune."

Her brow creased. "I thought you detested such things."

Adrian took a deep breath. "Very well. You force me to confess a most lowering fact: I am deeply superstitious. Despite my dedication to science, I have never been able to relinquish my belief in otherworldly truth."

That was quite possibly the most mendacious and senseless sentence he had ever uttered. Doubt crossed Mrs. Stanhope's dewy features.

"Taking a wife is a momentous step," Adrian explained. "With all due respect to your match-making skills, I wouldn't mind consulting another authority on the subject. The tarot is as good as any."

Her gaze narrowed. "Forgive me for mistrusting you, Mr. St. Ledger, but you've given me the distinct impression you could not care less whom you marry. Why would you seek the counsel of the cards?"

Adrian shrugged. "Hypocrisy is one of the many flaws in my character."

She stared at him, and Adrian had the distinct impression she was consigning him to the devil. But her voice bore the same labored patience she'd used with him all afternoon. "Very well. I shall undertake a reading at your next appointment. But you must be in a receptive frame of mind; I'll not tolerate ridicule."

"I've gotten us off to a bad start, haven't I?"

She gave him a rueful smile. "This is quite possibly the worst relationship I've had with any human being."

" 'Tis not as bad as all that."

"It is."

For a moment, Adrian was caught up in contemplation of the faint sparkle in her eyes. Then he remembered the task at hand. "Did you give Mr. Burwell a reading?"

The sparkle vanished. "No. Perhaps I should have."

"You think you would have foreseen his demise?"

She looked down. "I don't know. I am not an accomplished fortune-teller; 'tis merely a skill I learned in order to keep a roof over our heads. It's possible I would have missed Mr. Burwell's sad fate entirely."

Her frankness surprised him. What surprised him more was how much he wanted to believe her. "You didn't give him a flyer, either?"

"No." She watched his face. "What is this about?"

Adrian was not ready to confront her with the menacing handbill found on Burwell. He'd have to move the conversation in a different direction if he was to gain her confidence.

"Nothing." He stared at her mouth.

This was the point at which he'd meant to sweep away her doubts with a kiss. But the few feet that stood between them might as well have been an ocean. He couldn't simply pull her into his arms; she'd die of shock. But if he leaned forward a bit, he might brush her lips . . .

"Do you feel faint, Mr. St. Ledger?" Her eyes filled with concern.

He stiffened. "I am quite well, thank you."

"For a moment I thought you were about to topple into that mud puddle."

Hell, he couldn't do this. It was beyond him. Women were beyond him—at least women like Emmaline Stanhope, contentious and independent and scornful. He could only imagine what she'd say if he tried to kiss her.

"I believe you *are* ill, sir. You are quite pale." Without warning, she put her hand on his forehead.

In one violent motion, Adrian grabbed her hand and pressed it to his lips.

Her little gasp told him he'd done something strange and unforgivable, but he couldn't stop from nibbling at her tapered fingers. She hadn't worn gloves, and her hand was chapped. Her palm was soft, though, with little pads of flesh that made his senses roar as he kissed her there.

"Mr. S-St. Ledger!" she stammered, her faint protest nearly obliterated by the rumble of thunder overhead.

This was what he'd thought of doing back in her parlor, when she was rattling on about those abysmal dance steps. She'd tried to take his hand then, but he'd shunned her touch because he sensed it would be dangerous.

He'd been right. Her hand, and the chafed skin that marked her as a woman locked in a station

in life far below his, made him reel with pleasure. It was warm and moist from the rain, and
Adrian thought he'd never experienced anything
quite so pleasurable.

God. It was only a hand, and a chapped one
at that. But as much as he told himself that Mrs.
Stanhope's hand could not be responsible for the
intense delight that filled him, he knew otherwise.

Even as that confused jumble of thoughts
raced through him, his lips started down the inside of her wrist.

"In heaven's name, sir," she said faintly,
"please control yourself."

Ah. *That's* what was wrong. Something in him
had come loose, making him forget the control
that kept him sane.

Instantly, he released her hand. Though he
wanted to slink away like a rat caught stealing a
loaf of bread cooling in the window, he forced
himself to meet her gaze.

Her eyes were wide with amazement. But
wait: There was something else. Her lips parted
slightly as she stared at him from twin pools of—
of what, dammit? He'd been too long by himself
to know how to read that very intriguing look in
Mrs. Stanhope's eyes.

She thought him a fool—that much was clear
from the stunned expression on her face. But—
and there *was* a but—he also saw . . .

Desire. Yes, there it was, hidden in the recesses
of those lovely green eyes. Adrian was quite sure
Mrs. Stanhope hadn't meant to show him that.

Doubtless she didn't realize she'd betrayed herself.

But the furtive flame of passion vanished, overtaken by her horror at having him touch her so fervently.

Wrapping her cloak around her, she turned away, giving Adrian the disapproving set of her shoulders and the rigid outline of her profile. The awkward silence stretched between them like a bad play that had spun itself to an embarrassing conclusion.

Just when he thought things could not grow worse, the ground beneath their feet sizzled with a strange, malevolent force. The branches of the oak swayed. For one heart-stopping moment the air grew still. Mrs. Stanhope looked up, her eyes filled with puzzlement.

They had a split second of warning, but only that.

Suddenly, the sky turned brilliant and deadly. The ground gave an answering rumble. Adrian tackled Mrs. Stanhope, sending them both into the mud.

A deadly cracking split the oak to its core. Acrid smoke assailed his nostrils as a branch fell, narrowly missing the spot where his body shielded hers. The tree's savage shudder told him their luck wouldn't last.

The cracking exploded into one violent roar, and Adrian put his arms around Mrs. Stanhope and rolled them away just as the oak tumbled over on its side.

They lay in the mud, his arms locked protectively, clutching each other like lifelines. Neither dared move as the storm raged around them.

Eventually Adrian realized the treacherous storm had become only a distant rumble.

Lifting his head, he stared into Mrs. Stanhope's lovely green eyes. Shock was written on her features. Mud splattered her rosy cheeks. Rain matted her hair against her head, and she was covered in mud from head to toe, as he must be.

"Dear God," she murmured in a dazed voice.

And there, amid the smoke and mud and rain, Adrian finally lowered his mouth to hers.

Chapter 9

Thoughtless man.

He didn't seem to care that she was muddy and wet and chilled to the bone, not to mention frightened out of her wits. His hand imprisoned her chin and his thumb moved over her mouth until her lips parted for another kiss.

Heavens, she thought, as Mr. St. Ledger slid his tongue between her teeth. The kisses her father's students had stolen were nothing compared with this.

What sort of man kissed a woman in a mud puddle? What sort of man nibbled a woman's fingers as if he hadn't eaten in a week? And why did she sigh with longing as he inflicted himself on her in such a lowering fashion?

Saving her life did *not* grant him the right to use her this way—yet a wild stirring inside made her cling to him more tightly. When his hand burrowed under her cloak and caressed her breast, she moaned with something that sounded shockingly like pleasure.

Abruptly, St. Ledger lifted his head. He stared

at her in utter horror. Then he rose stiffly and reached down to haul her up.

Her mouth felt bereft. Her knees shook. Her breathing was ragged. When he released her hand, she nearly cried out in protest.

"This," he said slowly, "has been a disaster."

He pulled the edges of her cloak together. When his hands lingered on the fabric, her treacherous body swayed toward him.

"Are you all right?" he demanded.

"Yes," she murmured as her chest made a brief, last contact with his fingertips.

He took a quick step backward. "Your cloak is ruined."

Emmaline looked down at the once-green wool, now a muddy brown. The lilac edging was similarly obliterated. "Yes, I suppose so."

"I will buy you another," he declared.

"That isn't necessary. 'Tis too much—"

"I can afford it. Hell, I could buy you hundreds of cloaks."

Emmaline lifted her chin. "Pray, do not trouble yourself. I do not need your charity."

"Madam, I *will* buy you a new cloak." His eyes glinted steel.

"Mr. St. Ledger," Emmaline said evenly, "there is a name for women who accept such presents from men, and I do not care to have it applied to me. I should not have accepted *this* cloak, but your card was quite persuasive."

"Was it?" His brow furrowed.

"You were kind enough to make it seem as if the responsibility for the ruin of my old cloak was yours."

"And I accept responsibility for ruining this one."

"I undertook to walk with you in the rain. The damage is my doing, not yours."

" 'Twas I who threw you into the mud."

"And saved my life," Emmaline replied. "I owe you a great debt. I'll not add another."

"You are a maddeningly quarrelsome woman."

Emmaline stared at him. She couldn't help asking the question uppermost in her mind. "Why did you kiss me?"

He looked taken aback. "I thought it the thing to do."

If she'd hoped for something more flowery, she'd certainly mistaken her man. Still, it would have been nice to hear him say he'd been carried away by the moment, that the danger they'd evaded had pierced his dreadful reserve. That nearly losing his life had driven him to kiss her, knowing that all they had was this time, this moment, this slender piece of longing that would not be denied. That some vast valley between them had been crossed during that kiss and that he saw, as clearly as he'd ever seen anything in his life, that they belonged together. That he now meant to pluck her from her penurious existence and carry her off to his grand house, her prince at last.

Balderdash.

When would she learn? St. Ledger was studying the mud on his jacket, not even looking at her. She was stunned at how far her imagination had taken her. She'd almost had them marching down the aisle—an appalling thought, for Mr. St. Ledger was not the sort of man she'd ever marry.

Emmaline wanted to stab him with the dagger of her disappointment, and if the wound was mortal, so be it. His kiss had unsettled her more than the storm or the disaster that had almost befallen them.

Slowly, his head came up.

With a muttered oath, he grabbed her elbow and propelled her across the street. He deposited her at the door of the cottage, then stalked off to his curricle. Since the top was folded back, the inside was undoubtedly as soggy as he was. He didn't say good-bye or hide his eagerness to remove himself from her presence.

But Emmaline did not want him to leave. What she wanted was another kiss.

What was wrong with her? St. Ledger was not a prince—nor even polite—and she, certainly, was no princess. But somehow, he'd conjured up those moldy fairy tales from her childhood, hurled them at her in a rush of hope and disappointment.

How dare he?

"What a muddy spectacle you will make driving through London," she called, suddenly furious at both of them. "But that is the way of your class, isn't it, Mr. St. Ledger? You do what you wish, and count on wealth to excuse it."

He'd been turning his pair, but at her parting shot he flung her a violent gaze filled with dark promise. Then he set his horses toward Brook Street and that grand house.

*　　*　　*

"Ah, Your Grace. I imagine you would like a bath." Gibbons gave no sign that he thought the appearance of his mud-encrusted employer unusual.

Adrian peeled off his boots. He doffed his jacket and dropped it next to them. His waistcoat came next. Finally, he removed his shirt, but kept his pants on.

A footman was summoned to take the offensive garments away. Others scurried about with buckets of water as Adrian climbed the stairs to his chamber. Once inside, he removed his pants, wrapped himself in a towel, and waited in a black mood for his bath to arrive.

It took an eternity, during which he excoriated himself for making a cake of himself over Mrs. Stanhope. Women did not care to be made love to in the mud. He'd been so possessed by the notion of kissing her that he'd lost all common sense.

"I thought it the thing to do." God. By now, she was probably regaling her aunt with the tale of his deranged behavior.

He'd never met a woman like Emmaline Stanhope, never kissed a woman who inspired such dread and longing, never felt he'd go mad if he didn't touch her.

He could cross verbal swords with her all afternoon and emerge unscathed. But one touch of her hand, her fingers, her mouth, and he lost all reason. *In the mud, for God's sake.* He must remember there was method to his madness, reason behind his scheme. He was charged with the task of discovering whether she'd committed dastardly deeds; it would not do to lose control in the process.

Reason. Control. Those bywords had pulled him from the brink more times than he cared to count.

When at last he sank into the hot, sudsy water, Adrian wanted only to shut out anything that reminded him of Emmaline Stanhope. He closed his eyes and began the number games he played to focus his will. *Ten, nine, eight . . .*

A scratching at the door shattered his peace. A boy of about ten entered, lugging a bucket of water.

"Mr. Gibbons said I was to help you bathe." The lad was slight, too slight to carry his burden easily. Water splashed onto the carpet, and he looked stricken.

"I've bathed myself my entire life, boy," Adrian growled. "Go, and tell Gibbons he's got straw for brains."

The boy gave him a horrified look.

"Don't tell me you're afraid of him."

"N-no, sir—I mean, Your Grace." The boy hesitated.

Damn it, he wanted to bury the day in suds and hot water. He did not want to sit in his bath and converse with the scullery boy. "What is it, then?" Adrian demanded.

Shyly, the boy took a step toward the tub. "Mr. Gibbons said I might help you. He said if I was very quiet you might let me."

The lad was painfully slim. Just then his dark eyes were a bit too bright, and the hand holding the bucket trembled from the weight of his burden.

"Put the bucket down, dammit."

The lad couldn't suppress a sigh of relief as he set the heavy bucket on the floor. His wide eyes looked out of a face too gaunt for a boy of his years.

"What's your name, lad?"

"Peter."

"What is your job?"

The boy drew himself up proudly. "I'm the scullery boy, Your Grace. Cook says I do a good day's work, better than the last one."

"What happened to him?"

"He ran off, I think." Peter looked uncertain. "Mr. Gibbons hired me a fortnight ago. Gave me a shilling to take home to my ma. She's right proud of me."

A shilling. A pittance. Doubtless the boy had a dozen siblings and an invalid mother dependent on his wages. Adrian steeled himself against whatever tale of woe Peter was about to bestow on him.

But the boy just stood there, staring at him in that direct and unnerving way children had.

"Can I help you with the bath?" he asked hopefully.

"No."

Peter's face fell.

"But you can fetch me some clean clothes."

The look of joy that crossed the lad's features made Adrian feel like a cad. "Mind that you don't drop my pants in the water," he added gruffly.

Peter opened the wardrobe and gave a low whistle at the garments hanging there. "*Satin*," he said in awe, staring at the shiny fabric. "You've got satin shirts."

"Not those. The muslin."

"But—"

"The fancy stuff belonged to my father. I've been meaning to have Gibbons get rid of it."

Carefully, Peter took out a plain muslin shirt and a pair of kerseymere trousers. "Is this all right?"

"Yes. Put them on the bed. Now let me be."

Either the boy didn't hear the dismissal, or he pretended not to. "This is a strange house," he ventured.

Adrian closed his eyes and concentrated on the water's enveloping warmth. "Oh?" he murmured without interest.

"My ma didn't want me to work here. Said it wasn't natural to have no women in a house. She's scared something will happen to me."

Adrian's eyes shot open. "Like what?"

Peter looked down. "You know. Something."

Adrian couldn't see Peter's face, but he didn't need to see fear to feel it. "Why did she let you work here, if she thought you wouldn't be safe?"

Peter looked up warily.

"No, don't answer that." The boy had to work because his mother needed the money. It was no more complicated than that.

Adrian leveled a gaze at him. "No harm will come to you here. Now I'd like to take my bath alone, if you don't mind. It's been a trying day."

Peter hesitated, but didn't speak. Adrian sighed. Half-truths and bland reassurances hadn't satisfied him at that age, so why would they satisfy this solemn young lad?

"It was my father who banned women from his properties," Adrian said gruffly. "He and my mother quarreled, and he couldn't stand the sight of women after that. He was mad, I think, but so are many men. It doesn't make them evil, though it sometimes makes them mean."

The boy absorbed this news in silence. "Are you mean, too?" he asked at last.

The answer was far more complex than the question. "I don't think so," Adrian said slowly, "but sometimes I wonder."

"Why don't you have women here? Are you angry at them, too?"

"No. I just don't plan to be around long enough to change things."

"My ma's a good cook," Peter added proudly.

"I'm sure she is. You have to understand that—" Adrian broke off. Why did Peter have to understand? *He* wouldn't have, at Peter's age. "Let me put it this way: Sometimes a man doesn't want distractions."

"My ma wouldn't be a distraction."

"I'm sure she wouldn't."

"My eldest sister, May, she's got a temper, but she knows how to be quiet, if she has to. You wouldn't be sorry if you hired her."

Adrian's bathwater was cooling rapidly, but he'd resigned himself to the fact that his bath wasn't going to go the way he'd planned. "A temper, eh?"

"Lizzy, now, she's the loud one." Peter sighed. "You wouldn't like her."

"No," Adrian assured him, "I wouldn't like loud. Or temperamental, or—"

"Jenny, though, she's a sweet girl. Even if she is my sister. 'Course, she's only six. Then there's Hetty and Betsy. They aren't old enough to do much work."

Apparently Peter *did* have a dozen siblings, or close to it. "Peter," Adrian said sternly, "I don't have time for—"

"Sorry, Your Grace." The boy looked sheepish. "Ma says I talk too much. Like Prudence—she's twelve. Two years older than me, but she thinks she knows everything. You know how it is with sisters."

"No. I had two brothers."

Peter looked wistful. "Wouldn't mind a brother or two. But Ma says no more babies."

"What does your father say?"

"Don't have one. None of us do."

Now *that* was too much.

Adrian reached for the bucket of cold water and poured it over his head. He welcomed the chill that spread through him, focusing his mind on a place far beyond this chamber. A place where there were no insistent boys, no annoying women, no absent fathers, no long-suffering mothers. A place where fears and hopes didn't reach, where pain had no meaning and the events of the day were only meaningless stones in a road filled with thousands like them.

An ascetic existence.

*   *   *

"There are seventy-eight cards," Emmaline began. "You mustn't infer too much from any individual card. Its import lies in the juxtaposition with the others."

St. Ledger looked bored. He'd made no reference to the muddy events of yesterday, or the angry manner in which they'd parted. Emmaline had half expected him not to appear for his afternoon appointment, but he'd presented himself at her door at precisely four o'clock. Aunt Heloise was napping, so they had the parlor to themselves.

Had that kiss affected him as it had her? Did he feel the tension, the awareness, the heaviness between them? St. Ledger revealed so little of himself it was impossible to know.

"Some say the cards have an uncanny ability to chart a subject's emotional and moral state," Emmaline said, determined not to let St. Ledger's brooding affect her.

"Ridiculous."

Emmaline glared at him. "There is no need to demean what you do not understand, Mr. St. Ledger. If you don't wish a reading, we can turn instead to our lessons—which," she added peevishly, "you are in sore need of."

"Am I?" His expression was unreadable.

Another quarrel with him was the last thing she needed. "Do you wish to proceed?"

"After you tell me what I am in sore need of."

Emmaline bit her lip. "I'm sorry. I was impertinent."

He shrugged. " 'Tis not a bad quality."

She had no idea how to interpret that remark. If it was a compliment, it had been delivered in typical St. Ledger fashion, so she'd never know.

"You were about to elaborate on my deficiencies," he reminded her.

Emmaline sighed. "Your conversation is blunt, your manners atrocious. Your dancing is abysmal, your ability to anticipate a woman's needs nonexistent." She slanted him a gaze to see how he was accepting this news.

"Go on." One of his brows arched almost imperceptibly.

"There is a great deal of work to be done to make you an acceptable husband. I do not know how else to say it, Mr. St. Ledger. You are self-centered, rational to the point of bloodlessness, and—"

"Women prefer bloodied husbands?"

"What I meant is that you do not care about anything except those rocks of yours."

"Your knowledge of my character is astonishing, Mrs. Stanhope."

Emmaline flushed. "I didn't mean to presume."

"That has never stopped you before."

"I only meant that you seem woefully ignorant—perhaps even incapable—of the little gestures women appreciate."

"Such as?"

Emmaline wasn't fooled by St. Ledger's bland look; he was obviously baiting her. "The usual things: flowers, notes, amiable conversation, a drive through the park. A woman likes to be tended to."

"Rather like a potted plant?"

"A bit more than that," she replied evenly.

"And you don't think me capable of this 'tending'?"

"There is always hope," she felt compelled to assure him, though she wasn't certain in his case. "We needn't reform you completely, just so you'll pass muster."

"What a relief."

"You are making sport of me again, Mr. St. Ledger. It is not kind."

"I am not a kind man."

Emmaline picked up the tarot deck and began laying out the cards. The man could go to the devil with her blessing.

"Now this is interesting." She was unable to hide her surprise. "I had expected the king of swords, but the knight is startling." She laid out another card. "And the queen . . ." Her voice trailed off.

"Out with it, Mrs. Stanhope," St. Ledger said solemnly. "What do you see?"

Emmaline was reminded of a cat, playing with his prey in the instant before delivering the killing bite. Her gaze narrowed. Very well. She'd spare him nothing.

"The king reveals you to be a logical and rational man, but unaware of the feelings of others and capable of cruelty. *That* is certainly no surprise."

He only smiled.

"You are possessed of an unfortunate rigidity, but the knight suggests a secretiveness, as well as imminent change. The way he is positioned here, next to the queen, suggests—"

"The change will be her doing," St. Ledger finished with a yawn. "And though she is intelligent and quick-witted, the question is whether or not she is trustworthy."

Emmaline leveled a gaze at him. "One might almost think you had done this sort of thing before. But if you had, you would have said so. You would not have allowed me to make a fool of myself by telling you something you already knew."

"You give me too much credit, madam." But he had the grace to look chagrined.

"Not at all. Perhaps you would like to return the favor, Mr. St. Ledger."

He frowned. "Favor?"

"I have just given you a reading. Now it's your turn. Pray, tell me what you see in the cards for me."

St. Ledger sighed. He picked up the cards, re-ordered them, and laid them out with the ease of one who'd done so many times. His mouth twisted wryly as he turned up the queen of wands.

"Obstinate," he declared. "Imagines wrongs."

"Independent," she countered. "Practical and kind."

He arched a brow. "Ah, but look, Mrs. Stanhope. The knight enters. Action. Change. A sudden departure."

Emmaline stared at the card. "A change of residence. How very odd. Perhaps we will be evicted after all."

"The queen is home-loving," St. Ledger pointed out. "She'll find another."

Emmaline crossed her arms over her chest. "Why don't you tell me how you came to know so much about the tarot?"

St. Ledger hesitated, and she braced herself for another of his cutting remarks.

"My mother was a client of Madame Le Normand and of other mystics on the Continent," he said. "I made it my business to learn all I could about the methods of the charlatans who treated her. Unfortunately, my knowledge came too late to help her."

St. Ledger's voice was flat, as if someone else had lived the past he was describing. "Years afterward, I thought to salvage something worthwhile from her experience. I showed Parliament how easy it was to mislead a willing subject with sleights of hand and carefully ambiguous words. But Charles Fox wouldn't be persuaded, and the Whigs lined up behind him."

"I am sorry," she said.

"The Tories wouldn't lift a hand either—not only because they didn't want to fight the Whigs over something so trivial, but also because one of my father's friends, the marquess of Ainsford, took particular pleasure in ridiculing my theories. He was—and still is—one of the most notorious practitioners of the occult in all England."

Emmaline touched his shoulder, offering comfort.

"Don't." He rose, putting himself beyond her reach.

The wretched man. "You don't need anyone, do you?"

"No."

She glared at him. "If you know so much about the tarot, why did you say nothing about the queen's power? You saw it. I'm sure you did."

" 'Tis only a card, meaningless by itself."

"Intriguing, though, isn't it?" Her temper was spinning her out of control. "The queen's power is ascending. She's dangerous."

"Be careful what you begin, madam," he said in a measured tone. "You may be required to finish it."

It was a warning, but of what? Understanding dawned. "You refer to yesterday."

St. Ledger's eyes transformed from translucent gray to smoke. Perhaps he wasn't as unaffected by that kiss as she'd thought.

"*I* started nothing, you'll recall," Emmaline retorted. She rose indignantly.

A mistake. Now only inches separated them.

The space between them seethed with a dizzying heat. St. Ledger's gaze held hers. Suddenly, Emmaline knew he was going to kiss her again.

But he only regarded her, catlike, from gray slits. "The tending," he said softly. "Is that difficult to learn?"

Why didn't he kiss her? Emmaline's body felt warm and fluid, her legs wobbly. "I-I don't know."

" 'Tis a game, isn't it, Mrs. Stanhope? This thing between men and women. I do not play it well." His finger touched her chin, then he recoiled.

Emmaline flushed. Did he have to make his scorn so very obvious? "Game or no, sir, half the world is made up of women. I'm afraid you must learn to live with us."

"It seems so."

Emmaline looked away. Did he desire her? Why would he? She wasn't beautiful. She possessed a sharp tongue, and she didn't scruple to use it. She had learned to fend for herself, not to flirt or charm.

But she wasn't a coward, either. Once more, she met his gaze. St. Ledger was staring at her with such ferocity, she almost thought he was going to strike her.

He lifted his hand, and his fingertip gently brushed her cheek, then grazed her lips lightly before retreating.

"Damn," he said, and stalked from her parlor.

Chapter 10

Emmaline Stanhope was no traitor. That much Adrian had decided. She was complex, but genuine. Obstinate, but kind. By some trick of fate, the cards hadn't lied.

She fascinated him. Her mouth was soft, alluring as a dream. Her skin was smooth, like fine pearls. But she wasn't fragile—he'd give her that. Neither his wealth nor his temper intimidated her.

Today, in her parlor, she'd nearly brought him to his knees just by standing so close. Furious at himself for allowing one woman to so affect him, Adrian headed for his study like a man bent on destroying everything in his path.

Lust. That was all that gnawed at him. Simple, everyday lust. He could control that.

As Adrian barreled into the study, a figure yelped in surprise. "Your Grace." Peter jumped away from the mantel. "We didn't expect you."

"What the devil are you doing in my study?"

"Watching Galahad," Peter said quickly. "Mr. Gibbons said I might."

A glance told Adrian the bird was engaged in his favorite occupation, preening in front of the mantel mirror. "I've told Gibbons I don't want that bird in here. I can't work with him chirping all the time."

"I was cleaning the cage and he got loose." Peter regarded Adrian fearfully. "I'm sorry, Your Grace."

The boy was trembling. Did he take him for an ogre? Adrian frowned. Where had he heard that term applied to him? Of course: the ever-insightful Mrs. Stanhope.

"Get him out of here. I have work to do."

"I've tried, but he won't come. He likes it here."

Was there no place in this enormous house where he could find peace? "A guinea for you, boy, if you can get that bird to follow you out of the room."

Peter eyed him in amazement. "A *guinea?*"

Damn. He had so much and the boy so little. And though Adrian had never sought his vast wealth, nor wanted it, the disparity appalled him. "A guinea," he confirmed gently. "Two if you accomplish the thing in the next minute."

Peter raced out of the room, and in moments was back with a handful of birdseed. Galahad gave a loud chirp and flew to the boy's shoulder. Peter shot Adrian a triumphant look. Was it imagination, or did the boy stand a little taller, hold his shoulders a little straighter?

Adrian reached into his pocket and pulled out two gold coins. "Well done, lad."

Boy and bird sailed out of the room, and it was difficult to tell who flew higher.

With a sigh, Adrian regarded the paper awaiting his attention. Compared to Mrs. Stanhope, fossils were supremely uninteresting. He wanted to kiss her again. Hell, he wanted to do more than that.

She made him want to betray his own iron will. And will was all that stood between him and the rush of emotions lurking in a place he did not care to visit.

Ever again.

Already, his thoughts drifted back to her tiny parlor, as if an invisible bond held him in her thrall. His mind's eye saw him kissing her wildly until she abandoned that stubborn defensiveness. He saw himself taking her on that divan until he went mad from lust.

She was dangerous. Like that damned queen of wands.

"You say he is wealthy?" Miranda eyed her skeptically.

"Quite," Emmaline replied.

Miranda sighed. "Just this morning I found— I am loath to confess it, but 'tis true—a *gray* hair!"

Since Miranda's hair was the color of straw, Emmaline could not imagine how her friend could distinguish a solitary silver strand, but she nodded sympathetically.

"A nabob seems too good to be true," Miranda continued. "He must have some flaws."

Emmaline hesitated. How to describe St.

Ledger's character? "He has a number of rigid habits."

"So you have said. But is he kind, Emmaline? I should not like to marry a man who isn't kind."

"I cannot say," Emmaline confessed. "He saved my life—twice, in fact—but I shouldn't count on kindness if I were you. He is very cold."

And yet not. Dear Lord, she had no idea what to think about St. Ledger. He conjured wild, unsettling images. Last night she had dreamed of kings and knights doing battle for her hand.

Her father would have laughed if she'd confessed to such nonsense. *"You see, Emmy? We all need to believe in the dream. True love is out there, waiting. You just have to find it."*

She didn't believe. Life was earnest and sometimes frightfully hard. Her landlady didn't accept dreams as currency. There was no room in the real world for fantasy or wishful thinking. Here and now, that's all there was. No castles, no kings, no knights. No happily ever after.

She wouldn't invest St. Ledger with virtues he didn't have, just to satisfy some misguided need for companionship or love. She'd not delude herself; Adrian St. Ledger wouldn't change. He wouldn't make any woman happy, unless that woman had long ago banished silly dreams. Unless that woman had her eyes wide open.

Miranda Manwaring was such a woman. She knew, as Emmaline did, that life offered few choices. They'd met at Lady Warwick's, when Miranda was a teacher's assistant. She was several years older than Emmaline, but still handsome.

"Part of me knows I must jump at the chance." Miranda sighed. "Another part of me wonders if it is ridiculous to hope for more."

Emmaline pressed her hand. "Think about it, Miranda. I shall call again in a day or two." She suspected Miranda wouldn't take long to ponder the matter. Chances like this didn't come along very often.

Outside, Emmaline stood on the street corner looking for a hackney, hoping it wouldn't take forever to find one. She was not very familiar with Guilford Street, although it seemed safe enough. The shadows were lengthening, though; their oppressive gloom was everywhere. A light rain had begun to fall. If only she and Aunt Heloise could afford a carriage, or even a horse . . .

No sense in brooding over the impossible; dwelling on one's hardships led nowhere. Still, at times like this she felt the loss of her father acutely. He'd made her yearn to believe that there was such a thing as a love that could survive the passage of time, even death.

Standing on the street corner as little raindrops turned into big ones, Emmaline fought back a tear. Love was for hopeless romantics like her father—thank the gods she was a practical woman. She'd put her own silly dreams where they belonged: in the pages of her diary. She had no trouble separating truth from fiction, reality from hope. She'd make her own way in this world without clinging to foolish hopes.

Emmaline was still congratulating herself when a horsehair blanket was flung over her head.

Rough hands shoved her into a musty vehicle. She screamed, and the hands fumbled under the blanket to stuff a rag in her mouth.

By the time the carriage started to move, the heavens had loosed a deluge. Amid the pounding rain and booming thunder came a quick burst of cool, damp air.

And then, silence.

Adrian dreamed of a canary pecking at his nose and when he awoke, found it was no dream. Galahad was perched on his chin, squawking loudly.

Moonlight streamed in his window, scattering its unearthly light over the bed as Adrian's gaze locked with the bird's.

"Go away," he growled.

Galahad flew to the table, but even as Adrian closed his eyes, he knew sleep wouldn't return. A hollow loneliness gripped him, the kind that engulfs a man late at night when he knows there is no one to blame for his isolation but himself, when he knows it will always be thus because any other way is unthinkable.

Still, something more than existential pain was at work tonight. Adrian stilled, trying to discern the source of his unease. Galahad's wild cries filled the room, but nothing was amiss—at least nothing Adrian could see.

And then, a word came to him: *Emmaline*.

No. It was not possible. He had not been pulled from sleep by a crazy canary trying to tell him something about Mrs. Stanhope. But there she was, her image clear in his mind's eye, and every time he sent the image away it roared back with painful clarity.

Mrs. Stanhope needed him.

Good God. Must the woman invade even his sleep?

He was too close to the world of dreams to think clearly. Reason had abandoned him. As Galahad circled the room, frantically beating his wings, something called to Adrian. He wanted to name it, but the only possibility that came to mind was ghastly.

"You suffer when she suffers, don't you, boy? I knew it. You're the type. Sensitive, fragile."

A word caught in his throat, and he opened his mouth to fling it to the powers of darkness: no and no and no.

Adrian threw his pillow across the room. He ripped off his covers. A murderous growl lodged in the back of his throat as he lurched to his feet. Peter had neglected to replace his bucket; there was no icy chill to pull him from the vestiges of slumber. No matter; mad rage would do.

His feet touched the soft Aubusson carpet.

"Gibbons!" he roared.

Adrian strode to the hearth and lit a rush candle from the banked embers. The thing sputtered, then went out. A beastly noise rose in his throat.

As he lit the candle a second time, his hands shook. He stared at them, wondering what insidious demon had possessed him. Then he strode to the wardrobe and wrenched it open.

He yanked a pair of trousers from the wardrobe, then tore a shirt off its hanger and threw it over his head. In the same wild, fumbling fashion, he donned a coat and the first pair of boots he put his hands on.

Adrian flung open the door of his room and marched into the hall. His boots clattered loudly as he stomped down the stairs.

"Gibbons!" he roared into the nocturnal silence.

Galahad fluttered after him, chirping and swooping chaotically. Adrian shouted again, and at last he saw the man, nightshirt flapping, running after him.

"Your Grace!" he said breathlessly. "What has happened?"

"I need a horse!"

"But . . . 'tis after midnight."

"Damn it, I don't need you to tell me that."

Gibbons stared at him. "It will take me a moment to dress, Your Grace. I'll come with you to the mews and—"

"Hell. I'll get my own damned horse." Adrian flung open the door and tromped out into the night, the canary following.

The stable lad Adrian roused from a sound sleep looked scared out of his wits. "Which one do ye want, Yer G-Grace?" he stammered.

Adrian had no idea. He pointed to the first horse he saw. To his consternation, his hand still shook.

The stableboy regarded him with a mixture of awe and surprise, which Adrian took as an ominous sign. He watched warily as the boy grappled with the enormous black that pawed impatiently at the straw. That sturdy back and finely muscled legs looked as if they could take a man to hell and back with no trouble.

As he swung himself onto the black, Adrian was vaguely aware of Gibbons signaling for another horse and of the canary swooping near his head.

Adrian set off.

Every jarring stone, every thundering step ripped through Adrian like a bullet. He bounced on the horse's back like a tumbling ball, wondering whether the horse sensed his lack of riding skill. He prayed the creature wouldn't throw him to kingdom come.

The horse's powerful muscles gobbled up the night with boundless authority. Balancing precariously in the stirrups, Adrian's legs finally surrendered to the force underneath. He let himself feel the horse's easy motion, the rhythm of the sturdy gait. And somehow, as the great animal bore him into the night, they became one.

One with a horse? He, Adrian St. Ledger, surrender to an authority beyond his own? A power that was unpredictable, almost feral in its intensity?

Never.

Still, there was something exhilarating about plunging headfirst into the unknown atop a beast whose name he didn't know toward a fate he couldn't even imagine.

Had he lost his mind?

Near the park they passed a hackney and revelers too foxed to pick themselves out of the gutter. The wind stung Adrian's face, mocked his sanity. The blood in his veins pounded furiously.

The horse thundered down the turnpike like a spirit let loose from purgatory.

A soaring thrill gripped Adrian as he flew recklessly into the night, enslaved by the rhythm of the horse and the wildness of his own need. Never in his life had he surrendered to the sweet, implacable terror that seized him now.

God. How he'd missed this.

Chapter 11

~~~~~

"I am in your debt, sir." Emmaline regarded the man in her parlor warmly. "I have no doubt you saved my life."

The ordeal had been horrifying. She'd been convinced she was about to die. But as the carriage began to roll, Emmaline had heard a man's refined tones and then the sounds of a struggle. When the blanket lifted, Mr. Deverell's pleasant features came into view. He'd driven her home and, when her legs wobbled as she tried to exit his carriage, had gallantly carried her to the front door.

The man looked quite out of place in their shabby cottage. He was obviously a gentleman, from his polished ebony cane to his curly beaver chapeau. His tousled blond hair gave him a youthful, carefree air, though his eyes were filled with concern.

He'd introduced himself as the Honorable William Deverell, and he'd seemed apologetic, even contrite, about rescuing her in such a violent fashion. He deeply regretted the fact that the abductor had whipped up his team and pulled away before the Watch could be summoned.

Though it was after midnight, her aunt insisted they treat Mr. Deverell to the bounty of their kitchen, which consisted of a few honey cakes and stale rolls. Her aunt produced a bottle of brandy she kept for special occasions and poured a liberal amount into Mr. Deverell's glass.

Mr. Deverell drank obligingly, then his distinguished features grew pensive. "Can you think of any reason someone would wish to make off with you, Mrs. Stanhope? Other than your obvious beauty, of course."

Emmaline flushed. She felt the strangest inclination to grin. "I cannot think that my appearance, whatever it may be, has anything to do with it."

"Perhaps something in your past?" He looked deep in thought.

"My past is very ordinary, sir."

"Something recent, perhaps. Has anything unusual occurred?"

"No," Emmaline replied. "We are two women who live quite simply, Mr. Deverell."

"A man met his doom at our very gate," Aunt Heloise announced dramatically. "Run over by the Mail."

If ever a man's eyebrows could be said to touch the ceiling, they were Mr. Deverell's.

" 'Tis true," Aunt Heloise added darkly. "And it's been nothing but hardship since. Investigators coming and going—'gentlemen of the shade, minions of the moon.' "

Mr. Deverell looked even more astonished.

"The death was an accident," Emmaline assured him, "but Mr. Burwell might have saved himself. Instead, he stood in the street, seemingly unaware of the approaching danger." To her great dismay, a small giggle escaped her lips. Emmaline clapped her hand over her mouth. The stress of her ordeal had obviously left her lightheaded.

"Most odd." Mr. Deverell pretended not to notice her strange behavior. "Did you have a connection to this fellow—what did you say was his name?"

"Frederick Burwell. He was a client of mine."

"Client?" Mr. Deverell frowned.

Emmaline blushed. He'd not actually suggested anything untoward, though the implication could be read into the inflection of his voice. "I run a matrimonial service. Mr. Burwell had every expectation—as did I—that I would find him an acceptable bride. It was all quite aboveboard."

"I see." Mr. Deverell appeared to consider this. "Forgive me, Mrs. Stanhope. It is none of my business, and yet . . ." His voice trailed off.

"And yet you fail to understand how a man can leave my house, then stand in the path of the Mail?" Emmaline sighed. "The investigators seem similarly baffled, sir. I have no explanation for Mr. Burwell's behavior."

"He did not impress you as a man in danger?"

"Not in the least. He appeared quite calm, even buoyed by the prospect of finding matrimonial happiness."

Mr. Deverell considered this. "Most likely the ruffian tonight had no connection to the man. On the other hand—perhaps I shouldn't mention it—from my vantage point across the street tonight, it seemed that your abductor had been watching you for some time."

"Watching me?" Emmaline blinked.

He hesitated. "Have you considered the possibility that you are being followed?"

Aunt Heloise put her hand to her chest. "Good heavens!"

"Doubtless my imagination was playing tricks," Mr. Deverell said quickly. "Nevertheless, it is prudent to exercise caution. I will call at Bow Street this very day and endeavor to learn more."

"Thank you. And let me say how fortunate it was that you were taking the night air tonight in Guilford Street."

"I wonder—" His gaze met hers. "Would you mind if I called upon you now and then? To bring you news from Bow Street, of course."

Mr. Deverell looked so hopeful that Emmaline could not help but smile. "Not at all."

His mouth curved in an answering smile. His brilliant blue eyes looked thoughtful. Perhaps she was only imagining the interest in them, but it was pleasant to contemplate a kind gentleman's regard.

"What the *hell* is going on here?" boomed a voice.

Emmaline jumped—indeed, all of them did. She gaped at the figure in the doorway. "Mr. St. Ledger! Whatever are you doing here?"

He stood silhouetted against the night, ushering in a wrathful gust of air from outside. His clothing was askew, and he wore the most amazing pink-satin shirt. His hair stuck out from his head at odd angles. His gray eyes gleamed wildly, and he looked like nothing so much as a feral cat about to spring at them.

"I have been"—his gaze slid from her to Deverell—"riding."

In the middle of the night? This rigid man who hadn't strayed from his daily routine in years? Emmaline tried to remember whether he'd listed riding after midnight as among his avowed preferences. No. Definitely not.

"Well," she said, at a loss for words.

A wary Mr. Deverell moved slightly to stand between her and St. Ledger.

Emmaline introduced the two men. "Mr. St. Ledger studies fossils," she added incongruously.

St. Ledger stiffened, as if suddenly recalled to himself. Within the span of a few seconds, he underwent an extraordinary transformation. The wild look in his eye vanished; his face assumed an expressionless mask. He ran a hand through his hair, smoothing it into place.

"I have a passing interest in science myself," Mr. Deverell said, apparently satisfied that Mr. St. Ledger did not intend to murder them. "You might call it an avocation," he added, dutifully trying to keep the conversation afloat.

St. Ledger felt no such obligation, however. "What the hell is he doing here?" he demanded.

"Mr. Deverell saved my life tonight," she explained.

"Oh?" For some reason, St. Ledger looked none too pleased.

She gave him a brief account of what had occurred, but instead of joining in her admiration of Mr. Deverell's heroics, he merely declared, "How convenient."

"What an odd thing to say," she said heatedly. "Mr. Deverell risked his life on my account and—"

"Here I am, sir," interjected a new masculine voice. "Ready for action, prepared to take the bull by the horns." Mr. Gibbons clicked his heels smartly, though he looked as haphazardly put together as his employer.

Mr. Deverell eyed her in bewilderment. "If you wish me to stay until these people leave"—he looked pointedly at St. Ledger—"I am happy to do so."

"We are quite safe," Emmaline assured him. "Please accept my thanks once more, Mr. Deverell. I am sure you must be greatly fatigued and in need of sleep."

Emmaline ushered the reluctant Mr. Deverell out of the house. Her aunt, looking well pleased with the new turn of events, studied Mr. Gibbons with a speculative gaze.

"Brandy," Aunt Heloise said quickly. She scooped up the bottle. "Oh, dear. There's hardly any left. Would you help me search for more, Mr. . . . ?"

"Gibbons," he replied with a questioning look at St. Ledger, who made no effort to detain him as Aunt Heloise pulled him down the hall.

Emmaline sank wearily into a chair. The light-headedness had given way to a headache.

St. Ledger perched rather gingerly on the divan. "Something odd happened to me tonight," he began.

"Yes, well, something odd happened to *me* tonight," Emmaline retorted, "but I have not invaded your home at an ungodly hour to inform you of it."

His gaze held hers. "You are in danger."

"You are late with that assessment," Emmaline snapped. "Anyway, Mr. Deverell rescued me. The danger has passed."

"It has not."

Emmaline put her hand to her forehead. "Can we continue this discussion at another time?"

"My conviction that you are in danger woke me from a sound sleep. You cannot know how that pains me. I am a man of science; I spend my life in the service of rational, provable thought. I do not believe in sorcery, or fortune-telling, or any of the chicanery people like you use to separate the unwitting from their money."

"What you call chicanery has fed us many a night," Emmaline said, bristling. "And who are you to declare such things invalid? Not everything in the world is as concrete as those ghastly bones of yours."

"Regrettably, you have hit upon a truth. Life holds such uncertainty that some people must search for meaning, for magic, for cures they wish to believe are out there, just beyond their ken. They delude themselves into believing that one's fate can be discerned, even overcome. I have never been among their number."

His stark gaze impaled her. "I spent many years trying to demonstrate that those who manipulate the mind do unspeakable harm. I impose a relentless control upon my own thoughts to banish the irrational. And yet . . ."

With a sigh he pulled something out of his pocket. "Do you recognize this?"

Emmaline glanced at the handbill. " 'Tis our flyer." She studied the drawing of the death card, the scrawled letters of Mr. Burwell's name, and frowned.

"It was in Burwell's pocket."

She eyed him in bewilderment. "What does this mean?"

"Apparently Burwell was involved in treason. Most likely he was murdered by those who feared he could expose them."

"Treason," Emmaline repeated, dazed. "Dear Lord! You cannot think that *I* had something to do with his death."

He watched her face. "The murderer knew the net was closing in on Burwell and that, consequently, his death would be examined from all angles. Was it suicide? An accident? Was Burwell drugged, mesmerized, or otherwise incapacitated so that he didn't know death was barreling down the road at him?"

"Heavens," Emmaline whispered.

"The murderer made sure that if anyone was looking for suspects, the path would lead not to him, but you."

Emmaline bit her lip. "No wonder there have

been so many investigators. Why haven't they accused me?"

St. Ledger shrugged. "No matter which way one comes at it, Burwell was killed by the Mail coach. There was no mark on his body that wasn't put there by a coach and six horses. There's nothing to implicate you, save that hand-bill."

She'd been so proud of those notices, pains-takingly copying each one, right down to the dis-tinctive "Gypsy Flora" lettering she had thought so exotic. Now someone had turned her work into something evil. "What will happen?"

"My uncle is one of Lord Castlereagh's top aides. He will be guided by my report."

"Report?" Dear Lord. Evidently nothing and no one—least of all Mr. St. Ledger—was as they seemed.

"You are in danger. The murderer may have decided you are a threat to him. Tonight's kid-napping was no accident."

Emmaline had thought her abductor a pro-curer or robber whose path happened to cross hers. She never considered that he'd been wait-ing for her. Mr. Deverell's claim that the man had been watching her now seemed frighten-ingly correct.

"You must leave this place," St. Ledger said grimly.

"Leave?" Emmaline gave a hysterical laugh. "And where must I go? To Mayfair, where your kind gads about? To Covent Garden, where a girl can do well enough if she's willing to sell herself for a shilling?"

He said nothing.

"Look around you." She gestured around the tiny parlor. "Is this the home of a wealthy woman? We are barely keeping our heads above water. You suggest safer ground. Well, there is no safer ground. There is no ground at all."

Emmaline's voice broke on a sob. "Why in heaven's name do you come here with your wild stories and your strange warnings? Leave me be."

"There is one place. A castle, actually. Not too far from town. I haven't been there in years."

"A castle." Emmaline stared at him in astonishment.

"Your aunt would come, too," he said stiffly. "I wouldn't want you to think the arrangement improper."

Emmaline let out a shaky laugh. "I doubt you know the first thing about what is proper and what is not."

"I will send Gibbons round in the morning to arrange things." He gave a nod of satisfaction and rose, as if everything was settled.

Emmaline grabbed his sleeve. "I would not go with you to the corner, much less a castle, Mr. St. Ledger. You are a bedlamite."

He stared at the spot where her fingers touched his sleeve, but did not pull away.

"You invade my house and fill my head with frightening tales and demand that I go with you to a castle. If I am in any danger, sir, 'tis from *you.*"

"It was not I who tried to kidnap you tonight."

"Somehow, that does not give me comfort."

Emmaline stared at him. "Dear Lord, what manner of man *are* you?"

He sighed in resignation. "I suppose there's no way to continue the masquerade. Once you see the castle, the servants, the peacocks—"

"*Peacocks?* Whatever are you talking about?"

He moved toward the door. "I will explain in the morning."

Emmaline tugged on his arm, forcing him to halt or risk dragging her out into the street. "It *is* the morning, you horrid man! Tell me this very minute."

He stood in the doorway, looking as if he wished to be anywhere else. "I am Trent. Not by choice or design."

"Trent?" she echoed, uncomprehending.

He coughed. "It is a, er, ducal title. There are several other useless titles lumped in besides."

Emmaline gaped at him.

"If it amuses you, you may bring your cards, or crystal balls, or whatever you and your aunt require." He edged out the door. "Though I detest false science, I shouldn't like to deprive you of your amusements."

"Amusements," she repeated numbly.

"We will leave at noon, after my lecture to the British Archaeological Society. Please have your trunk waiting on the stoop."

With that, he was gone. In the next moment, Mr. Gibbons rushed past in search of his employer.

Emmaline sank into a chair. "A ducal title," she repeated slowly. "Mr. St. Ledger is a *duke.*"

"I once knew a duke." Aunt Heloise regarded

her from the doorway. "He had a special fondness for my Katherine. Imagined himself as Petruchio." She clasped her hands and struck a pose. " 'Be it moon, or sun, or what you please. And if you please to call it a rush candle, henceforth I vow it shall be so for me.' "

Her aunt sighed. " 'Tis a notion that works better on stage than in real life, dear. The cursed man expected instant obedience. That's the trouble with dukes."

Emmaline put her head in her hands.

Chapter 12

"Lovely woman. Lovely."

Adrian balled his trembling hands into fists to hide them from Gibbons's sharp eyes. He even managed a decent glower. "Did I ask your opinion?"

"No, Your Grace."

They were quite a pair, Adrian in the pink-satin shirt and Gibbons in his red nightshirt tucked into tan breeches. They'd returned home to find bleary-eyed footmen and Peter cajoling a squawking Galahad into the house.

Adrian barely registered the chaos. He was still trying to comprehend what had happened to him tonight. He'd been ready to play gallant knight to her captive princess. And when he'd discovered another man in her house, a beast within wanted to rip the man to shreds.

Thank God Mrs. Stanhope had not been in a forgiving mood. Her angry confusion had been just the tonic he'd needed to get himself out of her house with his dignity intact. Condescension

153

and pride tamped down the disturbing emotions that spiraled within him.

Why the hell were his hands shaking?

Adrian sank into a chair and the bird flew to his shoulder with a cheery chirp. He wished he knew what strange force was at work between him and the canary.

He downed a glass of brandy.

"I want this destroyed." He fingered the laces of the ridiculous shirt. "I want every piece of my father's clothing disposed of immediately."

A slight frown crossed Gibbons's features. "I do not believe the late duke would have liked—"

"As you have pointed out more times than I can recall, *I* am duke now, Gibbons. My father's wishes are irrelevant." Adrian closed his eyes, trying to summon the vestiges of his control. Instead, he was beset by an image of a pink-clad knight racing toward an irate princess.

Gibbons coughed delicately. "He had his flaws, Your Grace, but which of us does not?"

Adrian massaged his temples. "No sermons, Gibbons."

"I'm sure I have never attempted such a thing," Gibbons replied stiffly.

Adrian regarded him with a bleary gaze. "Why the devil do you work for me, Gibbons?"

Gibbons looked surprised. "We Gibbonses have always been privileged to serve the dukes of Trent."

"Some would think that a curse, not a privilege."

"Each generation has brought its own challenges and rewards," Gibbons replied in a neutral tone.

The man must be nearly sixty, the age his father would have been if he'd condescended to take the pox vaccine. Gibbons might make excuses, but his father had been a beast. When Portia had taken him to the Continent on her strange odyssey, Adrian had not missed the cruel tyrant he'd known only from a distance.

Only later had Adrian surmised the truth: His mother had done something that so enraged the duke that he'd essentially banished them. His father's anger hadn't ended with Portia's death. Years later, when Adrian returned to England to try to persuade Parliament to outlaw the mystics who'd put her through such pain, the duke wouldn't see him.

By then Adrian had surmised that his father thought him the product of an illicit union between the duchess and a secret lover. It explained the years of coldness, the fury his father never tried to conceal in his presence. His mother never hinted of such a possibility, but the scenario fit. His father was not a man to play the cuckold. He'd never forgive such a betrayal, or the product of it.

Yet for all his anger, the duke had never disinherited Adrian, never made him out a bastard. Perhaps he simply considered the odds of Adrian's inheriting so unlikely he hadn't bothered. Perhaps his mother hadn't been unfaithful after all. Perhaps Adrian only persuaded himself she had, to explain why his father despised him.

Whatever the reason, the title had come to

Adrian untainted by rumor or innuendo.

It was his goal, once he put the estate in order, to retreat to Oxford, immerse himself in his studies, and leave the follies of a dukedom behind. Since he'd been in London, Adrian had been deluged with invitations to this ball or that rout, all of which he'd declined. He had no interest in frivolity or in the women he knew would put themselves in his path simply because of his title.

Mrs. Stanhope was different.

He'd never met a woman who had adapted to life's vicissitudes with such determination. His mother had never been strong, not in the way Mrs. Stanhope was strong. Over the years, Adrian had come to understand how people could ruin their lives in the service of guilt; he realized that much of his mother's pain was self-inflicted, that she must have been punishing herself for breaking her marriage vows and foisting a bastard on her husband.

Sometimes Adrian would find himself in the middle of the night wondering whether he could have saved her. What if he'd launched himself at her tormenters? Clawed at their maniacal faces with his young fingers, exposed them for the frauds they were?

He'd tried it once, with disastrous results. Should he have tried again? Or would she have perished anyway, determined to atone for her sins?

A tactful cough made Adrian realize that Gibbons was watching him. "Yes?" he said wearily.

"About the arrangements," Gibbons said.

"What arrangements?"

"Your offer of sanctuary to Mrs. Stanhope. I don't believe you have seen the Essex property in years. It is not quite up to snuff."

Adrian's gaze narrowed. "Out with it, Gibbons."

"It's an abomination."

"The castle? But my father kept it in prime condition. He prided himself on the battlements, the tapestries—even had his coat of arms painted on every shield. He'd never have let it go to ruin. That castle made him feel like a damned king."

Gibbons hesitated. "I believe the property came to have unpleasant associations for His Grace. After you and the duchess departed, he let it go to ruin."

That surprised him. "Why?"

"I couldn't say, Your Grace."

Adrian suspected the man knew far more than he was telling. "The servants, the peacocks—they're all gone?"

"Yes."

"I've just invited Mrs. Stanhope and her aunt to stay in a rotted pile of stones?"

"I'm afraid so."

And needlessly confessed the truth about his title.

"They were beautiful peacocks," he said in a musing tone. The castle had seemed grand and impregnable, like a young boy's fantasies.

"Quite lovely," Gibbons agreed. "His Grace even had an albino peacock. The duchess often said it was her favorite. She had a fondness for renegades."

Renegades? Adrian would never have put it quite that way, but perhaps Gibbons had more insight into her character than he'd had as a child.

"I don't suppose you have a way around this problem, Gibbons."

"Your mother preferred the small dower house at the edge of the property. She lived there during her last years in England. The house and gardens have been maintained, thanks to a provision in her will. Mrs. Stanhope and Miss Alcott would be quite comfortable there."

Memories stirred within him. He vaguely recalled the neat little house that had been so very different from that vast, imposing castle. "Very well," he said. "We'll put them there. I will manage at an inn. You'll stay at the dower house."

"*I?*" Gibbons looked dismayed.

"They'll feel safer with a man in the house—though after tonight, whoever tried to abduct Mrs. Stanhope is probably licking his wounds. He'll stay away until he feels it's safe to surface. That's why we need to act quickly. While he's pondering his next move, we'll spirit the women off to the country. He won't have a clue where she's gone."

"May I respectfully suggest that your presence would be far more reassuring to the ladies than mine?"

Adrian eyed him incredulously. "Mrs. Stanhope and me under the same roof? Unthinkable."

Gibbons said nothing.

Adrian wanted nothing more than to be alone,

but Gibbons made no move to leave. Instead, he handed Adrian a small ledger.

"You might care to examine this. It's a catalog of the books in the castle library. His Grace often bought old texts from colleges that needed an infusion of funds. The castle is moldy and dank, and these books ought to be rescued. Perhaps you could use them in your research."

A library catalog was the last thing he cared to look at. He waved it away. "I trust you'll make the appropriate arrangements for tomorrow?"

"Yes, Your Grace."

"And find out what the devil happened to my bucket."

"Your bucket?" For a moment, Gibbons looked confused. "Of course, Your Grace. Right away."

With great dignity, Gibbons turned and left the room, as if he weren't wearing that spectacle of a nightshirt, as if his employer weren't a vision in pink satin.

At the knock, Emmaline flung open the cottage door. "Liar!" she declared passionately.

"I beg your pardon, madam."

Emmaline reddened when she saw the man on her doorstep. "I am sorry, Mr. Gibbons. I thought you were Mr. St. Ledger—er, the duke."

Gibbons bowed. "His Grace elected to ride."

Emmaline's gaze flew to the street, where the duke of Trent sat on a frisky black horse that seemed barely in check. A grand carriage emblazoned with the ducal crest stood outside her weather-beaten gate. A coachman held the team of horses, and a footman stood at the carriage door. A second vehicle, which she took to be the baggage coach, also stood at the ready.

Never had Emmaline traveled in such a fashion. She felt like Cinderella about to be driven to the ball.

Except that she loathed the prince.

She marched out to the street until she stood looking up at him atop that enormous beast. "Tell me, Your Grace. Has anything you've told me been the truth?"

"Almost nothing."

And that kiss? That strange madness in the mud that felt so demanding and desperate and real? That couldn't have been genuine, either. A duke would never hunger for her kiss.

His gaze held hers. Emmaline tried to fathom the meaning in those gray depths, but he'd proven how little she knew of him. " '*I am an innocent, an utter innocent,*' " she quoted in a mocking tone. "What a lie. You must have thought me witless."

"I prefer to call it a ruse."

"Call it what you wish, 'tis still a lie."

He shrugged. "My uncle asked me to investigate you. I have expertise in those of your ilk. Are you ready, madam? My horse grows skittish."

Her *ilk?* Emmaline glared at him. The man looked utterly self-possessed, arrogant, and unapologetic. Why hadn't she seen the truth of his lineage before?

Emmaline turned on her heel and strode briskly to the carriage. The footman assisted her and her aunt inside, then they were off. Down the turnpike, toward an uncertain future.

"It won't do you any good, you know," her aunt said. "A woman can only be angry for so long, particularly when the target of her anger is a man she adores."

Emmaline made a strangled sound. "I do *not* adore Mr. St. Ledg—the duke of Trent."

"Why not?"

Emmaline stared at her in disbelief. "The man is a liar. He used me."

"And what woman does not use a man, I want to know?"

"I'm sure I have never used a gentleman in my life," Emmaline retorted.

"Poor girl. You can't know what you've missed." Aunt Heloise regarded her pityingly. "Some of my most memorable liaisons were well used."

"He has the disposition of a snake," Emmaline muttered. "Scorn is the only emotion he knows."

" 'What a deal of scorn looks beautiful in the contempt and anger of his lip.' " Aunt Heloise sighed. "Now *that's* what you need to work on, dearie. The man's lips."

Emmaline shook her head. "You are not taking this seriously, Aunt. You cannot see—"

"Oh, but I do, dear. I see quite a lot. He wants you, you know. Desperately."

Emmaline stared at her.

"By the time a woman reaches my age, she knows these things," Aunt Heloise said. "Em, dear, the man needs you."

"He detests me," Emmaline muttered.

"Doubtless that is why he is spiriting us away

to his castle." Her aunt arched a brow.

"Aunt, I love you dearly, but you see things the way you wish them to be. Life isn't a play, where you can fiddle with the ending."

"Nor is it as dreadful as you wish to make it."

Emmaline sighed. " 'Tis no use. We'll not agree on this. You have a soft spot for the man, and I—"

"You should let him make love to you, dear. It would be the making of you. No, don't look at me that way. I know I'm just an aging actress with a scandalous past, but I know a thing or two about love. Without it, life would indeed be the dreadful, humorless existence you seem determined to make it."

Emmaline fell silent. Her aunt's eccentric views no longer shocked her, but there was still a world of difference between Aunt Heloise's notion of love and hers.

Why was it so horrible to wish that a man be honest, caring, and kind? She could never care for a man as dishonest as St. Ledger had been.

"You never told him, did you?" her aunt asked.

"Told him what?"

"That you're not a widow. That you've never been married. That you lied when you said you had." Aunt Heloise gave her a bland smile.

Mutely, Emmaline shook her head.

"Oh, dear. I guess that means you are both liars. Tsk-tsk. What *will* he think of you?" Aunt Heloise sighed and began to study the view out the carriage window. "Do you think he will be pleased to discover the truth?"

"I don't care," Emmaline declared.

Aunt Heloise eyed her solemnly. "Anger can be so stimulating, dear. Each of you raging at the other, sublimating desire into hostility. Imagine his gaze wide with fury at your deceit, his lips curled in scorn, his hands wild with outrage. Imagine him putting those hands on you, wanting to shake you into submission, but capturing your face for a searing kiss instead."

Emmaline gaped at her.

"That's right, dear. Try to imagine—though there is so much you can't imagine, because you haven't experienced it. But trust me, Em. Rage is one of the very *best* emotions. Do let me know when you find that out."

With that, her aunt resumed her placid scrutiny of the scenery.

Chapter 13

I nstead of peacocks, he had rats.

As Adrian stepped into his father's castle, memories he'd thought long gone flowed through him: dozens of servants, hunt parties that lasted for days, noble steeds that could jump any fence or hedgerow.

This decrepit pile of stones bore no resemblance to his memories. Gargoyles who'd presided with proud menace from atop the turrets lay in chunks of crumbling stone at his feet.

"Heavens!" Mrs. Stanhope stared at the rat that ran across her path. Her voice held no panic, and Adrian suspected she'd seen her share of them. Her gaze traveled around the great hall, with its decaying walls and tattered tapestries. "This was your home?"

Adrian shook his head. "I never lived here." Only dreamed of earning a place here and basking in the paternal love that went so unreservedly to his older brothers.

"It is . . ." She was at a loss for words.

"Satisfactory," Aunt Heloise interjected. "We

find your home most satisfactory, Your Grace."

Mrs. Stanhope frowned. "I cannot imagine being—"

"Anything but enormously gratified with your generosity." Miss Alcott shot her niece a stern look.

Adrian hadn't yet informed the ladies they wouldn't be staying in his rat-infested castle, and he was most interested in the ensuing battle of wills. That was denied him, however, when Gibbons intervened.

"It is His Grace's desire that you ladies stay in the dower house that was his mother's home. It is at the foot of the hill beyond the woods. You will find it in immaculate condition."

Mrs. Stanhope gave Adrian a measuring gaze, but said no more.

The brief drive through the woods was accomplished in silence. The dower house was everything Gibbons had promised, a haven of cosy warmth. Cheerful curtains hung in the parlor, and the furniture bore not a speck of dust.

Miss Alcott pressed Gibbons into helping her inventory the kitchen pantry. She firmly rebuffed her niece's offer of assistance, so Adrian soon found himself alone with Mrs. Stanhope in front of a blazing fire that failed to warm the chilly reserve between them.

Adrian sensed her uneasiness, then wondered in disgust when he'd become such an empathetic idiot. *You're the type. Sensitive, fragile . . .*

Impossible. There wasn't a sensitive bone in his body, and he sure as hell wasn't fragile. He was a man now, impervious to wounds of the heart.

Still, he didn't know what to do about Mrs. Stanhope. Violent urges swamped him; her frosty veneer failed to dampen the desire that clawed at him with unseemly urgency.

Even now, with her aunt and Gibbons only a room away, he fought the overpowering urge to sweep her into his arms.

"I trust you will be comfortable here," he said abruptly. She had been staring into the fire but looked up at his words. "Good day," he added gruffly. He'd not stand around mooning over her lovely person.

"I will come with you as far as the garden," she said.

He eyed her in suspicion but said nothing as they walked outside. The carefully tended flowers were vibrant; their heady scent made him keenly aware of her. He found himself thinking about her husband, and whether the man had made her happy. He wondered how long it had been since she'd known a man—best not to wander down that road.

Why must it be *this* woman who'd opened the floodgates in him? Why couldn't he leave her be?

"We are in your debt," she said suddenly. She bit her lip, and Adrian found himself coveting that pink flesh. "I realize that I have seemed ungrateful—"

"I must have you," he growled.

"I-I beg your pardon?" she asked faintly.

"I said I'm happy to have you," Adrian corrected quickly. "Here, that is—at the dower house."

"Oh." She eyed him warily.

Her lips were lovely, moist, full. He imagined kissing them as they deserved to be kissed—not in the mud, but here and now in this garden full of beautiful, fertile things. For her kisses he would slog through a million mud puddles and battle legions of rats. He imagined himself freeing her breasts from the confines of her bodice, running his thumb over the nipples, making them stand erect and proud . . .

Then he'd return to his studies and cottage in Oxford. Life couldn't return to normal until he'd possessed this woman. Why hadn't he realized that earlier?

"Is something wrong?" she asked, when he continued to stare at her.

"Yes—no. That is, I should have made matters clear beforehand." Damn. He sounded like a mumbling fool.

She frowned slightly. "What matters?"

Adrian took a deep breath. "I'm afraid I cannot rest until I've had you, Mrs. Stanhope. I've never kept a mistress before—never had the time for one. I'm prepared to be generous. What is the, er, going rate?"

She stared at him incredulously. Two bright splotches of red appeared on her cheeks.

"My aunt and I," she said in a tight voice, "will remove ourselves from your property immediately."

God, the woman was mercenary. He saw through her ploy, of course. She wanted to hear about the money. "Fifty pounds should be more than enough, especially since I'm providing you room and board." He'd happily pay for the pleasure of bedding her. Hell, he'd pay any price she named. "You'll not have a better offer," he added.

Mrs. Stanhope raised her lovely chapped hand and slapped his face.

"Let me tell you something, St. Ledger or Trent, or however you style yourself," she said in a quavering voice. "I have only contempt for men like you. You have the wealth and title to do or be anything you wish. You could better society. You could make it so that people like Aunt Heloise, who have given audiences such pleasure, do not have to spend their last days in poverty. You could find her a physician who isn't out to take her last shilling."

Her chest heaved in rage. "You could make it so that women like me, who have so very few choices in life, do not find themselves living off the kindness of a deceitful lecher with the understanding of a flea."

Through the fabric of her gown, Adrian saw the outline of her breasts. They were pleading for his touch. Heedless of her fury, Adrian pulled her into his arms.

She burst into tears.

Adrian hated tears. Controlling one's emotions was such a simple, basic thing; there was no reason for her to turn into a watering pot.

She batted at his hands ineffectively. "Only a cad would try to seduce a woman he'd offered shelter to in her hour of need."

That gave Adrian pause. "I may be a bit clumsy," he conceded. "I believe I mentioned that once."

"It's the only honest thing you've said to me," she flung at him.

He tried to look contrite but was fairly certain he hadn't pulled it off.

Her eyes were stilettos of hot fury. "A woman would have to be out of her mind to want a man as insensitive as you."

All right. He'd been clumsy, perhaps even crude—but he had to have her. It was the only way to banish this obsession, to regain the control he'd spent years perfecting. He'd not let his pride get in the way. "I'm not averse to more lessons."

"Lessons?"

He cleared his throat. "Flowers, conversation, dancing . . . the things we discussed before."

"*Before*, I thought you an unworldly man in search of a wife. Now I know you for an incorrigible liar."

"I never claimed to be perfect," he said stiffly.

"Then perhaps your soul will burn in hell for only a few thousand years, rather than an eon."

She turned on her heel and started for the house. Adrian caught her hand.

"Do you mean to force me?" she demanded. "I warn you: That's the only way you'll have me."

Rape? God's blood. She couldn't think him capable of that. "It's just that—" What? That he'd lost all control, behaved like an animal, thought with his anatomy instead of his brain? He released her.

"I'm, er, sorry."

His words surprised him as much as they did her. Her gaze narrowed, as if she couldn't believe her ears. She stood there uncertainly, toying with the edge of her sleeve.

"It's useless to quarrel," she said at last. "In my business, I have learned that what one woman may find horrendous, another may adore. One woman's flowers may be another's weeds."

"You've put me in with the weeds, I suppose."

She gave him a watery smile. "A dandelion, I think. One moment of splendor, then lost to the wind."

"If there was a moment of splendor between us, I believe I missed it."

She slanted a gaze at him. "You've probably seduced scores of women."

"No." He couldn't remember any other women anymore. Only her. *Emmaline.*

"Dozens, then."

"Is this a game?" he demanded. "If it is, I'd like to know the rules. You don't want me to touch you, yet you continue in this provocative vein."

Her smile vanished. "Perhaps I'm looking at you with new eyes."

"Why?" He'd missed something, some nuance.

"I'd like to see if it's possible to find someone likable underneath that horrid shell of yours." Her lips curved upward.

Adrian had a sinking feeling that he was about

to get his head handed to him on a silver platter. Yet he couldn't resist that intriguing gleam in her eyes. If she was setting a trap, he'd walk into it willingly if it meant assuaging this rampaging desire.

"You'll consider my offer?" he asked cautiously.

Her gaze held his. "Perhaps."

"I will call on you tomorrow," he announced, daring her to deny him.

"Until then." She gnawed on her bottom lip.

Little did she know she'd just set his soul afire.

"You mean to make him *grovel?*" Aunt Heloise looked at her in horror. "Em, dear. That is *not* a good plan."

Emmaline stuffed a posy into the cornflower blue vase she'd found on a shelf. "He thinks I am beneath him. He thinks he can do anything he wishes because I have nowhere else to go."

"He was very generous to set us up in this house."

Emmaline ripped another posy from the bouquet she'd picked this morning. "He wants to make me his mistress." Her face grew warm.

"Of course," Aunt Heloise replied easily. "He wants you madly."

"That is what I am counting on."

"I see. You mean to lead him down the garden path, so to speak."

"I only wish to give him a taste of his own medicine. The man needs a comeuppance. He is so arrogant, so sure of himself, so very much a *duke.*"

To think she'd actually believed that a man of Mr. St. Ledger's obvious assets would need help finding a wife. She'd let her desperate need for the money erode her common sense.

Aunt Heloise pursed her lips. "The man can hardly help his pedigree."

Emmaline set the vase on the table with a thump. "No, but he ought to do something with his wealth and position. All he does is dig for old bones."

"Is there something wrong with that?"

"He doesn't care for anyone. He takes whatever suits him, yet chooses nothing." *Fifty pounds should be more than enough.* "He's cold and empty, like that horrid castle."

"And he makes your heart flutter wildly."

Emmaline flushed. "He is nothing to me."

"He is everything you've ever wanted, dear. He's the prince who's come to claim you."

Emmaline eyed her in disbelief. "With all due respect, Aunt, you are mistaken."

Aunt Heloise smiled. "My dear Emmaline. There are many things of which I am completely ignorant. Love is not one of them. Nor lust, for that matter."

"I am neither in love nor in lust with the duke of Trent."

"Then why have you embarked on this revenge? If the man is nothing to you, you would not expend such effort to humble him."

"I mean to teach him a lesson, so that he will never treat another woman the way he has treated me."

Aunt Heloise eyed her consideringly. "I'm not

quite sure what it is you think he has done to you."

"What has he not done?" Emmaline shook her head in disgust. "He has thrown me into the mud—"

"He saved your life."

"Insulted my honor by offering me carte blanche—"

"He thinks you a widow, a woman of experience. It hasn't occurred to him to propose marriage."

"Who said anything about marriage?"

Aunt Heloise merely smiled, and Emmaline fought the urge to stamp her foot like an angry child. Her aunt could not possibly understand how infuriating the man was. He needed a comedown, and she was just the woman to provide it.

"Be careful, dear," Aunt Heloise warned. "You might get caught in your own trap."

Emmaline laughed. "There is no danger of *that*." She studied the vase of posies, satisfied at her handiwork.

"Being a man's mistress is not the worst thing in the world, Em, dear."

Dear Lord. She'd been thoughtless. Her aunt had had any number of liaisons in the past, which she'd never kept secret. "Oh, Aunt. I did not mean to suggest . . ."

"That I've done anything tawdry? No, I'm sure you didn't." Aunt Heloise regarded her calmly. "I don't fit most notions of a lady, dear. I've had a full life, and if it were to end tomorrow, the only thing I'd regret is leaving you alone."

Tears came to Emmaline's eyes, and she wrapped her aunt in a hug. "Nothing will happen to you. I swear it."

"Tsk-tsk. Ladies do not swear." Aunt Heloise gave her a mischievous smile. "They make promises, which they sometimes break."

"I won't break mine," Emmaline insisted.

"Not the one you've made to me. But perhaps you will find it more difficult to keep that vow of revenge against the duke. He's a diamond in the rough. I should hate to be you when he gains a little polish."

Emmaline lifted her chin. "There's nothing he could do to me."

"I fear he's already done it."

Emmaline frowned, uncomprehending.

"He's made you hope—you won't forgive him that. I imagine that's why you're so intent on bringing him to his knees. But have a care: A groveling man can be positively *lethal.*"

Aunt Heloise moved the vase to the other side of the table. "Close your mouth, dear. You'll let in flies."

Chapter 14

❦❦❦

"**N**ow, now. His Grace has lovely rats. You'll adore them." Emmaline tucked the squirming cat more securely under her arm.

Thomas gave a loud meow. "He won't welcome a complaining guest," she chided. "Make yourself amenable, or you won't have those kidneys again, I promise you."

That morning Mr. Gibbons had gone to the village and returned with a basket of food—kidneys, flaky biscuits, fresh eggs, and a loaf of bread that was still warm from the oven. He'd also let slip the fact that his employer was spending the afternoon in the castle library.

With her stomach pleasantly full, Emmaline felt up to the task of matching wits with the duke. He would learn that she was a person to be reckoned with. She imagined the glorious moment when he'd admit he couldn't live without her, when he'd confess himself enslaved . . . when she'd turn and walk out the door. For all the princes who had never followed her to the ends of the earth, for all the knights who had ignored her dragons, she'd enjoy this small, mean-spirited revenge.

She'd not let the flirtation get out of hand, nor allow herself to contemplate what it would be like to truly win his love. She silenced the small voice inside warning that she was better than this, that she ought not let herself be ruled by anger at the inequities between them or the hopelessness of truly capturing his heart.

Besides, she didn't want the duke's heart. A gentleman like Mr. Deverell was more to her liking. She'd sent him a note before they left London informing him of their travel plans, in the event he had news from Bow Street to report. It hadn't been forward to do so, she told herself, only considerate.

When the door to the castle creaked opened and the duke himself stood there, Emmaline almost lost her nerve.

"Good afternoon," she said cheerfully. "I brought Thomas."

He stared, uncomprehending, and made no move to fill the awkward silence.

"He will help with the rats," she hastily explained. "Thomas is an excellent mouser."

"He's outnumbered. They'll send him packing."

Emmaline wasn't sure whether he was jesting or no. She'd never seen a man who found it so difficult to smile. Did his regimented existence contain any joy?

"This way," he said.

It was a library like none other. Scores of

shelves rose to the ceiling, holding books with finely tooled leather bindings that looked to be in good condition. Someone had gone to great effort to preserve the library, if not the building itself. Shroudlike cloths covered the furniture, except for the desk and chair he'd been using. The drapes had been opened to allow in light.

He wore a preoccupied air; Emmaline soon discovered why. "I've discovered one or two medieval works on archaeology," he told her. "I'm eager to study them."

Not eager to flirt with her. Had she misread the signs of his interest? No, he'd been quite insistent. Fifty pounds was an enormous sum. He'd not have offered it to a woman he didn't find alluring.

"There's a catalog, if you'd like to peruse it." He pointed to a thin volume on the desk.

Emmaline set Thomas down and picked up the catalog. Hundreds of titles had been listed in a precise, neat hand, something she suspected was foreign to dukes.

"The Romans uncovered fossils at Cornwall." His voice held a note of barely contained excitement. "I've found a book containing engravings of the specimens."

Emmaline had never heard him speak with such animation. It struck her that she didn't know this man at all. Faced with a choice between her and a rock, he'd undoubtedly choose the latter. She might as well try to enslave the moon. "How . . . nice," she said.

Her tone must have conveyed her disappointment, for he turned and studied her. "Tell me about your husband," he said abruptly.

Startled, Emmaline looked up to see a sudden spark of interest in his gray gaze. Confessing her lie would only drive that intriguing gleam from his eyes. "He was . . . young."

His brow furrowed. "Young?"

"We knew each other as children. He wasn't a child when we married, of course." Heavens. She was making a muddle of this.

"How did he die?"

"The war," she improvised, feeling less worthy by the minute. "He perished on the Peninsula. At, er, Salamanca."

"No children?"

"None—not any." She prayed he wouldn't notice her discomfort.

"You were happy?" His gaze was suddenly unreadable.

She nodded, hoping her lies had not doomed her to eternal torment.

He watched her face. "It's your eyes. They reflect a myriad of feelings all at once. And the dimple to the left of your mouth—it gives you a whimsical air."

"Dimple?"

His mouth twisted in amusement. "Didn't you know?"

She'd looked in the mirror hundreds of times but never seen anything more than a slight, flawed indentation. "No."

He moved to her side. "Do you miss him?"

"My husband? No—yes, of course. But it's been a long time. I hardly think of him now."

Heavens. She sounded like a callous idiot.

And though the duke was worlds above her, though he'd never see her as an equal, Emmaline could not suppress a sigh as she studied the smooth planes of his face, the firmness of his jaw. Without thinking, she reached up to touch it.

He stiffened. His startled gaze met hers.

"I beg your pardon." Instantly, her hand withdrew to the protective folds of her skirt. Clearly, one did not presume to touch a duke without first obtaining his permission.

"I'm sorry," he said. "I hadn't expected—"

"I see," she said tightly, cutting him off. She'd been wrong about his wanting her. Fifty pounds was an absurd amount of money for the favors of a woman so far beneath him; he'd probably regretted his rash offer as soon as he'd made it.

"You can't possibly."

Temper and humiliation gave her voice an edge. "I'm sure I have sufficient intelligence to understand that my very touch makes you recoil in distaste."

He sighed. "Sit down."

Emmaline was not at all certain that she should; the man was so wretchedly inscrutable, so devastatingly desirable that she was quite out of her element.

But his eyes held an intensity that compelled her. She seated herself in the chair. What now?

"Have you ever heard of Father Maximilian Hell?"

Whatever she'd expected, it wasn't that. "A priest?"

"Yes. A physician of sorts. My mother was under his care for several years and I studied at the Jesuit school he founded in Vienna. He was an . . . exacting teacher."

He crossed the room, putting the desk between them. "Like Franz Mesmer, Hell believed that magnetic force cured illness, but his experiments were less benign than Mesmer's. He induced pain in a patient, then used magnets to try to draw out the pain."

"Did it work?"

His mouth pulled into a grim line. "Let me put it this way: After her sessions with Hell, my mother no longer thought about her illness. His favorite technique for inducing pain was to apply a lit cigar to the skin."

Emmaline stared at him. "He tortured her?"

"I believe so. But I was young at the time and unable to challenge the great Hell—though I tried. The first time he came at my mother, I fought him. He locked me in a closet for a week."

"A *week*?"

He nodded. "He demanded that I watch her treatments, said it helped her to have me there. By the time he let me out of the closet, I was ready to agree to anything. So I learned to control myself, to watch and not react. I swore I'd avenge myself on him one day—but he was old and died before I got a chance."

Emmaline covered her mouth in horror.

"That was years ago." He smiled thinly. "I bear no lasting scars."

"Except the loathing of closed spaces," she said slowly, as truth dawned.

"And an aversion to . . . affection. I'm at sea

around any man or beast that demands it." A stunned look came into his eyes. "I've never told that story to a soul."

Something caught in Emmaline's throat. It must have shown in her eyes, for he turned away. "Don't pity me. I'll not have that."

But it wasn't pity she felt. It was something far more complex, and it put to shame her small-minded plan for revenge. It coiled around her heart like a caress, daring her to confront her own duplicity, demanding that she see this man as he was, not as she'd imagined. Against the courageous honesty he'd just shown her, she had no defense.

Confusion gripped her. She wasn't brave enough to face the thing that had slipped into her heart like an arrow aimed sure and true.

"I . . . I need to return to my aunt." She rose.

"I will escort you." He moved to her side.

"That's not necessary," she said quickly.

"Wild boars run in those woods. I'll not leave you unprotected."

What a strange notion. She'd never had a protector, though she had fielded one or two offers of another, more unsavory sort of protection. Indeed, the duke himself had extended one yesterday.

But he appeared to have nothing like that in mind as he walked her down the hill, through the woods, and to the dower house. He said little, but as she put her hand on the door, he covered it with his.

"That was quite possibly the longest conversation we've ever had."

Emmaline had been momentarily lost in contemplation of his profile. "Conversation?"

"About your husband. And . . . the other matters."

"Oh—yes." The burden of her dishonesty weighed heavily on her shoulders. "Your Grace . . ."

"Adrian," he corrected. "My name is Adrian."

She stared into his eyes and swallowed hard. "Adrian, then."

"I think of you as Emmaline. Do you mind?"

"N-no," she stammered.

He hesitated. "About yesterday, in the garden—"

"It's not necessary to apologize," she assured him.

His eyes were churning dark seas of gray. "You're a very touchable woman, your prickly nature notwithstanding."

"Your apology is accepted." Emmaline shot him a too-bright smile.

"That wasn't an apology."

Emmaline blinked. She waited for him to leave, but he didn't move—just stood there, an arm's length away, watching her with those brooding eyes.

His fingertip touched the shoulder of her frock. Then it moved lightly down the profusion of tiny buttons that ran the length of her back.

"You have so many of these," he murmured. "Do you need them all?"

Liquid heat seared her insides, turning her brain to mush and her muscles to quivering jelly.

"Yes," she whispered. "I am quite sure that I do."

"A pity," he said.

He turned and was gone.

Adrian had been too intrigued by the library to leave the castle that afternoon. Gibbons was right: It was a treasure trove of ancient scientific thought. Still, Adrian didn't much care for sitting in the near darkness. The single oil lamp didn't begin to illuminate the shadows, and they were rapidly closing in. His breathing had accelerated. His heart pumped violently. It was almost as if he were back in that closet, waiting for Hell to finish with his mother.

His cadences and mind tricks had deserted him. He sensed he wouldn't get them back, not as long as Emmaline occupied his mind and dominated his will. He'd deposited her at the dower house a few hours ago; surely he could wait until the next day to see her again. He'd be damned if he'd let one woman change the habits of a lifetime.

Yet, twenty minutes later, he stood at the foot of an old birch tree behind the house, over-whelmed by a longing that ran swift and true to the core of his being.

The bewitching Mrs. Stanhope had loosed a strange magic. He didn't understand the source of her power. She wasn't a mystic—her knowledge of the tarot was only superficial. If anything, she was too much of the world; her fearless grasp of the human condition threatened every trick he'd devised to keep the world—and her—at bay. He'd held himself apart from that world, immersing himself in his work, whereas she'd done just the opposite, taking up the challenge of keeping herself afloat by any means possible.

Where he was rigid and fixed in his habits, she was fluid, adaptable. Where he had locked himself away, she'd spent a lifetime accumulating keys to open the next door, the next possibility. Adrian very much feared that she held the key to his soul.

Surely all that was between them was lust. Why else had she come to his castle today? *"I'd like to see if it's possible to find someone likable underneath that horrid shell of yours."*

Adrian didn't know what deep game she was playing, but he feared he would have to take the bait she offered.

Perhaps this very night.

Chapter 15

The shadow brought her awake. Its deadly stillness pierced her dreamless sleep. Someone was in her room.

Emmaline opened her mouth to scream, but the sound locked in her throat.

The duke of Trent stepped out of the shadows.

She sat up and clutched the covers to her chest. Dear Lord. She'd meant to provoke him, but she hadn't known, hadn't guessed, hadn't been prepared for *this.* "My aunt—"

"Is snoring peacefully in the next room." He watched her face. "Do you wish me to leave?"

Of course she did! But strangely, she couldn't find the words. He stepped into a treacherous beam of moonlight that painted him in harsh angles and fathomless shadows.

In another step he was at her bedside. He wore no jacket, only a plain lawn shirt. The sleeves were pushed up, revealing the sinewy power of his forearms. The laces had come undone, exposing the curve of his chest muscles.

She ought to be afraid, but all she could think

was how magnificent he looked. He'd come to her this night because he hadn't been able to stay away. He'd realized she was the woman of his dreams, the grand passion for whom he'd been waiting all his life. He didn't care that she was so far beneath him. Her heart had called to him, and he'd heard. And now he'd come to carry her off, to worship her with his love. They'd live happily ever after and—

"You sleep with your mouth open."

Emmaline's reverie crashed to a halt.

"Snore, too. I could hear you out in the hall." His gently seducing tone robbed the words of any sting.

Emmaline held her breath, waiting.

"Your nightgown is not what I imagined."

She looked down at her old cotton night trail, then lifted her chin defiantly. "I'm sorry it doesn't live up to your expectations."

"I don't have any expectations, Mrs. Stanhope. None that I'd care to mention."

Mrs. Stanhope. He hadn't even used her given name. Where was the man whose candor and vulnerability had tugged at her heartstrings this afternoon? Bitter loss rose in her throat.

"Please go," she said quietly.

Instead, he sat on the bed. Moonlight and shadow warred within his gaze. His hand reached for her, then halted, his fingers hovering mere inches above her breast. Emmaline scarcely dared to breathe. What sort of beast had she awakened? And why did she so yearn to know him?

He pulled the frayed ribbon at the neck of her

gown. Obediently, the gown fell open to expose her shoulders and a wide swath of her chest. His gaze roved over her, seeing all that his hands had not yet uncovered. Slowly, his fingertip trailed over the rise of her breast.

Emmaline thought she would die of longing.

"Get up," he commanded softly. "I want to see all of you."

His eyes never left hers as she slipped out of bed. Her knees nearly buckled; surely he did not mean to strip her naked. As she rose, her gown slid off her shoulders. He hooked a finger under the fabric and eased it down until it pooled at her feet. Desire, silent but unmistakable, gleamed in his eyes. Shame filled her—and anticipation.

He arched a brow in silent query. That single gesture, with the arrogance it so effortlessly conveyed, brought home the appalling gap between them.

How dare he make her hope that he cared?

"I hope you brought the money," Emmaline said with quiet fury. "I'll not let you have me on credit."

He went still. The tantalizing gleam in his eyes vanished. His lips thinned on a scowl.

Then he was gone, leaving only the shadows, empty and bereft.

Moonlight illuminated the lifeless fabric on the floor. A shattering sense of loss filled her. She ought to be grateful that he'd spared her, but she couldn't summon anything like gratitude.

Mechanically, she picked up her nightgown, put it over her head, and retied the ribbon. Then she got into bed and buried her head in the pillow to cry.

Not in his wildest dreams had he imagined how beautiful she was. Her body was slender and lissome, her breasts small and round with nipples that yearned for his touch. Her legs were long and lean, and he'd not been able to stop his eyes from following them upward to that place where they met.

Thank God he'd jeopardized nothing, lost no piece of himself to passion. He'd barely touched her, gazed upon her, but had given nothing away. She'd brought him to his senses.

Emmaline.

Such a lovely, lilting name. It flowed like music off the tongue. She deserved flowers and priceless gowns and servants. She deserved a real man, not someone so mired in the past that he couldn't let himself make love to the woman he wanted so very badly. He'd held himself back, but it had only made the longing worse.

He'd thought her a woman of the world, one who understood that the pleasures of the flesh were separate from the needs of the heart, that they could never overlap.

But her eyes had held something vulnerable and new. And when she'd taunted him, he'd recognized the false bravado behind her words.

As he walked through the copse of trees, bound for his rat-infested castle, shame stalked him like a dark angel.

* * *

"He did *what?*" Aunt Heloise stared at her.

"The duke of Trent came to my room last night," Emmaline said calmly. "He removed my gown, stared at me for a few moments, then left."

With several sleepless hours to think about what had happened, Emmaline had reduced the events of the night to that bloodless summary.

Aunt Heloise's fork fell to the plate with a clatter. "Why in the world did you let him leave?"

Emmaline blinked. "Surely you wouldn't expect me to—"

"No," her aunt said with a sigh. "I suppose not." She took a bite of the biscuits Mr. Gibbons had brought them. "Emmaline, my child, you let a golden opportunity walk out the door. I must think on this."

"There is nothing to think about," Emmaline insisted. "The man humiliated me. We must leave immediately."

"Must we?" Her aunt studied her.

"Of course. You cannot think I mean to remain? Not after he treated me with such arrogance and—"

"Deference," her aunt corrected. "Can't you see the truth, dear? A man does not walk out on a naked woman, especially if he was the one who brought that state about, unless he is suffering mightily."

Emmaline stared at her. "Suffering? Aunt, I don't think you understand the situation—"

"I understand perfectly. 'Tis you who are birdwitted. Now, hush for a minute. I must think about what is to be done. I will consult Mr. Gibbons. He will be back from the village soon."

"Mr. Gibbons? Aunt, you cannot be serious! I would die of humiliation if anyone even guessed—"

"Good morning, ladies." In the doorway, Gibbons bowed courteously. He held a basket of food.

Aunt Heloise rose. "Well met, sir! I have an urgent matter that requires your assistance."

"I am your servant, madam."

"My niece has suffered mightily at the hands of your employer," Aunt Heloise said sternly, ignoring Emmaline's horrified expression. "I do believe the man has a screw loose."

"His Grace is brilliant," Gibbons replied, frowning. "His papers are widely accorded to be without equal. In his field he is considered a visionary."

"I was speaking of his abilities with women."

"Oh." Gibbons looked mournful.

"He came to her room last night," Aunt Heloise said.

The soul of tact, Gibbons did not even glance at Emmaline, who decided to pretend she'd grown deaf.

"Nothing came of it," her aunt continued mercilessly. "The man is impossible."

Gibbons cleared his throat. "His Grace has a good heart."

"So you have said."

Watching the two of them spar, Emmaline realized that this was not the first time Mr. Gibbons and Aunt Heloise had discussed the subject.

" 'Tis true," Gibbons returned. "Unfortunately, his difficult past has blighted his ability to relate to those around him, especially to those of the female gender."

Aunt Heloise regarded him pointedly. "Many of us had difficult pasts. Nevertheless, we have avoided turning into idiots."

"I must take offense on my employer's behalf." For the first time, Gibbons displayed a hint of temper.

"You may do as you wish, Mr. Gibbons. But if the duke is the paragon of character that you say, he will rise above his difficulties. So far, he has shown no sign of doing so. Something must be done. I refuse to allow my niece to be treated in such a thoughtless fashion."

"No, we cannot have that," Gibbons conceded.

Aunt Heloise pointed to a chair. "Do sit, Mr. Gibbons. You look a bit peaked."

Gibbons hesitated. "Oh, no, madam. I could not."

"Nonsense, I never stand on ceremony." To Emmaline's surprise, Aunt Heloise took Mr. Gibbons's hand and led him to a chair.

He sank into it gratefully. "I do not know what to do, Miss Alcott. I am at my wit's end. You know what they say: You can lead a horse to water but not make him drink."

"Because you haven't provided the drink he wishes," Aunt Heloise retorted. "Emmaline is pure champagne, an elixir most rare, to be prized above all others."

Emmaline closed her eyes in mortification.

"We could force him into marriage," Aunt Heloise said in a musing tone. "He did compromise her, after all."

"Aunt!"

"Although he does think her a widow," she added. "Compromise is a thin claim under that circumstance."

"Yes," conceded Mr. Gibbons. "But if Mrs. Stanhope were to tell His Grace that she has never been married, I feel sure he would listen to reason."

Dear heavens—her aunt had told Mr. Gibbons about her lie. Emmaline was mortified.

"Not yet. His Grace must spend more time in her company. Alone. He'll come about." Aunt Heloise turned to Emmaline. "You must carefully time your confession, dear. Too soon, and he runs for his life. Too late, and your claim of innocence will be moot."

Emmaline stared at them. "Please tell me that you and Mr. Gibbons have *not* been scheming to bring us together."

Her aunt regarded her fondly. "Why, of course we have, dear. I always said you should marry a duke, and so you shall. Once I presented the matter to Mr. Gibbons, he agreed that you and Trent would be perfect together."

"You have an admirable spirit, Mrs. Stanhope," Mr. Gibbons put in. "I saw that from the first. I was also very taken with your father's writings. They combine intelligence with a true understanding of the heart. His Grace is sore in need of such a balance."

Emmaline stared at him. "You read my father's papers?"

"Of course." Mr. Gibbons seemed surprised that she would think otherwise. "The duke's welfare is always uppermost in my mind. I researched your family with diligence."

"Then you must know we have no pretense to grandeur," Emmaline said. "Surely the duke should have a bride of his own class."

"I've never found class to be the true measure of a person's worth." Mr. Gibbons smiled. "A gently bred debutante would bore the duke to tears."

"That man needs a real woman, dear," her aunt put in.

"Forget this outlandish notion," Emmaline pleaded.

"His Grace does not do well in certain areas, but I hope I have not given you reason to think any less of him, Mrs. Stanhope," Mr. Gibbons said. "He is an admirable man, worthy of the highest respect. It will take patience and understanding to draw him out of his shell. I pray that you have both."

"I'm afraid I have neither," Emmaline said wearily.

Mr. Gibbons allowed himself a sigh. "I beg you will reconsider, madam. You would be the making of him."

"And he would be the ruin of me." Emmaline rubbed her temple. "Forgive me, Aunt. I have the headache. I believe I shall lie down."

"Of course, dear. And do not worry: you may leave everything to me."

That was exactly what Emmaline was afraid of.

* * *

The engraving was wondrously detailed. The
tooth was clearly from an unknown species. It
had been found four hundred years earlier and
lavishly described by an unknown scholar whose
work had been entitled "Notice on the Strange
Tooth from Tilgate Forest." Adrian had never
heard of Tilgate Forest, but if it contained teeth
such as these, he intended to mount an expedition there as soon as possible.

So absorbed was Adrian that he did not at first
notice the shadow that fell over his chair.

"Your Grace?"

Adrian's heart did a somersault in his chest.
With a deep sense of foreboding, he looked up.
"Mrs. Stanhope," he acknowledged. He couldn't
bring himself to call her Emmaline. After last
night, he needed distance.

"May I speak to you about an important matter?" She looked grim, determined.

Adrian rose quickly. "About last night—"

"I bear some measure of blame, for I had allowed you to think that I . . . I would welcome
your advances." She regarded him coolly. "In
fact, I never intended to allow you to touch me."

He stared at her. "I see."

"I envisioned you crawling to me on your
knees, begging me for kisses, which I intended
to refuse. I wanted to have the pleasure of humbling you, making you grovel. That was mean-
spirited of me, and I regret my action. You are
in no way to blame for last night."

The pleasure of humbling you. How very sweet.
Adrian opened his mouth to consign her to the

devil, but she spoke before he could.

"Further, you should know that Mr. Gibbons and my aunt have been plotting to unite us in matrimony. Until this morning I had no inkling of their scheme. I hope it will reassure you to know that I will make no claim of compromise, nor attempt to force you into marriage. I have no interest in marrying you, and I am certain you have no interest in someone of my station."

No, of course he didn't. The notion was ludicrous. He would put a stop to Gibbons's interference immediately.

"My aunt and I will return to London," she continued. "If you will allow us the use of your carriage for the journey; I promise our paths will never cross again." She fell silent.

His gaze narrowed. "Is that all?"

"Yes."

"I have just made a startling discovery, Mrs. Stanhope. An ancient tooth was discovered in England hundreds of years ago and may, in fact, have come from creatures linked to the fossil I discovered earlier this spring. Out of such revelations comes knowledge, madam—the knowledge that our planet is far older than we think, that creatures who no longer exist walked this land millions and perhaps billions of years ago."

She frowned. No doubt she'd lost the thread of the conversation. Come to think of it, he'd lost it, too.

"Do you know what that means?" he demanded. "It means that we are just tiny grains of sand on an enormous beach. Or, if you prefer, mere pinpoints of light in a vast and infinite sea of stars. Our affairs are meaningless. Insignificant. The world goes on, and creatures come in and out of existence. Time passes, and it is as if we'd never been."

"I . . . I don't know what to say, Your Grace."

"Adrian, dammit!"

Before he could control his spiraling temper, before he could remind himself that what happened between them was indeed utterly meaningless, Adrian caught her face between his hands. Then, though it was extremely foolish, he kissed her the way he'd never kissed any woman—with all the longing of a lifetime.

He didn't want to; he shouldn't have. But last night he had stood in her chamber and beheld her naked. No man had that much control.

Her hands stole around his waist. Adrian crushed her to his chest, wanting her to feel his heartbeat thundering out of control.

Emmaline. Emmaline. The drumbeat would not be silenced.

He broke the kiss at last, put his hands on her shoulders, and gave her a shake so she would know that he meant every word.

"I will return you to London myself," he growled. "You are nothing but trouble to a man who learned long ago that passion is but a trick of the mind. The sooner you are gone, the better."

Her eyes were wide, her cheeks flushed, her lips swollen from his kiss. Her hair had tumbled down around her shoulders.

"You had no business coming through those

woods again," he snarled. "You might have been killed."

She looked dazed.

"Doesn't that prospect bother you?" he demanded softly. "It bothers me. Because if you'd been killed, there'd be no one to drive me out of my mind. And I would miss that, Mrs. Stanhope. Very much, indeed."

With a muttered curse, Adrian hauled her out of the library.

Chapter 16

Mr. Deverell was in the parlor of the dower house.

Emmaline stopped short of the doorway in the futile hope she could slip upstairs before anyone noticed what the duke's kiss had done to her hair. But Adrian, who had come inside when he'd seen Mr. Deverell's carriage, stood at her back, barring any retreat.

Aunt Heloise spied her immediately. "Come in, dear."

"Mrs. Stanhope," said Mr. Deverell, bowing politely. "It is a privilege to see you again."

"Unctuous, isn't he?" Adrian muttered behind her.

"Stop it!" Emmaline whispered.

Mr. Deverell's alert gaze went from her to the duke. The disappointment in his eyes filled her with remorse. He was a very nice man, and so handsome. Any woman would be fortunate to gain his affection. She wondered why he didn't make her pulse race as Adrian did.

"I have come as promised to report that I have

learned the identity of the person who hired your abductor," he said. "Credit must go to Bow Street, of course. The runner I employed has been most diligent."

"Oh, dear," Emmaline said. "It was a great expense, I'm sure. I will reimburse you as soon as—"

"Have the bill sent to me," Adrian barked.

Once more, Mr. Deverell studied the two of them. His gaze lingered on her disheveled hair. With a little sigh of regret, he nodded. "The fee was not large, but I am happy to share the cost with this gentleman, who, it appears, has staked a claim to it."

"Indeed." Aunt Heloise smiled. "Mr. Deverell, I fear you two were not properly introduced that night in our cottage. May I present the duke of Trent?"

Mr. Deverell looked surprised. "Then perhaps the situation can be dealt with after all, for the man who paid your abductor was none other than the marquess of Ainsford. The marquess moves in circles well above my touch—though I do have the honor of being received in Almack's."

"Ainsford?" Adrian's eyes narrowed.

Deverell nodded. "He hired one of the Fleet Street denizens to do the job. The culprit hasn't surfaced, but those who'd heard the man boast about the money were all too happy to talk to Bow Street."

Emmaline frowned. Where had she heard the name?

"I can hardly believe he would abduct a young

woman," Mr. Deverell continued. "Still, he is a dangerous man. I had the distinction of serving as Lord Ainsford's secretary for several years. He can be quite ruthless."

Now she remembered. Ainsford had been opposed to Adrian's bill in Parliament. A proponent of the occult, he'd said. A shiver rippled her spine.

"Why would he wish to abduct me?" she asked.

"Perhaps he happened upon you in Guilford Street and couldn't live without your charms, though. I'm sure you will excuse my bluntness in discounting that possibility." Adrian's expression was grim. Emmaline flushed.

"It's obvious there is a link between your abduction and Burwell's death," he continued. "Perhaps Ainsford has ties to Burwell he doesn't care to have revealed. He may suspect the man told you something that could lead to him."

"If that's so, Lord Ainsford must be involved in—"

"Something unsavory," Adrian finished with a warning glance.

Treason, she'd been about to say. He'd cut her off just in time. She wondered whether his caution was due to the presence of Mr. Deverell, who was obviously a most upright gentleman, or her aunt, who had not a discreet bone in her body. No contest there, she decided.

"Gentlemen," Aunt Heloise said, as if on cue, "I have the perfect solution to this problem. I know exactly how to discover what the shady marquess is up to."

Oh, dear.

Her aunt was in her element. "The cast is assembled, the playwright inspired," she said happily. "All we lack is the audience, and that we shall have shortly. Emmaline? Mr. Deverell? Are you with me? I promise you won't wish to miss this performance."

"With all due respect, ma'am," Mr. Deverell said, "I am thoroughly confused."

"Confusion is but a lack of the coherence that comes with practice. Mr. Gibbons, do join us. We were just about to launch our little plan."

All eyes went to Mr. Gibbons, who had brought his usual basket. "Which plan would that be, Miss Alcott?" he asked politely.

"To turn your employer into a proper duke, so that he can lead us into the very den of the beast who would do Emmaline harm."

"I am as proper as I wish to be," Adrian growled.

"Nonsense," Aunt Heloise replied. "Mr. Gibbons and I had thought to nudge you in the right direction, but you have greatly disappointed us. Since I am in charge now, there will be no missteps. I am a stickler for plot."

Emmaline put her hand to her temple. "Aunt—"

"Quiet, dear. And do not worry: I have parts for all of you. Mr. Deverell, you shall play Trent's friend. I believe you can carry that off; you have the right touch of breeding and aristocratic bearing."

"Thank you, madam," Mr. Deverell said gravely.

"The duke, however, is in need of coaching. Mr. Gibbons, you and I will take on that job. Emmaline, you may assist us."

Emmaline could only shake her head.

"Don't be difficult, dear." Her aunt smiled. "I will need very little preparation for my role, as I am naturally inclined to dominate the stage. 'Tis a gift, alas."

"Miss Alcott, what the devil are—"

"Tsk-tsk, Your Grace. You must learn to wait for your cues. Now, where was I?"

"I'm afraid none of us understands what exactly you are planning," Emmaline said gently.

"Actually," put in Mr. Deverell, "I am beginning to get the gist of it."

Aunt Heloise beamed. "I knew you were a quick study, sir. You will be of invaluable assistance."

Emmaline sensed Adrian's gathering rage. A disaster was brewing. "Perhaps you can be more precise, Aunt."

" 'Tis quite simple. The duke of Trent has decided to bring his fiancée to London—"

"*What?*" he thundered.

"Fiancée?" Emmaline echoed weakly.

"—to introduce her to society and help her gain a bit of town polish. Regrettably, she is orphaned, so there is only her dear aunt to act as chaperone. With the help of this astute aunt, a woman of high moral character and excellent breeding, the duke is able to turn his fiancée out in proper fashion. Hmm, perhaps I should have a title myself. Lady Alcott. Yes, I like the ring of that. I shall be the widow of Lord Alcott, who would have been"—she paused to think for a moment—"your father's elder brother—if he'd had one, of course." She beamed at her cleverness.

"The *ton* welcomes them with open arms, gratified to have the duke take his proper place in society at last. In making the social rounds, the duke and his fiancée—and her aunt, of course—encounter the marquess of Ainsford."

Mr. Deverell hesitated. "I don't mean to be critical, Miss Alcott, but how does one move from a brief encounter with Ainsford to discovering what he is up to?"

"Well . . ." Aunt Heloise began uncertainly.

"I have an idea." Emmaline's expression was thoughtful. "Adrian—er, the duke—says Lord Ainsford is a student of the occult."

"Oh, my." Aunt Heloise smiled in delight, then hesitated. "How exactly does that help us, dear?"

Emmaline looked at Adrian. "I'm not sure."

Adrian looked resigned. "Ainsford is notorious for his 'clinics,' where a favored mystic purports to cure ailments for the entertainment of Ainsford's friends."

When they eyed him blankly, Adrian sighed. "You did say that your aunt was ill?" he prompted Emmaline.

"Ah." Aunt Heloise clapped her hands. "A brilliant plan, Your Grace. I am to be the bait for the marquess. I am quite accomplished at dying; my Desdemona won acclaim all over London."

"I trust you will not need to go that far."

"What if Lord Ainsford recognizes me?" Emmaline asked.

"Would you recognize him?" her aunt countered.

"Certainly not. I've never seen the man."

"I imagine he has never seen you, either, dear. A wealthy man like that does not do his own evil deeds. He doubtless dispatched someone else that night to, well, dispatch you. Anyway, you will look like a soon-to-be duchess, not an impoverished fortune-teller. Costumes work wonders."

"I hope you do not propose to carry off this masquerade from Oxford Street," Mr. Gibbons put in. "His Grace's betrothed would never live at such an address."

"No, indeed," Aunt Heloise replied. "We shall move into His Grace's house. I hope there is room?"

"Oh, yes," Mr. Gibbons assured her. "And may I say that I am filled with admiration for your cleverness."

"Thank you." Aunt Heloise beamed.

The room fell silent. Adrian's brooding gaze locked with Emmaline's. "About my betrothal to Mrs. Stanhope—"

"We shall call her *Miss* Alcott, I think," Aunt Heloise interjected with a sly glance at Emmaline.

"The betrothal is only a pretext?" he asked warily.

"Oh, yes," Aunt Heloise assured him.

Emmaline noticed the quick, conspiratorial glance between her aunt and Mr. Gibbons.

Adrian looked grim. The prospect of ingratiating himself with the man who had blocked his crusade on his mother's behalf must be abhorrent. "I will speak to my uncle," he said finally. "If he agrees, 'twill be done."

"Couldn't your uncle have Ainsford investigated through official channels?" Emmaline asked.

"Ainsford is very powerful. He might block an official investigation," Adrian replied. "A word from him against my legislative petition was enough to doom it. At the time, though, I was only my father's youngest son. The situation is different now."

"A battle between the highest noblemen in the land," her aunt said happily. "High drama, enormous stakes. We will sell out the house!"

Emmaline did not entirely trust Adrian's easy capitulation. " 'Tis revenge, then, that lends your support to my aunt's plan?"

"It doesn't matter why he's agreed to help us, only that he has," her aunt said. "Now, let me think. Time is of the essence. For all we know, Ainsford may be plotting Emmaline's doom this very minute. Will a week be enough time, Mr. Gibbons?"

Mr. Gibbons eyed Adrian dubiously. "I fear not . . ."

"Nevertheless, we shall rise to the occasion. We leave for London one week from today. In the meantime, we must be diligent. No sloth will be tolerated, we have a performance to prepare for."

Aunt Heloise turned to Adrian. "You will

move into this house. We rehearse morning and night. Mr. Deverell, I am sorry we do not have room for you."

"I shall put up at an inn," he said graciously.

"Thank you. Now—"

"I have no intention of staying here," Adrian declared.

Aunt Heloise sighed. "Do not be difficult, Your Grace. Somehow, over the next week, we must reform you. It is an immense task that will require every spare minute. We cannot pull it off if you are elsewhere."

"I do not care to be reformed," he said evenly.

"Of course not. That was only a figure of speech." Aunt Heloise gave him a brilliant smile.

Dear Lord, thought Emmaline. *The fat is in the fire now.*

He and Mrs. Stanhope under the same roof. His mother's house, overtaken by a mad actress and her irresistible niece.

Adrian surveyed the small but adequate room he'd been assigned. It would be more comfortable than where he'd slept last night—on the hard ground outside the castle with his rolled-up jacket for a pillow and the stars for cover. He'd been too drained to travel to the inn. Now he wished he'd staked his claim to those rooms before Miss Alcott had a chance to put Deverell in them.

But alas, the deed was done. Mrs. Stanhope was next door in the room he'd occupied as a child. She slept in the bed in which he'd tossed and turned so many nights.

His mother wouldn't have minded the new occupants of the house. She'd have found common ground with Miss Alcott—nothing like madness to bring people together—and admired Emmaline's spunk.

His uncle would doubtless think Miss Alcott's plan insane, but damned if they wouldn't pull it off anyway. Fate had given him another chance to avenge his mother's death, and he meant to take it.

The last time Adrian had seen her, she was being carried off to a sanitarium that had swallowed her whole. Word of her death had come later, at the school he'd been sent to in Belgium. The headmaster had come to Adrian's room, bringing the local priest in case Adrian had need of him. He hadn't.

They explained that the duchess of Trent had jumped out of a window. When he shed no tears, they stared at him as if he were an unfeeling monster. They didn't know that crying was beyond him, that his mother's end came as no surprise. Even as a boy, he had known that she'd set herself on a disastrous path. She had put herself through so many agonies that death, when it came, was a mercy.

None of the harrowing treatments had eased her pain—or his as he'd watched most of them. She had wanted him with her, she said, for he was her last and dearest child. How he'd wanted to believe that.

Ainsford wasn't to blame for her death, but he had made it possible for the unscrupulous to continue to manipulate the weak. For his mother, for all those who hadn't the strength to prevent the dark forces of evil from ravaging their souls, Adrian would go after Ainsford.

He wouldn't lose this time. A man didn't get many second chances, yet here it was: ill conceived and reckless, but too tempting to refuse.

Leave it to a woman to figure out how to ruin a man.

I can scarcely believe he's in this house . . . Such an intriguing name, Adrian. Melodious, like his voice—

"What is that you are scribbling?"

Emmaline slammed her diary shut. She hadn't heard Adrian come into the parlor. "Meditations and the like."

"Meditations? Are you a philosopher?"

"No. I just put down the odd trivial thought."

"May I read it?"

"Certainly not." *Heaven forbid.*

"This is for you." He held out a book.

Intimations of Romantic Love in Selected Fairie-Tales, by Robert Ulysses Alcott. "Where did you get this?" she whispered.

"Gibbons brought it over from the castle. Strange, that he knew of your father's work. Perhaps he and your aunt have been plotting again."

With trembling hands, Emmaline opened the book. She knew her father's arguments by heart, for he had honed them over many a supper. Yet the written word somehow took on a persuasive elegance his oral arguments had not:

The ordinary world of Perrault's tales is occupied by fairie godmothers, talking animals, and strange longings that beset the protagonists. Romantic love, a concept foreign to Perrault's time, nevertheless emerged in the dark, mysterious, and not-to-be-denied power that transformed beasts into princes and scullery maids into princesses. The meaning of these otherwise austere tales lies in their thrilling proof of the human need for love—even when it had no name.

Oh, Papa, Emmaline thought. So loyal to love, so unwilling to let it be obliterated by life's hardships. He was born a dreamer and had died one still. Unexpectedly, a sob welled in her throat.

He thrust a handkerchief at her.

"Thank you." Emmaline tried to stop her tears, but they spilled over onto her cheeks.

To her dismay, he sat beside her. "You are a writer, too."

Emmaline shook her head. "I scribble meaningless entries about insignificant things that have happened during the day. I don't know why I feel the need to do so. Perhaps to make sense of them."

"Ah. We must do that, mustn't we?"

"My father wrote about love." Emmaline felt an absurd need to defend him. "He believed it held the secret to happiness, long life, and the salvation of the eternal soul. It was the prism through which he saw everything else. For many years I thought it a blind spot."

"And now . . . ?" His gaze met hers.

She looked away.

"Have you written about me?" His tone conveyed a complete indifference to the answer.

"Such conceit! Why would I do such a thing?"

He shrugged. "I suppose it is commonplace to have a man invade your room at night."

Emmaline flushed. "Of course not."

"Did you write about it?"

"No."

"Not trivial enough?" One brow arched rakishly.

"You are deliberately baiting me."

"It is either that or kiss you, and you haven't welcomed the latter." His burning gaze robbed his words of their insouciance. "You feel it, don't you?"

"I have no idea what you mean."

"The very air between us—it is alive with passion."

"It is not." Again she turned away, but he caught her hand and brought it to his lips.

"Emmaline." His voice wrapped around her name, said it like a caress. "I lied to you."

Yes, that was it—an argument would distance him. "Of course you did," she retorted. "I have never met a man who has told so many lies as you, Your Grace."

"Adrian," he said softly. "A-dri-an. Three vowels, three consonants. Nicely balanced, don't you think?"

"I suppose."

"I'm not an innocent: that was the lie. I've had women, though not nearly so many as you might imagine."

"I have not imagined any such thing." Emmaline kept her tone light to show that this conversation was meaningless.

"The truth is, I never wanted any of them the way I want you."

Emmaline prayed for divine intervention—an angel, perhaps, to swoop down and fly the man far away. Failing that, she'd settle for an interruption from Mr. Gibbons or her aunt.

None came.

"I suppose it's an honor to be wanted by a duke," she said scornfully.

"To humble a duke," he corrected. "Isn't that your goal?"

"Certainly not."

"You wanted me crawling on my knees, begging for your kiss. Wasn't that how you put it?"

Emmaline flushed.

"I shan't crawl," he said gravely. "Or beg. I am a master of control."

Irony, self-mockery, or truth? The slight upward curve of his lips revealed little.

"Then again—" he cocked his head—"perhaps I will crawl after all, just to satisfy your insatiable need to humble me. Would you like that?"

"It doesn't count if you do it like that," she said petulantly.

"Like what?"

"With that mean-spirited irony of yours."

"I see." He watched her face. "Nothing less

than full, unadulterated submission will do for you."

Emmaline rose. "I'm sure I am needed in the kitchen."

"You are not. Gibbons hired two villagers to cook for us."

"Stop it, Adrian."

"I am trying to make you see that you want me, too." He caught her hand. "Maybe I *am* an innocent, after all." His gaze dropped to her mouth. "I've never been touched, not in the way I want you to touch me." He kissed the back of her hand, then turned it over and kissed her palm. "You won't deny me that, will you, Emmaline?"

He took her other hand and kissed it, too.

Longing filled her. She was a heartbeat away from letting him show her the ways he'd never been touched. But it was folly to think she could be anything more to him than someone to satisfy his lust.

Emmaline snatched her hands away. "I *will* deny you that, and everything your black heart demands. I am a woman to be reckoned with, not a toy for your pleasure. And now, if you do not mind, I will go to my room."

Chin held high, she made an exit worthy of Aunt Heloise.

She completely forgot to take her father's book. And the diary that lay so invitingly on the sofa where she'd left it.

Chapter 17

•••

"**D**on't you possess something more stylish, Your Grace?" Miss Alcott sighed. "You wore such a nice shirt that night you rode to our cottage. Pink, I think—and satin. A lovely fabric. Catches the light well."

Adrian prayed for patience. "I will not array myself like a peacock, ma'am."

"Very well. Let us turn to something else." She examined the list she'd prepared. "Emmaline tells me she covered the area of conversation with you, but . . ." She eyed him critically.

"But?" Adrian prompted with a sense of foreboding.

"Forgive me, Your Grace, but you are prone to abruptness. Long silences. Even rudeness. I've never heard a pleasantry from you, not even something so commonplace—"

"As the weather?" he suggested darkly.

"There. That is just what I'm speaking of. You interrupt. You are no respecter of gender, nor the trappings of polite society."

Mr. Gibbons cleared his throat. "That is a trait I have found common to dukes."

"Hmmm. Now that I think on it, my Petruchio *was* rather abrupt." Miss Alcott smiled. "You may keep your rudeness."

"Thank you."

She and Gibbons had been having a go at him for nearly an hour. He'd received lectures on the social graces, the proper way to greet a woman, and the various entertainments to which a fiancée should be squired. Gaming hells were out, as were cockfights. Crushing routs and balls were in. These evidently required dozens of clothes Adrian had no intention of wearing: gaiter pantaloons, cossack trousers that looked like balloons on a man's legs, high-necked cravats capable of choking the breath out of him.

Deverell, whom Miss Alcott viewed as a paragon of gentlemanly behavior, had tried to persuade Adrian to commission a many-caped cloak like the ones worn by fashionable whips, but Adrian would have none of it. He was not and would never be a nonpareil.

Trying to reason with Miss Alcott was like trying to stop Fulton's blustering new steamship. Moreover, under her ministrations, Gibbons had bloomed into a complete nuisance. The man longed to have a proper duke to tend, and he was clearly hoping Miss Alcott would present him with one. Adrian decided that Gibbons's judgment, so reliable before, was not to be trusted. The man would have him wearing that pink satin if he wasn't careful.

"After dinner," Deverell was saying, "it is customary for the ladies to retire and the gentlemen to drink port and discuss the issues of the day."

"Nonsense," Adrian grumbled. "The ladies retire to gossip and the men to drink themselves to such excess that they miss the chamber pot provided for their convenience. Any pretense at conversation swiftly dissolves into what is quite literally a—" He broke off, suddenly recalling his audience.

"Pissing contest," Miss Alcott finished for him. She looked quite put out. "I must add Proper Language Around Females to the list. Is there no end to what we must accomplish?"

"His Grace has a point," Deverell conceded, ever the gallant peacemaker, "but most gentlemen endeavor to conduct themselves with decorum."

Not those who'd visited his father. They'd been too drunk to notice the small boy who hid under the table to observe manly rituals on the rare evenings he was allowed to sleep overnight in the castle.

"Now, as to the rest: Emmaline tells us you have some unusual, not to say unnatural, behavioral habits."

The woman made him sound like an aberrant toad. "I have no idea what you refer to, Miss Alcott."

"You possess a dread of closed spaces, is that correct?"

Emmaline had indeed been thorough in her reporting. "Yes," he admitted.

"You are superstitious?"

Adrian drew a blank. Then it came to him: the

lie he'd used to get her to give him a tarot reading. "Not at all."

Miss Alcott furrowed her brow. "Emmaline was most clear on that point."

"Perhaps she exaggerated." Emmaline knew he'd lied, of course. She'd probably taken great delight in adding yet another foible to the long list her aunt was compiling.

Miss Alcott pursed her lips. "She also described you as a hypocrite. Not a very charitable observation, but—"

"Quite true, I'm afraid." Adrian waited for her to ask him to elaborate, but she merely arched one eloquent brow, as if to say she was on to his tricks.

"Do you dance, Your Grace?"

"Not if I can help it."

Miss Alcott shot Gibbons a sympathetic gaze. "My heart goes out to you, Mr. Gibbons."

"Your niece tried to teach me once," Adrian added. "I stepped all over her toes. It put her in a miserable temper."

"This man is hopeless," Miss Alcott declared.

"I'm afraid you must accept me as I am," Adrian said. "I'll have none of those airs and fribbles you want to hang on me."

He turned to Gibbons. "By the way, there was no bucket of ice water in my room again this morning."

Miss Alcott frowned. Adrian tried to explain. "My disposition requires ice water each morning. Thomas Jefferson swore by it. In fact—"

"I believe we've done enough work for now," she said, massaging her brow. "Please go and, er, get your drink of ice water, or whatever you require."

Adrian strode outside with the relief of a man spared the firing squad. He needed to be alone with his thoughts—and more importantly, with Emmaline's diary, which he'd purloined from the parlor after she left in a huff. He'd been dying to read the thing, but Gibbons and Miss Alcott had cornered him so swiftly after Emmaline left that they must have been lying in wait for him.

Adrian sat under the canopy of the old birch. He had no qualms about reading the journal; a man must know his opponent, after all. Perhaps he'd learn how to defeat this strange power Emmaline had over him.

Looks alone didn't account for it. More handsome than beautiful, her features bespoke a feminine power that emanated from within, not from the exterior, comely though it might be. Her eyes, twin pools of jade, reflected fire and inner strength. Her hair, auburn shot through with red, was one of her loveliest assets, and she didn't wear it in ringlets or other silly styles. Nor was she partial to the ghastly arsenic face powder he'd seen on some women. She had no need for counterfeit charms.

One kiss. One inelegant, clumsy kiss had done this. No matter that it had been a kiss in the mud, it had spawned an inexorable force he could no longer deny. It called to him like a siren across a sea of emotions that bubbled like a brew of erotic mayhem.

He was, quite simply, a quivering mass of longing.

The journal was an opening into her soul, and perhaps the weapon he needed to fend off this all-consuming desire. It would reveal her flaws, her vanities, her shifting allegiances, her true intent.

With a shooting thrill of anticipation, Adrian opened Emmaline's diary. It fell open to a well-worn page:

He kissed me. It was muddy. It was heaven . . .

Adrian's heart leapt to his throat.

"Good night, Em, dear." Aunt Heloise kissed her cheek. "We'll start in the morning with the proper behavior at a ball. You and His Grace will report to the music room at precisely nine o'clock."

Panic rose in Emmaline's throat. "Can't you do this without me? I don't want to see him, and he certainly has no wish to see me—"

" 'O, youthful eyes that see so little, and yet how they confess the secrets of the heart.' " Aunt Heloise gave her a hug. "My dear, you are made for each other. I feel it here—" she gestured to her heart.

Emmaline shook her head. "He is but amusing himself."

"The man is anything but amused, dear. Trust me on that. Now good night, and if you hear any strange noises from my end of the hall, put them out of your mind. I am a restless sleeper, as you know."

Emmaline knew no such thing, but her confusion vanished as she saw her diary lying on the bed, half-hidden by the quilt.

Had it been here all along, hidden in the folds of the bedding? She thought she had left it downstairs, but a search had revealed nothing. Had someone taken the diary, read it, and tucked it under the covers to throw her off?

Surely not. If the duke had read her diary, he'd have confronted her with the contents, since so much of it was about him. He'd never have returned it to her room and made it appear as if it had been there all along. Yet here it was, apparently undisturbed, as if it had lain under the quilt all day.

As she picked up the diary, a piece of paper tumbled out. It held two lines of bold script. Her fingers trembled as she read:

Sweet Helen, make me immortal with a kiss. Her lips suck forth my soul; see, where it flies!

Marlowe.

Emmaline sat on the bed in a state of utter shock.

Someone was pacing out in the corridor, not in bed slippers but in loudly clomping boots. Sleep, already elusive, was impossible. Adrian ripped the covers off, strode to the door of his chamber, and flung it open.

The corridor was empty. At the far end near the stairs, he saw a snippet of fabric as the culprit rounded the corner.

Adrian wrapped his dressing gown around him and set off after the stomper. At the top of the stairway, he caught another tantalizing glimpse of fabric on the landing below. But by the time he reached the first floor there was no one to be seen.

Who was playing this game? Miss Alcott? Gibbons? Emmaline?

He climbed the stairs again. When he reached his room, he saw that Emmaline's door was open. He hesitated. He didn't intend to cross that line again—not without encouragement, anyway. But he couldn't resist one peek, just to see if she was sleeping soundly.

She was not. Emmaline stood near the door, not two feet away. The flannel night rail covering her from head to toe did not halt the sudden heat that shot to the pit of his stomach.

"I . . . heard a noise," he said lamely.

"So did I." Her gaze was riveted on him.

The conversation immediately faltered. They stared without speaking for a good ten seconds.

"Thank you," she whispered at last.

"You're welcome," he ventured, with no idea what sterling deed she was thanking him for.

"I've always adored poetry."

Poetry? He frowned.

"You read my diary." She looked down.

Shame filled him. "Just a passage or two. I didn't mean to—" No, he wouldn't compound the deed with a lie. He'd meant to, all right.

"You understood," she said softly.

Understood? No, that wasn't the word. He'd

been horrified, shamed, and humbled by what
he'd read:

*I did not want him to stop. His kisses make me
weak. They bring on a strange lethargy . . .*

At first he'd thought she was writing about
someone else. But the mud was unmistakable.
He didn't know what to do about the shard of
joy that ripped through him as he read those
words, so he had just closed the journal and gotten rid of it as soon as possible. He'd held his
breath as he slipped it into her bedcovers this
afternoon, praying no one would find him out.

"I am sorry for my anger this morning," she
said. "It's just that . . . well, one moment I think
you despicable, the next moment I—" She broke
off, biting her lip.

"Yes," he murmured. "That, too."

"Who are you?" she demanded suddenly.
"The infuriatingly remote man who cares for
nothing but his fossils, who has no use for sentiment or anything approaching kindness?"

She took a step toward him, and any defense
he might have offered dissolved in a wave of
simmering desire.

"Or are you a man capable of eloquent tenderness, who refuses to let it emerge?" She
touched his sleeve.

Eloquent tenderness. Surely she had someone
else in mind—but no, she was eyeing him with
wistful yearning. "Which is it, Adrian?" she said
softly. "Who are you?"

"I—" His voice sounded hoarse.

Her hand moved to his shoulder. Warning bells sounded in his brain. She was too near, too ... everything. With all the strength he could gather, Adrian took her hand and gently removed it from his shoulder. This night would end badly, if he wasn't careful. "Emmaline, I—"

"It's all right. I don't believe in fairy tales, either." She smiled sadly. "But I do like Marlowe. Thank you."

Adrian wondered if it was possible that wanting her had affected his hearing. She thrust something into his hand. He looked at it, uncomprehending.

Marlowe. Then at last he understood.

But she'd already closed the door, and he couldn't bring himself to knock on it and explain. If he saw her again tonight, he wouldn't be able to let her close that door against him.

He returned to his room, the note clutched in his hands like a counterfeit draft used to purchase a rare jewel. He might have congratulated himself for not pressing the advantage that note would have gained him, except that he didn't feel virtuous; he felt bereft.

For the first time in his life, he despised his self-control. He closed his eyes and consigned it to oblivion, but he was too much the coward to really let it go.

If he made love to her, he'd never recover. All the cadences in the world couldn't ward off the thing that clawed at him, the lurking monster who'd stalked him since boyhood—biding its time, waiting for the day Adrian found the one woman in the world he could love.

He felt as if he'd aged forty years in one night. He took off his dressing gown and slowly got into bed like a man who doesn't know if he is dreaming or awake. Then he saw it: the lovely red rose, resting on the soft pillowcase like a benediction for the damned.

"Did you hear anything?" In the shadows at the top of the stairs, Aunt Heloise furrowed her brow, listening.

"Not for some time now," Gibbons replied. "Racing down those stairs almost killed me, Heloise. I don't think this plan is working."

"Nonsense, John. You must have faith in my methods. Poetry is food for the soul; Emmaline must have been entranced. Marlowe understood a woman's heart."

"You don't know the duke. His childhood . . . Such a sad little lad. It tore my heart in two."

She studied him. "I do believe that is a tear in your eye."

He didn't deny it. "I've always been fond of the boy."

"The *boy* is thirty years old, John. It's time he faced the truth. He and my Emmaline are meant for each other."

"I don't know about that. . . ."

"*I* do."

Gibbons's eyes narrowed. "Heloise, you are a conniving woman."

"I've never denied that." She fluttered her lashes at him, but he merely returned an unreadable gaze.

"You know, John," she said in a low, husky

voice, "you could have me for a song."

His arched brow put her suddenly in mind of
Trent. "I've never been able to carry a tune, Heloise. Leastwise not a fancy one."

"Perhaps you only want coaching."

Gibbons shook his head. "I'm too old to learn
new ways."

"Isn't that just like a man? You sound like the
duke himself!" She glared at him.

"Do I?" He stroked his chin consideringly.
"That's something to think about, isn't it? Good
night, Heloise."

She watched him disappear down the hall into
his room. With a sigh she gathered her skirts and
returned to her chamber.

Chapter 18

❝**M**rs. Stanhope. A word with you, if I may.❞

Emmaline looked up from the rosebush she was tending. She loved roses and had often wished that the cottage had a garden. She sat back on her heels and regarded Mr. Deverell with an inquiring gaze.

He looked so well-dressed and proper, whereas her face was flushed from the morning's sun and her hands very much the worse for wear. With gentlemanly aplomb, he offered his hand to help her up.

"I am glad you are alone, Mrs. Stanhope. I have been waiting for a chance to speak privately with you." His features were grave. His hand lingered on her elbow.

"Yes?" Emmaline asked with some alarm. Had he news of the marquess?

"I was honored that you wrote to let me know of your travel plans. I hoped that—" He hesitated. "I wonder," he said at last, "whether you could find it in your heart to think of me in a way—what I mean is that I am excessively fond of you, Mrs. Stanhope."

Emmaline's eyes widened. She'd not expected this. "Mr. Deverell, I do not know what to say."

He kicked at a clump of dirt. "I know that your affections are otherwise engaged. I only wish to know whether that is a temporary state, and whether I might hope to claim your regard at some time in the future, perhaps after this masquerade is done . . ." His voice trailed off.

Emmaline's heart went out to him. He was so nice and looked so miserable. She knew, nevertheless, that she could not return his regard. She'd written that note to him out of fury at Adrian; now she saw how wrong it had been to give Mr. Deverell hope. She remained silent, searching for words that would not hurt his feelings.

"Ever since we met—under difficult circumstances, to be sure," he continued, "I have admired your courage and independence. A man of my meager means has few choices when it comes to planning his future, but I wondered whether you might consider a liaison at some later date."

Emmaline stilled. "A *liaison*?"

"Under other circumstances, I would propose marriage," he quickly assured her. "But I can scarcely marry a widow. You see, I am in line to inherit a viscountcy. Fourth in line, but one never knows what will happen, does one?"

"No," she agreed softly, "one does not."

"As used goods, a widow would be inappropriate for me to wed. Any child of our union would be under a shadow as to its paternity. As a potential heir, I must marry a virgin. Nevertheless, I could keep you in style. I have several profitable investments. I also dabble in chemistry, which allows me to supplement my income now and then."

Emmaline took a deep breath. "Used goods," she repeated slowly. "Yes, I suppose I am that."

"I did not mean anything derogatory," he assured her. "I am filled with admiration for you, madam. I only hope you can envision a time when you can make room for me in your affections. After you and the duke have parted, of course. I should not like to share another man's mistress."

"Certainly not." Closing her eyes, Emmaline took another deep breath.

"Have I offended you?" he asked anxiously.

Emmaline opened her eyes and regarded him calmly. They needed Mr. Deverell's cooperation. For now, she'd hold her tongue. Except for one small matter.

"I admire your candor, Mr. Deverell, but I am afraid I cannot give you reason to hope."

His face fell. " 'Tis as I thought. One can hardly compete with a duke."

"No," she said, "one cannot."

"Forget I spoke, Mrs. Stanhope."

Emmaline studied him. "May I give you a word of advice, sir?"

He smiled at her. "I yield to your superior knowledge, madam. Was I too eager? Unpolished? Too complimentary?"

Emmaline felt old beyond her years. "No. But

I must advise you against speaking of a woman as 'used goods,' at least to her face. 'Tis—how shall I say it? Alienating. Yes, that is just what it is."

Mr. Deverell flushed. "I didn't mean—"

"I'm quite sure you didn't. Don't worry, Mr. Deverell. I am not offended." *Wounded to the quick,* she thought grimly, *but not offended.*

He bowed politely and hurried away.

"He'll take your advice to heart," said a familiar voice. "Deverell's a quick study."

Emmaline's heart sank as Adrian emerged from the shadows of a birch tree. He'd obviously heard everything. "Eavesdropping scarcely becomes a duke," she said petulantly. "Why didn't you simply come out and join the conversation?"

His eyes narrowed. "You didn't need help."

"No," she agreed bitterly. "I'm perfectly able to handle things myself."

"How the devil can I keep you safe when you're sending notes to half of London announcing your whereabouts?"

Emmaline lifted her chin mulishly. "I wrote only to Deverell. I might add that since our arrival here, the only person I've needed protection from is you."

He sighed. "About last night . . ."

Unexpectedly her eyes burned. "If this is another of your backhanded compliments—"

"The poetry. I didn't send it."

Emmaline bit her lip, hoping the pain would prevent her from feeling this latest wound of the heart. She lifted her chin. "Perhaps I have a secret admirer," she said with a brittle smile. "I suppose he will be the next one to ask me to be his mistress."

"I don't mean to wound you," he said gruffly, "but I couldn't let you believe that I—"

"Wound *me?* I assure you, that is quite impossible." She waved a dismissive hand. "I'm a woman of the world, used goods, don't you know?" Her voice broke.

His gaze held hers. "I would never call you that."

"It doesn't matter what you call me, Your Grace—"

"Adrian, dammit." He took a step toward her.

"Adrian, then. It doesn't matter, because there is no changing the gulf between our stations."

"If I sent you poetry," he said in a rough voice, "it wouldn't be Marlowe."

"Oh?" Her voice quavered. "Who, then?"

"Herrick, maybe. 'Give me a kiss and to that kiss a score; then to that twenty, add a hundred more. A thousand to that hundred—' " He broke off. "Good God. Here I am quoting poetry to a woman I—"

"Don't even like? Want only to bed?" Emmaline offered acidly. "The possibilities are many."

Storm clouds gathered in his gray gaze. "Be careful, Mrs. Stanhope. You know not what beast you may bestir."

"Dear me." Emmaline tossed her head. "My knees are positively trembling in terror, Your Grace."

"I suspect your aunt sent the poem," he said evenly. "She hoped you'd think that I—"

"Cared for me?" she offered disdainfully.

"You need not fear: I would never be so stupid as that."

"I found a rose on my pillow last night. Undoubtedly Gibbons placed it there, hoping I'd assume you'd done it."

She gave a bitter laugh. "Know this, sir: if I sent you flowers, it wouldn't be roses."

He studied her. "What then?"

"Something large and menacing, with a bite to it. Stinging nettle, perhaps, or deadly nightshade."

"You would poison me?" He arched a brow.

"Merely give you enough to make you deathly ill."

Emmaline turned away, but he caught her hand and reeled her in like a fish.

"Do you hate me so very much?" His thumb brushed her lips.

"I don't hate you."

His gaze raked over her. "Then we are . . . friends?" He said the word with such irony she knew he was mocking her.

"N-Not friends."

"Lovers, then."

Her eyes widened. "I don't . . . want that."

He ran his fingers through her hair, pushing the hairpins out as easily as she'd put them there hours ago. "Are you certain?"

Certain? No, she wasn't certain of anything. What was this delicious sensation that swept through her? Despite her best efforts, her secret heart had long dreamed of a man who would move her like this. But this arrogant, uncooperative, bloodless man? If he was her Prince Charming, it was fate's cruel joke.

His hands met at her waist and traveled slowly up her sides to cup the underpart of her breasts. A small moan escaped her.

"You like that, don't you?"

Vain, conceited man. Yet something wild and reckless held her spellbound as he began to work the laces of her frock.

Slowly, he pushed the fabric down her shoulder, baring a breast. "You are lovely," he whispered.

She batted at his hands and tried to cover herself. "Someone will see us."

" 'Tis only fear of discovery that gives you pause?" He imprisoned her hands in one of his. He nibbled at her earlobe, then trailed kisses down her neck.

Emmaline mustered a final shred of resolve. "You cannot think I derive any pleasure from— dear heavens!"

He lifted her into his arms and carried her to the far side of the tree. "There," he said, sliding her body down his length as he set her on her feet. "No one can see."

His strong, firm body felt so very . . . *necessary* against hers. "I will scream," Emmaline threatened.

He merely arched one brow.

"I can handle men like you, don't think I can't."

"Can you?" Deftly, he freed her other breast from the confines of her bodice.

"Y-yes. And I did not say that you could do . . . *that*."

His lips grazed the rise of her breasts in a kiss that was so soft, yet erotic, Emmaline scarcely dared to breathe. Slowly, his tongue encircled the tip of one breast. She fought back a whimper as he took her nipple into his mouth. He was a monster to do this to her, only yards from the house, where anybody might see. Yet the desire he'd ignited left her weak with a need that damned caution.

He crushed her against him, cradling her against his arousal, daring her to resist.

She wanted moonlight and roses and poetry and flowery declarations of love and a promise of ever after. She deserved that, not this gritty wildness against a tree, not his hands using her in such relentless fashion.

Yet she was helpless against the raw pleasure he'd aroused. She wanted the touching—though it could only be fleeting, not forever.

A sob escape her.

He tilted her face upward. "Poor Emmaline. You really don't want me, do you?"

Tears streamed down her face. "N-no."

"I was only imagining those little moans of pleasure."

She sniffed. "Yes."

"When I touch you here"—he drew a lazy circle around her breast, then lightly weighed it in his palm—" 'tis awful, is it not?"

"Yes," she said in a small voice.

He turned his hands over, allowing the back

of his fingers to graze her nipples. "And this must be dreadful."

He *knew*, the wretched man, knew he was driving her wild with longing. Her treacherous body arched toward him.

Slowly, he bunched the fabric of her skirt until it was up around her waist. Emmaline closed her eyes as a dangerous shard of anticipation shot through her. He wouldn't—he *couldn't*—do this to her.

One of his hands moved to cup her buttocks. The other descended to her abdomen, applying the slightest bit of pressure there as he stroked her possessively. She shuddered with need. His hand moved on down her thigh, then wandered in desultory fashion until it settled at the white-hot heat centered at the juncture of her legs.

"And this?" he said softly.

"H-h-horrid," she stammered. This wasn't real. She couldn't be here, now, feeling this exquisite pleasure with an arrogant duke who had so little regard for her—

"I beg your pardon." His hands fell away from her.

Emmaline cried out in dismay.

Their gazes locked—his knowing, hers bereft. With a heartfelt sigh, she abandoned all pretense and put her arms around his neck.

He found her again, and his slow, delicious rhythm made her knees buckle. She leaned against him, hating the fact she was more than ready to be well used.

His fingers toyed with the moist folds of her sex, spawning sensations that drove her beyond speech, beyond protest, beyond her wildest fantasies. His sorcery controlled her, and she could only plead for more of this rough, dangerous magic he controlled so well. She had neither the strength nor desire to stop him.

The first inkling she had of his true power came with the tiny, tantalizing waves that began where his hand touched her and rippled toward some unknown ecstacy. The waves grew and grew, until pleasure swamped her all at once, filling her with joy. Resistance flowed out of her, replaced by an inexorable and undeniable sense of fulfillment.

She was his. Now and always. At that moment, she despised him with a passion that equaled the primitive pleasure he'd unleashed.

Suddenly his hand covered her mouth. Had she cried out? "Your aunt," he whispered.

"Emmaline," Aunt Heloise called from the edge of the garden. "Is that you, dear? Nuncheon is ready."

Emmaline took a deep breath, then realized Adrian's hand was still under her skirt, still stroking that most intimate part of her such that—

"Tell the duke that Cook has made a trifle for dessert," her aunt added.

Emmaline fought her laughter because she knew it would end in tears. Though this unexpected passion had forever changed her, for him she was merely a trifle to satisfy his carnal appetites.

"I'll be right there," she called in a shaky voice.

Aunt Heloise gazed thoughtfully at the rose-bush, then returned to the house.

"I must go," Emmaline said. But she didn't move.

"Must you?" He didn't release her. Instead, he cupped her sensitive flesh, spawning another wave of glorious pleasure even as she shook her head in angry denial.

God's blood. He'd stood Emmaline against a tree and pawed her like a desperate animal.

Gibbons had been studying him with a speculative gaze all afternoon. Miss Alcott was beaming like a lighthouse. Everyone knew, or thought they did.

Maybe they'd enlighten him, for Adrian had no idea what had happened to him this morning under that old tree. Something had escaped its cage, had driven him like a madman. It wasn't about to rest until he had Emmaline in his bed and banished whatever dark desires had led him astray.

Worse, a dangerous exuberance filled him when he conjured the image of Emmaline swept by the pleasure he'd wrought.

In his years of ruthless asceticism, he'd allowed himself only the occasional indulgence, always with women who understood the rules— the chief being that the pleasures of the flesh were ephemeral and meaningless, though occasionally necessary. But touching Emmaline was exquisite torture, as necessary now as breathing.

" 'Bait the hook well! This fish will bite.' "

Adrian looked up from the book he'd been

staring at blankly for half an hour. Miss Alcott, her face a mask of bland innocence, was regarding him from the doorway of the study.

"I've been rereading *Much Ado About Nothing,*" she said pleasantly. "It so perfectly captures the raw edges of passion, the delicious tension between desire and fulfillment, love and hate. 'Tis such fun watching Beatrice and Benedick discover that the other side of their anger is desire and need, a true passion for the ages." She paused to give her words their full effect.

Adrian did not pretend to misunderstand her meaning. "A comedy of errors, madam, nothing more."

"Yet the attraction we feel for those we profess to despise makes fulfillment that much sweeter, does it not?"

Adrian gave her a pained look. "Miss Alcott, may we speak of something else?"

She settled herself into a chair. "Why, Your Grace, I did not think we were speaking of anything in particular. But if there is something that bothers you, why, you must be sure to tell me. I am the soul of discretion."

In a pig's eye, Adrian thought grimly. "I have decided to return to London tomorrow."

"We have spent but two days preparing for our roles," she protested. "There is no substitute for a proper rehearsal."

A week sharing this house with Emmaline was sure to destroy him. In London, at least, he had a huge mansion in which he could disappear for a time.

"Nevertheless, I have business that demands

my presence," he said, though he couldn't think of a thing that fit that description. "If you and your niece wish to remain here," he offered hopefully, "that is up to you."

She put her hand to her breast. " 'Whither thou goest, we will go,' " she recited in a dulcet tone. "Do not worry, Your Grace. We will not abandon you."

Adrian's gaze narrowed, but Miss Alcott merely smiled at him with cherubic innocence. She was, he decided, a remarkable woman.

Chapter 19

Sir Harry stared at his nephew. "Ainsford? You can't be serious. The man's an intimate of the Prince."

"Hardly a sterling character reference."

Something was different about Adrian. His nephew seemed more . . . human. Yes, that was it. More human. Less cold, but more volatile.

Perhaps it had something to do with that canary, which perched on the desk as if it was his right, or Mrs. Stanhope, who—for reasons that escaped him—was ensconced in Adrian's house.

"Ainsford has more to recommend him than that woman does," Sir Harry groused. "Damn it, man, I sent you to investigate her, not bring her home."

"By 'that woman' I assume you refer to Mrs. Stanhope?" his nephew asked softly.

Definitely more volatile. Sir Harry had not reached fifty years of age without knowing when danger was nigh. "If she is innocent, by all means show me the proof," he said in a conciliatory tone.

"She is."

Sir Harry waited, but apparently Adrian didn't intend to offer any. "As you requested," he continued, "I've had Deverell checked out. A worthy gentleman by all accounts. He's the fourth son of the earl of Pembroke; he did indeed serve for several years as Ainsford's secretary. We're trying to find the runner Deverell hired, but the man has evidently been sent on another case."

He shook his head. "Damn it, Adrian. I can't accuse Ainsford on your say-so. Lord Castlereagh will not care to embarrass one of the Prince's friends." He regarded his nephew intently. "Perhaps you're letting personal bias interfere with judgment. I'm well aware that Ainsford led the fight against your bill."

"If Ainsford is a traitor, neither Castlereagh nor the Prince will support him." Adrian's eyes were cold. "He tried to abduct her. That in itself is a crime."

"Perhaps he merely wanted to make her his mistress and seized on a novel way to go about it—what the hell?"

His nephew closed the gap between them so swiftly that Sir Harry barely registered the sudden movement that brought Adrian's hand to rest, heavily, on his shoulder.

"Mrs. Stanhope is no man's mistress," he said softly.

So that was the way of things. Sir Harry eased himself away from Adrian's hand. "Very well. Don't expect me to make excuses for you if the plan goes awry. Do you really think you can beat Ainsford at his own game? He's quite extraordinary with that mesmerizing thing. I don't understand any of that nonsense."

"I do." Adrian fixed him with a look of such intensity that Sir Harry quickly grabbed his hat and made for the door. His nephew, so pitiful as a child, had grown into the very devil himself. Complete with a familiar, which squawked loudly as he dashed out of the room.

Her first ball. Emmaline could hardly believe she was about to enter the glittering world of the *ton* on Adrian's arm. She stared at her reflection in the mirror. She certainly didn't feel like the elegant young lady who peered back at her.

"A bit dated." Aunt Heloise studied the jonquil silk gown Gibbons had fetched from the attic, "but many will look at you and think of the duchess herself, which is all to the good. When the new clothes from the modiste arrive, you'll set your own style."

"They are costing the duke a fortune," Emmaline said worriedly.

"He has a fortune and then some. I cannot think of a better way to spend it." Aunt Heloise preened in the mirror, wearing another attic discovery she had pronounced fashionably gaudy. Her wayward red curls had been tamed into a dramatic upsweep crowned by a tiara Mr. Gibbons had provided. She made a convincing dowager viscountess, which was what Mr. Gibbons had decided she must be.

"Lofty enough to command respect, obscure

enough to confound any swift attempt to verify the title," he'd declared.

Not for the first time, Emmaline wondered whether Mr. Gibbons and her aunt were conducting a romance. Aunt Heloise had never been bashful about her flirtations, but Mr. Gibbons wore a quiet reserve that Emmaline suspected ran deep in his character. He'd been scrupulously proper when dealing with her exceedingly improper aunt.

But who knew what might happen? Emmaline's life had changed so much in the last few weeks that anything seemed possible. The cheval glass gave her an image she didn't recognize. Her hair was piled atop her head, held there by a profusion of pins and two jeweled combs Mr. Gibbons had found in a box of the duchess's jewelry.

Adrian had hired two maids to help them with their toilettes. Emmaline had never had a maid, never imagined she could look like this. Though her slippers were satin, not glass, Emmaline felt like Cinderella readying herself for the ball.

As she descended the staircase, her hands trembled. She couldn't believe she was in a grand London house, looking and living like a future duchess. The illusion would vanish after they sprang their trap for Ainsford. Still, she couldn't help but wish the magic might last.

At the foot of the stairs, Mr. Gibbons bowed deeply. "You look lovely, madam," he said quietly. "Much like Her Grace, the first time I saw her. She wore that gown on Michaelmas the first year of her marriage."

"Thank you, Mr. Gibbons." Emmaline flushed at the unexpected, obviously heartfelt compliment.

But it was Adrian, standing in the shadows a few feet away, whose riveted gaze sent her heart to her throat.

Tall and uncompromising, he was the very portrait of ducal grandeur. His stark black breeches and white-silk shirt fit him perfectly. His cravat was tied in an intricate but understated fashion. He expression was stern, his jaw defiant, his eyes unreadable. His dark hair had been tamed, though an unruly shock of it dared to infringe on his forehead.

The molten heat in his eyes told her he was thinking of that day in his mother's garden, when she'd lost her dignity and pride to his clever, seductive hands. By tacit agreement they had since avoided each other, as much as two people living in the same house could.

When had this game between them grown serious? When had the jibes and parries become a prelude for passion? When had the wit of argument transformed into something not in the least amusing?

Wordlessly he moved toward her, his gaze now a careful blank. When he offered his arm, Emmaline swallowed hard and placed her gloved hand on his sleeve. He escorted her outside and down the steps, and assisted her into the waiting carriage. There she waited for Aunt Heloise, while Adrian stood on the drive with Mr. Deverell. Several minutes later, Aunt Heloise emerged from the house.

"Go ahead, dears," she called gaily. "I need another minute. Mr. Deverell can drive me."

Mr. Deverell managed a game smile at her aunt's transparent attempt to put Emmaline and Adrian in the carriage together. Since there was nothing to be done, Adrian climbed into the carriage and sat opposite Emmaline on the polished leather seat.

Their knees touched, briefly.

They eased away from each other so that unfortunate lapse wouldn't happen again. The coachman signaled to the team, and with a lurch, they were off.

Adrian made no attempt at conversation. Even though she could scarcely look at him without turning scarlet, Emmaline was not about to remain silent in deference to his loathing of closed spaces. They had to talk sometime; it might as well be now.

"You like this, don't you?" she challenged. "You like being closed, withdrawn, a recluse. You're afraid to be anything else."

Slowly, his eyes came into focus as he turned his head to look at her. His gaze held equal parts annoyance and consternation. A growl sounded somewhere in his chest.

Emmaline ignored it. "Deep inside, you're still the frightened boy who was locked in that closet, aren't you?"

"I don't know what you mean," he said coldly.

"It's simple," she said, gathering her courage. "Like it or not, what happened in the garden changes things between us. You ought to face that."

When he didn't respond, she couldn't stop a surge of anger. "Grow up, Your Grace. Embrace life. You will be the happier for it."

For a moment he said nothing. Then slowly, an uneven smile spread over his features. She'd been prepared for his anger, but not for this fey smile that sent her heart to her throat.

"You've got me figured out, haven't you, Emmaline?" he said softly. "You've told yourself that I'm damaged, that I can't care for anyone other than myself. You've told yourself I'd make you miserable, but you don't know for sure, do you? You're all dressed up in your borrowed finery and you're afraid you'll come to like it. And me."

Emmaline was stunned. In one eloquent moment he'd voiced her deepest fears, humbled her with such searing truth she could only shake her head in helpless sorrow.

Suddenly he left his seat to sit next to her, though the bench offered scant room for a man of his size and a woman in a fancy ball gown. Their hips touched, their legs brushed. Emmaline met his gaze uncertainly.

His eyes held longing and concern, as if she actually meant something to him, when she knew all he really wanted was to make her his mistress. She turned away, afraid to see that truth in his eyes.

When his fingertip brushed her cheek, she shivered.

"You are cold," he said.

"No." But she drew her shawl more tightly around her.

He put his hands on her shoulders, massaging them through the light cashmere. "You are as fine as any duchess," he murmured. There was no irony in his tone.

"Leave me alone." Tears threatened to betray her.

"You *do* mean to make me grovel, don't you?" he asked softly.

Emmaline stared at the faint sparkle in his eyes and knew that her foolish heart was lost to him forever.

The carriage rolled to a stop. Adrian held out his hand, his attention riveted on her as if she were the only woman in the world. Emmaline knew his attention was for the benefit of their hostess and her guests; that didn't stop her pulse from racing.

Their gazes met, hers shy and hesitant, his probing. When his hand went to her waist as she stepped from the carriage, his touch robbed her of breath.

Her father's words bounded across the years like a misbegotten genie conjured from some cast-off lamp.

Her Prince had come. Never mind that he looked and sometimes acted like the very devil, never mind that he was worlds above her touch.

He'd kissed her awake from a deep and dreamless sleep, banished the evil witch, trampled the cruel stepsisters, turned the pumpkin into a fine coach and four, transformed her dreams into spun gold.

All that was missing were the glass slippers.

*   *   *

Adrian was desperate to make love to her. He yearned for Emmaline as he'd never yearned for anything in his life. And he'd have her, by God, even if she stuck out her dainty foot and tripped him as he was falling head over heels in love with her.

Love. Good God. Anything but that.

She walked gracefully into Lady Higgenbotham's house, shoulders squared and head high, as if she'd moved in these lofty circles all her life. She looked every inch the duchess, whereas he felt awkward in his grand clothes, especially the stiff neckcloth Gibbons had constructed around his neck.

He caught up to her just as obsequious footmen moved to take her shawl, and glared at the servants so fiercely they quickly backed away. He wanted to be the first to feast his eyes on those perfect shoulders, to study how the fabric descended daringly to the cleft between her breasts; he didn't want to give anyone else that privilege.

They waited in a vast receiving line to greet their hostess, whom Adrian had never met. He'd known almost none of the senders of the many invitations that had come to him. Apparently a ducal title opened all doors.

Sure enough, the moment the majordomo announced Adrian's identity, the room fell silent. The churning sea of elegantly attired lords and ladies parted to make way, as if the duke of Trent and his fiancée were royalty.

Miss Alcott, who had finally arrived with Deverell, immediately immersed herself in her role.

Ostensibly their chaperone, "Lady" Alcott flirted shamelessly with every man who entered her orbit. Deverell made himself scarce.

Ainsford, the target of their foray into society, was surprisingly easy to find. In fact, he sought them out.

"Trent." Ainsford's gravelly voice intruded on Adrian's contemplation of the tulips of the *ton* who clamored for Emmaline's attention several dozen feet away.

A man should have *some* dignity, Adrian thought darkly, as a dandy with grotesquely padded shoulders maneuvered himself next to Emmaline, where he had the same gratifying view of her neckline Adrian had had earlier.

"I hadn't heard you were betrothed," the marquess said, following Adrian's grim gaze.

Adrian forced his attention away from Emmaline and her court. "Ainsford," he acknowledged. His gaze returned to Emmaline.

"Ah, so *that's* the way of things. You have my sympathies, Trent. A love match always ends badly for one of the parties. Alas, affection is rarely returned in the measure it is given."

Adrian gave Ainsford his full attention for the first time. The man had always cut a dashing figure, with dark hair and brushy eyebrows that lent him an almost satanic air. He was only a decade older than Adrian but looked old and haggard.

Bloodshot and turbulent, Ainsford's eyes reflected a misery that almost wrung a drop of pity from Adrian. Whatever had happened to the marquess since their paths crossed ten years ago had exacted a heavy toll. Lines of worry marked his face; his shoulders were in the process of becoming stooped, like an old man whose course was run. His once-lustrous hair was shot through with gray. Age had claimed him prematurely and relentlessly.

Doubtless Ainsford's dissolute ways had finally caught up with him. Hardening his heart against the unexpected sympathy, Adrian regarded his former nemesis coldly. "Miss Alcott is most constant in her affection."

"Of course," Ainsford returned easily.

Adrian waited for a ponderous second or two. "Unfortunately, she also has a prodigious interest in metaphysics."

The marquess stared at him as if he could not believe his ears. "Metaphysics? By which you mean . . . ?"

Adrian shifted uncomfortably. "The more obscure, er, arts. Prophecy, mesmerism, mysticism, and the like. Her aunt is sick. She is anxious to find a cure, even an unconventional one."

Ainsford burst into laughter. "Good God, man. What wondrous poetic justice is at work to saddle *you* with such a bride?"

The marquess seemed genuinely amused. He gave no sign of recognizing Emmaline—but then, no one would recognize that elegant goddess as the penniless fortune-teller abducted in Guilford Street.

"I couldn't say," Adrian replied coolly. Ainsford was taking the bait like a fish who hadn't eaten in weeks.

"We must do something about this, Trent."

Ainsford wiped a tear of mirth from his eye. "We cannot let this young lady's passions go unaddressed. Come to my salon on Thursday. I promise she will see enough to whet her appetite. Perhaps we'll even find a cure for that aunt of hers—though if that is the lady holding forth in the corner, she doesn't look very ill."

"Her sickness comes and goes," Adrian improvised.

"Most of the mysterious ones do. The body can turn against itself, you know. I don't claim to know all the answers, but we've had some extraordinary results at our sessions. We will do our best for her."

As easy as that, the fish was caught. Adrian managed a scowl, though elation filled him. "I won't be a party to anything unsavory, Ainsford."

The marquess cast a speculative eye at Emmaline. "No, of course not," Ainsford said. "She must meet my wife. You remember Yvette, do you not?"

"I'm afraid not. You and I move in different circles."

"That was long ago, Trent. I hope you're not holding that bit of old history against me." The marquess smiled as he watched Emmaline. "Yvette will adore her."

Adrian decided not to make a show over Ainsford's peace offering, since too much sudden friendliness would make the man suspicious. "Is the marchioness here?"

A shadow darkened Ainsford's features. "She is indisposed. When you are wed, Trent, you will see how a woman's whims can rule a man's life."

After Ainsford left, Adrian watched Emmaline dance with a dandy who clutched her hand with more warmth than he liked. He was tempted to cut in, but he didn't have a clue how to perform the steps. He wished he'd paid more attention to those dance lessons.

Hell. He wasn't about to stand here and watch Emmaline in another man's arms—not when his own ached to touch her. Adrian decided to seek out the punch bowl. The sooner he put Emmaline out of his sight, the better. He shot one last, furtive glance at the dance floor.

She was gone.

She'd been there just a moment ago, doing some intricate step he hadn't a prayer of imitating. She couldn't have vanished.

But she had.

And Adrian knew, from the gut-wrenching fear that seized him, that Emmaline was right: His life had changed irrevocably and would never, ever be the same again.

Chapter 20

⟨⟨∽◯∽⟩⟩

Emmaline stomped the inside of Mr. Steed's foot, which caused him to release the very improper hold he had on her. "Contrary to your claim, sir, my aunt is *not* waiting for me out here. Indeed, I see no one in this courtyard but us."

Steed smiled through his pain. "Forgive the lie, Miss Alcott. I was desperate to be alone with you. I know you are spoken for, but you would not be happy with Trent. He is reputed to be strange, even cruel. I would never treat you thus."

"No, you would lie and invent tales to lure unsuspecting women to dark and private places. Begone, sir, and thank your stars that the duke is not here." Emmaline turned her back on the man, and he slunk away like a chastened puppy.

What was wrong with the men of the *ton*? As far as she could see, they were either drunkards or dandies. For a moment she'd let their admiration go to her head. It had been nice to be surrounded by fawning gentlemen. But they didn't know her, she reminded herself; they didn't admire *her*, but only an image they'd formed in their heads. They coveted what the duke had, as if by association they could elevate themselves to his standing.

Emmaline sighed in disgust. There was not a man here to compare with Adrian. Unfortunately, he cared nothing for her. Oh, he'd shown her a passing affection—even lusted after her in his odd way. But when this madcap adventure was over, he'd turn them all out and reclaim his house as a bastion of masculinity. He'd go off and search for fossils, and that would be that.

How could she return to a life without him? Their quarrels masked an inescapable attraction she hadn't been willing to acknowledge. But it wasn't just the sensual currents between them that made him so compelling. She'd come to realize that his forbidding veneer masked a deeply wounded and heroic heart.

Rescuing her from those dandies at the Argyle Rooms was only the beginning. He'd saved her during that storm, and rushed to her side the night of her abduction like a knight in shining armor.

To be sure, he'd lied about his identity, but she'd lied about hers, too. They were quite a pair. No. *Not* a pair. They'd never be what they were pretending to be now: betrothed, in love. She must stop wishing for what could not be.

Emmaline knew she must return to the ballroom and make pleasant, meaningless conversation with society's glittering elite. Beyond those enormous French doors, substance was forfeit to style, and the only man she longed for had not even bothered to ask her to dance.

"Don't move." Adrian's low voice hit her like a thunderbolt.

She froze.

"Turn around. Slowly."

Emmaline complied, swallowing hard when she saw his face, which was rigid with rage.

His smoky gaze traveled from the jeweled combs in her hair to the exquisite slippers on her feet and back again, lingering on the neckline of her gown. His finger touched her lips.

"Not a word," he commanded. "Not one word."

Lanterns lined the far reaches of the courtyard, casting a soft, hazy glow that could not disguise the hard brilliance and white heat in Adrian's eyes. Some other emotion besides anger lurked in those murky gray depths.

"Take my arm," he ordered, "and remove that look from your face. If we see anyone, I don't want it to appear that you aren't enjoying the night air with your betrothed."

He had to mock her, did he? Had to remind her that this masquerade was only that.

"This way." He took them through the garden behind Lady Higgenbotham's house. Emmaline didn't ask why they weren't returning to the ball. It didn't matter really, for they'd not travel the same road together in the end.

An alley ran behind the house. He led her into it, but her slippers weren't fit for walking over anything harder than a polished parquet floor. Emmaline stubbed her toe on a rock and gave a little yelp of pain.

Abruptly, he lifted her into his arms, looking none too pleased about it as he carried her to the end of the alley, where his carriage waited. A footman rushed to open the door. Adrian tossed her into the carriage as if he were glad to be rid of his burden.

"Where are we going?" Emmaline demanded.

He didn't answer. Instead, he nodded to the footman, who sprang up to the box next to the coachman. With the crack of a whip and a lurch, they were off.

Adrian sat across from her, arms folded across his chest, his face a mask of indifference save for his brooding eyes. Anger, disgust, and vengeance lurked in that gray gaze.

The carriage barreled through the streets. Her uneasiness increased when the vehicle did not slow at Brook Street. It sped past the park and the more sedate carriages whose fashionable inhabitants were returning to their homes.

Emmaline clung to the bench as the coach rocked with each turn. They'd break a wheel at this rate, but Adrian gave no sign of concern for the fate of his carriage, or her. He stretched out his legs, bracing them against her bench so they took the brunt of the rough ride. At every curve in the road, she slid across the bench, her legs stopped only by his, as immovable as stone.

When the houses grew fewer and the lights dimmer, Emmaline realized their destination was far from London.

"Where are you taking me?" she demanded.

"Don't talk." His voice was cold, hard. His lips moved slightly with whatever he was silently reciting to distract him from the confines of the carriage.

"I see. You don't wish to be inconvenienced by the chore of speaking to me." Her scorn held a desperate edge. What in the world was he about? "*My* wishes are obviously trivial."

His brow grew thunderous. Indeed, the nuisance of a closed carriage looked to be the last thing on his mind. With his brooding scowl and elegant attire, he was a portrait of ducal displeasure. Emmaline was determined not to be intimidated. "I insist upon an explanation. I won't go another mile without one."

His gaze slid over her.

"I am not a woman to sit here calmly while you make off with me to parts unknown."

He didn't say a word.

Arrogant man. "Very well. If you do not care to speak, I shall do the talking for both of us. Indeed, I feel a monologue coming on." She eyed him defiantly. "Shall I tell you about my evening, Your Grace? I have never been to such a grand event. It was quite a spectacle, but the people were—how shall I say it?—thin of substance. I was required to tell no fewer than a dozen young ladies where my gown was made.

"I didn't care to confess that it was borrowed from your attic, so I embellished. I told them it had been made for me in France at the behest of no less a personage than the Empress herself. No one questioned how I managed to persuade Napoléon's consort to commission such a creation.

'Tis quite possible the ladies were unaware that England and France are at war."

His hooded gaze gave no sign he'd heard a word.

She gave him a reproachful look. "I can see that you mean to be difficult, so I shall simply have to fill in your part of the discussion. Unfortunately, it won't be as witty or intelligent as you yourself might devise. A common fortune-teller could never match wits with a duke."

One of his brows arched.

"There: you see? I could never manage that perfectly raised brow. It expresses *so* much feeling—which I can only guess at, since you choose not to enlighten me."

Emmaline gave an exaggerated sigh. "Where was I? Oh, yes: tidbits gleaned at the ball. Lady Melton has commissioned Turner to paint a portrait of her eldest daughter. Turner is all the rage, you know. And Lady Jersey has changed mantua-makers. I believe she thought Madame Celeste too plebian. But how silly of me to think you would be interested in comments from the ladies. Shall I tell you about the men, then?"

"No."

She eyed him in mock surprise. "So you *do* possess the power of speech! I cannot say how much this fills me with anticipation. I should love to have your comments on the compliments that came my way tonight. A woman lacks perspective on her own attributes. For instance: Did you know that my eyes sparkle like diamonds? Indeed, they vastly outshine the stars in the sky. My complexion is like smooth alabaster, my disposition radiant, my beauty likened to Helen of Troy. What do you think, Your Grace? Shall I take these comments to heart? Or could these gentlemen have exaggerated a teeny bit?"

Emmaline paused dramatically, as she imagined Aunt Heloise might.

Adrian's implacable gaze held hers. Briefly, it occurred to her that it wouldn't be wise to push him too far. But tonight her reckless temper ruled. She pursed her lips in a mock pout. "Perhaps I was too hard on Mr. Steed. It is hardly his fault that his passion for me overwhelmed him. If you turn this carriage around, I shall return to the party and apologize. What—no thought of going back? No matter, I shall simply pretend you are he."

Emmaline mustered a simpering smile. "Mr. Steed, I have been remiss. Did you say you could not control your desire for me? Perhaps you could apply to the duke for instruction. He has a will of iron, you know, never lets the tiniest emotion get the better of him. Control? He epitomizes the word. Desire? No, Mr. Steed, the man has none. No desires, no uncontrollable urges."

She paused. "Well, maybe one, now that I think on it. He detests closed spaces—oh, and everyone around him. He has no use for the human race, you see; thinks we're all a waste of time. But he does adore fossils. You ought to see his collection; it is magnificent."

Emmaline sat back against the squabs, quite out of breath—and furious. The more she'd talked, the angrier she'd become. How dare he snatch her up and take her heaven-knew-where on a whim?

To her great surprise, Adrian met her gaze with a barely perceptible curve of his mouth that might have been, but surely was not, a smile.

"No," he said softly.

"No?" She stared at him in disbelief. "Is that all you can manage, sir? One paltry 'no'? I am insulted."

"No, they did not exaggerate."

Emmaline frowned. "If you persist in speaking in riddles, Your Grace, I do not see how—"

"Your eyes. They *do* sparkle like diamonds."

Emmaline stilled.

"And vastly outshine the stars in the sky."

Her mouth fell open.

"Alabaster, radiant, Helen of Troy," he said softly. "All those things, and more."

Thunderstruck, she stared at him. "You are making sport of me."

"You are more than words can measure, Emmaline. Add to that courage, cleverness, and a practical, unsentimental nature—admirable qualities, all. But, my dear, you have the disposition of a crocodile."

His simmering gaze robbed her of breath. "You once asked me what sort of woman I admired. A phlegmatic one, I said. But you're not that, Emmaline. You possess too much passion. It unsettles me." He paused. "It drives me wild."

His calm tone belied the depth of emotion in his words. "You may tell Mr. Steed I have no lessons to impart—if you see him again, which I promise you won't."

"I'll not have you selecting my friends," Emmaline said mutinously.

The pupils of his eyes constricted. "Friends? No. But lovers? Yes, I will choose those."

Slowly, provocatively, his gaze roamed over her. "There will be only one," he said in a husky voice. "Me."

Suddenly it all became clear, this mad flight into the night. "You are abducting me," she whispered. "You mean to . . ." Her voice trailed off uncertainly.

He leaned toward her, his eyes liquid fire. "Did you think I would let you be?" he asked softly. "First Deverell, then all those men tonight. You captivated them as you've captivated me, Emmaline. Didn't you know? After that day in the garden, there's no going back."

Captivated *him*? No, she wouldn't believe it. Yet his eyes held no mockery, no amused disdain; he looked deadly serious.

"Where are you taking me?" she asked breathlessly.

His molten gaze never left hers. "To a place where I can make love to you."

Emmaline stared at him. "No."

His lips thinned into a slow, sensual smile. "My dear Emmaline," he said softly, "do not make the mistake of thinking you have any say in the matter."

Chapter 21

Adrian had not been to the cottage in three months, but his landlady had kept it neat and clean in his absence. On his desk lay a treatise on sea fossils he'd meant to study, notes for the paper he was to deliver this fall, and the spectacles he sometimes used for reading.

Two spartan rooms with plain furnishings would never have served the duke of Trent, but they had been all Adrian St. Ledger required.

Who was he tonight? A little of both men, perhaps, but mostly a man in thrall to a woman he couldn't do without.

Emmaline's ball gown filled the doorway as she stood at the threshold and surveyed the cottage. She'd never known the man who lived here; she'd only known his counterpart, who'd gained a dukedom he never wanted.

He had been happy here with his books and his papers. Hadn't he? But he'd been ignorant then of how a woman could grip a man's soul. The man who'd created this monastic existence no longer existed.

"Come in."

She didn't move.

Adrian schooled himself to patience. He was a civilized man—a scholar, a teacher, a gentleman. "Come in," he repeated.

Something was wrong with his voice. He'd meant to sound calm, even kind. The words came out ragged, hoarse.

Emmaline lifted her chin, daring him, defying him.

She wanted her pound of flesh, it seemed. Very well. He'd apologize for abducting her, an act so desperate and imprudent it baffled him. He wasn't given to rash acts.

At least St. Ledger wasn't. The duke of Trent was apparently quite intemperate. There was no doubt in Adrian's mind which man she'd riled.

"Get the hell in here," he growled.

She stepped inside. The rustling of her gown spawned erotic images of the fabric pooling at her feet, of her stepping out of it and into his arms.

St. Ledger might have made her tea. Trent didn't bother. "There's no use looking for help there," he snarled, when she cast an uncertain eye back at the departing carriage. "My men have gone for the night."

Her eyes widened. He ought to feel guilty for frightening her, but that would be the response of a civilized man. He'd lost any pretense of that the moment he'd seen her with that lascivious oaf in the courtyard. Emmaline didn't belong to any man but him.

"I demand that you let me go," she said coolly.

She was pluck to the bone; he'd give her that. But she didn't know how desperate he was. He took a step toward her.

"Demand whatever you want. It won't change a thing."

Her eyes narrowed. "What right do you have to keep me here?"

The right of a man who would die without her touch, who'd go insane if he didn't have her this day, this hour, this minute. His hand trembled as he touched her cheek. She didn't flinch, didn't turn away, but continued to stare at him from those challenging green eyes.

Somehow she *knew*, damn her, that though he'd abducted her, it was she who held him captive.

His fingertips brushed her mouth. It was smooth, pliant. The merest touch made him shudder with desire.

Her lips parted slightly. Involuntarily? He couldn't tell. Her eyes held surprise, distrust. He ran his fingers through her hair, clumsily knocking a comb out of place. It fell to the floor in a flash of diamonds that might have been coal, for all he cared.

Her hair tumbled down. Adrian stroked the silky mass one of Peter's sisters had disciplined into place only hours ago. An errant tendril curled around his finger, but he abandoned the silken wisp to trace the neckline that had tantalized him all night.

"Stop," she whispered.

He slipped the fabric off her shoulders. "I can't."

"Can't, or won't?" Her voice quavered.

"What does it matter? You're mine, Emmaline."

The bodice of the gown fell to her waist. His finger traced a path around her nipple, coveting her. He cupped her breasts, allowing the softness to fill his palms. He brushed his thumbs over the erect buds, but that wasn't enough.

He pushed the gown lower, over her hips, and when the dress balked, he rent the fabric in a desperate urgency that only escalated when he saw the curve of her hips, the swell of her backside, the lush triangle between her legs.

"You are horrid." She sounded perilously close to tears.

"No," he said softly. "I'm what you want."

"You don't know what I want." That catch in her voice threatened to unman him. "You've never once asked."

Adrian inhaled deeply. He forced his roving hands to be still. "Very well. What do you want?"

"Flowers. Poetry. Promises. Things you couldn't give me in a million years. And respect. That, most of all." She clutched the edges of his waistcoat. "I want the dream, Adrian," she said fiercely. "And you're not it."

"I don't believe in dreams."

"I don't, either—not really. But you could pretend. You could damn well pretend." Her sob rent him in two.

"I'd buy you a kingdom if that would help," he rasped. "I'd write you poetry, send you flowers, dance if you teach me. But that wouldn't change anything. I'd still be the man who couldn't let you go. Dress it up with flowers if you wish, but damn it, Emmaline, *you've got me on my knees*. Don't you see, woman? You've won."

She stared at him, her troubled eyes probing for honesty. Slowly, Adrian lowered his mouth to hers. He gave her a kiss so sweet and pure he hadn't known it was in him, but his insides shook with desire that wouldn't be denied.

"I must have you," he whispered. "There's your victory, don't you see? I won't free you because I can't. You've ruined me, Emmaline. You've made my life a living hell."

Her eyes flashed. "Well, that's some consolation, isn't it?"

With a low growl, Adrian swept her off her feet. He carried her to the rope bed that had been adequate only a few months ago, but which now seemed too small and hard.

"Emmaline." Her name tore from him like a prayer as he covered her body with his. "This is all I can give you."

Her defiant green gaze locked with his. "Then I'll take a voucher for the rest."

A voucher for the rest. He didn't know whether to make love to her or strangle her, so he settled on something in between. His hands toyed with her hair, then trailed down her neck along that sensual path he'd marked in the garden that day. When she arched upward, pleading with undisguised desire, a thrill unlike any he'd known swept him.

He had won, too. For he'd brought her here to

his small, hard bed, and she was looking up at him from eyes glazed with passion. She couldn't deny her need any more than he could.

He'd have taken her to a palace if he'd had one, but she only wanted a flower or two and a pretty verse to go with it. Yet as simple as those things were, he couldn't provide them. In the place inside him where there should have been feeling, there was only vast emptiness and a hard, bitter regret for all he could not be.

But the passion—that, they could share, and the rare exuberance that for a moment made everything all right.

With the certainty of a man who knows he's won the battle but lost the war, Adrian prepared to claim the woman of his lost, desperate heart.

Emmaline didn't care that the mattress wasn't thick enough to cushion her backside from the ropes underneath. Her senses had ceased to acknowledge anything but Adrian's touch.

The fine silk of his shirt, the ties of his knee breeches, the ribbing of his silk stockings, the starched muslin of his cravat—all were unwelcome barriers between them. She wanted him naked, too, wanted to feel his skin next to hers. Desire made her bold. She fumbled at the unfamiliar fastenings of his clothing, then realized she had no idea how to manage all those laces and ties.

"Help me," she pleaded, clutching the edges of his shirt in her frustration.

"Begging becomes you," he murmured, lowering his mouth to hers. "You must do it more often."

She might have kicked him, had his insistent lips not robbed the words of any sting, had his hands not chosen that moment to trail over her abdomen.

"*Adrian,*" she gasped.

With swift, masculine efficiency, his shoes were off in two seconds, his stockings in one. The intricate cravat and impeccably tailored breeches followed. All the trappings of his station, gone. There was only this small bed that he'd made a cradle for their passion.

Their gazes met—his burning with desire, hers glazed with need. With trembling hands, Emmaline put her arms around his torso and clung to him. His skin was smooth and firm, every taut muscle evidence of his masculine power. And yet, he trembled, too. That awed her.

You've got me on my knees, he'd said. But this didn't feel like victory. This felt like magic, sprinkled over with fairy dust.

His touch was gentle, but she saw the effort restraint cost him. His breathing was labored; his eyes churned with passion. His hands shook as they ran the length of her body, claiming her as his.

Love and longing had taken her over. A strange urgency drove her on. His fingers found the places he had coaxed to unwilling ecstasy in the dower-house garden; they began to spin that wondrous magic anew. Tonight she didn't need coaxing; she was beyond that.

"Adrian." Passion lent an unfamiliar huskiness

to her voice. She clutched him fiercely, made sure he saw the truth in her eyes as the restless knot of tension inside her grew tighter still. *"Adrian."*

All their battles suddenly condensed into this one, shimmering moment: Adrian poised over her, searching her eyes before he entered her, reducing her world to the sum of his touch, yet expanding it into a place so large it defied reduction into words or thought.

He felt impossibly large, but her body opened to him as if this raw invasion was the most natural thing in the world. She'd thought nothing could surpass the magic he worked with his hands; she was wrong. As he filled her, her body thrilled to this strange new pleasure, which felt so utterly *right*.

Slowly, he pushed deeper. His back muscles tensed under her hands as he disciplined himself to restraint.

Defiantly, Emmaline arched upward, drawing him deeper still.

With one great shudder, he flung restraint to the devil and drove himself into her. Emmaline felt his power all the way to her womb.

She hung on for dear life as he set them on a mad flight to the center of that white-hot heat he'd ignited. Gentleness fell by the wayside; that rough magic drove them on and on. Locked with him in a duel of desire, Emmaline followed his rhythm, matched his fire with hers.

Suddenly, the passion between them exploded in shards of pleasure beyond her wildest imaginings. And in that soul-shattering moment, there was nothing in her world but Adrian and the exquisite joy that made them whole.

Tears streamed down her face, of happiness and of sorrow for the union that would never last into happily-ever-after. She clung to him, trying to shut out all but the wonder of what they had done.

Adrian's fingers brushed away the tears. Emmaline closed her eyes, trying to hide the joy and despair that warred within her.

"Emmaline." The sound of her name on his lips filled her with hope. But when she met his gaze, she saw a torment there that mirrored hers.

She turned away, unwilling to shatter this stolen moment, but he touched her chin and made her face him.

"Why are you crying?" He shifted his position so that he could nestle her in the crook of his arm.

"Because this is so . . . so *much*."

He pondered that. "Did I hurt you?"

"No."

His hand stroked her shoulder. "I wondered," he said. "You seem very . . ." His voice trailed off.

The words hung there. Very *what*? Had her inexperience been noticeable? Had she done something clumsy and inept?

"It has been a long time, hasn't it? Since your husband died." He watched her face.

Husband. Dear lord. She'd forgotten. He mustn't know that she'd lied. And yet, why not? What was the use in pretense now? Emmaline took a deep breath.

"I had no husband. That was a fiction I invented to provide a measure of respectability, to keep my gentlemen clients from pressing me for"—she sighed wearily—"*this*. I took the name Stanhope from a newspaper account of Lady Hester Stanhope's travels."

She looked away. How silly she'd been then, imagining herself leading Lady Hester's dashing, independent life. She'd thought nothing of the lie all those months she'd styled herself a widow. But here, in this bed that was suddenly much too small for them, the lie seemed immense.

"You've never known a man, have you?"

There it was, damning in its blunt truth. "Don't worry," she said bitterly. "I won't claim compromise, Your Grace. Your dukedom is safe."

"I see." The edge in his voice almost broke her heart.

Emmaline met his gaze. "Is that disappointment I detect in your tone? No? Anger then. Yes, I'm quite sure that's it. You don't like it that I lied—though you are doing an admirable job of controlling your temper. My compliments, Your Grace. But control is everything with you, isn't it?"

And just like that, she'd put them on hostile footing again. This time, she'd make sure they stayed there.

"I wouldn't worry, John. Emmaline is perfectly able to take care of herself."

Gibbons made an impatient sound. "It's not her I'm concerned about. It's the duke."

Heloise frowned. "You speak of the man as if he were a child. He's not, I assure you. By now, he's doubtless illustrated that fact to my niece."

Gibbons sat in the chair next to the divan, where Heloise had spent the morning lying down. Last night's ball had been splendid, but she'd overdone it. For the first time in weeks, she felt too tired to move. Even a spirited discussion with Gibbons about the couple's mysterious disappearance hadn't cheered her. She'd forgotten how it felt to be this weary. Maybe she *was* getting old, after all. This dreary thought had barely formed when the door swung open and a footman stood on the threshold.

"The marchioness of Ainsford," he announced.

"Oh, no," Aunt Heloise groaned. "Tell her I'm not at home."

But it was too late. Lady Ainsford sailed into the room. Gibbons immediately rose.

"I quite understand your reluctance, Lady Alcott," the marchioness said. "Rest assured that I am accustomed to dealing with the sick."

"How comforting," Aunt Heloise murmured. She tried to sit up, and Lady Ainsford rushed toward her.

"You must not exert yourself on my account. I am here to tell you that your illness can be cured and to invite you to a session at our salon Thursday evening. You will see what wonders can be worked on your behalf."

Lady Ainsford's birdlike features gave her a beady look and condescending air. Heloise had no intention of letting such a person seize the advantage. With an effort that cost more than she let on, she sat up.

"I have been to doctors. Not one of them has come up with anything approaching a cure. Indeed, I find myself distrustful of those who promise miracles."

Lady Ainsford was all sympathy. "I understand your reluctance, Lady Alcott. But we are honored to have Monsieur Rigaud staying with us. He is a cousin of the celebrated Madame Le Normand, forced to flee his country because of the war. He is wise in the ways of unconventional cures. His specialty is the mesmerizing method. Why, he rid me of my dreadful headaches in only a few sessions."

Heloise studied her. "No doubt additional sessions are required to maintain the cure."

Lady Ainsford colored. "Monsieur Rigaud is very thorough."

"But of course."

Gibbons had been standing awkwardly at attention, hoping to remain unnoticed, when Lady Ainsford's gaze settled on him.

"I have not met your gentleman friend," she said.

"Gibbons, my lady," he said quickly. "I am a servant in this house."

"A servant?" Lady Ainsford's assessing gaze moved from him to Heloise and back again. "How . . . droll."

"Don't worry, Lady Ainsford," Heloise said regally. "Convention has not been breached." She paused for a heartbeat. "Alas, he won't have me."

Lady Ainsford gaped at Heloise before quickly recovering her poise. "I had best leave you to your rest," she said faintly. "I hope you will come Thursday."

"We wouldn't miss it," Heloise said solemnly.

With a wan smile, the marchioness swiftly departed. A pregnant silence settled over the room. Gibbons eyed Heloise sternly. "That was not well done, madam."

"It was wonderfully done," Heloise retorted. "Never say I can't deliver a wicked line when one is needed."

He pondered that. "No, I would never say that. But at times, Heloise, you are far too uninhibited. A little restraint—"

"Would bore me to tears," she said. "I have no intention of living what's left of my life as a tediously proper spinster. When has restraint ever brought happiness?"

To her surprise, a shadow settled over his features. "The world does not adapt to us, Heloise. It is we who must do what the world bids. Anything else is unthinkable. I do not hold with those who maintain that the divisions among the classes should be erased. Rules exist because anything else invites chaos."

"A little chaos is necessary to happiness," Heloise said firmly.

"I have had my ration of chaos. I vastly prefer propriety."

"Do you?" She studied him. "Why don't you tell me about your ration of chaos, John? I am intrigued."

Gibbons colored. "I have no intention of confessing my youthful indiscretions. Suffice it to say that I made mistakes, grave ones. I have lived with the consequences of those mistakes. Indeed, I shall never escape them."

"You are very hard on yourself, John."

"Not hard enough." His eyes clouded. "I betrayed a trust, Heloise, one established long ago. I abandoned duty for desire. That mistake has haunted me since."

Heloise pursed her lips. "I see your suffering in your eyes, John. You have a very revealing face."

"I hope not," he said, alarmed. "A man in my position must maintain a certain equanimity. My paltry troubles must be subsumed in the higher duty of serving my employer."

"That sounds more like servitude than serving."

Gibbons eyed the door as if he were contemplating a swift retreat.

"Sit down, John," Heloise said.

"No. I have been guilty of a grave lapse in propriety as it is. I have allowed myself to think of myself as your equal, when, in fact, I am your servant."

"You are not my servant. You are the duke's servant."

Gibbons did not respond.

"Furthermore," Heloise said softly, "if you think you occupy a lower rung in society than I, allow me to disabuse you of that notion. I have lived a rich and full life, John. The only times I've comported myself as a lady have been when the part called for it. No man has mistaken me for a real lady in a very long time."

"That is their loss."

She studied him. "Why, John, I believe that was a compliment."

"I admire you a great deal, Heloise. You have more courage than most men—certainly more than I."

"You have more than you think, else you wouldn't be here now." Her gaze was speculative. "Indeed, I begin to suspect that beneath that excruciatingly proper facade beats the heart of a renegade."

"Certainly not."

Heloise sighed. "I am not quite myself today, or I would show you the truth. For now, would you sit next to me, John? I picked up a volume of plays from Adrian's library. I am too tired to read them myself, but I would dearly love to have one read aloud to me."

Concern swept his face. "Can I get you something for your illness? A tisane, perhaps, or camomile tea?"

She shook her head. "The play, John. Just the play."

He sat on the divan and opened the book. Clearing his throat, he began to read: " 'Hung be the heavens with black, yield day to night . . .' "

"Not that dreary thing. Let me see." She flipped the pages until she found something suitable. "Try this." She handed him the book.

" 'If music be the food of love, play on . . .' " Gibbons looked up uncertainly.

"Oh, yes," she said, sighing. "Yes, indeed."

Chapter 22

I want the dream, Adrian. And you're not it.

Of course not. He had nothing to give. She'd exposed his control for what it was: an excuse to avoid facing the turbulent and painful emotions she brought to the fore.

"Your Grace?" Peter, his mop of brown hair in its usual disarray, peeked around the door of Adrian's study.

"What is it?" Adrian demanded gruffly. The boy was another one he ought not get too attached to.

"I'm wondering . . . that is—" he broke off awkwardly.

"Stop stammering. Out with it."

"It's about my mother."

That was about the last thing Adrian wanted to hear. "Look, boy—Peter—I'm very busy." He shuffled his papers, as if those reptiles couldn't wait another few million years.

"She wants to meet you."

Adrian frowned. "Why?"

"Ever since you hired May and Lizzie to assist

Lady Alcott and Miss Alcott, I think she's been worried about their, er, virtue." Peter flushed.

"No one here has any intention of harming them."

"Ma says the road to hell is paved with good intentions."

After last night, Adrian couldn't argue with that.

"She wants to meet you, to make sure you won't let anything happen," Peter said. "You know, with all the men around . . ."

"I doubt your mother will accept my assurances, but have her come. Hell. Have her bring the whole damn family."

Peter brightened. "You mean that, sir? About the whole family? Prudence and Jenny are hard workers, too. And Ma's a fine seamstress. Ma wouldn't worry about us if she was here to watch over everyone. And she wouldn't complain about not having enough food to put on the table."

Adrian held the boy's gaze. "Exactly how many females do you have at home?"

"Twelve."

"You're the only boy?"

"Yes, sir."

"They're good workers?"

"Except for Maggie. She's lazy as sin, Ma says. Maggie loves music. Fancies herself an expert on the clavichord just because she worked in Lord Pembroke's house for a few weeks when his was being tuned. When I told her you've got one of the new pianofortes, she was green with envy."

Adrian sighed. "Ask Mr. Gibbons to attend me."

"I am here, Your Grace." Gibbons stood in the doorway, an expectant look on his face.

How the devil did the man anticipate his every whim, as if some invisible bond lay between them? Even this afternoon, when Adrian had brought Emmaline home from their disastrous trip, Gibbons was his usual, unruffled self. He'd merely inquired whether they cared for nuncheon, which they declined, Emmaline having no wish to lay eyes on him again, least of all over a plate of kidneys.

Now Gibbons's dark eyes held a glimmer of agitation. Adrian wondered what had caused it, but he'd never embarrass the man by asking.

"Gibbons," he said, "do I need a house-keeper?"

"Unquestionably."

That took Adrian by surprise. He'd thought the house ran well enough as it was. "Can the house accommodate another dozen servants?"

"Oh, quite," Gibbons replied. "The attic rooms are empty, you know."

Adrian didn't know. His gaze narrowed. "Why do I have the feeling that you are not telling me something?"

Gibbons hesitated.

"Peter, take Galahad away and give him some exercise," Adrian said.

The boy gave a whoop of delight and, in a few moments, had Galahad and cage well in hand. Adrian waited until the boy's footsteps died away and he could no longer hear Galahad's happy chirp.

"Something is afoot. What is it?"

Gibbons hesitated. "I collect that you are considering hiring Peter's family, which is all to the good. This house has been too long without women. Indeed, the timing is fortuitous, for I have decided I can no longer remain in your employ. It is best that you move ahead with a new staff. Peter's mother will make a fine housekeeper."

Adrian blinked. "Your family has served mine for generations."

"I have tried to atone for my sin," Gibbons said quietly. "But I cannot change the past, and I find it haunts me more and more these days. I'd thought to remain here forever, watching you move toward your destiny. Indeed, I sense you are close to finding the happiness that has eluded you since childhood. I cannot tell you how gratifying that is. But for reasons I do not entirely understand, I find it agonizing to remain here."

Sin? Atone? Destiny? Adrian had no idea what Gibbons meant, only that the words did not fit with the calm, quietly forceful man who'd made himself so indispensable.

"You will stay until after we trap Ainsford." He leveled a gaze at Gibbons, daring him to disagree.

"I will stay until my replacement is trained," Gibbons corrected mildly.

"No one can replace you, as well you know."

"Thank you, Your Grace." Not a shred of emotion shadowed his placid features. Adrian could almost persuade himself that he'd imagined their conversation, except that the odd phrases still rung in his ear. *You are close to finding the happiness that has eluded you . . . your destiny.*

What the hell was going on? And why did he sense that disaster lurked around the bend?

"Miranda! How delightful to see you." Emmaline rushed to embrace the young woman who stood in the foyer looking uncertainly at the vaulted ceiling and gilded staircase.

"I came as soon as I got your note," Miranda said. "I don't understand—"

"Never mind that now. We have so much to talk about." Emmaline hustled her friend into the parlor, where Miranda perched gingerly on a damask-covered divan.

"You are the duke of Trent's fiancée? And . . . living in his house?"

"Aunt Heloise is here," Emmaline hastily assured her. "She is an excellent chaperone."

Actually, her aunt was a deplorable chaperone, but even if Aunt Heloise had been a stickler for propriety, nothing would have stopped what had happened last night. The drive back from Oxford had been one long, awkward silence. She'd seen nothing of Adrian since.

"But what of Mr. St. Ledger?" Miranda looked confused.

"The duke presented himself as St. Ledger, which I believe is his family name, in order to investigate me. It seems I was the chief suspect in a murder."

"Oh, no!" Miranda put her hand to her mouth.

"It is a confusing tale. Adrian pretended to be seeking a bride—"

"Adrian?" Miranda frowned.

"St. Ledger. The duke. But then I was abducted—"

"Abducted!"

"Briefly. He decided I wasn't a murderess, so we have all embarked on a grand scheme to catch the real villains." Emmaline shot her friend a too-bright smile. "I am masquerading as the duke's fiancée in hopes we might trap the actual murderer."

"Heavens!"

Emmaline took a deep breath. "Oh, Miranda, it is all such a pickle. Here I thought I'd found the man for you and he was not what he seemed."

"A *duke!*" Miranda stared at her in amazement. "You are living in a duke's house."

"Only for a short time. When this business is done, I will—" Emmaline broke off. "Well, I don't know what I will do, but—"

"What is he like?"

"The duke? Like any other man, I suppose." Emmaline bit her lip. Adrian was unlike any other man, which is why she couldn't stop remembering how his hands felt on her, how his eyes glinted with an unquenchable fire as he—

"You are in love with him."

That brought her up short. "Of course not," Emmaline replied. "I'll agree that this is all very odd. I seem to have awakened in a fairy tale, except that this is real life and there is no such

thing as magic, and anyway..." She sighed.
"Yes, I fear I am."

Miranda rose and enfolded Emmaline in her
arms. "Oh, Em, I am so sorry."

"No need to feel sorry for me." Emmaline held
back her tears. "I have acquired a new wardrobe
and am living in the best of circumstances. I
want for nothing."

Miranda watched her with wide, sympathetic
eyes.

"I need to plan my future, however," Emmaline said quickly. "When this is over, Aunt Heloise and I will make our way as we've always
done. That is why I wrote to you. I feel very
badly that I disappointed you, Miranda. I didn't
know that Mr. St. Ledger was not who he
seemed. I truly thought you two could make a
match of it."

"Emmaline—"

"Now, now. Don't go saying it's all right when
it isn't," Emmaline interjected. "I've promised
you a husband, and I will find you one. In fact,
I have a candidate in mind. He is handsome and
fairly well fixed, not the deepest of minds, perhaps even a bit shallow, but his heart is good."

"I've never seen you like this, Emmaline."

"He is everything a woman could want," Emmaline continued ruthlessly, though her voice
wobbled. "He will make a fine husband, and
your children—"

"Stop it," Miranda said firmly.

"—will be beautiful." Emmaline burst into
tears.

A sound at the threshold drew their attention.

William Deverell stood there in all his well-tailored glory. "Mrs. Stanhope! I came as soon as I could. Whatever has hap—"

"Miranda Manwaring, meet William Deverell," Emmaline sobbed. "You are p-p-perfect for each other."

Then a dreadful hiccup escaped her and she ran from the room, leaving Deverell and Miranda staring after her in amazement.

You're all dressed up in your borrowed finery and you're afraid you'll come to like it. And me.

Oh, yes, Emmaline thought grimly as she pulled the brush through her hair, she'd come to like it. *And* him. But it was worse than that, as Miranda had made her realize. She'd given her heart to a man who didn't want it. Or didn't think he did.

Making love with Adrian had been wonderful—until she'd ruined it for them—but the magic they'd created wasn't enough.

She'd never met a man so guarded and enigmatic and mesmerizing. He'd intrigued her, and like a fool, she'd taken the bait. For ignoring common sense, for dancing too close to the flame, she had no one to blame but herself.

You've got me on my knees . . . you've won. She'd won nothing except heartbreak.

Alabaster, radiant. Pretty words, but borrowed flattery. The despicable Mr. Steed had said them first, on the dance floor.

The passion in you drives me wild. Had she really fallen for that old line?

I won't free you because I can't. Emmaline flung her brush on the floor.

When all is said and done, you'll have ruined me . . . made my life a living hell. Now *that*, she decided grimly, opening the door to the hall, was more like it.

Adrian sat on his bed, staring at the boots he'd just taken off. To his amazement, he'd worn a mismatched pair—one brown, the other black—all day. How had his orderly life dissolved into such disarray?

For that matter, no one had replaced the bucket of ice water at his bedside. How else was a man supposed to wake up in the morning, instantly ready for the tasks ahead?

Galahad, meanwhile, had practically adopted him. Despite Peter's diligent attention, the canary seemed to prefer Adrian. The cage was now a permanent fixture in his study. Another cage had been found for Adrian's bedroom so that the bird could spend as much time as possible gazing on his host with birdlike gratitude.

"All I did was fish you out of the hearth," Adrian grumbled. "A simple thanks would have been sufficient. You needn't grace us with your presence permanently; there must be families all over London who'd be delighted to have a bird of your talents."

Galahad gave a happy chirp, then began his nocturnal serenade. If someone had told Adrian that at the ancient age of thirty he would have a bird singing him lullabies, he'd have called the notion preposterous.

There had been so many unsettling changes in his life lately; most could be laid at Emmaline's door. Orderliness and precision were essential to his days, yet he'd lately found himself in the midst of wildly unplanned endeavors, like last night's excursion to Oxford.

Moreover, they had little in common. He'd never share her love of furry and feathered creatures. Galahad was amiable enough for a bird, but Adrian disliked Thomas's cloying habit of rubbing up against him when hungry.

Animals, mismatched shoes, women in the house, mad abductions—what next? Gibbons, it seemed. Though as a child, Adrian had barely known the man existed, the thought of Gibbons's departure filled him with a profound sense of loss. Could that be laid at Emmaline's door, too?

He'd reason it out later. A good night's sleep would help—he hadn't gotten one last night. After they'd made love, then quarreled, sleep had been impossible. The distance between them pierced him like a stiletto in the place that, if he'd had a heart, would surely be in shreds by now.

Fortunately, he was heart-whole. Or was that shriveled, barely beating thing inside him a heart at all?

He snuffed the candle at his bedside, lay back against the pillow, and decided not to let Emmaline haunt his dreams.

But fate had another plan.

The door swept open, and Emmaline stood on the threshold in a thick flannel gown that covered her from neck to toe, yet which was inexplicably the most erotic thing he'd ever seen.

"Wake up, Your Grace," she said softly. "There are one or two things to settle between us."

Hell. Where was Gibbons when he needed him?

Chapter 23

❦❦❦

"**C**ourage, Your Grace," Emmaline said. "This will be over soon."

"One can always hope." The shadows hid his face.

"Ah. The man with the biting wit is with us once more. Pray, tell him not to go anywhere. I've one or two things to settle with him, too."

"We are all ears."

Emmaline wasn't about to let him take refuge in irony. "Which is worse?" she demanded. "That you touched me at all, or that I wasn't the merry widow who'd admit you to her bed and make no claim on your affections?"

"It was *my* bed, as I recall."

"Answer the question."

"Either way, you'd make me out an insensitive clod."

"You *do* catch my drift! How gratifying to know we can truly communicate."

"As I've said, sarcasm doesn't become you."

Emmaline ignored that, but when he swept the bedcovers aside, her heart skipped a beat.

"Abducting me was such a grand gesture." Her voice dripped with scorn. "Surely, I thought, it takes a Man of Great Feeling to do something so outlandish. Then I realized the truth: There wasn't an ounce of genuine feeling in what you did."

He crossed his arms, which strained the fabric of his nightshirt and allowed her a tantalizing glimpse of his chest. "How do you know?" he asked softly.

An edgy awareness of him beset her as he swung his feet off the bed. Emmaline affected a casual tone as his feet touched the floor. "Doubtless you got the notion from the abduction Mr. Deverell foiled. Too bad Mr. Deverell wasn't around last night to stop this one."

"Deverell isn't stupid enough to stand in my way," he growled, moving toward her. "I had a failure of will last night. I shouldn't have made love to you."

"But you did," she retorted.

"Nothing has changed." Inches stood between them now.

"You're wrong." Emmaline touched her palm to his chest. The warmth of his skin sparked an answering heat in her. "I don't want borrowed flattery. I want something genuine. And I'll have it from you, Adrian St. Ledger."

He didn't pretend to misunderstand. "Not love, Emmaline. It's not in me."

Her hand trailed down the lapel of his nightshirt. "I'm not one of your precious fossils come to you cold and remote, centuries in the making.

I'm a woman who has touched your heart. I see it in your eyes."

His gaze narrowed. "Emmaline—"

"It's raw, isn't it?"

"Raw?" He frowned.

"The feeling. Raw, pure, absolute. That's why you don't like it. The passion. The love. It's frightening."

"No." His voice was clear, cold, a denial. His expression revealed not a shred of emotion. "You don't know what I feel. You're just guessing."

"Am I?" She studied him. "Do you know what it's like to have everything you've ever wanted in life—every dream, every prayer, every promise you've not dared to believe—summed up in one pure moment of passion?"

He closed his eyes.

"Yes," she whispered. Her fingers slid down his nightshirt. "You do know. And you're going to admit it."

"No." The denial was stark, final.

Her hand reached his thigh. "You're going to learn that I love you. That you can't stop it. That there is magic between us. Not the stuff of fairy tales: better."

"Emmaline." His voice was hoarse, dry.

"Touch me." She placed his hand on her breast and felt the slight but unmistakable shudder that betrayed him. "You make me tremble, too. The whole world is contained in that spot where you touch me."

He withdrew his hand, but she caught it.

"Do you know what stands between us?" she whispered. "The control you worked so hard to build. The magic I spent years denying. You're mine, Adrian. Touch me and know that above all else."

"I can't."

"You *will*."

Slowly, Emmaline unlaced her nightgown. She let it slip to the floor. His brittle gaze swept her, taking in her nakedness, drinking in every detail.

He made no move to touch her. His eyes were hard, implacable. He wouldn't give an inch. She stared at him.

An eternity passed.

Slowly, Emmaline bent to retrieve her nightgown. Tears streaked her face as she grabbed a fistful of flannel. Just as she turned, he caught her hand.

"Come here." His voice was low, seething with passion.

She froze.

He turned her around and backed her against the bed. White-hot fury sharpened his gaze to polished steel. "If I'd known you were a virgin, I wouldn't have touched you."

"Don't blame me for your mistakes," she shot back.

He looked as if he might throttle her, but the anger in his eyes was edged with pain. "Even if you hadn't lied, I'd have found some other reason to push you away. I can't be close to a woman. To anyone."

"Perhaps you haven't found the right woman."

"I don't want to find her."

"Coward."

His mouth curved upward. "I've only loved one woman in my life, Emmaline. At least I think I loved her. In the end, I was never really sure."

"How imprecise of you." Tears stung her eyes, but she refused to look down. "I'm sure she was gratified."

"I was speaking of my mother."

She blinked. "Oh."

He put a finger under her chin, tilting her head up so their gazes met. "I've no use for love. It's never brought me anything but pain."

The words hurt, but they also made her furious. "I'm sorry for your past, for the cruel childhood that made you the man you are," Emmaline flung at him. "My heart goes out to the boy who felt he failed to protect his mother and then learned not to care. But you're not that boy anymore."

"Emmaline—"

"I'm angry for the pain you suffered, angry at the people who hurt your mother, at the father who didn't care." She couldn't stem the rush of words. "But most of all, I'm angry at you, Adrian. Because you've mired yourself in the past. You've lived a sterile, cold existence that only perpetuates the mistakes your parents made—"

"Damn it," he barked. "That's enough."

"Angry, are you?" she taunted.

"Hell, yes," he snapped. "You can't accept any truth that doesn't fit with yours. Stop trying to figure me out. It will end badly, I assure you."

Emmaline rose on tiptoes, so her face was almost level with his. "Will it?" she murmured against his lips.

He inhaled sharply.

"Rage. Fury. Outrage," she said breathlessly. A wild searing heat spiraled though her. "We can build on that, Adrian. Oh, yes, we *can*."

The anger between them exploded. Adrian ground his mouth into hers, turning the kiss into a battle of wills he quickly won. Then he lifted her off her feet and tossed her roughly onto the bed. Instantly, he was there, straddling her, forcing her arms above her head.

"I don't give a damn about the future or the past," he growled. "I want you *now*."

Emmaline arched upward, urging him, daring him. With a hoarse cry, he ripped off his nightshirt.

His hands were everywhere, relentlessly claiming her. Emmaline gloried in the savage strength that left her no choice but to writhe in delicious agony beneath him.

Again she arched upward, taunting him. "You see?" she whispered. "You can't control it."

With a primitive cry, he thrust his tongue into her mouth, invading her, daring her to defy him. But it wasn't enough, and Emmaline wasn't about to settle for less. She'd never been so angry, so determined, so *aroused.* By the time this night was done, he would know how little choice he had in this passion between them. If he thought her the only captive, he was about to discover otherwise.

"Now," she whispered. "*Now.*"

He lifted his head. A stunned look came into

his eyes, as if he'd suddenly realized where this wild lust had taken him. Steel swept his gaze, threatening to banish the molten heat there. One last bid for control.

Slowly, Emmaline's hand closed around his arousal.

His feral growl nearly unnerved her.

With a predatory cry, he positioned her to accommodate his burgeoning hardness, then thrust into her with savage fury.

It was a taking, nothing less. Yet even as his wild need overwhelmed her, she gloried in the ruthlessness of the power that would not be denied. He'd lost control. She'd done that. Desire had defeated that stubborn will.

Her nails dug into his flesh as she clung to him, no less a prisoner to her own raging desire. She'd never wanted anything more than she wanted him now. Her mind emptied of all save the stampeding need that fed on their anger, then purged it. He drove them to a furious ecstasy they'd doubtless repudiate by dawn.

Suddenly, it was over.

Scarcely daring to breathe, they lay still, limbs coiled around each other possessively. Then, incredibly, the drumbeat of passion started anew. Faintly at first, then in a deafening cadence that left no room for thought or regret. Over and over they spiraled through the night, exhausting each other.

After the taking and giving had cleansed them of all but a troubled peace, sleep gathered them in its tentacles. Just as Emmaline drifted off, the memory of her aunt's wisdom floated into her head.

Rage is one of the very best emotions, Em. Do let me know when you find that out.

"If Ainsford produces a tarot deck or any other artifice, you will be amazed and attentive." Adrian regarded Miss Alcott sternly. "Do not reveal your knowledge of such things."

"Don't worry," she assured him cheerfully. "I never overplay my hand. Sometimes the best acting requires disciplining oneself to understatement."

Adrian was willing to bet that Miss Alcott had never in her life disciplined herself to understatement. He had a bad feeling about tonight, but perhaps that was for other reasons. He'd had a sinking sensation inside ever since he'd awakened this morning with Emmaline in his arms. Daylight had cast the night in shades of regret.

What had he done? Had what they'd shared been love? Were the passion and anger two sides of the same emotion? Had the barbed dance between them all these weeks led inexorably to the moment when he took her in his arms and prayed the night would never end?

His gaze settled on Emmaline. Her face was unnaturally pale. She didn't say a word when he took her arm and escorted her to the carriage. She didn't look at him as she settled herself on the seat. He wanted to take her in his arms and apologize for that wild, violent fury that had seized him last night. The fury *she'd* instigated.

With an effort, he forced his mind away from

last night. Tonight's dangers would demand his full attention.

Deverell had thought it prudent to skip this outing; he said his presence might make Ainsford suspicious, as their parting last year had not been amicable. "He flaunted his mistresses before Lady Ainsford," Deverell had said grimly. "As his secretary, I handled the financial arrangements for these women. Conscience dictated that I leave his employ. I have never regretted it."

Judging by the tipsy woman Adrian had seen on Ainsford's arm at the Cyprians' Ball, the marquess hadn't mended his ways. But that didn't concern him tonight, graver matters were at stake.

To Adrian's amazement, Gibbons had insisted on coming. He and Miss Alcott had developed a friendship of sorts, and if that helped the lady do her best tonight, so be it. But they made for a very odd lot as they pulled up to Lord and Lady Ainsford's house. It sat back from the street behind a pair of iron gates, over which two grotesque stone mastiffs presided. Servants instantly took charge of the carriage, leading the horses to the large mews that ran behind the house.

"So glad you could make it, Trent," Ainsford declared heartily as he greeted them at the door. "And with such a delightful company, too."

Lady Ainsford's brittle gaze surveyed them all, lingering a bit longer than necessary over Gibbons. "Do you bring your servant *everywhere*, Lady Alcott?"

"Oh, yes," Miss Alcott assured her. "Mr. Gibbons tends to me morning and night."

Emmaline's aunt smiled benignly as a flustered Lady Ainsford fanned herself. Adrian stole a look at Gibbons, who looked decidedly irked.

Monsieur Rigaud, a thin man of indeterminate age and saturnine features, waited silently as greetings were exchanged. His only acknowledgment was an assessing, penetrating gaze directed at Miss Alcott, as if he were measuring her susceptibility to his art.

Ever alert to her audience, Miss Alcott put a lacy handkerchief over her nose and swayed slightly. Lord Ainsford rushed to her aid, but she waved him off.

" 'Tis what I have Mr. Gibbons for," she said weakly.

"This way, madam," Rigaud said solemnly.

Leaning on Gibbons's arm, Miss Alcott followed Rigaud into the music room. Rigaud sat on a chair next to a divan. He wore a light gray robe trimmed with gold lace. One of his feet was bare; a golden sock adorned the other. He plunged his bare foot into a wooden bucket filled with water.

A solitary violinist played softly in the corner. Rigaud took a metal rod, inserted the lower end into the water, and began to rub the upper end in a rhythmic stroking motion. At last he turned to Miss Alcott.

"Please recline on the divan," he said in heavily accented English, "then remove the slipper of your foot nearest me."

Miss Alcott gave no sign that she found this instruction odd. Her solemn countenance matched only by Rigaud's, she lay back on the divan and allowed Gibbons to remove her shoe.

Adrian had seen Rigaud's like before. Wealthy benefactors sometimes opened their homes to such people, who in turn provided hope that illnesses could be cured and the future foreseen. But even Mesmer had abandoned this particular parlor trick some years ago. Adrian hoped Miss Alcott would be able to keep a straight face during what was to follow.

"What are your symptoms, madame?" Rigaud asked.

"Fatigue," Miss Alcott responded with a weary sigh. "A great and endless fatigue. It has sapped me of my life's force. With it have come headaches, the most dreadful kind. Sometimes I despair of living." Her voice broke slightly on that last. Adrian's estimation of Miss Alcott's acting abilities rose a notch.

Rigaud nodded. "I think I can help you, but first I must see whether you are a good candidate for the cure. Alas, many bring a skepticism to the *baquet* that closes their minds to my methods. Those I cannot help."

Miss Alcott regarded him with a worshipful gaze. "My mind is completely open to you, Monsieur. This condition has caused me such difficulty that I am at my wit's end."

With a nod to the violinist, Rigaud rubbed the metal rod with renewed vigor, then touched it to his arms and torso. The music grew faster, more intense. Rigaud wore the look of a man in great concentration, but Adrian thought Miss Alcott the better actor, for Rigaud had not quite managed to disguise the greed in his pale yellow eyes.

Lady Ainsford, Adrian noticed, paid special attention to the lavish manner in which Rigaud rubbed that metal wand over his body.

As the violinist plunged into an *allegro,* Rigaud seized Miss Alcott's hand, then her toe. Then he alternated between the two, rubbing the metal rod all the while.

Adrian had seen something similar years ago, when a mesmerist more advanced in his art had put Adrian's mother through a full *baquet.* She and several other patients had held hands around a large wooden tub filled with magnetized water. Protruding iron rods allowed each patient to press a rod against the part of the body in pain or distress. Seizures sometimes resulted, even deaths, though some patients had inexplicably gotten better. Adrian suspected they possessed a heightened suggestibility and had simply talked themselves into a cure.

Miss Alcott's eyes were closed; Adrian could not tell whether she'd been drawn into a trance or was feigning one.

At last the violinist bowed a soft, mournful coda. Rigaud withdrew from his patient.

Miss Alcott's lashes fluttered open. She gave Rigaud a bewildered smile. "I feel—it is difficult to explain—relaxed, I think. Very relaxed."

A smug smile settled over Rigaud's thin lips. "Did you feel the magnetic force, Lady Alcott?"

"Oh, yes. I felt the most amazing warmth running through my limbs. It was almost—I blush to say it—*pagan.*"

Ainsford arched a brow. Lady Ainsford seemed to be studying the drapes, as if deciding whether they needed washing.

Rigaud removed his foot from the bucket and a towel was instantly provided for his use. As he dried his foot, Rigaud watched Miss Alcott carefully.

"I believe I can help you. I may require several sessions to achieve a full trance. We will begin tomorrow, if madame is willing. There is a modest fee, but—" He waved his hand as if to suggest it was a minor concern.

"I will pay all expenses. Money is not an issue where Emmaline's well-being, and that of her aunt, are concerned," Adrian declared gruffly.

This statement drew an amused look from Ainsford, who no doubt found delicious irony in the situation. "Brought to the bit by love, eh, Trent?" Ainsford's gaze moved from Adrian to Emmaline, who flushed and tried to smile lovingly at her future husband.

What deep play they were engaged in, Adrian thought. Ainsford looked as if he would gladly murder Rigaud, and perhaps Lady Ainsford, too. Obviously the marquess had not missed the simmering awareness between those two. Perhaps that accounted for Ainsford's haggard look these days.

The possibilities for treachery here were many. Rigaud was an expatriate Frenchman with an avaricious eye. He'd be alert to any chance; would he draw the line at treason? Lady Ainsford had the warmth of a toad and the nerves of a high-strung filly. Were she and Rigaud partners in crime as well as lust?

Ainsford himself was a slippery character. Adrian didn't put much stock in the man's show of friendship after all these years. The marquess looked brittle and unstable, like a man burdened by a dark secret. Had he tried to abduct Emmaline, to silence forever the possibility that Burwell had said something indiscreet? If so, who had helped him—his feckless wife or the greedy Frenchman?

For now, all hope of finding out rested with Miss Alcott. Blind adoration settled over her features as she looked up at Rigaud. Adrian decided that she was an excellent actress, after all. Either that, or she'd really been taken in by the man.

Adrian looked at Emmaline, to see if he could read the truth there. But what he saw in her eyes was the one truth he didn't want to see.

Love.

Chapter 24

"**S**trange as it seems, I feel much better."
Aunt Heloise perched on the edge of
her bed. "Perhaps Monsieur Rigaud is on to
something."

Emmaline eyed her in alarm. "Never say
you've fallen under his spell? I thought you were
only acting tonight."

"Of course, dear. But it was quite invigorating
to have the man stroke my toe so *insistently*. No
wonder Lady Ainsford is so on edge. Rigaud
must have quite a following of females."

"Why would Lady Ainsford be on edge? And
why would women like an unpleasant worm like
Rigaud?"

Aunt Heloise sighed. "My dear, you are such
an innocent. Rigaud and Yvette are embroiled in
an affair, of course. Ainsford knows and doesn't
like it one bit. Rigaud is one of those deceitful
manipulators who revel in playing one lover
against the other."

Emmaline stared at her. "How can you know
such things? We weren't there above an hour."

"Because I know the secret recesses of the human heart," Aunt Heloise replied. "Which is why I also know you have fallen in love with the duke."

Emmaline turned away.

" 'Tis nothing to be ashamed of."

"He does not care for me. He doesn't want me."

"Wrong on both counts. I'll grant you this: he's a difficult nut to crack, though he's shown signs of doing just that since you returned from Oxford. We'll soon be planning your wedding at St. George's."

Emmaline shook her head. "The last thing he wants is a wedding. And I'll not enslave myself to a man who doesn't know how to love."

"Enslave, is it?" Aunt Heloise's gaze narrowed. "Things have gone further than I thought. Leave everything to me, dear. I'll bring him around for you."

"No, Aunt. I've made a cake of myself and let my own feelings go too far. I've acted shamefully, like some brazen doxy. Why, last night I actually went to him and—" Emmaline broke off, red-faced.

"Now, now, Em. Where's the romantic in you? Where's your father's spirit? Life is too short to spend on regrets."

Emmaline held her tongue. There was no sense discussing it further. She'd gone to Adrian with full knowledge of the vast chasm between them.

"I'm glad you're feeling better." Emmaline mustered a weary smile. "May I get you a glass of warm milk to help you sleep?"

"Thank you, but I've already sent for some sherry."

Emmaline kissed her aunt's cheek. "Don't stay up too late. Remember, we agreed to accompany Lady Ainsford shopping in the morning."

"We did, didn't we?"

Emmaline didn't like the mischievous gleam in her aunt's eye. It would be just like Aunt Heloise to plead a headache, leaving Emmaline to accompany the tedious Lady Ainsford alone. But that was tomorrow's problem. For now, she had the night to get through.

This time, she'd spend it in her own bed. Alone.

At the knock, Heloise looked up from the plush comforter she had arranged around her in the bed. She still had the figure of a young woman, she decided, fanning herself. Well, perhaps not a young woman, but a woman in the prime of mid-life. Her breasts, like every other part of her, had grown fuller with time. Fortunately, most men appreciated maturity.

She'd found a lovely green night rail laid out for her tonight by one of those nice maids. The silk confection was cut rather low, which suited her just fine. With all her props in place, Heloise gave a regal command: "Enter."

As the door swung open, she suppressed a smile. He'd brought it himself, as she'd known he would.

"Your sherry, madam," Gibbons said.

"Thank you, John. You may put it here." Heloise indicated the bedside table.

"The girls had been sent to bed, or I'd have had them bring this," he said.

"Of course." Heloise was not surprised, as she had told the maids not to wait up for her tonight. "They are young. They need their sleep."

Gibbons put the sherry on the table and stepped back quickly. "If there is nothing else—"

"You seem rather tense tonight, John. Is anything the matter?"

Gibbons stiffened. "Not at all."

"Not in the least?"

"No."

"I am so relieved. For a moment I thought you were angry at me." Heloise lowered her lashes demurely. With a small sigh, she reached for the glass of sherry. Her motion allowed the comforter to slip down to her waist and exposed some of the very mature aspects of her figure. She took a sip, savoring the pungent liquid and its amber heat. With a breathless sigh, she licked an errant drop from her lip.

"What are you about, Heloise?" Gibbons said sharply. "I swear if I have to stand here and endure more of your tricks, I—"

"Tricks, John? I don't know what you mean." Heloise pursed her lips.

"Don't do that, Heloise."

She reclined against the pillow. "I am yours to command, John. You don't like my expression? I'm happy to change it. I do so adore a masterful man."

Gibbons scowled. "Stop it."

Heloise took another sip of sherry. "No, John. You are too much fun to bait."

"You are a shameless flirt, Heloise. I do not care to be another of your conquests. Besides, we are past our dancing days."

"Nonsense," she said in a husky voice. "I still dance as well as I ever did. Perhaps better."

"You know what I mean."

Heloise sighed. "It was the toe, wasn't it?"

Gibbons blinked. "I beg your pardon?"

"My toe. The way Rigaud touched it, stroked it, *owned* it in his unique way. You didn't like that, did you John? You were jealous."

"Heloise, you are the strangest woman I have ever known."

"Ah, but you have *not* known me, John—in the biblical sense. That is the problem, isn't it?"

He stood at her bedside, rigid with something that might have been anger, but to Heloise seemed likely to be something else altogether. She took another sip of sherry. It really was an excellent vintage, a bit fruity but with assertive undertones. She'd not had sherry like this since that duke she'd known so long ago.

My goodness. Time passes so quickly. The thought made her wistful. For even as she watched John's wonderfully expressive eyes, knowing that he would soon be hers, she could not help but wonder how much more time was left her, and how much of it would be spent in flirtatious games like these.

Would there ever be a man who wished to keep her? Not for a week or a month or even a year, but for all time? What was time, anyway, but a measurement of one's presence in the world? Had any of those performances she'd thrown herself into with such abandon meant anything when all was said and done? She had her memories, but the memories would die with her. Had it all been a waste?

Suddenly, and quite unexpectedly, her eyes filled with tears. Bewildered, she looked up at John. She'd planned to turn him into another in a long line of conquests who had helped her pass the time until her time came to an end. She'd always pretended it didn't matter, that she was using them as much as they were using her.

"I'm sorry," she whispered.

His brow furrowed. "For letting Rigaud stroke your toe?"

"For thinking you would wish to have anything to do with me. You are too fine, John, much too fine."

He shifted awkwardly. No doubt he was trying to figure a way to leave without seeming rude. Heloise decided to spare him that difficulty. "Good night. Thank you for the sherry."

It was a clear dismissal. She threw in an insouciant smile, just to show him that she didn't care, that there was no reason for him to stay.

He didn't go. He stood looking down at her as if there was something he meant to say. Must he make this difficult? Must he stand there and with every breath force her to see how tawdry she was, how far he was above her?

Heloise deliberately looked past him to the door. "It is late," she said in a cool, unemotional voice. She'd not lost her acting skill, that much was certain.

To her amazement, he sat on the bed. His gaze

moved from the curls she'd arranged artfully over her shoulders to the neckline of her gown. Heloise suddenly felt horribly exposed. She'd worn less on stage, but then she'd not had John staring at her from such solemn brown eyes.

"That gown becomes you," he said.

Heloise's heart gave a tiny little flutter.

"But you must not wear it again."

Her spirits came crashing down to earth.

"It belonged to the duchess. It should have been discarded when she died."

Of course—she was not worthy to wear the gown of a duchess. Heloise reached for the comforter, intending to cover herself. She only prayed that John took himself off before she burst into tears.

"I have a story to tell you," he said. "I've never told it to a soul, but it seems right that I should tell you."

"I don't want to hear your confessions, John," Heloise said angrily. Did he mean to make her endure a litany of the reasons why he could not stay with her?

"Nevertheless, you will. It's important, Heloise. It's what stands between me and everyone else in the world. You, Adrian—everyone."

Heloise saw the genuine anguish in his eyes. "Very well, John. Confess away." She managed a weak smile.

His gaze slid to the glass of sherry. "May I?"

Heloise nodded. She watched in fascination as he brought the glass to his lips, drained it, and returned it to the table. She'd never envied a glass as much as she did this one for its fleeting, intimate knowledge of him.

"It started on a night long ago, when His Grace consumed three bottles of port . . ."

The canary was standing on his manuscript. Adrian picked up the bird and set him elsewhere. "You'll have to behave," he said sternly, "or go back in your cage."

An indignant chirp was the only response.

"Don't think I won't," Adrian groused as he picked up his pen and reread what he'd written this morning. The paper was coming along nicely. The notion that the large bone derived from some ancient reptile had inspired him. He couldn't wait to mount an expedition to Tilgate Forest.

Galahad perched next to Thomas, who napped on the table next to his desk. Strangely, the bird and the cat tolerated each other. That surprised him almost as much as he'd surprised himself by tolerating them in his study. To be sure, he didn't like finding cat hair on his chair or yellow feathers on his papers. Nor would he want the animals around permanently. When Emmaline left, she'd take Thomas. He intended to give Peter the canary.

When Emmaline left. An unsettling thought.

He'd not gone to her room last night. He couldn't bear the thought of seeing her love for him in her eyes.

You don't have the slightest idea what to do with those feelings. How very true.

Do you know what stands between us? That con-

trol you've worked so hard to build. Control had been his only refuge since the age of ten.

"I've fallen in love with you." But all the love in the world didn't give a man the power to alter the past or protect those he loved. And in that hard fact lay the only truth he knew: Love hurts, always and forever, and the only way to stay heart-whole was to avoid it at all costs.

Do you know what it's like to have everything you've ever wanted in life . . . summed up in one, pure moment of passion?

Oh, yes, he knew. Emmaline made him long to believe that life was more than just moving in orderly fashion from one paper to another, from one dig to another, marking time in precisely measured tasks. She made him wish there was something more, something enduring.

Adrian tried hard to immerse himself in the world of enormous lizards. Had they lived here, in the very spot where his father's mansion sat in the most fashionable part of London? Had the earth been so very different then, such that all creatures then and since were mere specks of sand on an endless beach in a vast, unfathomable universe? Was life some great continuum, connecting the past and present across an unfathomable expanse of sky?

If so, how did the love of a woman and a man matter in such an endless sea?

Adrian stared at Galahad, wondering what his ancestors had looked like. And Thomas—was he descended from some fierce feline, larger than either of them could imagine? These were questions he'd never solve, answers he'd never find.

But he did know one thing: his feelings for Emmaline defied everything he'd worked to build: discipline, order, logic—his very character. And yet, he couldn't help but wonder whether he'd built his life on a house of cards. A deep, abiding uneasiness stole over him.

"Your Grace."

Adrian hadn't heard Gibbons come in. He forced his eyes to focus on the man. "Yes?"

"It's Mrs. Stanhope." Gibbons wore a worried frown. "She went shopping this morning with Lady Ainsford, and—"

Isn't back yet. Dear God, he'd known the words before Gibbons said them. Had he become so attuned to Emmaline that he knew when she was in trouble?

"Lady Ainsford is here," Gibbons continued. "She says Mrs. Stanhope vanished during their shopping trip."

Adrian's trembling hand dropped the pen. *Please don't let anything happen to Emmaline.*

"Has Bow Street been notified?" He rose, ready to turn heaven and earth upside down until he found her.

"Oh, Your Grace! I am so distraught." Lady Ainsford rushed into the room, her hands clasped around a handkerchief she'd already wrung the life out of. "One moment she was with me at Madame Celeste's looking at patterns. The next minute—oh, I cannot bear to go on!"

"Try," Adrian said evenly, ready to choke the story out of her.

"She and Madame Celeste's assistant were discussing the latest fashion plates from *La Belle As-*

semblée. Miss Alcott commented that the new styles were nicely understated, yet elegant."

"And then?" he growled dangerously.

"There was a commotion in the street. I pointed it out to her. Several carriages were involved in an accident, and the drivers were at fisticuffs. Miss Alcott stepped outside to see what was the matter, and that's the l-last I saw of her. Oh, this is terrible!" With a loud sob, she buried her face in her handkerchief.

"Gibbons!" Adrian roared, though the man was only six feet away. "Have a horse saddled."

"Done, Your Grace. I've ordered a horse for myself as well."

"Have someone see Lady Ainsford home." Adrian strode from the room. His heart was pounding with dread. What if she'd been murdered? What if even now she was beyond his prayers?

He hadn't kept her safe. And she'd left the house this morning thinking he didn't care.

Did fools get second chances?

As he strode down the hall Miss Alcott touched his sleeve; her face told him her fears matched his.

"Don't worry," he said, trying to convince himself as much as her. "I'll find her."

"I doubt you'll have to look far."

"Oh?" He itched to be on the horse, riding to Emmaline's rescue, doing something—anything—to get her back.

"That woman is the worst actress I've ever seen."

Adrian's gaze narrowed. The marchioness's

sobs spilled out of the study into the hall. He had not thought it possible for anyone to sob that loudly.

"I'll leave her to you," he said.

With a grim smile, Miss Alcott moved toward the study. "I'll take care of her."

Chapter 25

"Gentlemen, this will be the performance of my life," Heloise declared.

"Be careful, Heloise." Beside her in the carriage, Gibbons looked worried.

"All of life is a risk, John. If we free Emmaline tonight, nothing else matters."

Watching Gibbons and Emmaline's aunt, Adrian wondered why he had never picked up on the deepening undercurrents between them. But for now, only one thing was on his mind: rescuing Emmaline.

He and Gibbons had ridden through half the streets in London today looking for Emmaline and anyone who might have seen her. They'd interviewed coachmen, pages, footmen, and maids on shopping errands in Bond Street for their employers. Other than the carriage fracas, no one had seen anything unusual.

Adrian had gone to Bow Street, thinking to hire the man Deverell had used, since he was familiar with the case. But he didn't have the runner's name, and the officer behind the large oak desk didn't have many answers. Several runners were away on assignments, Adrian was told, but he was welcome to question them when they returned. Meanwhile, Adrian paid a large sum of money to put two of Bow Street's finest on Emmaline's case.

Instinct told him that Ainsford and his wife had her, or Rigaud and Lady Ainsford, or any combination of the three. When Ainsford sent a note offering to cancel tonight's session in view of Emmaline's disappearance, Adrian sent the marquess a firm reply stating they'd present themselves at eight o'clock as planned—to seek assistance from Ainsford and Rigaud in finding Emmaline.

"Don't they know we suspect them?" Heloise asked.

"Probably," Adrian said. Whatever game Ainsford was playing, they'd all be part of it before this night was done. "Remember: Shut out Rigaud's voice. Do not focus on whatever device he uses to mesmerize you. Control your thoughts."

"I am *always* in control during a performance. If only I'd gone shopping with her. I didn't really have the headache, I was just fatigued." Heloise's voice broke. "I have a terrible feeling that if we aren't successful tonight, I'll never see Emmaline again."

"Now, Heloise," Gibbons said sternly. "That's no way to talk. You have a performance to give."

Heloise took a deep breath. "I'm ready."

The fierce stone mastiffs over Ainsford's iron gates looked especially ominous tonight. "The devil's den," Heloise muttered as their carriage rolled up the drive.

"It's just a house." Gibbons patted her hand. "Inside is just an audience, like many you've faced. I have absolute confidence in you."

"Stop distracting her," Adrian growled. Heloise was staring at Gibbons as if he were King George himself.

"I am not distracted," Heloise retorted. "Indeed, I am never more focused than just before a performance."

Adrian leveled a gaze at her. "Your words must compel every eye, demand every feeling. No one must notice what I am about."

Heloise lifted her chin a notch. "When *I* am on stage, there is nothing else to notice."

As she descended the carriage steps with queenly grace, Adrian prayed she was right. He'd stake his life on the fact that Emmaline was somewhere in Ainsford's house. He intended to search every nook and cranny.

Ainsford himself met them at the door, his expression grim. "I'm sorry for your trouble, Trent. Yvette has been trying to remember anything that might shed light on Miss Alcott's disappearance. And Rigaud has offered his full assistance. He is nothing if not eager to please."

The marquess's usual self-mocking smile was not in evidence. He seemed genuinely concerned, but perhaps the man was as skilled an actor as Heloise. It took all the control Adrian could muster not to grab Ainsford around the throat and demand that he confess all.

Instead, he forced himself to perform his part

in this charade. "Lady Alcott believes that because she and Emmaline are very close, she might, with Rigaud's help, divine Emmaline's whereabouts."

Ainsford looked dubious. "I've heard of such things, of course. We've done the odd séance now and then, along with mind-reading exercises, but for the most part they've been parlor tricks, nothing more." The marquess's candor surprised Adrian, though that, too, might be only a pose.

An eerie wailing came from the music room. Ainsford led them toward the sound, which Adrian recognized immediately. Sure enough, Rigaud sat before a glass harmonica, one of Mesmer's favorite instruments. Filled to varying levels with water, the glasses emitted unearthly sounds when rubbed. The instrument was intended to establish the mood and facilitate the trance.

Lady Ainsford, looking more nervous than any innocent woman should, patted Adrian's sleeve. "Don't worry," she whispered. "If anyone can find her, 'tis Rigaud."

Adrian seriously doubted the man could find his way out the front door. Ainsford, meanwhile, studied Rigaud with a cold, speculative gaze that suggested he knew of Rigaud's relationship with Lady Ainsford. Adrian wondered why the Frenchman had not discerned the considerable danger to himself. He ought to be packing his bags, rather than lingering under Ainsford's roof. Perhaps he'd made the mistake of believing in his own illusions.

At last Rigaud left off his playing. "Be seated, Lady Alcott," he commanded.

Heloise sat on the divan. Gibbons sat next to her, which deepened Rigaud's moody scowl. Before Rigaud could object, however, Heloise took his hand.

"Please, Monsieur." Her voice was husky with emotion. "You alone can help us."

Rigaud allowed himself a moment to bask in her adulation. "I will do my best, Lady Alcott." He turned to the others. "I must have absolute silence."

Adrian stationed himself near the music-room door. When Heloise provided the opportunity, he would slip away to search the house.

Rigaud pulled out a shiny watch. Was there an original bone in the man's body? Adrian wondered in disgust. Every mesmerist from Vienna to Belgium used a pocket watch.

"Concentrate solely on this." Rigaud's voice was low, soothing. He swung the watch to and fro in front of Heloise's eyes. "You will feel relaxed, peaceful."

"Yes," she murmured.

"Mine will be the only voice you hear," Rigaud said. "You will be deaf to all others."

He's a charlatan, Heloise. Remember that. Adrian willed his thoughts her way, knowing he was a fool to place stock in such measures. Still, it was better than standing around waiting, with nothing to occupy his mind but thoughts of what Emmaline must be enduring.

"Your eyes will remain open, but it is my face alone you will see."

Emmaline's face, Heloise. Not that French idiot's.
Slowly, Miss Alcott nodded.

"Your hands are heavy. You cannot raise them."

Nonsense. You can raise them whenever you wish.
After a while, Rigaud lifted Heloise's hand, then let it drop lifelessly into her lap. "Excellent. She is mesmerized," he announced solemnly.

The pompous ass. *Heloise? Are you still there? Don't forget your part. Emmaline's life may depend upon it.*

Lady Ainsford sat on the edge of her chair, looking like a frightened rabbit. Ainsford stood nearby, watching his wife like a hawk. The room was silent and still.

The stage is set, Heloise. Do your best.

"You are in a dark room," Rigaud said softly. "It is not of our world, but a world where form is meaningless. Spirits inhabit that world. They are trying to reach across the divide to you. They have something to tell you."

The distraction, Heloise. Don't fail me.

"Yes," Heloise said in a flat voice. Her eyes were glazed, unfocused. Adrian prayed she'd bested Rigaud, that she'd been able to retain control.

Emmaline needs you.

"Your thoughts are for your niece," Rigaud continued. "They know that. They wish to help."

She nodded.

That's right, Heloise. Keep them in your thrall.

"One in particular is near," Rigaud whispered. "He wishes to speak."

There was a long silence. No one moved.

Everyone leaned toward Heloise, waiting to see what would unfold.

Adrian held his breath. Was Heloise mesmerized, after all? Had they failed?

"*She*," Heloise corrected softly. "*She* wishes to speak."

Adrian's heart leapt to his throat. *That's the way, Heloise. You've got them now.*

Rigaud looked taken aback. "Er, *she* wishes to speak. What does she wish to tell you? Is it about your niece?"

Adrian edged to the threshold of the music-room door.

"She wishes to speak of marriage, of men, of ... love." Heloise's voice grew husky. "Nay, not love. *Lovers.*"

"Heavens." Lady Ainsford wrung her hands.

Perfect, Heloise. Keep it up.

"The spirit has known many men," Heloise murmured. "She is skilled in the sexual arts."

Lady Ainsford's eyes widened.

Adrian surveyed the room. Everyone but Ainsford was hanging on Heloise's every word. The marquess looked edgy, restless. He met Adrian's gaze and frowned. Adrian relaxed against the doorframe in a pose that suggested his utter disdain of the proceedings. Ainsford's lips curled, but he kept his gaze on Adrian, as if he didn't wholly trust Adrian's intentions.

Come on, Heloise.

"What does she want?" Rigaud prodded Heloise.

"To speak." Heloise cleared her throat. "Venus," she said in a flat monotone, "gave me my lust—"

"Dear Lord." Lady Ainsford paled.

"—and alas, though I knew better, I never could withdraw my Venus-chamber from a good fellow."

Lovely, Heloise. Lovely, lovely, lovely.

Stunned, silent shock radiated around the room. Every eye fell on Heloise. "Is that the only spirit who wishes to speak?" Rigaud demanded.

"Nay." Again that unblinking, lifeless countenance. She stared straight ahead, at no one in particular. "There is another."

"Thank God," Ainsford muttered.

"Let him—or her—come forward," Rigaud ordered.

Now, Heloise.

"She has a message for—" Heloise paused.

"Yes?" Rigaud demanded impatiently.

"The message is for Lady Ainsford."

The marchioness put her hand to her mouth. Rigaud frowned. Ainsford's sharp gaze impaled both of them.

Now!

Heloise took a deep breath. In a searing, unearthly voice, she intoned: "Clytemnestra, for her lechery, caused her husband's death by treachery."

Lady Ainsford's hand went to her heart.

"Oh, treacherous wives, who'd slain their husbands in their beds—"

"Good God," Ainsford muttered.

"—and copulated with their lovers while their husbands' corpses lay scattered round."

Lady Ainsford slumped to the floor. Rigaud gasped. Ainsford dropped to his knees, clutching his wife's hand.

Adrian slipped from the room. Anyone who saw him would surmise he'd gone to fetch help, but every ounce of his being was focused on Emmaline.

He took the stairs two at a time.

"Thank God, I've found you."

Emmaline looked up from the pallet on which she'd been lying, her limbs trussed like a goose at Michaelmas. Her stomach felt queasy, her head ached. Her memory was fogged. She remembered stepping outside Madame Celeste's shop to see what the commotion was. She'd felt a cool breeze, then all was blank.

Her face lit up. "Mr. Deverell! How glad I am to see you. Do you mean to make a habit of rescuing me?"

He smiled. "So it seems, Mrs. Stanhope. So it seems."

"It has been a very trying day, Mr. Deverell, but I cannot seem to remember most of it. Would you be so kind as to untie my bindings? Where am I?"

"On Lord Ainsford's property." Strangely, Mr. Deverell made no move to free her.

"Then we were right? Ainsford is behind this evil?"

"It wouldn't surprise me in the least."

Emmaline frowned. Everything was just a bit off. Mr. Deverell's voice, his demeanor, the incomplete manner in which he answered her questions. "If you could just release my bindings, Mr. Deverell?"

"What? Oh, of course. My mind was wandering." Deverell bent down and, with a large, lethal-looking knife, swiftly cut the rope around her ankles.

Emmaline flexed her cramped feet. "Thank you. How did you find me, Mr. Deverell?"

"I know Ainsford's house well. As his secretary, I made it my business to know everything. Actually, this isn't the house, but an old section of the stables."

Emmaline stared at him. Mr. Deverell no longer resembled the polite, respectful gentleman who'd rescued her in Guilford Street. His usually neat hair was tousled, his jacket askew. His cravat had come undone, and the ends sagged like wilted lettuce. "Mr. Deverell? Could you please . . . ?" She held out her wrists, which were still tightly bound.

"I'm afraid not." His tone was devoid of sympathy for her plight.

"Mr. Deverell, what in the world are you about?"

"Money, Mrs. Stanhope. A great deal of money."

A frisson of fear rippled her spine. Emmaline willed herself to remain calm, sensing that distress might provoke him.

"Ainsford has so much of it, yet he pays his secretaries a pittance," Deverell said. "Still, there were advantages to working for him. A marquess's aide moves in exalted circles."

A horrifying certainty came to her. "You abducted me today, didn't you, Mr. Deverell?"

He looked pleased. "I knew you were an intelligent woman. You've figured out my plan,
haven't you?"

"Er—not exactly, I must confess. Perhaps you
could explain it." Emmaline tamped down her
fear. If she could keep him talking, perhaps
someone would find them. *Adrian, please come.*

Mr. Deverell smiled. "A man so rarely meets
a woman who approaches his intellect. It is too
bad you formed an attachment to Trent. He
won't make you happy, you know."

"You think not?"

"Too remote and unfeeling. I'm not that way
at all, Mrs. Stanhope. Still, I can see Trent's appeal. Money covers a multitude of sins—isn't
that what they say?"

"Charity," Emmaline corrected automatically.

"What?"

"I believe it's charity that covers a multitude
of sins."

He frowned.

"Then again, perhaps I have it all wrong," Emmaline said quickly. "I do not have my aunt's
aptitude for remembering lines."

"No, she is quite extraordinary." Deverell
studied her. "Are you certain Trent claims your
heart?"

"The only thing I am certain of at this moment
is that my wrists are being scraped raw by this
rope. Can you not loosen it a bit?" She flashed
him a hopeful smile.

"Do not try to cajole me, Mrs. Stanhope. Your
fate has been decided."

Emmaline hesitated. "And that would be what, exactly?"

He studied her thoughtfully. "Death by stiletto."

Her heart slammed into her chest, but she kept her voice calm. "My abduction in Guilford Street—you engineered that, too, didn't you?"

"You are very smart for a woman. Yes, I needed to discover if Burwell had told you anything that would lead to me. Pretending to rescue you gained me your confidence. I can be very ingratiating, you know—it comes from being fourth in line to a title. Ladies adore me until they realize I have no inheritance to speak of."

The hemp dug into her flesh, but Emmaline was past feeling the pain. "You are the traitor," she said softly.

"'Traitor' is a very harsh word. I merely made the most of an opportunity. Through Ainsford, I met men in high positions with similarly underpaid staffs. Burwell was such a man. He'd found a post in the War Office but lacked the insight to profit by it. Over the years, I've invested in the smuggling trade along the coast. As any smuggler knows, War Office secrets are in great demand. Burwell and I formed a mutually satisfying partnership."

He sighed. "Alas, Burwell was indiscreet. His activities drew the suspicion of his superiors. I had to get rid of him."

Deverell's cold, emotionless tone made her shiver.

"H-how did you get him to stand in the path of the Mail?"

"Nitrous oxide—in my opinion, the most useful discovery of the last decade. One merely heats ammonium nitrate in the presence of iron filings. The resultant gas induces a number of interesting sensations—euphoria, exhilaration, giddiness. And, most importantly for my purposes, a complete loss of motor control."

Emmaline blinked. "I have never heard of it."

"Allow me to enlighten you. I only dabble in chemistry now, but for a while I made a living as an apothecary. 'Tis a lowering occupation. A physician is considered a gentleman, but the apothecary a mere tradesman. Selling medicines provided me neither money nor position. As the son of a viscount, Mrs. Stanhope, I am entitled to live well."

Why, Emmaline wondered, had she never noticed the lack of true warmth in Mr. Deverell's eyes?

"Shall I tell you about my invention?" he asked abruptly. "It is ingenious, if I do say so. A small bellows attached to a rubber tube sprays the gas from a canister. I activate the spray by compressing my arm against the bellows. The entire device can be hidden up a coat sleeve. The gas can't be seen, though it is quite cold."

That blast of cold air. She'd felt it during both abductions, along with a strange light-headedness. And Mr. Burwell had wrapped that scarf around his neck as if he'd taken a chill.

Emmaline's mind gave her the image of poor Mr. Burwell, smiling happily while the Mail bore down on him. He hadn't escaped his fate because he couldn't move—and was too giddy to realize the danger. Traitor or no, he hadn't deserved to die like that. "You were there—in the street. But where? I didn't see anyone."

"Burwell was kind enough to stop and give a feeble old lady directions. Did you like my disguise?"

The hunched-over woman in the voluminous cloak . . . wrapped carefully around her so as to prevent scrutiny. Emmaline stared at Deverell. He was actually smiling. "You tried to make it appear I was involved in his death."

"Yes. Because of their suspicions about Burwell, I knew the authorities would be disinclined to accept an apparent accident at face value. I'd taken one of your flyers from along the turnpike, added some sinister things—the death card was a nice touch don't you think?—and stuffed it in Burwell's pocket while he gave me directions. Clever, don't you agree?"

"Appallingly so."

"Such spirit," Deverell said wistfully. "I would have enjoyed taming you."

He toyed with the blade of his knife. "Everything would have worked out had it not been for St. Ledger. I'd satisfied myself that Burwell had told you nothing incriminating. For a brief period, I even thought you and I would become . . . closer. But alas, St. Ledger turned out to be a duke, with all of the advantages that brings."

"His title has nothing to do with my feelings for him," Emmaline said indignantly.

Deverell gave her a pitying look. "I am not stupid, Mrs. Stanhope. A dukedom is surpassed only by a kingdom. I saw the way Trent looked at you. I knew he'd let nothing rest until he solved Burwell's death, cleared your name, and protected you from harm."

Adrian, Emmaline thought desperately, *where are you?* "You made us think Ainsford was behind my abduction," she said, playing to his vanity.

"Brilliant, wasn't it? I did my research, Mrs. Stanhope. Once Trent entered the picture, I was determined to find his weaknesses. When the political skirmish with Ainsford turned up in Trent's past, I knew I could work the marquess into my plans. Trent readily took the bait, as did you all. But alas, there were complications."

"He means me," said a thin voice.

Lady Ainsford stood in the doorway, a pistol pointed at Deverell's heart. "What a mess you've made of things, William."

Mr. Deverell's gaze narrowed. "Don't do anything foolish, Yvette. Remember how very much you have to lose."

"I've already lost," Lady Ainsford said bitterly. "My husband hates me, you are a traitor, and Rigaud is an imbecile."

The hand holding the pistol trembled as she stepped into the room. The situation was too volatile for Emmaline to feel relief at the woman's arrival. That thought was confirmed by Lady Ainsford's distasteful glance in her direction.

"William threatened to tell my husband about my involvement with Rigaud if I didn't help him abduct you. I tossed that blanket over you in Guilford Street and made struggling sounds, so you'd think William had fought your abductor.

This morning my job was simply to lure you outside the shop so William could spray you with the gas."

Mr. Deverell had spun a vast web of treachery very quickly.

"Ainsford already knows about Rigaud." The marchioness glared at Deverell. "I can see it in his eyes. I'm going to tell him what you've done, William, what you've made me do. He'll destroy you. And maybe, in time, he'll forgive me."

"It won't work." Deverell's eyes narrowed. "Ainsford won't save you, Yvette. All he cares about is himself."

"That's not entirely true," said a ravaged voice.

Now Lord Ainsford stood in the doorway. With his heavy scowl and lined features, he didn't look like anyone's notion of salvation. "Yvette's right, Deverell. I knew about Rigaud. I've known about all of them. Even you."

Lady Ainsford paled.

"You didn't like it when I terminated your employment, did you?" Ainsford asked softly. "But it was either dismiss you or kill you for seducing my wife."

Lady Ainsford gasped.

"You made a remarkable recovery from your fainting spell, my dear," Ainsford observed. "No doubt I have Rigaud to thank for that. The man is a wonder, isn't he? But a shade too greedy. The butler tells me he's stolen every candlestick in the house. You ought to have picked a lover with a bit more class."

He hesitated. "I don't hate you for straying,

Yvette. I've wronged you more times than I can count. I'd like to make it up to you, if you'll have me."

Lady Ainsford lowered the pistol. "Oh, Richard," she sobbed, throwing herself into Ainsford's arms.

It was all the opportunity Deverell needed. He lunged for the weapon. A split second later, a shot went off.

Chapter 26

◆◆◆◆◆

Adrian had seen coffins bigger than this.

"We are almost there," Rigaud whispered. The man sounded scared to death—as well he should, since Adrian had nearly strangled him.

Piles of crumbling stone formed the tunnel walls, and they were literally closing in. Each step took Adrian into a space smaller than the last. The air was fetid and suffocating, and the farther Rigaud led him into the bowels of the earth, the more it seemed to Adrian that he was descending into hell itself.

"Where are we?" The voice didn't sound like his own.

"Under the mews. We'll emerge on the far side, where no one can see us from the house. It's a bit of a maze, but you English love mazes, *n'est-ce pas?*"

"And you French go to any lengths to bed a woman."

Rigaud looked indignant. The solitary candle gave his face a ghostly pallor. "Using the tunnel was Yvette's idea. She feared Lord Ainsford would discover us if we risked a rendezvous in the house. No one inhabits the older part of the mews—the stableboys sleep in the newer section. The tunnel is the only way to get to the old mews at night undetected. The stable yard has those bright new gaslights, you see. Most inconvenient."

"So you traversed this filthy tunnel each night to roll around in the manure?"

"I do not find that amusing, *monsieur le Duc*. There is perhaps a slight odor, but one gets accustomed to it. And it was not every night. A man must get his sleep."

"Oh, yes. A man's got to be rested and alert to steal all that silver." Adrian forced himself to keep talking. It would not do to be alone with his thoughts.

Something scurried across his foot. He tried not to think of the creatures that lurked in the darkness and to focus instead on Rigaud's miserable existence. The man was no spy, just a petty thief pilfering his way through England's aristocracy. During his search of the house, Adrian had discovered a trunk full of candelabra, jewelry, and other treasures in Rigaud's room.

That, in addition to the grip Adrian applied to Rigaud's scrawny neck, had persuaded the Frenchman that cooperation was advisable. Rigaud readily admitted his affair with the marchioness and volunteered to show him the tunnel to the mews, the only place Adrian hadn't searched.

Now he wished they'd chanced the gaslights.

"Legend has it your King Charles—a stupid man, *non*?—had these tunnels built all over London. But what use were they? The man lost his head anyway."

He tried to focus on Rigaud's prattle, but the tunnel robbed his mind of everything but the terror.

"Yvette enjoyed the drama of sneaking through the tunnel to meet me," the Frenchman continued. "Me, I did not like it so much. It is a little confining, *non*?"

Adrian fought a wave of nausea.

"But sometimes," Rigaud added, "extreme measures are needed to make a woman—how do you say it?—come around. Truth be told, she was reluctant. I think she really loves Ainsford." He shrugged, as if to say there was no accounting for tastes, or the vagaries of love.

Extreme measures. Sometimes necessary, yes. Sweat poured over him, had done so ever since they entered the tunnel from Ainsford's basement. Adrian forced his feet to take him deeper into the darkness. A feral chatter sounded very near his ear. Bats, perhaps.

Or demons.

"It is just ahead," Rigaud said at last.

Adrian stilled. Muffled voices, too faint to identify, came from somewhere above them. At least one of them belonged to a woman.

"It must be Yvette," Rigaud whispered. "But why would she be involved in Miss Alcott's abduction?"

Dear God, Adrian prayed. *Do not let Emmaline be harmed.*

"*Zut!*" Rigaud halted as he rounded a curve in the tunnel. "The rains must have done this."

After holding back the earth for nearly two centuries, the walls had finally bowed to nature. Crumbled stone blocked their path. Only a small opening remained, one that would have to be navigated on hands and knees.

Hell's revenge, Adrian thought grimly. Somewhere, the Jesuit's spirit was rubbing its hands in glee.

Scurrying insects crawled over his flesh as he groped his way after Rigaud, inching toward the voices above. His mind had ceased to function; discipline was gone. The cadences had been replaced by an endless terror. Instinct alone—the certainty that Emmaline was in danger—drove him on.

"Here," Rigaud whispered. He pointed to some steps that led upward, then extinguished the candle in case anyone kept watch on the other side. They emerged into a small, dark closet.

Adrian rose shakily to his feet. He inhaled, trying to calm his breathing. Emmaline needed him. He couldn't abandon her to his childhood fears. *You're not that boy anymore.*

Trembling, he took another steadying breath. The air was rich with the odor of manure, which he'd take over the confines of a tunnel any day.

On the other side of the closet door, voices were raised in anger. Adrian recognized Deverell's and Lady Ainsford's. He did not hear Emmaline's.

His heart thudded in terror. Then a muffled gunshot split the night.

"Yvette!" Lord Ainsford knelt over his wife, his face white with fear. A patch of blood stained the shoulder of Lady Ainsford's gown where she'd been shot.

His dagger gleaming in the candlelight, Deverell watched them with a curious detachment. Emmaline's hands shook as she fumbled desperately with the rope at her wrists.

"It's no use thinking you'll escape, Mrs. Stanhope," Deverell said. "To be sure, things are more complicated now. I'd hoped to pin your abduction and murder on Rigaud. The authorities would have no trouble accepting a Frenchman as their spy. They'd have ignored his protests of innocence. But with all the commotion, Rigaud has probably fled. Moreover, there are now three of you to dispose of. So I must make an adjustment. Never let it be said that I am not a flexible man."

Emmaline stared at him. "You are a monster."

"Not really. I merely strive to achieve the financial stability that should have been mine all along. The inheritance laws are so unjust, aren't they?"

"If you've killed her," Ainsford snarled, "I'll see you in hell."

Deverell looked surprised. "I'd never have taken you for a devoted husband, Ainsford. Alas, I cannot stay to discuss this startling development in your character. I imagine someone has already raised a hue and cry about that gunshot. Unfortunately, since all of you know what I've been up to, all of you must die."

"You won't pull it off," Ainsford growled.

"On the contrary. Let me just think this through: Rigaud abducted Mrs. Stanhope in the belief Burwell had told her something that could incriminate him. Lady Ainsford—an unstable woman, as everyone knows—discovered Rigaud and Mrs. Stanhope together in this little hide-away. By the way, Yvette, quite a few people know about this room. I myself spent a lovely afternoon here with your abigail several years ago. And with you, of course. But I digress.

"Enraged over what she assumed was a lovers' tryst, Yvette ran to get Ainsford's pistol and shot Mrs. Stanhope. That gun is only a one-shot affair, unfortunately, so we must think of another way to kill the rest of you."

Deverell ran his fingertip along the hilt of his dagger. "Ainsford heard the shot. When he came to investigate, Rigaud stabbed him and Lady Ainsford, then fled."

"No one will believe that," Ainsford said.

"Nonsense," Deverell replied calmly. "It's an amusing comedy of errors."

"You are deranged," Emmaline said. "Utterly deranged."

Deverell regarded her pityingly. "That may be, madam, but unlike you, I shall live to see another sunrise."

"I wouldn't count on that," growled a voice.

Deverell whirled. Adrian's foot shot out and

kicked the knife from his hand. With an angry cry, Deverell launched himself at his assailant. They crashed to the floor in a battle each man knew was to the death.

Emmaline almost died herself when Deverell's hand snaked out for the dagger, mere inches away from his fingers.

But Adrian moved so swiftly she scarcely saw his hands as they vaulted him upward for the kick that left Deverell motionless at last.

And as quickly as that, the nightmare was over.

Adrian's hands would not stop shaking. His fingers would not hold the pen. His brain would not manage the orderly thought processes necessary to his work. The papers on his desk sat blank and useless.

Emmaline had left today. She'd kept to herself all morning, busy with the final stages of packing. Her good-bye had been calm, impersonal.

He should go to her, say something to make her stay. But what? He'd already told her about Ainsford's note, saying Lady Ainsford was improving, and both had vowed to heal the breach in their marriage.

His uncle had stopped by last night to inform them Deverell was recovering from his injuries, although slowly, as conditions at Newgate were not charitable to the infirm. Rigaud was nowhere to be found, and Sir Harry was happy to apportion any residual blame to the absent Frenchman.

All in all, the entire matter was neatly wrapped up. Adrian could return to his fossils and papers; Emmaline and her aunt could get on with their lives.

Adrian had insisted that Emmaline take her new clothes. He had paid the rent at the house Gibbons had found for them in a respectable neighborhood. Never again would she live in a cottage on the turnpike.

He had not yet told her about the money deposited in an account for her at the Bank of England. The hard knot of sorrow in his chest told him he'd done too little, too late. Emmaline didn't want clothes or a fancy house or a bank account.

She wanted love.

Strange, ungovernable feelings assailed him, they left him unable to do aught but wonder how he'd gotten so very far off course. He'd never felt so lost.

Emmaline was more important to him than life itself.

But she'd settle for nothing less than his heart, and that, he couldn't give. He couldn't allow anyone that power over him. He'd be walking on eggshells the rest of his life, waiting for happiness to be destroyed. Besides, in the end, he'd failed to protect her, from Deverell.

In the week since the events at Ainsford's, Adrian had not spoken to Emmaline about these matters. He knew she was hurt by his silence. She didn't understand that almost losing her had destroyed the man he'd been, that there was no one to put in his stead.

Adrian sensed, rather than saw, Gibbons in the doorway. "Yes, Gibbons?"

"Heloise has persuaded me that I must speak to you. It is a matter of some importance."

Age had settled over the man almost overnight. His face was lined and somber; his eyes seemed dull and lifeless. His silver hair had lost its luster. Or perhaps it was just a trick of this mausoleum of a study, with its drawn drapes and flickering candles that sucked the life out of the room.

"Very well." Adrian tried to look attentive, though it was difficult for him to focus.

Gibbons closed the door behind him. "It's about your father, Your Grace." He hesitated. "Loyalty demands that I not continue, but my conscience dictates otherwise."

"The man is dead—loyalty is meaningless. Please continue." The last thing Adrian wanted to discuss was his father, but he'd not tell Gibbons that. Not when Gibbons was looking at him with such heartfelt distress.

"Your parents' wedding was the event of the season, you know." Gibbons had a distant look in his eyes. "King George himself sat in the royal pew."

Adrian made a tent of his hands and studied Gibbons over his fingertips. "That's not what you came to tell me."

"No." Gibbons looked away, seeing the past. "They settled in at the castle. Your father loved the pageantry of the place. He thought there was no better grouse to be found than on his land. He lived for the hunt. Truth be told, he preferred the company of men like himself—robust, hearty, strong—to any woman's. After your mother gave him two sons, the duke took to surrounding himself with his fellow hunters. They were a coarse and unruly lot, fond of drink."

"My father was a drunk," Adrian said bluntly. "He neglected my mother, so she moved to the dower house. I surmised that years ago. Get to the point." He had no wish to relive his childhood.

"Your mother did not move to the house because His Grace neglected her. She did so because one night he drank too much port and came to her door, which she'd taken to locking against such a possibility."

A chill crept over Adrian. "I see."

"I don't know what happened that night, but in the morning she moved to the dower house. I helped her set up her household, though His Grace never knew of my involvement. He banished the female servants from the castle and all of his properties, vowing he'd not have anything more to do with women in this life. I found them other positions. Several moved into the house with your mother. She was happy there for some time."

Adrian remembered snippets of his childhood in the dower house. He did not remember seeing his mother happy.

"Your mother was a woman of grace and charm," Gibbons continued. "She tried to make the best of things, and although her marriage had been a disaster, I think she'd almost forgotten she had a husband."

Tentacles of dread snaked around Adrian's

heart, as if something he'd known all along was moving inexorably toward him.

"I served His Grace's household, but truth be told, there was little for me to do. Your father had lost all interest in anything but drink and hunting. Your brothers were sent away to school." Gibbons paused. "Your mother, on the other hand, needed my assistance. In some ways she was quite fragile—too fragile, perhaps, to survive marriage to a man like the duke."

A hard edge of anger suffused Gibbons's voice. "She was quite alone in the world. Neither her parents nor her friends dared defy the duke. Everyone simply vanished, leaving her to the isolation of the dower house."

Adrian stared at Gibbons, as if seeing him for the first time. "She had no one," he said slowly, "except you."

"Gibbonses have always served Trents. It was my duty to serve the duke and duchess. The fact that they lived apart did not change that."

Adrian remembered the baskets of food Gibbons had brought to Emmaline and her aunt. "You took care of everything, didn't you?"

"It was my responsibility."

"But it was more than that, wasn't it, Gibbons?"

Gibbons hesitated. "Yes."

"You fell in love with her."

A slow flush crept over Gibbons's features. "I kept my distance. The idea of breaching the boundaries of my class was unthinkable."

"Was it?" Adrian studied him.

"I was a servant. She was far above me. I was

content to worship her from afar." Gibbons closed his eyes. "Until that night."

Adrian's innards constricted.

"His Grace had begun his slow descent into spirits that would rule him ever after. One night, after a particularly rowdy party at the castle, he rode his horse down to the dower house and"— Gibbons took a deep breath—"assaulted her."

Adrian knew the word was intended to spare him from the truth. Instead, all was suddenly and brutally clear.

That was the night he'd been conceived. *Rape.* It explained his father's remoteness, his mother's fragility. Her anguish had turned inward, literally making her sick. All those years on the Continent, searching for a cure to her mysterious illness, she'd been trying to rid herself of the violent stain of his conception.

Adrian looked away. "It cannot have been easy for you to tell me such a thing," he said wearily. "Frankly, I could have managed without knowing, but I suppose the truth does not like to stay hidden."

"That is what Heloise said." Gibbons held his gaze. "I am not done with the story, Adrian."

Startled, he stared at Gibbons. His man of affairs had addressed him by his given name. Not that he minded, strangely, but Gibbons had never committed such a lapse.

"As I said, I'd kept my distance," Gibbons continued. "But after that night, everything changed."

Realization stabbed Adrian like a dagger. Rage rose in him. "You touched her, didn't you? You took advantage of her when she was defenseless and broken."

"No. Not then." Gibbons's voice held anger, too. "Yes, she was broken and helpless. And if I'd been any kind of a man at all, I'd have marched up the hill and killed your father after I found her the next morning huddled in the garden, bleeding and bruised and crying her heart out."

Adrian closed his eyes. Damn Gibbons for giving him this.

"But I wasn't that kind of man," Gibbons said softly. "I wasn't strong that way. It was not in me to strike His Grace. Instead, I took her inside. I dismissed the servants and prepared her bath myself. I . . . I bathed her. Gently, washing away the blood as if I could somehow wash away the cruelty. I hoped to help her in the only way I knew—by serving her.

"She . . . she was never the same after that night. She'd shut herself into a chamber of her mind and never really came out of it. I brought her flowers, fresh fruit, trivial pleasures—all that was within my power to offer. I wanted to please her, to make her laugh. But he had destroyed her spirit."

Adrian turned away, his anger blunted by Gibbons's agonized confession. Yes, that was the mother he'd known. Broken and locked away from him, from everyone. Now he understood. A child of her rape, he'd been a constant reminder of the cause of her misery. She'd been damaged irreparably the night he was conceived.

It had never been within his power to save her.

He hadn't failed, so much as tried the impossible. How self-centered he'd been to think that he, a mere child, could bring happiness to a woman who'd been so horribly wronged.

But where he should have felt a heavy weight lift from his shoulders, he did not. His birth and his mother's sorrow weighed on him with a bitterness that would not be dislodged. He wanted to turn back the clock, to demand another chance, now that he knew the source of her despair. He wanted to repudiate his father's heritage, to denounce the man as the criminal he was, a criminal who had passed on his blood legacy to his son.

"Adrian."

He felt Gibbons's hand on his shoulder. Damn it, why did the man always know when he was needed? Adrian shrugged it off. He wasn't about to break down and bawl like a child. He'd bear his burdens like a man.

"I don't know how to say this," Gibbons said. "I've thought of this moment for years. Now that it's finally here, I don't know what to do."

"What the devil are you talking about?"

Gibbons took a deep breath. "I did love your mother. I fancy that in the weeks after the assault—"

"Rape," Adrian corrected angrily.

"Be silent, boy!" Gibbons roared.

Boy? Adrian blinked.

Gibbons took a deep breath. "Maybe I don't want to think of it that way. Maybe I can't."

Mesmerized, Adrian watched Gibbons's face.

"Your mother had no chance of happiness

with that man," Gibbons said bitterly. "Her fate had been settled long ago by people with other priorities. I didn't want to fall in love with her; there was no future for us. A duchess does not run off with a servant, Adrian. She'd have been forever ruined, dead to the world she came from. I knew that. She knew that. But . . ." Gibbons covered his eyes.

"But *what*, damn it?" Adrian leapt to his feet, ready to wrench Gibbons's hand away from his face. He *had* to see those eyes. They were so anguished and caring and . . . real.

"After that night, we grew close." Gibbons met his gaze. "I looked after her, tended her—"

A woman likes to be tended to. The notion, so elusive before, was now suddenly so very clear.

Gibbons sighed. "I thought I could give her a measure of happiness. Indeed, she seemed to respond. For the first time in days she laughed. She even flirted with me. She had a song she used to sing. Her voice was pure and sweet. I could listen to it forever."

He reddened. "I couldn't help myself, Adrian. I thought she loved me, too. I put aside the training of a lifetime, everything I'd ever believed about right and wrong. I made love to her."

Adrian stilled.

"I won't defend my actions, except to say that I thought I had a chance of making her happy. I was wrong. We had our moment of glory, a few days, nothing more. Then she sent me away—I never knew why. Eventually I came to see that it was because she felt herself unworthy of love. The duke had robbed her of any feelings of

worth. I returned to his staff and kept busy in
London to prevent myself from coming to see
her. I respected her wishes, but it broke my
heart."

Gibbons leveled a gaze at him. "Then you
were born."

A crazy thought occurred to Adrian.

"I've told you more than my pride wanted to,
but there's one thing more, Adrian." Gibbons
took a deep breath. "You might be my son."

A crazy thought that just might be true.

"Good God." A lump rose to Adrian's throat.

"I don't know for sure," Gibbons added. "The
timing . . . you could just as easily have been the
duke's from that awful night. I'm sorry. Perhaps
I shouldn't have spoken, but I've had a lifetime
to think about this, and somehow it seems right
that you know."

Gibbons hesitated. "I know this puts you in an
untenable position. You're a duke, and for all I
know entitled to be one. I have no proof, no reason to think otherwise. And yet, something deep
inside makes me proud to confess that I might
be your father."

The lump in Adrian's throat threatened to
burst.

"I'll never mention this to another soul—
though I've told Heloise. She helped me see that
the truth was more important than pretending
I'm nothing more to you than a servant. I've
watched you from afar for years, Adrian, always
wondering if you're mine. I kept my distance,
knowing that you and Portia would fare worse
if I came forward to confess all. Then she took

you away, and I had no contact with you at all. When she died—"

Gibbons paused. "I hoped that one day you'd return," he said at last. "I corresponded with your instructors—in your father's name, of course—to keep track of your studies and interests. I bought all those old texts and catalogued them, thinking you might need them for research. I visited your landlady to see whether you seemed happy. When the duke died, and your brothers soon after, I knew I had to bring you back."

He met Adrian's gaze unflinchingly. "In my eyes you'll always be mine, no matter who sired you."

Adrian took an unsteady step forward. Gibbons retreated to the doorway.

"I wouldn't blame you for hating me for what I've told you. I've already found another position. To the north—we need never cross paths again. And I'll go to my grave with this secret. I know you haven't wanted a dukedom, but you're entitled to have it. For what you and your mother suffered, for the pain that's been forced on you, you deserve the title no matter whose blood runs in you."

Gibbons stepped into the hall. In two strides, Adrian was at the door. "Gibbons!"

Gibbons froze.

"Damn it, man, look at me," Adrian growled.

Slowly, Gibbons turned.

"You . . . you don't know whether I'm really yours?" Adrian watched his face.

Gibbons shook his head.

"There's no proof one way or the other?"

"No."

"So . . . so I might choose, as suits my fancy?"

Gibbons regarded him warily. "I—I suppose."

A strained and prolonged silence descended. They stood there awkwardly, each trying to divine the other's thoughts.

Adrian cleared his throat.

Gibbons cleared his.

"Well . . ." Adrian's voice trailed off.

Gibbons waited.

"Hell." Now the burden *did* lift from Adrian's shoulders. "I choose you."

Gibbons opened his mouth, but whatever he meant to say was lost as his son enfolded him in a violent hug.

Chapter 27

This must be how Cinderella felt after the ball, Emmaline reflected grimly. It was the third day she'd spent in the new house, the third day she'd tried to make a life without Adrian in it.

"Why such a long face, dear?" Aunt Heloise surveyed her reflection in the mirror. As she had hoped, the peach-colored gown flattered her complexion. "Are you going to wait an eternity for that man to come to his senses?"

"It serves no purpose to dwell on what might have been," Emmaline said resolutely.

Aunt Heloise slipped on her new kid gloves. "It serves every purpose."

Emmaline eyed her curiously. "Are you going out?"

"Did I not tell you? John sent a note round this morning asking if I'd drive with him in Hyde Park. All the *ton* goes there to parade in their finery." Aunt Heloise smiled. "With my new clothes and the splendid curricle Adrian purchased for us, I look the equal of any duchess.

347

Did I mention I intend to remain Lady Alcott for a while?"

Emmaline sighed. "We can't live on Adrian's kindness forever."

"Kindness? Em, dear, the man is besotted, bereft, desperately in love. He'll not rest until he has you back."

She shook her head. "He feels nothing for me."

"Tsk-tsk. I've done my best with you, but sometimes even *I* despair of making progress. At all events, I can't talk now. John will be downstairs. There was a time when I'd keep a man waiting with bated breath, dangling at the end of a slowly twisting rope, but no more." She walked to the window. "Yes, there's Adrian's carriage now."

"Adrian—here?" The words came out a squeak.

"They were to drive over together," Aunt Heloise replied. "My goodness, Emmaline, one would think you were a shrinking violet instead of a woman of substance."

Emmaline's heart lurched. "I can't see him. Look at these circles under my eyes. I've hardly slept since we left his home. Whatever will he think?"

"If you don't quit babbling, you'll never know." Aunt Heloise rolled her eyes. "I have better things to do than concern myself with the woeful state of your love life, dear. I have my own suitor. I fancy we'll have an announcement soon."

"Oh, Aunt!" Emmaline embraced her. "You and Mr. Gibbons? That is wonderful!"

Gently but firmly, Aunt Heloise removed Emmaline's hands from around her shoulders. "Careful, I have no intention of spoiling this dress until John sees it."

"Why didn't you tell me he's asked you to marry him?"

"He hasn't." Aunt Heloise gave a last look at her reflection and sailed out of the room. "But he will."

Aunt Heloise was so very confident, and she such a coward. Emmaline couldn't bring herself to go down and face Adrian. She'd have one of those servants who seemed to be everywhere inform him she was indisposed.

Oddly, none of the servants were around, she quickly discovered. The house seemed unnaturally silent. She glanced out the window. Adrian's carriage was gone.

He hadn't waited for her. Perhaps he hadn't even accompanied Mr. Gibbons. Perhaps he was in his musty study this very minute working on his papers. Perhaps he no longer thought of her at all.

Well, there was no sense in wallowing in self-pity. She ought to congratulate herself for not succumbing to false hope. She wasn't Cinderella, or any of those other helpless heroines waiting to be elevated from their pitiable state by a man. She was capable of making her own way in the world—which was fortunate, for if her aunt married Mr. Gibbons, she'd be quite alone. Still, she'd never begrudge Aunt Heloise her happiness.

Emmaline looked at the bandboxes stacked in

her room. She'd never owned anything so fine as these new clothes. Adrian insisted he had no use for them; since they'd mattered so little to him, Emmaline had persuaded herself it was no crime to keep them. Now they served as a reminder of how much he'd given her—not the material things, so much as the love and longing he'd inspired in her.

Why had she ever thought him cold and passionless, when it was his deep love for his mother—a love that wouldn't die no matter how much he suffered—that had ruled him for so long? When had his fine, wounded heart reached out to envelop *her* in its love?

He didn't like the word, but each time he touched her, she'd seen love in his eyes. The night he'd rescued her from Deverell, that love had blazed fierce and true for all to see. He'd come to her aid like a knight in shining armor, his fighting skills graceful and deadly. He'd been that dauntless hero all along, if she'd but noticed.

But she had been too busy trying to fit him into her silly image of love. Flowers, poetry, dancing—all so superficial. *I want the dream, Adrian, and you're not it.* Foolish, foolish woman. The man she loved had a heart as big as the sky.

Emmaline went downstairs. She hadn't yet accustomed herself to the house's spaciousness; the empty silence unsettled her. Perhaps tea would ease her nerves.

A heady scent assailed her as she reached the foyer. It came from the parlor. Hesitantly, Emmaline peeked in.

Roses and lilies and a profusion of other flowers bloomed from vases in every corner. In their midst stood Adrian.

He looked positively dashing.

The canary yellow waistcoat showed his physique to excellent advantage. The curly beaver chapeau under his arm had a dapper yellow feather affixed to its brim. He held an ebony cane, at the top of which sat the brass image of an odd reptilian creature.

"Do you like it?" he asked, following her gaze. "I commissioned the head from an old engraving I found."

"W-where is your carriage?" was all she could say.

"Gibbons wanted privacy during his drive with your aunt, so he took it to the park instead of your new curricle."

The burning intensity in his gaze was so at odds with their mundane conversation that it robbed her of speech.

"I bought out every flower stand between here and Grosvenor Square." His sudden, sheepish grin made her breath catch in her throat.

"They're l-lovely," she managed.

"About the tending," he said abruptly.

Emmaline blinked. "What?"

"The tending. You know, the things a man does for a woman he . . ." He broke off. Emmaline stared at his mouth, imagining it on hers. She swayed toward him.

"Do you feel faint?" he asked.

Emmaline gave a ladylike cough and straightened her shoulders. "No. I—why are you here, Adrian?"

"I want to give it a try."

"Give what a try?"

"The tending. I've been an ass, Emmaline."

This was not possible. The love of one's life did not walk into one's parlor bearing flowers and a declaration. Emmaline turned away from the mesmerizing spark in his gaze. Her heart ached. "Adrian, spare us this agony. I don't need flowers, or a big house, or fine clothes. If you're trying to assuage your guilt—"

"Guilt?" He frowned.

"For seducing me." Strange, how hard it was to say those words, as if the admission was as costly as the deed.

"*Seducing you?*" He eyed her in disbelief. "It's *you* who seduced me. I haven't had a moment's peace since you entered my life."

" 'Twas *you* who entered mine, and under false colors at that." Emmaline lifted her chin.

"You sailed under false colors yourself, madam."

What was she doing? He'd come to her with flowers, and she'd picked a fight, all because she was so very angry at herself for pushing him away. "I'm sorry for my words. Let's not bicker. Let's part as friends."

"I have no intention of parting as friends."

"Now, *that* wasn't nice." Emmaline felt her temper boil.

"I am not a particularly nice man."

"As always, Your Grace, I am in awe of your perceptiveness."

"Damn it, Emmaline, leave off the sarcasm." A muscle tensed in his jaw.

"It's the only defense I have," she confessed. "Otherwise, I might look at these flowers and think you cared for me."

"We wouldn't want you to think that, would we?" he asked softly.

Something in his tone made her world still. "Not unless it was true," she said in a small voice.

"If it was, would you marry me?"

"Is—is that a joke?"

"You know I have no sense of humor." Was that the faintest smile about his mouth?

"Why would you wish to marry me?" she asked carefully.

"For the usual reasons."

"Companionship? Money? Lineage? I don't have the last two, so it must be my company that draws you."

He caught her hand. "You've forgotten passion." His fingers stroked the inside of her wrist, then trailed up to the sensitive inner part of her elbow.

"Passion alone isn't a reason for marriage," she said breathlessly.

"No," he agreed. His hand wandered to her side, where it stopped a heartbeat away from her breast.

Emmaline closed her eyes, trying to find the strength to deny him. Passion was all he'd own up to. He didn't want to marry her, only set her up as his mistress.

And what was wrong with that? she thought suddenly.

What did it matter what the world thought of

her? She'd thought him rigid, but it was her fixed notions of love and marriage that had almost cost her the man she loved. She'd be a fool to send him away, when he was looking at her like . . . *that*.

"I want to make love to you," he murmured.

She'd have years to ponder the rashness of her judgment. People would speak of her in disapproving tones. A fallen woman, they'd say. Maybe one day a relative would pore over her journal as she'd done with her father's writings and think that Emmaline Alcott had been an incorrigible, reckless dreamer.

So be it.

"Touch me, Adrian," she said in a wobbly voice. "You don't have to pretend to want marriage."

"Damn it," he growled. "I'm trying to tell you that I love you."

"Love?" she echoed weakly.

"I'll have you no other way than as my bride."

"Br-bride?" This *was* some cruel joke. She'd fallen into one of the Grimms' tales, where the magic invariably had a darker side.

Adrian brought her hand to his lips. His mouth lingered there, as if it were some wondrous delicacy. A rush of desire, potent and overwhelming, forced a moan from her lips. He arched one eloquent brow, then bent to kiss her.

At first his kiss was slow, indolent. Then it erupted with a wild, insatiable passion.

It was then Emmaline knew the truth: If he'd held a glass slipper, it would've fit her foot perfectly.

She burst into tears.

*   *   *

Heloise squinted out the carriage window at the elegant landaus and dashing curricles that drove by. It was too bad no one could see her new peach bonnet. "I wish we'd taken the new curricle, instead of Adrian's closed carriage," she groused good-naturedly. "Besides, I thought he had a loathing of closed spaces."

"He's trying a new approach. By riding in the coach as much as possible, he thinks that over time he might become less sensitized to the fear."

Heloise regarded Gibbons admiringly. "How intriguing. Was that your idea?"

"Hardly. I'm just a humble servant." But he smiled.

"I'm glad Adrian took the news well. About his paternity, I mean."

"His *possible* paternity. We'll never know for sure."

Heloise patted Gibbons's hand. "Perhaps not. But he's lucky to have you, John, no matter what."

"You were right to urge me to tell him. I still can't believe what's happened. In less than a week, it seems I've gained a son and a future. Suddenly, the world holds endless possibilities."

"Like what, dear?" Heloise adjusted the brim of her bonnet to a particularly rakish angle.

"The chance to get to know Adrian better, to share in a future with him." Gibbons hesitated. "The chance to love a woman."

Heloise regarded him steadily. "Would that be me?"

Gibbons pulled her close. "How have I managed to live my life without you?"

"To tell you the truth, John, I don't know," she said. "You've had a very spartan time of it, haven't you?"

"I made choices I had to live with."

"I respect you for that, John. But life is short."

"Meaning?"

Heloise gave him a saucy smile. "That one must take pleasure where one finds it."

"I've been intending to talk to you about that, Heloise." Gibbons eyed her sternly. "I'll not have my wife regaling people with bawdy poetry."

"Whatever are you talking about?"

"That séance at Ainsford's. If I hadn't been so scared that I'd give you away, I would have taken you outside and washed your mouth out with soap."

"You have much to learn about the theatrical arts, John." Heloise gave him a pretty pout. "My company once performed Chaucer at the Royal, of all places. I myself had twenty curtain calls that night. They loved my Wife of Bath. I've forgotten more lines than I remember, but I acquitted myself well enough at Lord Ainsford's, don't you think?"

"Yes, but that's over and done, Heloise. I'll not be hauling my wife off stage while some dandy in the pit claws at her skirts."

"That's the second time you've said that word 'wife.' Are you asking me to marry you, John?"

"I thought that was clear. Now that I've resolved things with Adrian, I am free to get on with my life. We'll wed as soon as I can get a special license."

Heloise studied him. "You assume a great deal, John."

Gibbons flushed. "I've not done this well, have I?"

"No, dear. I'm afraid you've fallen in love with a peacock, not a pigeon. I require a little embellishment, even in love. *Especially* in love. I do apologize if that is inconvenient."

"It is I who must apologize. I've been preoccupied with my own troubles. When Adrian opened his arms to me, it was like . . ." His voice broke. "Like a miracle. He actually welcomed the possibility I might be his father."

Heloise patted his knee. "That shouldn't surprise you. You are a good man, John, kind and true."

"I've let you down, Heloise. You deserve to be courted, to be surrounded with flowers and sonnets and all that a man is capable of doing to show a woman how much he loves her." He hesitated.

"Go on," Heloise prodded softly.

"I've wanted to make love to you, Heloise. I've wanted to stand beneath your window at night and sing hymns to your exuberance. You live life to the fullest."

"Yes," she acknowledged wistfully. "But I have a past, John, as you know. Perhaps you do not wish to saddle yourself with a soiled dove."

"Peacock," he corrected gently. "Not soiled, but gloriously painted in the colors of life. 'Tis humbling to know you care for me."

Heloise beamed.

"But . . ." Gibbons trailed off.

She frowned. "But?"

"You are not well, Heloise. I shall understand if you do not wish to consummate our marriage. It may be too taxing for you, too uncouth."

"*Uncouth?*" Heloise stared at him.

Gibbons shifted awkwardly on the seat. "Perhaps that was not the best word—"

"No, indeed," Heloise declared. " 'Tis true my health is indifferent, John, but I am by no means at death's door. Indeed, Monsieur Rigaud's magnet treatment made me feel quite splendid. I have great hopes for it. I shall insist that Adrian teach me the technique."

Gibbons regarded her dubiously. "I shouldn't like to take odds on it, but if anyone can persuade him, 'tis you."

"In the meanwhile, there is another treatment that comes to mind. An actress I knew swore by it. May I show you?"

"Show me?" Gibbons looked startled.

"Don't worry, dear. No one can see us in here." Heloise glanced out the window, then returned her attention to him. "We face each other like so. I bring my knees close, so that they are between yours."

Gibbons regarded her warily as she inserted her knees between his.

"A bit closer, John. Yes, that's right." She caught his hand. "Put your hand here. The energy must flow between us."

"Heloise," he began, his face scarlet as she placed his palm over her abdominal region.

"It helps if you move your hand like this." She guided it lower. "Try a stroking movement." She inhaled sharply. "Yes, that's quite acceptable."

"Is there no end to what you can teach me, Heloise?" His expression was unreadable.

"Probably not," she murmured. "Put your other hand here, around my body. Lean forward. Closer. Yes, like that. We are close enough to kiss, aren't we?"

Gibbons needed no further invitation. A long moment later, Heloise looked up at him through the fringes of her lashes.

"Do you wish to try the rest, John? This is very daring, isn't it? 'Tis not even dark, and we are only a stone's throw from the nearest carriage."

"I would like to try the rest."

Heloise shivered. "John, you make me tremble with excitement."

"I can't begin to describe what you do to me, Heloise."

"The stroking," she said a bit breathlessly, "should be lower. In the region of my ovaries."

"I have not the slightest idea where a woman's ovaries are, Heloise, but I think I can take it from here."

"You are *so* masterful, John. There is just one thing."

"Oh?"

"I hesitate to mention it," she murmured.

"Don't. Let me guess."

Heloise eyed him dubiously. "You can't possibly."

Gibbons merely smiled, his sharply arched brow reminiscent of the duke's. " 'If music be the food of love,' " he murmured into her ear, " 'play on . . .' "

"Oh, *John!*"

Emmaline took the handkerchief Adrian offered, blew her nose, and wiped her eyes as her wrenching sobs gradually faded to soft hiccups.

Adrian had surprised himself as much as her when he'd blurted out his love. It was as if a dam had burst, unleashing a torrent of feelings that had been pent up inside him. First Gibbons, now Emmaline. He'd been surrounded by love and never known it.

But she'd turned into a watering pot. How could he get through to her? Maybe if he did the thing properly. . . . He caught her hand and went down on one knee.

"Emmaline, I've tried to control my feelings, but—" She looked up, her gaze soft and vulnerable. "But control is not an option," he finished raggedly.

"Passion isn't love, Adrian."

"It's part of love. Let's make a new start." He knew he was speaking too fast. "I won't make love to you until you say so and—oh, hell, I can't promise that. Say yes, anyway, Emmaline. Please."

She shook her head in disbelief. "Oh, my, Adrian. Are you . . . are you groveling?"

"A lady I know insists upon it," he growled.

Her laughter dissolved into a new round of tears. Damn. He knew as much about crying women as he did about being a duke. Or being in love.

"There's just one thing," he said gravely. "You have to grovel, too."

"*Me?*" She blinked.

He arched a brow. "You can't think I'd accept anything less."

Emmaline looked uncertain. "What must I do?"

He pretended to consider the matter. "Come down here."

"On the floor?"

"The very best groveling is done on the floor."

Hesitantly, she knelt on the rug facing him, her skirts getting tangled with her legs.

"Let me help." Adrian put his hands around her waist and pulled her close, so that their bodies touched from shoulders to knees.

"This doesn't feel like groveling," she pointed out, as he nuzzled her neck.

He feigned surprise. "Of course it does. Now ask me to marry you."

"Oh, Adrian." She wiped away the last of her tears.

His hands began a slow descent along her spine. "Say it with passion—as if you couldn't live without me. As if I were all you'd ever wanted or dreamed of."

"All that, Adrian," she murmured. "All that and more."

He brushed her lips. "I love you, Emmaline."

She turned her head away. "But life isn't a fairy tale. People don't change overnight."

"You want me to change?"

"No, but . . ."

"*What?*" he demanded, his heart in his throat.

There couldn't be any buts. There couldn't.

"Isn't your first love fossils?"

"Sweet Jesus, Emmaline." He stared at her. "I'd take you over a fossil any day."

She flushed. "That's not what I meant. It's just that . . . well, you're too rational for love."

"Rational men don't fall in love?"

She sat back on her heels and eyed him accusingly. "You're twisting my words."

"You haven't reformed me, if that's what you're thinking. You recall that from the first, you allowed the possibility of less-than-perfect results." He caught her hand and pulled her closer. "I'm not claiming perfection, Emmaline. I don't know much about love. But I'm going to stay here, on my knees, until you say yes."

She took a deep breath. "Yes."

"*Emmaline.*" He bore her down to the floor.

Hell, it didn't matter how little he knew of love; they'd teach each other. He was poised on the edge of a precipice so sheer and magnificent it took his breath away. Below was something so wondrous he could hardly comprehend it.

"Adrian," she murmured as he eased her gown off her shoulder. "The servants—"

"I sent them away." He nibbled at her earlobe. "There's no way out for you now."

Her slow smile sparked an exquisite heat. "I know," she whispered.

A wild, reckless exuberance gripped him. The blood in his veins pounded furiously. The vast uncharted territory of the heart beckoned. Never had he surrendered to a siren song as sweet as the promise of Emmaline's love.

Peering over the edge of that steep precipice, he saw a yawning canyon that held the true mysteries of life: love and all that it brought.

He took a deep breath.

And jumped. With all his heart.

Epilogue

"**O**bstinate." Adrian arched one arrogant brow as he studied the card. "Imagines wrongs."

"Independent." Emmaline countered. "Practical and kind."

They glared at each other.

"Difficult," he said.

"Impossible," she added.

They burst into laughter. Scarcely aware of anyone else in the room, they sat close together on the sofa, the tarot cards between them.

"Did you know the Belgian canary is prized above all canaries?" Peter asked suddenly, looking up from a book. "It says here that the Belgian canary has had a lot of influ ... influ ..." He glanced at Gibbons.

"Influence," Gibbons prompted.

"In-flu-ence ... influence on English breeds." Peter grinned proudly.

"You're doing very well," Gibbons said. "We'll start you on the classics next."

"Oh, look, Adrian," Emmaline said. "The page of wands. And the eight, too. What do you suppose that means?"

364

"Hmm. A messenger bringing exciting news. Life-altering, perhaps." He gave her a speculative gaze. "Could indicate the coming of a child. But you've not mentioned anything along those lines."

Emmaline flushed. "Do you think the cards know something we don't?"

"I should be wary of abdicating reason for intuition."

"And I should be wary of reason altogether," Emmaline responded with a sly smile.

"Haven't you learned by now that heart and mind should exist in balance?" Adrian was thinking of last night's spirited debate on the Corn Laws, which ultimately ignited a long night of lovemaking. Judging by Emmaline's blush, she was remembering, too.

He adored the flush of scarlet that warmed her cheeks in the throes of passion. He could scarcely wait to get her upstairs again.

"Did I tell you I've found a husband for Miranda?" Emmaline said calmly, as if her gaze was not roving over him in a provocative fashion. "It's that nice professor who visited you last week to discuss the Sussex dig. I invited them both to dinner next week. He'll be perfect for her. So charming—"

"Careful, my love," he warned. "You'll make me jealous."

"I adore romantic men." Emmaline lowered her lashes. "Especially those who exude a certain . . . magnetism. And there is one particular man— well, I blush to confess it—but he positively makes my toes curl."

Adrian studied her. "Does he, now?"

Oblivious of the others, he leaned over and gave Emmaline a searing kiss. She returned the kiss with an intensity that ignited the magic between them anew.

Cards forgotten, Adrian pulled Emmaline to her feet. Neither of them remembered to say good night to the others.

Heloise beamed. "You see, John?" She nudged Gibbons. " 'All's well that ends well.' " Her brow furrowed. "Or is that 'all the world's a stage'?"

Gibbons leaned over and kissed her cheek. "A little of both, my dear. A little of both."

Author's Note

Franz Mesmer's discovery of hypnotism sparked a raging debate that continues to this day. Is the hypnotic trance real or an illusion? Do magnets promote health? For that matter, what is the connection between mind and health?

By the time the eighteenth century arrived, physicians had developed theories of a healing cosmic fluid, which Mesmer later adapted to his own philosophy. Mesmer himself was no mystic. He continually looked for scientific explanations for illness. Still, science then was not what it is now. Mesmer theorized that a "universal fluid" causes the gravitational pull in the heavens, as well as magnetism, electricity, light, and heat. From there, it is a quick jump to Mesmer's notion of "animal magnetism," a force he believed present in humans and animals and which he thought explained behavior and health.

The Vienna of Mesmer's time was alive with ideas, creativity, and pleasure-seeking. Mesmer became one of Mozart's patrons and enjoyed great success for a time, but his practices eventually came under increasing attack. His *baquet*, in which patients stood in a tub of magnetized water to improve their health, drew ridicule. In the laying on of hands that was part of Mesmer's treatment, some saw a sexual subtext. The trance itself, which Mesmer viewed as an integral part of the healing process, was deemed highly erotic. His séances consisted of group hypnosis in which patients often fell into convulsions or screams of ecstasy. His peers took a dim view of these sessions; some condemned Mesmer's ways as unscientific and immoral.

Needless to say, Mesmer had his imitators. Some experimented with magnets, like his early rival, Father Maximilian Hell. Others practiced faith-healing. Alchemists hocked elixirs they said would restore youth and aid in speaking to the dead. Secret societies promoting mesmerism sprang up in England and on the Continent.

Mesmer himself appears to have been a diligent and dedicated physician. Many of his patients had illnesses that today would be viewed as psychosomatic in origin. And though his theories are flawed, his discovery of the hypnotic trance stands as a major step in the development of the study of the mind. To this day, scientists debate whether hypnosis is real or just the result of a canny hypnotist and a highly suggestive mind.

One footnote: Mesmer believed animals had an abundance of magnetic fluid. He liked to hypnotize them and, in fact, had a pet canary that was especially susceptible to his powers. The canary slept in an open cage and woke him every morning by landing on his head. Mesmer died in 1815 in his eighty-first year—just as a gypsy fortune-teller had foretold. Afterward, his canary would neither eat nor sleep and was soon found dead in its cage. I've shamelessly stolen the loyal creature as the model for Galahad.

As to the other bits of history I've woven into this book, I cannot leave without mentioning the dinosaurs, my son's first love as a toddler. Englishman Robert Plot is believed to have discovered the first dinosaur fossil, a large bone, from a quarry in Cornwall in 1676. Plot did not know what he had, which may explain why he eventually lost the specimen. Centuries later, the fossil was identified from an engraving as a femur, probably from what early paleontologists called a megalosaurus, or "great lizard."

Other dinosaur fragments turned up in collections in the eighteenth century, but it was not until England's Regency period (1811–1820) that scientists found and documented fossils as belonging to an ancient, extinct order of giant lizards. British anatomist Sir Richard Owen later coined the term *dinosaur* in 1842.

And finally, I should say a word about Aunt Heloise's mysterious disease, lest readers be concerned about her fate. Her symptoms—fatigue, aches, chills, and memory difficulties—waxed and waned with puzzling inconsistency; today they would probably be diagnosed as fibromyalgia, a chronic illness for which diagnosis is elusive and treatment a matter of trial and error.

Many patients lead normal lives as long as rest, exercise, and diet are maintained. Others swear by magnet therapy. I suspect Aunt Heloise would be among their number.

Dear Reader,

What if you had to get married but there were no good prospects in sight? That's the problem facing Lady Gillian in Victoria Alexander's newest Regency-set historical THE HUSBAND LIST. Gillian and her friends make a list of the *ton's* most likely bachelors, but they're all unacceptable to her—until she meets the very sexy . . . and wildly unattainable . . . Earl of Shelbrooke.

It's evening, you've just settled down, there's a knock at the door—you open it, and could it be Mr. Right? In Hailey North's PERFECT MATCH pretty Lauren Stevens not only has one man vying for her affections . . . she has two—and to make matters more complicated, they're brothers! But for Lauren, Alistair Gotho is nothing but trouble . . .

Go west, young woman! And Rachelle Morgan's MUSTANG ANNIE is the perfect western gal—sexy, sassy . . . and determined not to fall for any old cowpoke that comes her way. But handsome Brett Corrigan is anything but old . . . he's completely irresistible.

Maximilian Chartwell made a promise he'd always protect his young cousin the duke, and he's not about to let an upstart American heiress trap the impressionable lad into marriage. But in Marlene Suson's NEVER A LADY it's Max himself who just might get trapped.

Enjoy!

Lucia Macro

Lucia Macro
Executive Editor
Avon Romance

AEL 0800

Avon Romances—
the best in exceptional authors and unforgettable novels!